PRAISE FOR
DARK DELICACIES:

"A wickedly crafted collection of terror...*Dark Delicacies* will prove a worthy addition to your bookshelf—you can already hear it screaming in the night!"

—Peter Normanton, *The Tomb* magazine

"Horrifying...veteran fans...should find this collection sufficiently repulsive, spooky and chilling...most (of the stories) are vividly conveyed narratives of terror, bloodletting and grisly death. Some even inject a bit of twisted humor into their nightmares."

—*Los Angeles Times*

"If, as Howison writes in his afterword, 'Horror has always been the blues of literature', then this anthology of 20 new tales of the macabre is an all-star concert whose performers work haunting riffs on gut-bucket themes...Howison, the proprietor of Burbank, Calif.'s Dark Delicacies horror bookstore, and Gelb, co-editor of the *Hot Blood* anthology series, have plundered their Rolodexes to recruit a formidable lineup of horror's top creative talents."

—*Publishers Weekly*

DARK DELICACIES 2: FEAR

MORE ORIGINAL TALES OF TERROR AND THE MACABRE BY THE WORLD'S GREATEST HORROR WRITERS

EDITED BY

DEL HOWISON AND JEFF GELB

WITH A FOREWORD BY

RAY HARRYHAUSEN

CARROL & GRAF PUBLISHERS
NEW YORK

DARK DELICACIES 2: FEAR
*More Original Tales of Terror and the Macabre by the World's Greatest Horror
Writers*

Carroll & Graf Publishers
245 West 17th Street, 11th Floor
New York, NY 10011

AVALON

"Uneasy Foreword to the Second Anthology" © 2007 by Del Howison
"The Act of Creation" © 2007 by Ray Harryhausen
"Sunrise on Running Water" © 2007 by Barbara Hambly
"Dog" © 2007 by Joe R. Lansdale
"The Accompanist" © 2007 by John Harrison
"Where There's a Will . . ." © 2007 by Robert Masello
"Stacy and her Idiot" © 2007 by Peter Atkins
"Amusement" © 2007 by Tananarive Due
"Great Wall: A Story from the Zombie War" © 2007 by Max Brooks
"Words, Words, Words" © 2007 by Gary Brandner
"Between Eight and Nine O'Clock" © 2007 by Ray Garton
"First Born" © 2007 by Penny Dreadful Ltd.
"A Host of Shadows" © 2007 by Harry Shannon
"What the Devil Won't Take . . ." © 2007 by L. A. Banks
"The Y Incision" © 2007 by Steve Niles
"The Unlikely Redemption of Jared Pierce" © 2007 by Joey O'Bryan
"Queen of the Groupies" © 2007 by Greg Kihn
"Season Premiere" © 2007 by James Sallis
"I Am Coming to Live in Your Mouth" © 2007 by Glen Hirshberg
"The Ammonite Violin (Murder Ballad No. 4)" © 2007 by Caitlin R. Kiernan
"Dark Delicacies Last Word—A Modest Proposal" © 2007 by Jeff Gelb

Simultaneous cloth and trade paperback first Carroll & Graf editions 2007

Library of Congress Cataloging-in-Publication Data is available.

Cloth ISBN-10: 0-7867-1950-8
Cloth ISBN-13: 978-0-78671-950-1
Paperback ISBN-10: 0-7867-1951-6
Paperback ISBN-13: 978-0-78671-951-8

9 8 7 6 5 4 3 2 1

Printed in the United States of America
www.perseusbooks.com

To Sue with love and affection. To Scott and Jason because they
made me, and to Joshua, The Guardian of the Gate
—Del Howison

To those who still enjoy a good scare on the printed page:
you—our readers!
—Jeff Gelb

CONTENTS

UNEASY INTRODUCTION TO THE SECOND ANTHOLOGY

DEL HOWISON

ELCOME TO THE second go-round of the *Dark Delicacies* anthology of horror and the unsettling. Once again our intent is to open that creaking door into the very personal wavering room of angst and horror, your mind. Are you uncomfortable? No? You will be. Pull up a chair. Here is a pillow to place behind your back. I hope nothing sharp is sticking out of it. The lamp is just right, casting its yellowed glow over your shoulder and into your lap. Wait! Are the curtains open? We wouldn't want anybody leering in at you while you read, would we?

Is that the faucet dripping? You could go into the kitchen and stop it, but it's so dark in there, and that may have been the rattling of the side door knob I heard a moment ago. Somebody checking on us to see if we're locked in and safe. I do hope we're alone in here. One last question before we get started. Do you have a pet? No? I thought I heard something walking on floorboards upstairs. It is probably just my imagination starting to run wild.

You know how things happen. Despite the cold wind outside, you're beginning to sweat. It could be that the heat is turned up too high. I guess that's why the furnace is making that banging noise in the basement. If it quits working, will we have to go down and fix it? A sudden lightheadedness, and your eyes don't quite focus right. A need to clear your throat, more for the noise than the swallowing. But your mouth seems awful dry. Maybe a glass of water will help. Oh that's right, it's still pretty dark in that kitchen, and the water continues to slowly drip. A steady rhythmic beat, beat, beat. Then it stops. How nice. Now the only noise is the sound of your own breathing

Something moves in the corner of the room just outside your field of vision. You felt it, and you almost saw it. But when you turn . . . no, no I guess not. There's nothing there. My mistake. Now the wind seems to be picking up outside. You can hear the shuffle and rattle of the bushes in front of the house. The sound of leaves skipping across the porch is a bit like shuffling feet, isn't it? You could turn on the porch light and peek out the front door. Oh, that's right. The light burned out last week, and you still haven't gotten around to replacing it. But I'm sure it's nothing. And that moan is merely the air rushing around the corner of the house. All old houses creak like that. It's the wood settling on its foundations. Nothing would be outside your door in this weather. Why, you would have to be a crazy person to go out on a night like this . . . wouldn't you?

It's a good night to be inside, curled up with a good book. Well, here it is. You're holding it in your hands. Clean the spots off of your glasses because they make it seem like there's something there when there really isn't. It's a shame that when you put on your reading glasses the rest of the room goes out of focus. The pillows over on the couch really take on weird shapes, don't they? They kind of look like animals when they're all fuzzy like that. Boy oh boy, one's mind can certainly dream up some pretty crazy stuff, can't it? Pull the lap blanket up over your legs. It feels snug and safer that way.

What's that? How did that moth get into the house? Isn't it fun how its flickering shadow grows small to large on the wall and ceiling. You can hear him banging into the lamp shade above your head, can't you? It'll die soon and drop, and then it will be peaceful again. That is, unless you want to go into the kitchen and get a rolled-up paper to squash it. Oh, that's right, the kitchen.

Well, let's just turn the page and start reading. That will make us forget about all of this nonsense. Wait. Damn that faucet. It's started dripping again. You're going to have to go into that kitchen sooner or later. Okay, later. It's time for a quiet little tale of terror first. A little aerobic reading to get your heart rate up. But, my, it's so high already.

Del Howison
September 2007
www.darkdel.com

FOREWORD:
THE ACT OF CREATION

RAY HARRYHAUSEN

Being asked to do a foreword for a book of horror stories is an odd thing for me. Although I have skirted the edge of horror when doing films based upon fantasy, mythology or when creating giant creatures, I have never actually been directly involved with horror in any of my films. I have created many bizarre creatures, but I have never jumped into the horror genre with as much enthusiasm as editors Del Howison and Jeff Gelb.

Horror is their thing, and it is what they do best. With their first effort together in 2005, they won the coveted Bram Stoker Award from the Horror Writer's Association for the Year's Best Anthology. They certainly have the pedigree behind them, as Jeff has edited almost 20 horror anthologies, and Del (along with his wife, Sue) owns America's horror book store in Burbank, California, for which this anthology is named. Also, they are both writers of horror.

The common denominator between us is the art of creation. Animators and writers have much in common—passion, imagination and the countless hours spent alone in small dark rooms. Both of our arts are born of imagination and created with the insight of observation.

Both stop-motion animators and writers must master some unexpected skills. For instance, I learned the art of fencing from a school in Hollywood before I began animating the skeleton sequence for *The 7th Voyage of Sinbad,* as I wanted to know how it felt to wield a sword, so I could project it into the model. A writer must also invest time researching the areas with which he is not familiar in order to bring life and reality to the story.

As I stated in my book *The Art of Ray Harryhausen,* I have always tried to instill character into my creations. To do that I had to observe how the character of a person or animal was expressed and then translate those observations into action. Because a writer needs to get into the character's thoughts as well as his actions, this kind of insight is the same for any professional writer, maybe even more so for people who do what I do.

Much as I go through multiple stages to get to the final product, an editor does the same. He outlines or lays out his book of tales and that produces a rough sketch. He traces the different stories he has chosen until everything fits into his mold of the book's structure. Then, whereas my final product is the animation in a finished film, the editor takes us on a journey through the arc or progression that the layout of the stories has detailed to end up with the finished book.

All in all, it is a creative process that parallels my own process for a very similar end: to tell a story and entertain. Usually, my stories are first of wonderment and fascination, but they may also frighten you or make you laugh. Del and Jeff want to frighten you first and then fill your mind with wonder. To accomplish that effect in this anthology, they have hired some of the finest writers in the genre.

I'm proud they asked me to write the foreword to their book. Maybe someday I'll design the monsters in this book for the movies. Who knows? It's in the lap of the Gods. In the meantime, I hope that these two "dark" editors continue their quest to bring you the macabre horror they know and love so well. So, until we meet again—sweet dreams.

—Ray Harryhausen
London

SUNRISE ON RUNNING WATER

BARBARA HAMBLY

The damn ship was supposed to be unsinkable.

Do you think I'd have set foot on the wretched tub if it weren't?

I embarked at Cherbourg for a number of reasons, chief among them being that the *Titanic* entered port from Southampton at sunset, and loaded in the dusk. I've never liked the thought of shipping myself in my coffin like a parcel, with the attendant risks of inquisitive customs-inspectors, moronic baggage-handlers, and all the tedious beforehand wrangling with a living accomplice who might or might not take the trouble to make sure one's coffin (or trunk—most of us prefer extra-large double trunks for travel) hasn't been installed in the hold lid-down under several thousand pounds of some imbecilic American dowager's frocks. Half the time one has to kill the accomplice anyway. Usually it's a pleasure.

"Are you sure you wish to do this, Napier?" inquired Simon, who had come down to the docks in a closed car to see me off. Being a century and a half older among the UnDead than I—one of the oldest in Europe, in fact—he is able to tolerate even more twilight, waking slightly earlier and, if need presses, can prolong his wakefulness for a short time into the morning hours, though of course only with adequate protection from the sun's destructive light. "You won't be able to hunt once you're on board, you know. The White Star Line keeps very accurate manifests of its passengers, even in third class. It isn't like the old days."

"Simon," I joked, and laid my hand on his gloved wrist, "you've been a vampire too long. You're turning into a cautious old spook—what do they call them these days? A *fuddy-duddy*."

I knew all about the passenger manifests. I'd studied them closely.

We'd hunted the night before, close to sunrise. I'd killed twice. I knew it was going to be a long voyage. Seven or eight days, from Cherbourg to New York. A span of time that bordered on dangerous, for such as we.

I hoped I wasn't one of those vampires who turn crazy after four or five days without a kill—who are so addicted to the pleasure of the death, as well as to its simple nourishment—that they hunt under conditions which are sure to bring them to the attention of authorities: for instance, among a limited and closely-watched group of people. But quite frankly, I didn't know. Without a kill every few days, we start to lose our ability to deceive and ensorcel the minds of the living, a situation I had never permitted to occur.

This was the first time in a hundred and forty years that I'd traveled very far from London. The first time since I had become vampire in 1772 that I had crossed the ocean.

When the UnDead travel, they are horribly vulnerable. Money has always provided some protection in the form of bribes, patent locks, servants, and social pressure (why do you think it's always Evil Lord So-and-So in the penny dreadfuls? It's astonishing how much interest bonds accumulate if allowed to mature for two centuries). But, as I was shortly to learn, accidents do happen. And the longer the journey, the more the chances accumulate that something will go fearfully wrong.

"There's a new world across the ocean, Simon," I said, making my voice grave. "Face it, Europe cannot go on as it is. War is going to break out. The Kaiser is practically jostling statesmen in doorways in the hopes of being challenged. You've seen the new weapons they have. Airships, incendiary bombs, cannons that can demolish a city from miles away. It's a wise man who knows when to make his break for safety."

Ninety-five hours later I was kicking myself for those words, but who knew?

Simon smiled, something he rarely does. "Perhaps you are correct, my friend. Be that so, I trust you will act in the nature of a scout, and send me word of the promised land. Now go, if not with God, at least with the blessing of an indifferent Fate, my Evil Lord . . ." He checked my papers for the name, ". . . Lord Sandridge." He put on his black-tinted spectacles and accompanied me to the barrier, where he added the subtle influence of his mind to mine in the task of getting my luggage through unchecked. I ascended the gangway, and from the rail saw him wave, a slim small form in dark gray, perhaps my only friend among the UnDead.

We are not, you understand, particularly pleasant company, even for one another.

Then I went down to the first-class luggage hold to make sure my coffin-trunk was both accessible and inconspicuous. Simon, I presume, returned home and slaughtered some unsuspecting immigrant en route for breakfast.

We put in at Queenstown on the Irish coast in the morning, before our final embarkation over the deep. It's always a damnable struggle to remain awake in one's coffin for even a short time after the sun is in the sky, but I was determined to make the effort, and it's a good thing I did. Shortly after I'd locked myself in for the day—we were still several hours from Queenstown at that point—I heard stealthy steps on the deck, and smelled the stink of a man's nervous sweat.

Of course someone had noticed the obsessive care I'd taken in bestowing my trunk, and had drawn the usual stupid conclusion that the living are prone to. Greedy sods. Skeleton keys rattled close to my head. I forced down both grogginess and the quick flash of panic in my breast—the hold was absolutely sheltered from any chance of penetration by sunlight—and fought to accumulate enough energy to act.

Get away from here, you stupid bastard! The living have no idea how commanding are the rhythms of vampire flesh; I felt as I had when in mortal life I'd gotten myself sodden-drunk on opium at the Hellfire Club. *This ship stinks with American millionaires and you're trying to rob the trunk of a mere Evil Lord?*

The outer lid opened, then the inner. I gazed up into a round unshaven face and brown eyes stretched huge with shock and fright.

I heaved myself up with what I hoped was a terrifying roar, wrenched the skeleton keys out of the young man's hand, and dropped back into the coffin, hauling the lid down after me and slamming shut its inner bolt. I heard outside a stifled gasping whimper, then heavy shoes hammering away across the deck and up the metal stairs.

I understand he abandoned ship at Queenstown and thus missed all subsequent events. A pity. Drowning was too good for the little swine.

It wasn't fear of robbery, however, that made me struggle to remain awake through the boarding-process at Queenstown, listening with a vampire's preternatural senses to every sound, every voice, every footfall in the ship around me. I had to know who was getting on the ship.

Because of course I had not been completely truthful with Simon as to my reasons for leaving England, or for embarking at Cherbourg for that matter. One never likes to admit when one has made a very foolish mistake.

Which brings me to the subject of Miss Alexandra Paxton.

I don't know under what name she boarded the *Titanic*. She knew, you see, that I'd be keeping an eye on the passenger lists and that I would have changed my own travel plans had I suspected she was on board.

It is another truism of the more puerile examples of horror fiction that the victims of Evil Lord So-and-So or the wicked Countess Blankovsky are generally of the upper, or at worst the professional, classes. This is sheer foolishness, for these people keep track of one another, particularly in a small country like England. (Another motive for choosing America.)

Vampires for the most part live on the poor. We kill people whom no one will miss. Regrettably, these people tend to be dirty, smelly, undernourished, frequently gin-soaked, and conversationally uninteresting. And we *do* enjoy the chase, the cat-and-mouse game: the long slow luring, for days and weeks at a time.

Which is how I'd happened to meet, and court, and flirt with, and take to the opera, and eventually kill Miss Cynthia Engle, only a few days before she was to have wed Lionel Paxton.

Lionel and his sister had sounded like a remarkably boring pair when Miss Engle had told me about them at our clandestine meetings, edged with danger and champagne. I hadn't allowed for my lovely victim's craving for the melodramatic, which discounted her suitor's native shrewdness. In any case, after a train of events too complicated and messy to go into, I had been obliged to kill Lionel as well.

Alexandra had been dogging me ever since.

She came aboard at Queenstown, at the last possible moment. This was an unnecessary inconvenience on her part, since, as I've said, the sun was high in the sky, and I couldn't have come up out of the hold even if I'd been awake. But I was aware of her, as I lay in the strange, clear awareness of the vampire sleep: smelled the distinctive vanilla and sandalwood of her dusting-powder, heard the sharp click of her stride on the decks.

And my heart sank.

There was no way I could kill her on board the *Titanic* without causing a tremendous fuss and possibly being locked in a cabin which might contain a window, which really *would* give the good Captain Smith something to write about in his log.

But *her* goal, on the other hand, was not survival. I knew from a previous encounter that she wore about her neck and wrists silver chains that would effectively sear my flesh should I come in contact with them, and carried a revolver loaded with silver bullets which she would not have the slightest hesitation about firing.

I also knew she was an extremely accurate shot.

I can't tell you exactly how the UnDead know when it's safe to emerge from their hiding places. There are those of us who can step forth in lingering Nordic twilights with no more than frantic itching of the skin and a sense of intolerable panic, others whose flesh will autocombust while the last morning stars are still visible in the sky. Our instinct in this matter is very strong, however—and those of us who lack it generally don't remain vampires very long.

I quit my coffin-trunk the minute I felt I could do so safely, around seven-thirty Thursday night, and ascended the several flights of steps past the squash court and through the seamen's and third-class quarters, down the long crew corridor known as "Scotland Road," and through a maze of passages and emergency ladders eventually reached my own B Deck stateroom in First Class. The advertising for the *Titanic* had strongly implied that no First Class passenger need be even aware that such things as lesser mortals existed on the ship—another reason I'd chosen the vessel for my escape. Sharp-eyed stewards abounded to make sure those who paid for elevation above the Great Unwashed achieved it, but they, like most of the living (thank God) were prey to appearances. I was deep in conversation with the young and extremely pretty wife of an elderly American millionaire when the door of the stair from below opened and Miss Paxton slipped through.

She was clothed in a gown that must have cost her at least half of what her unfortunate brother had to leave: blue velvet with a bodice of cream-colored lace. A little aigret of blue gems and cream-colored feathers adorned the springy thickness of her mouse-brown hair. She was a tall girl, of the sort referred to by Americans as a "fine, strapping lass;" her jaw was long, her nose narrow, and her blue-gray eyes cool and daunting. She carried a blue velvet handbag and a trailing mass of lace shawl draped in such a fashion as to conceal her right hand and whatever might have been in it, and I fled like a rabbit before she even got a glimpse of me.

"That young person," I said to the head steward as I pressed a hundred dollars American into his hand, "is an impostor, a confidence trickster who has been harassing me for a number of months. I do not know under what pretext she will attempt to get near me nor do I wish to know. Only keep her away from me, or from any room that I am in, for the duration of this voyage. Understand?"

"Yes, sir. Certainly, Lord Sandridge."

As I slipped through into the dining saloon an American matron's Pekingese lunged at me in a fury of yapping. They really should keep those nasty little vermin locked up.

Of course that wasn't the end of Miss Paxton. Having guessed I'd be traveling first-class, she had invested God knows how much in a first-class wardrobe, so I was never sure I could avoid her merely by sticking to the A Deck promenades. Nor could I afford to keep to my stateroom during the night hours when I was up and about. She would, I guessed, be looking for me. By whispers overheard from the cabin stewards and maids—and believe me, a vampire can hear whispers through both locked doors and the conversation of American socialites—I guessed she had garnered allies among them by some tale of disinheritance, persecution, and attempted rape.

She stalked me most of that first night, for she had a constitution of iron; I was eventually reduced to donning an inconspicuous pair of trousers and a tweed jacket and hiding out on the third-class deck among the Irish.

At sunrise I retired to my coffin-trunk again, but I did not sleep with anything resembling peace.

All through that day and the next I heard her footfalls, smelled her blood and dusting-powder, in the dark of my dreams as she moved through the holds.

I dreamed about her.

And I dreamed about the sea.

As Mr. Stoker so obligingly pointed out in his book *Dracula,* we—the UnDead—cannot cross running water, except at the hour of astronomical midnight, and at the moment when the tide turns. He is quite right. It was more than dread that seized me, when I and my vampire master stood on the threshold of London Bridge and he ordered me across. It was a sickness, a weakness that paralyzed me, as if death itself were rising from the moving river below us like poisoned mist. My master laughed at me, the bastard, and we took a hackney cab across the river to hunt. In later years we'd take the Underground. He'd keep me talking, to school me to focus my mind against the panicky disorientation that flowing water produces, but like all vampires I hate the temporary loss of my powers over the minds of the living.

That was the thing that most worried me during that April voyage. That while I could cajole, or manipulate, or charm, or bribe those luscious-smelling, warm-blooded, rosily-glowing morsels with whom I was surrounded every night, I couldn't alter their perceptions of me, or of what was going on around them.

I couldn't make them fall in love with me, so they'd be eager to do my bidding.

I couldn't lure them in a trance into nooks and corners of the hold, nor could I stand outside their cabin doors and tamper with their dreams.

Except for the fact that I retained some, though not all, of the superhuman strength of a vampire, I was to all intents and purposes human again, and indeed a trifle less so. The touch of silver would sear and blister my flesh; the touch of sunlight set me ablaze like a screaming torch.

And if this wretched young woman—who was as tall as I, and strong for a mortal—managed somehow to tip me overside, once in the water I would be paralyzed. I would sink like a stone, Simon had warned me, for the vampire state changes the UnDead flesh and we become physically perfect: all muscle, no fat.

Fat is what floats a body. (Simon knows things like that. He's made a scientific study of our state, and is fond of parading his knowledge, solicited or not.) Even in the sunless black of the deep ocean, I would not die, though crushed by the pressure of the water and frozen by its cold. Nor would I be able to move, save for the few minutes after midnight, or when the moon passed directly overhead and turned the tidal flow. Then the magnetism of the moving water would conquer again, and the sluggish currents push me where they would.

I would be conscious, Simon had assured me. (How the hell would *he* know?) I could think of no state closer to those described by Dante in his book of Hell.

And if Miss Paxton shot me with a silver bullet, even if it did not strike my heart, the logical place for her to dump my then-unresisting body would be into the drink.

All these things wove in and out of my dreams, with the clack of her shoe-heels on the storage-hold deck.

It was altogether not a pleasant voyage, even *before* 11:39 P.M. on the night of April 14.

I'd put in a brief appearance in the dining-room that Sunday night, enough so that no oversolicitous fellow-passenger or cabin steward would come inquiring for my health during the daytime. My story was that I was too seasick to eat. Most older vampires come to despise the stench of human food. I enjoyed it, and enjoyed too the spectacle of my table-mates shoveling away quantities of poached salmon with mousseline sauce, roast duckling, squabs and cress, asparagus vinaigrette, foie gras, and éclairs—to say nothing of gallons of cognac and wines. The flavors linger for many hours in the blood, another reason, incidentally, that we prefer to sup when we can on the rich rather than the poor.

My custom on the *Titanic* was to spend most of my night moving from place to place in the first-class accommodation. I hadn't seen Miss Paxton anywhere on the A or B Decks since Thursday night, but twice, once in the Palm Court outside the First-Class Smoking Room and once in the corridor near my suite, I'd caught the lingering whiff of her dusting-powder. She was still finding her way up onto the First Class Decks.

She could be waiting for me, gun in hand, around any corner.

For that reason I was on the bow deck of the ship—as far forward on B Deck as I could get and a goodly distance from what might have been supposed to be a gentlemanly lurking-place in the First-Class Smoking Room—when I saw a dark mass of almost-clear ice lying straight in the path of the ship.

Being on open water hadn't affected my ability to see in the dark, any more than it affected my ability to detect Miss Paxton's cologne. The iceberg, though several miles away, would be almost invisible to human eyes, for there was no moon that night and the ocean lay flat calm, eliminating even the telltale froth of waves breaking around the dark ice's base. The previous night, in my ramblings around the ship, I'd heard the men discussing a warning of heavy pack ice received from an American steamer coming east, and around dinner time the temperature of the air had dropped.

I worried no more than did anybody else onboard about the *Titanic* actually sinking, of course. Her hull was divided into water-tight compartments that could be closed at the touch of a button. But I did worry about there being a period of confusion in which one passenger—that is to say myself—might easily be incapacitated (say, with a silver bullet in the back) and dropped overboard without anyone's seeing it happen. An investigation might later focus on Miss Paxton's purported vengefulness, but that wouldn't do *me* any good.

I descended to the C Deck well and down the stairs to the cargo holds, where the "Scotland Road" corridor would lead me, eventually, to the Grand Staircase, and so up again eventually to the Boat Deck, at the rear of which lay the bridge.

And there she was, stepping out of the door of a servants' stair, blocking my path.

She said softly, "I have you, villain."

I said, just as softly, "Bugger."

She brought up her hand and I saw the gun in it. Down here surrounded by the crew quarters the sound of a shot would have brought everyone running, but at thirty feet it wasn't likely she'd miss. If she didn't get me through the heart the silver would cause such extraordinary damage as to both incapacitate me wherever it hit, and to cause great curiosity in the ship's doctor. On land I could have rushed her before she fired.

But I didn't trust my reflexes. I wheeled and plunged for the transverse passageway that would take me—I hoped—down the smaller crew corridor, and so to another stairway up. Her heels clattered in pursuit as I darted around the corner, fled down the brightly-lighted white tunnel. I debated for a moment simply stepping into the shadow beside the nearest stairway and taking her as she came past—this late at night it would be easy to drop *her*, unconscious (or dead—I hadn't fed in four days and I was ravenous), over the side.

But she had the gun. And I knew from the past that she was a lusty screamer. I darted to the nearest downward stairway and found myself lost in the mazes around the squash court and the quarters of lesser crew on F Deck. I could hear her behind me still, though farther off, it seemed. It was astonishing how those metal corridors reechoed and tangled sound, and down here the thumping of the engines confused even the uncanny hearing of the UnDead. The main stairway led up through the third-class dining hall but that, I knew, would be the logical place for her to cut me off. There was another, smaller stair by the Turkish Bath, and that's where I was, halfway up, when a shuddering impact made the whole ship tremble and knocked me, reeling, off my feet and nearly to the bottom of the steps again.

I don't think I doubted for an instant that we'd hit that wretched iceberg.

Only a human could have missed it that long. It towered above the ship, for Heaven's sake, glistening but dark: it was almost clear ice, as I'd seen, not the powdery white of ice that's been exposed to the air. I understand (again, from Simon, who wasted not a moment after I finally reached London again in telling me, *I told you so*) that when the upper sides of icebergs melt sufficiently to alter their balance they sometimes flip over, exposing faces that are far less reflective, especially on a moonless night. Even so . . .

I clung for a moment to the stair-rail, listening. The lights still blazed brightly, and after the first long, grinding jar there was no further shaking. But as I stretched my senses out—out and down, to the decks below me—I could hear the dim confusion of men's voices, the clatter of frenzied activity.

And the pounding roar of water shooting into the ship as if forced from a fire-hose.

I thought, *Damn it, if it floods the first-class luggage hold I'm sunk.* I blush to say that was the very expression that formed itself in my mind, though at the time I thought only in terms of my light-proof double trunk and the two handsome windows in my stateroom. I had no idea what the White Star Line procedure was for keeping track of passengers and luggage on a disabled ship until another vessel could come alongside to take everyone off, but there was no guarantee that any of that would happen until after daylight.

On the other hand, I thought, depending on how much confusion there was, it would now be very easy to dispose of Miss Paxton without anyone being the wiser.

Trunk first.

First-Class luggage was on G Deck, at the bow. The gangways were sufficiently wide to get the trunk up at least as far as the C Deck cargo well. I was striding forward along a corridor still largely deserted—crewmembers sleep whenever they can, the lazy bastards—when the heavy beat of the engines ceased.

Silence and utter stillness, for the first time since we'd lain at Queenstown, filled the ship, seeming louder than any thunder.

I wasn't the only one to find the silence more disturbing than impact with thousands of tons of ice. Doors began opening along the corridor, men and women—most of them young and all of them tousled from sleep—emerged. "What is it?" "Why're we stopped?"

"Hit an iceberg," I said. I pulled a roll of banknotes from the pocket of my tuxedo jacket, and added, "I'll need assistance getting my trunk from the First-Class hold. It contains papers that I cannot risk having soaked." I could have carried the trunk by myself, of course, but if seen doing so I could kiss good-by any chance of remaining unnoticed, unquestioned, or uninvestigated for the rest of the trip.

"I'm sorry, Lord Sandridge." Fourth Officer Boxhall appeared behind me, uniformed and worried-looking. "We may need the crew to stand by and help with the mailroom, if the water comes up onto the Orlop Deck. If you'll return to your stateroom, I'll have a man come there the moment we know one can be spared. At the moment there doesn't seem to be much damage, but we should know more within half-an-hour."

I could have told him there was water pouring into what sounded like several of the water-tight compartments down below, but reasoned he'd have the truth very shortly. One of the stewardesses was looking closely at me, a thick-chinned, fair-haired Yorkshire girl whom I'd seen more than once in conversation with Miss Paxton. She moved off swiftly down the corridor, slipping between the growing gaggles of crewmen. So much for any hope of waiting in my stateroom.

Still, I thought, midnight was only ten minutes off. If there were crewmen hauling sacks of mail out of the way of floodwaters in the First-Class cargo hold, I'd be able to divert their attention from me while I rescued the trunk myself.

Or killed Miss Paxton.

And by long before sunrise, I reflected as I strode toward the stair, I'd know whether I was going on another vessel, or staying hidden in some sun-proof, locked nook on the *Titanic* while repairs were effected. With any luck I'd be able to get an immigrant or two in the confusion as well.

Miss Paxton would be up on B Deck, headed for my stateroom. On C Deck some of the Swedes and Armenians from steerage were still laughing and playing with chunks of the ice that had been scraped off the iceberg. On the B Deck promenade a few people were prowling about, dressed in their coats and their thickest sweaters; a young man in evening-clothes showed me a piece of ice, then dropped it in his highball: "Saw the thing go past. Bloody amazing!"

"You don't think there's been any damage to the ship?" asked an elderly lady, doddering by on the arm of her superannuated spouse.

"Good Lord, no. God himself couldn't sink this ship."

Simon would have crossed himself, vampire or no.

If I ever find myself in a similar situation again—God forbid!—I will do so, too.

By this time I realized—and the UnDead are more sensitive to such matters than the living—that the deck under my feet was just slightly out of true. With all that water in the compartments below that didn't surprise or upset me. I climbed to the Marconi shack on the Boat Deck—the room where the telegraphers sat pecking frantically at their electric keys. "We've sent word to the *Californian,* but she hasn't replied," said one of the young men, when I asked. "Probably turned off his set and went to bed. Bastard nearly blew my ears off earlier tonight, when I was trying to deal with the passenger messages. The *Carpathian*'s about sixty miles south of us. She'll be here in four or five hours, to take the passengers off."

Four hours would put its arrival in darkness, I reflected as I made my way toward my own stateroom and what I hoped would be a rendezvous with my pursuer. Five hours, at dawn.

Which meant that the moment Miss Paxton was safely out of the way I would have to get that trunk, one way or another. And be where I could get into it come first light. Never, I vowed, would I travel again if I could help it: it was just one damn complication after another.

I could scent Miss Paxton's dusting-powder as I entered the corridor leading to my stateroom. The scent was strong, but she was nowhere in sight. In the other cabins I heard the murmur of voices—a woman complained about having to go out on deck in the cold, which was prodigious—but there was certainly neither panic nor concern. I took a few steps along the corridor, listening, sniffing.

She was in my stateroom.

Of course. She'd got the maid to let her in.

This would be easier than I'd thought.

I closed my eyes as midnight moved into the icy heavens overhead. Reached out my mind to hers, where she waited in the comfortable darkness of my room. Laid on her mind, one by one, the fragile veils of sleep.

Gently, gently . . . I'd done this to her before, back in London, and had to be all the more subtle because she knew what it felt like, and would resist if she recognized the sensations again. But she was tired from prowling the ship by night in quest of a clear shot at me, by day in search of my trunk. I could feel her slipping into dream. I murmured to her in the voice of the River Cher, beside which she and her idiot brother Lionel had played as children; whispered to her as the breeze had whispered among the willow-leaves on its bank.

Sleep . . . sleep . . . you're home and safe. Your parents are watching over you, no harm can come to you . . . .

One has only about ten minutes, at the very outside, at those turning-hours of noon and midnight, when the positions of earth and stars (as Simon has explained it to me) are strong enough to counterbalance the terrible influence of the tides. It was excruciating, keeping still, concentrating my thoughts on those of the young woman in my stateroom. Feeling those seconds of power tick away, calculating how many I'd need to stride down the hall, open the door, and bury my fangs in her neck . . .

An image I had to keep stringently from my thoughts while my mind whispered to hers. *Sleep—rest—you'll sleep much easier if you take off those itchy heavy silver chains around your neck. It's safe to do so—you're safe . . . They're so heavy and annoying . . .*

I felt her fumble sleepily with her collar-buttons (why do women persist in wearing garments that button up the back?). Saw her in the eyes of my heart, head pillowed on velvety hair half-unbound on the leather of the armchair. Fingers groping clumsily at her throat . . . *Sleep—*

The catch was large, solid, and complicated. Bugger. She must have chosen it so, knowing it wasn't easy to undo in half-sleep or trance. Damn, how many minutes—how many seconds—left . . . ?

Gentle, gentle, Lionel is asking for the necklaces. *You have to take them off to give them to him—*

I heard her whisper in her heart, *Lionel,* and tears trickled down her face. In her dreams she saw her brother, plump and fatuous as he'd been in life, holding out his hand to her. *Got to have silver to wear to my wedding, old girl. Not legal if the groom's not wearing silver. New rules.*

She let the revolver slide from her fingers, brought up both hands. The catch gave, silver links sliding down her breasts. Seconds left, but enough—

I strode forward down the corridor and that God-cursed, miserable, miniaturized hair-farm of an American matron's Pekingese threw itself out of the door of a near-by stateroom and fastened his teeth in my ankle. The teeth of such a creature would hardly imperil a soggy toast-point, much less a vampire in full pursuit of undefended prey, but the UnDead are as likely as any other subject of Lord Gravity to trip if their feet come in contact with a ten-pound hairball mid-stride. I went sprawling, and although I caught myself as a cat does, with preternatural speed, the damage was done. The Peke braced his tiny feet and let out a salvo of barks, his mistress appeared in the stateroom door just as I was readying a kick that would have caved in the little abortion's skull, and shrieked at me, "How *dare* you, sir! Come to mummy, Sun!"

And the next second Miss Paxton, collar unbuttoned, hair tumbling over her shoulders, and gun in hand, was in the door of my stateroom, taking aim at a distance of six feet . . .

And midnight was over.

I fled. Mrs. Harper (I think that was her name), straightening up with her struggling hell-hound in her arms, effectively blocked the corridor for the instant that it took me to get out of the line of fire, and I pelted down the staircase, into the nearest corridor, with Miss Paxton like a silent fury at my heels.

There were people in the corridors now, my fellow-passengers in every imaginable variation of pajamas, sweaters, coats, bathrobes, and life jackets, all of them carping about having to go out on the boat decks, and all of them impeding Miss Paxton from taking aim at me—and me from getting far enough ahead to lose her. I strode, dodged, slithered bow-ward along the B Deck corridor, making for the cargo well that would give me swift access to the bowels of the ship. The lights were still on, but if they went out—as I thought they must, with the holds flooding—she would surely be mine.

The deck was definitely sloped underfoot when I reached "Scotland Road" on D Deck again, now milling with crewmen. At the head of the spiral stair going down to E and F, I stopped short with a jolt of sickened shock. Beneath me a pit of green water churned, eerily illuminated by the lights that still burned on the levels below.

That water looked awfully *high*.

The gun cracked behind me, and I spun; there were still crewmen in the corridor, but none were between me and the emergency ladder from which Miss Paxton had just emerged, and not a single one attempted to stop her. I don't think the mad bitch would have cared if they had. Maybe her tales of my perfidy had spread widely among the crew: maybe they had a better idea of what was going on below our feet than the passengers or I did. The fact remained that she had a gun and a clear shot, and I knew that even a glancing wound from it could prove fatal. I hadn't drunk the blood of thousands of grimy peasants, factory workers, prostitutes, and street-urchins over the course of fourteen decades to let myself be put out of the way by an enraged middle-class virago.

I did the only thing possible.

As she fired I fell against the rail, tipped over it, and dropped straight down into that seething jade-green seawater hell.

It was every bit as cold as I'd been led to expect.

My mind seemed to fracture, to go numb. I screamed, and my mouth and lungs flooded with water—it's a damn good thing I'd quit breathing many years previously. I remember staring up through the green water and seeing Alexandra Paxton looking down at me, gun still in her hand.

I was conscious, but I felt my ability to act at all—to summon my limbs to obey my disoriented mind—bleeding out of me like gore from a severed femoral artery. I couldn't move until she left, until she was convinced that I was dead, and she seemed to stand there—gloating, I expect, the miserable cow!—forever.

Then she spit at me, and turned away.

It took what felt like minutes of slow, clumsy thrashing before I could thrust myself to the door into what I think was F Deck. My fingers were like cricket bats, and I don't know how long I spent simply trying to get the door open. My brain was like a cricket bat, too, trying to fish a single wet noodle of orientation—where the hell was the stairway up to E Deck?—from the swirling maelstrom of horror, shock, terrifying weakness, and nightmare panic.

And I knew with blinding certainty that, watertight compartments be damned, the ship was going down.

Voices, impossibly distant, came to me from all parts of the ship.

Voices that said, "She's sinking by the head."

Voices that said, "You must get in the boat, Mary. I shall follow later."

Voices that said, "Get back there, you. Women and children first."

Nearer, feet thudded amid a frightened yammering of Swedish, Gaelic, Arabic, Japanese: third-class passengers trying to find their way up the maze of stairways to the decks above. Crewmen shouted at them to go back, to stay in their cabins, they'd be called when it was time for them to get in the lifeboats. But I'd gone to sea, God help me, as a living man all those years ago, and I knew jolly well how many people could fit into a boat the size of the mere sixteen that were in *Titanic*'s davits.

I had to get up to the decks before they started letting those foreign swine take up boat space that I'd paid for with my first-class ticket. And I had to get there before the foreign swine realized that there wasn't going to be enough room for them in the boats, and took matters out of the crew's hands and into their own dirty paws.

The struggle was literally Hellish: I refer specifically to the Fifth Circle of Dante's Hell, where the Sullen bubble in eternal stasis in the mud beneath the waters of the River Styx. I can only assume that the Styx is warmer than the Atlantic ocean in mid-April. Water at a temperature of thirty degrees has exactly the same effect on the UnDead as it would on the living, only, of course, more prolonged, since the living wouldn't survive more than a few minutes even were breathing not an issue. Beyond the paralyzing cold, there was the sheer hammering disorientation of ocean water—living water—itself. For long periods I became simply immobilized, my brain shrieking, fighting to make a hand move, a foot thrust against the metal walls that hemmed me in; it was like trying to remain awake in the final extremities of exhaustion. I'd come out of it, twist and thrash and wrench myself to push along a foot or so, then sink back into an inactivity I couldn't break no matter how frantically I tried.

Those periods got longer, the moments of clumsy, horrified lucidity shorter and shorter. And around me I could feel the walls, the hull, the decking tilting, tilting, as the weight of the water in the bow doubled and quadrupled and quintupled, and I hung there helpless, aware of the sheer, horrifying *depth* of the ocean below.

I wonder why I didn't go mad. Not with fear that I would die when that final hideous tipping-point was at last reached and the ship began her lightless plunge to the bottom: with the appalling certainty that *I would not and could not.*

Ever.

Whether because the water conducted sound, or for some other cause, as I spastically, intermittently, agonizingly crept and pushed my way toward the stairways and survival, I was completely aware of everything that was passing on the decks above. Even above the cheerful ragtime being pumped out by the ship's band, I could hear with nightmarish clarity every conversation, every footfall, every creak of the tackle as the crew loaded up the lifeboats and lowered them to the surface of the sea far below. The ships' officers kept saying, "*Women and children first*," and the women and children— brainless cretins!—kept finding reasons to remain on the main vessel where it was warm. A number of men got into those early boats unchallenged, since there were so many women who weren't inter- ested: I learned later one of them was sent off with only twelve people in it. The miserable Mrs. Harper got off accompanied not only by her husband but by her wretched Pekingese.

But around me the walls changed their angle, with what to me seemed to be fearful speed, until even those first-class idiots on deck (I use the term advisedly) realized there was something greatly wrong. By the time I dragged myself at last, shaking and dripping, up a main- tenance ladder onto D Deck, and stumbled toward an unguarded crew ladder to go above, the bow of the ship was underwater and all but four of the boats were gone.

I won't go into a detailed description of the behavior of the some two thousand men and women in competition for the approximately one hundred and sixty available passes out of the jaws of death. Anyone who has lived for close to two centuries in a major city like London has had ample occasion to view the behavior of mobs, and the passengers of the *Titanic* actually acquitted themselves fairly mildly, all things considered. Yes, the crew members had to form a cordon around one boat and threaten to shoot any non-lady who tried to board; yes, the men did rush another of the boats (I was too far back in the mob to get on, damn those other selfish bastards to Hell).

Astonishingly, the lights remained on, and the band continued to play, giving an eerie disjointedness to the scene, but somehow, I think, keeping everyone just on the human side of total panic. God knows what it would have been like in darkness, with no sound but the groaning of the ship's overstrained armature readying itself to snap. I had long since given up any thought of getting my trunk to safety, or of Alexandra Paxton. I learned much later she'd gone straight from shooting me (as she thought) to the Boat Deck, and had gotten off fairly early in the proceedings. She returned to England and lived, I regret to say, happily ever after.

The bitch.

For my part, my only thought was getting into a boat and trusting to luck that the rescue ship would arrive while night still lay upon the ocean. The richest people in the world were aboard the *Titanic,* for God's sake! Other vessels must be racing one another to pick them up.

Mustn't they?

In addition to the regular lifeboats the *Titanic* carried four canvas collapsible boats, and two of these were assembled and put in the lifeboat davits as the last of the wooden boats was lowered away. The other two, lashed uselessly to the top of the officers' quarters, were too tangled up in rope to be dragged to the side, but men swarmed over them, trying to get them into shape to be floated off if and when, God help us all, the ship went under.

And under she would go. I knew it, could hear with the hyper-acute senses of the UnDead the snapping creak of her skeleton cracking under the weight of water pulling her down, and the whole stern end of her—God knows how many tons!—that was by this time lifted completely clear of the glass-smooth, obsidian ocean. The lights were beginning to glow red as the generators began to fail. As I fought my way through the mob to one of the collapsibles, a dapper little gentleman who'd been helping with the ropes turned to the officer in charge and said, "I'm going aboard." When the officer—who'd been fighting off would-be male boarders for some minutes—opened his mouth to protest, the dapper gentleman said, "I'm Bruce Ismay; President of the White Star Line." He stepped into the boat.

As it swung clear of the deck I reached the rail: *You may be President of the White Star Line but if there's room for you, there's room for me . . .*

And I froze. I could have batted aside any of the officers who tried to prevent me, and the leap would have been nothing. For one moment, just before the men began to lower, less than two feet separated the boat's gunwale from the rail; with a vampire's altered muscle and inhuman strength, I've cleared gaps four and five times that with ease.

Two feet of space, with running water not all that far below.

Had I been assured of the return of my immortal soul by so doing, I could not have made that jump.

And by the time I fought my way to the place where the other serviceable collapsible was being lowered, it was away. A number of passengers jumped at this point, when the boats were close enough to have picked them up. If you walked forward, it wasn't all that far to the surface of the sea. I made my way to the roof of the officers' quarters and joined the struggle to get the remaining two collapsibles unraveled from the snarl of ropes, get their canvas sides put up (the designer of the damned things is another on the long list of persons I hope will rot in Hell), and get them to the rails: if one fell upside-down (which it did) it was too heavy and too clumsy to be righted. I could feel the angle of the deck steepening, could tell by the dark water's advance that the ship was being pulled forward and down.

At 2:15 the bridge went under. A rolling wave of black water swept over the roof of the officers' quarters and floated the right-side-up collapsible free. I scrambled aboard, fighting and clawing the army of other men trying to do the same thing; glancing back I could see the *Titanic*'s stern, swarming with humanity like ants on a floating branch, lift high out of the ocean. It was a fearful sight. Voices were screaming all around me and if I'd ever had a doubt that a vampire could pray, and pray sincerely, it was put to rest in that moment. I shrieked God's name with the best of them as I threw myself into that miserable canvas tub, and we oared away, gasping, from the great ship as she snapped in half—dear God, with what a sound!—and her stern crashed back, the wave propelling our boat on its way.

I saw her lights beneath the water as the bow pulled down, dragging the stern after it. The stern rose straight up for a moment, venting steam at every orifice and wreathed in the despairing wails of those wretches still trapped aboard; pointed briefly like a stumpy accusing finger at the beacon-cold blazons of the icy stars . . .

. . . then sank.

With my trunk aboard.

And no rescue-boat in sight.

It was twenty minutes after two in the morning. Dawn in the north Atlantic comes, in mid-April, at roughly five A.M.; first light about a half-hour before that.

Dear God, was all I could think. *Dear God.*

The men—mostly crewmen—around me in the boat were praying, but I was at something of a loss for words. What I really wanted was for a light-proof, unsinkable coffin to drop down out of the heavens so I could go on killing people and drinking their blood for another few centuries. Even in my extremity, I didn't think God would answer that one.

So I waited.

The collapsible's sides never had been properly put up. We started shipping water almost immediately and barely dared stir at the oars, for fear of altering the boat's precarious balance and sending us all down into those black miles of abyss. This consideration at least kept the men in the boat from rowing back to pick up swimmers, whose voices hung over the water like the humming of insects on a summer night. Some sixteen hundred people went into the sub-freezing water that night—I'm told most of the other boats, even those lightly laden, held off for fear of being swamped. One American woman tried to organize the other ladies in her boat to stage a rescue at this point and was roundly snubbed: so much for the tender-heartedness of the fair sex.

The cries subsided after twenty minutes or so. The living don't last long, in water that cold.

Then we could only wait, in fear perhaps more excruciating than we'd left behind us on the *Titanic,* for the canvas boat to slowly fill with water, and sink away beneath our feet.

Or in my case, for the earth to turn, and the sun to rise, and my flesh to spontaneously ignite in unquenchable fire.

It was small consolation to reflect that such an event would briefly keep my fellow passengers warm and, one hoped, would take their minds off their own upcoming immersion.

Should the boat sink before I burst into flames, I found myself thinking, my best chance would be to guide myself, as best I could, toward the *Titanic* wreck. The short periods of volition permitted by even a long succession of noons and midnights would never be enough to counteract the movement of the slow, deep-flowing ocean currents. Staying in the wreck itself would be my best and only chance.

I could hear Simon's voice in my mind, speculating about how divers were already learning to search for ships foundered in shallow waters, for the sunken treasures of the Spanish Main and the ancient Mediterranean. *In time I fancy they shall discover even Atlantis, or at the very least whatever galleons went down chock-full of treasure in mid-ocean. You can be sure that whatever science can invent, treasure-hunters will not be long in adapting to their greed.*

The richest men and women in the world had been my fellow passengers. Very few of them stuffed their jewels in their pockets before getting into the lifeboats. Of course the treasure-hunters would come, as soon as science made it possible for them to do so.

And even as I thought this, I sent up the feeblest of human prayers: *Please, God, no . . .*

As if He'd listen.

At 3:30, far off to the southeast, a flicker of white light pierced the blackness, followed by a cannon's distant boom.

A slight breeze had come up, making the ocean choppy and the air yet more bitterly cold. Tiny as a nail-clipping, a new moon hung over the eastern horizon. Men had begun to fall off the collapsible, which was now almost up to its gunwales in sea-water that hovered right around the temperature of ice: fall silently, numb, dead within sight of salvation. I could see all around us the ocean filled with the pale-gleaming blobs of what the sailors called "trash" and "growlers," miniature icebergs the size of motorcars or single-story houses, ghostly in the starlight. Among them, or west and south in the clearer water, I could make out the dark shapes of the other lifeboats. Could hear the voices of the passengers in them, tiny occasional drops of sound, like single crickets in the night.

It wanted but an hour 'til first light. I think I would have wept, had it been possible for vampires to shed tears.

The sky was staining gray when one of the lifeboats was sighted, slowly inching toward us. How far we'd drifted I don't know; I'd sunk into a lethargy of horror, watching the slow growing of the light. It might have been the effect of the water in the boat, which was up to our knees by this time; there were only a dozen men left, and a woman from third class. I could barely move my head to follow the lifeboat's agonizingly lentitudinous approach.

Everything seemed to have slowed to the gluey pace of a helpless dream. It was as if time itself were slowly jelling to immobility with the cold. Far across the water—perhaps a mile or two, in the midst of the floating ice—loomed the dark bulk of a small freighter. All around it the lifeboats were creeping inward, some from miles away, like nearly-frozen insects painfully dragging themselves toward the jam-pot that is the Heaven of their tiny lives.

And I could see that, even if the lifeboat reached us—and each second it seemed that we'd go down under their very noses—there was no way under God's pitiless sky that it would reach the freighter before full light.

Don't make me do this, God. Don't make me . . .

Like the laughter of God, light flushed up into the gray sky, turning all the icebergs to silver, the water to sapphire of incredible hardness and depth. At the same time my frozen flesh was suffused with unbearable heat, my skin itching, writhing . . . my flesh readying to burst into flame.

Hiding in a boiler on the wreck, curled in some corner of the grand staircase or the Palm Court Lounge, I would have only to wait for the treasure-hunters to come.

The cold and darkness would only *seem* eternal.

Would hope in those circumstances be more cruel than the comfort of despair?

I closed my eyes, tipped myself backward over the side.

I was about to find out.

DOG

JOE R. LANSDALE

Jim Aaron thought maybe he ought not to go riding because the front tire of his bike felt as if it might be losing air. Nothing serious, but a long ride could cause problems. He had noticed that the tire felt a bit flat when he checked it yesterday morning after his ride, but this morning, after the fight with his wife over some stupid, unimportant thing, he had forgotten all about it. He was just glad to leave the house. If he wanted to put air in the tire, he had to go in the house to get the air pump out of the closet, and he didn't want to do that, lest he stir things up again.

He sat on the bike at the end of his drive and looked back at the brick house with its well-trimmed shrubs and felt something he couldn't identify. Anger. Disappointment. He couldn't place it, but whatever it was, it was gnawing at his insides like some kind of trapped, starving rat.

He felt that he should be happier than ever. Six months ago, he had become a millionaire, and through no effort of his own. He had been working as a columnist for a newspaper, and it was a job he enjoyed, but then came the discovery of oil and gas on land he had forgotten he owned. Some godforsaken piece of wilderness out in the sticks, covered in brush and woods and full of snakes and chiggers. But just before his aunt died, she had sent in the oil and gas researchers, and by the time they got to it, found gas and oil, his aunt was gone, and she had left the land and the oil to him. It was pumping enough every month to give them more money than he made in a year as a humor columnist. A few papers had picked up his column, and it looked as if it were on its way, but now there was no need. He was up to his neck in money.

Thing was, he and his wife fought all the time now. Over money, of course. How it should be spent, what they needed to own. The house they had now was very nice, very comfortable, and they had a gardener, but somehow it hadn't made things better. They had been living okay, not special, but okay, and they were happy then, and now they had plenty of money, so why weren't they happy? Even sex, something they enjoyed a lot before and were good at, had gone out the window. As of late he had begun to feel emasculated, and he felt his wife sensed it and responded in kind, treated him like a neutered pet instead of a man.

The money had made him worthless, and he missed writing the column, wished now he hadn't quit the job when the money came in. Should have stayed at it, he thought. He considered possibly getting his old job back, or maybe trying to write a humor book. Right now, however, it was all just a daydream from the seat of a bicycle.

Whatever the problem, Jim decided he didn't want to go back into that house for the air pump, or for that matter any other reason, at least not for a while. Not until Gail cooled off and he did the same. Besides, the exercise was good for him. Made him feel good, kept him healthy. He just wouldn't ride far, spare the tire, come back to the house, and find some way to make it up to Gail. Fact was he couldn't quite remember what it was they were fighting about.

Jim eased the bike out onto the street. It was a small street, and the traffic was near non-existent this time of morning, and only picked up in the afternoon when residents of the neighborhood came home from work. Besides, he had discovered at the far end of the street a little path that went off in the woods, and he could ride there without worrying about traffic at all. He wouldn't go too far, in case the tire was actually losing air through a small hole instead of by common wear and time, but it would be a nice short ride, something to get the blood pumping and maybe clear his head of domestic cobwebs.

He pedaled off, coasting mostly. It was a great day, with only one dark cloud in the sky. It looked as if someone had wadded up a piece of carbon paper and tossed it into a blue box full of huge puffs of white cotton. He lifted his head and looked up at it, felt the heat of the sun on his face.

A dog barked as he rode by the Langston home. It was their poodle, Cuddles. Cuddles was white and untrimmed. He looked like a small ball of soft white wire. Cuddles continued to bark and run alongside for a while, then finally left the chase to go back home.

It only took about twenty minutes to reach the end of the street, and by that time, Jim had worked up a pretty healthy sweat. He didn't feel the least bit winded and had pedaled a lot of his frustration out. He thought of Gail, decided he had to make things up to her somehow, get back on track. Besides after six years of marriage, they couldn't be that far off track, not in just six months, when they should be happiest of all. He realized he was losing focus again, falling back into thinking about this morning, and that wasn't what he needed. What he needed was to be in the moment, feel the wind on his face, feel his body working the bike, the road beneath the wheels bouncing him along.

The woods at the end of the road were thick, and the road was of white sand, but it had not become so hot yet that it was like powder. Later in the year the East Texas sun would hammer it until it came apart, and if you were to pick up a handful of sand, it would run through your fingers like water. Now, however, there had been enough rain, and spring was not a complete memory, so it was packed solid.

Jim eased off the street and onto the narrow, white sand path and stopped long enough to look at his watch. He wanted to time himself from here till the end of the path. He figured that would take about twenty, to twenty-five minutes. The path got bumpier as you went in, ran alongside a creek on its right-hand side, and to the left the woods were thick with brambles with a few paths cut through them for hikers and bike riders. At least that was the intent. The place was considered community property, and the division manager, Gad Stevens, had cut paths through the woods for the kids to ride their bikes. Or to be more exact, he had roughed out some paths; their completion was some time away. The paths had to be trimmed wider, needed to be raked down. They were way too bumpy for bikes, and unlike the white sand path, they were of clay, and though they could be hard, they could also attract and hold water. He had heard Gad discussing the matter with a fellow at the filling station up the street, across the highway, while he was pumping gas next to him. They had talked, and he had listened. It wasn't that wonderful a conversation, but Gad was a loud talker, and as a columnist, over the years, Jim had learned to be observant, at least in certain ways. All kinds of tidbits could become columns.

He checked his watch. It was thirty seconds off the hour. Maybe, he thought, it might be a good idea to only ride to the big hill and back. That way, if the tire went down, he wouldn't have to push the bike as far. He pushed his weight down on the handlebars. If the tire was low, it didn't feel that low. It seemed sturdy. Maybe it had been his imagination.

As he was considering on this, he looked back over his shoulder, saw something that surprised him. Trotting down the street was what at first he thought to be a calf, but was in fact a very large, black and tan dog. He had never seen the dog before. It was the size of a Great Dane, but it was much wider. It moved in powerful strides, held something in its mouth he couldn't make out. It looked like a mop head. A very dirty mop head. The dog spotted him, stopped, turned its head slightly and studied him.

Heavens, thought Jim, that dog is really, really big, and its breed . . . Jim couldn't tell. A mixed dog. Maybe part Dane; part Saint Bernard . . . German Shepherd? The animal seemed to have attributes of all those dogs, yet appeared to be something quite alien. A real mutt.

Jim turned back to his watch. He had let the second hand pass the hour mark.

To hell with it, he thought, eased the bike onto the path and began to ride at a brisk, if not full out rate. As he rode, he heard something that at first made him think of the tire, that it might be losing air. But no, it was coming from the rear.

He glanced back, saw the source of the sound. Behind him, he saw the huge dog, loping along, the mop in its mouth. It was gaining on him, and the dog's paws striking the path were making a kind of thudding sound. Jim biked on, glancing back from time to time, and one of those times he was surprised to see just how close the dog was, and now he could see what was in its mouth, and it caused Jim to let out with an involuntary burst of air.

It wasn't a mop in the big dog's jaws, it was Cuddles. And Cuddles was long past it. His head drooped, and his tongue hung out, and he was covered in dirt and blood. The damn dog had killed Cuddles, who was about as harmless as a silk pillow.

Glancing back again, Jim saw the dog drop the poodle and really begin to run. Jim started peddling hard, began to pull well ahead of the dog, but he wondered how long he could keep it up. In a long run, if he got far enough ahead, he could beat the dog, but in a short run, the dog might well catch up with him. It was taking long, loping strides, and there was a look about the dog that was strange, and the way its paws hit the trail, it was like an elephant stampede, dust flying up from what Jim thought of as pretty hard ground.

Jim started breathing heavy, then checked himself. He was hyperventilating, feeling the beginnings of fear. He came to a deep drop in the road, what he had been waiting for, and as he went over it, he heard the dog panting, he was that close. The drop caused him to gain speed, and he went down the hill very fast, faster than the dog could go. It was a long ways down, and he felt the bike building speed. Normally, he liked to just let the drop carry him along, but now, with that thing behind him, he didn't pause at all, but pedaled very hard, adding more speed to the momentum of the dip in the trail.

He was going so fast, when he reached the bottom of the hill he nearly lost the bike, felt it skid out from under him, way out, almost to the point of no return, but hc was able, by sticking his leg out and gently pegging the ground, to knock himself back on course. As he turned the curve around a dark wad of trees, near the creek, he saw the dog, having gained too much momentum from the hill, tumble and fall, go twisting and rolling into the briars on the left side of the road. In fact, the dog was going so fast, it rolled completely out of sight. Jim could hear the dog tumbling, coming up against something with a smack.

Jim didn't know if he should feel good or not. There was no guarantee the animal was after him. It had killed poor Cuddles, but that was dog stuff. Cuddles had probably come out to bark at him on the road, and the dog had reacted by instinct, probably didn't even realize the mop was a dog. The big dog pursuing him could be nothing more than a playful game of chase.

Still, as a precaution, as the road leveled out, Jim bent over the handlebars and began peddling hard.

He looked back. No dog. Still, he kept peddling at a brisk rate.

A long, black chicken snake was writhing across the road. Not poisonous, but it was a snake. Jim tried to miss it, but it was too late, he hit the snake causing it to twist up and hit the spokes, and then in the next moment, Jim was skidding and sliding onto his side, barely getting his leg out from under the bike in time.

When he got up, he saw that the knees of his sweat pants were torn and that the chicken snake was twisted up in his front spokes, thrashing about, trying to free itself. If he grabbed it, it might bite him, venomous or not.

Jim found a stick by the side of the road, and by snapping off a couple of limbs, he had a forked tool that he thought he might be able to use to push the snake's head down with, then uncoil the rest of it from the spokes, though the idea of touching a snake went against Jim's grain, made his skin crawl.

He went back to his bike, and after a few misfires, was able to get the fork against the snake's head and push it down to the ground. About a foot of the long snake was twisted up in the spokes, and gritting his teeth, Jim took hold of the snake with a shudder, tried to twist it out of the spokes, the tail slapping against his hand, making him recoil with revulsion.

As he worked the snake free, he suddenly felt uncomfortable. His first thought was that the snake's family was creeping up on him, but when he lifted his head and looked, he saw the big dog. It was trotting down the trail, but when it saw him, it stopped and stared. It was a good ways off, but there was something about the way it stood, the way it looked, that caused Jim to tug hard at the snake. The snake tightened on the spokes even more. The dog began to trot again. Jim dropped the stick and, using both hands, began to yank at the snake.

The dog was picking up speed, starting to drop its head low to the ground, like a lion creeping up on an antelope. Jim jerked the snake as hard as he could, snapped it free of the spokes, whipped it into the woods, grabbed his bike, got on it, and started off.

When he looked back, the dog was gaining.

Jim really began to crank down and then he had an uncomfortable and sobering thought. The road would come to an end soon. Maybe ten minutes if he were going all-out. What was at the end of the road besides woods? That would be the end of his ride, and he would be at the dog's mercy.

He wondered if he could he fight the dog off? Would it even bother him? *Maybe,* he thought, *I'm getting worked up over nothing. I do that a lot. Like this morning. The whole thing with Gail. It was silly. What was it? Hell, why do I care?*

Thoughts shot through his mind like machine gun bullets, but none of the bullets struck anything important. He just kept peddling. And then he remembered the little paths. They led down to the lake. Gad, what had he said? Something about working the paths through to the lake with the chainsaw and the tractor . . . Something like that, and that not all of them had been cut through. He remembered that. Yeah, Gad had been standing out by the gas pump, putting in gas, talking to the man in the truck, telling him how he hadn't yet ran all the paths to the lake.

What if he took a path and it was the wrong path?

Could the dog smell him on the bike if he was well ahead of it? Oh, sure. Sure, it could. He had seen on the *Animal Planet,* how dogs had this super sense of smell, and with him all worked up, sweaty, he was like a hot lunch on the move.

He saw one of the narrow, red clay paths coming up. He hesitated only a moment, and took it.

The path was so rough he felt as if it would bump his guts out, and there were bogged tire marks from a motor bike, probably made when it was wet. The ruts had dried, making the going even worse.

The path came to an abrupt end against a wall of trees and briars and brush. Jim felt panic set in as he worked the handlebar brakes. He glanced over his shoulder. The path was empty. Perhaps he could go back, find another trail. But he had to go all the way back, and what if he was riding right at the dog? He looked left and right. To his left the woods were thick, same as in front, but on the right there was a small gap in the trees and brush. It was still twisted up with some thorns and brambles, but it seemed passable with a little work. Beyond the brambles, twenty feet away, he could see another path. If he could make it through, he could take that route. Maybe it went all the way out to the lake.

Jim lifted his bike, used it to push down some of the brambles. Out of the corner of his eye he sensed movement. The dog. The blasted dog was at the end of the trail, slinking toward him, not fast, but steady, making the stalking fun.

Jim shoved the bike forward as a shield against the foliage, but it twisted and caught in his socks and poked his flesh, and one whip-like piece slipped out from under his bike and snapped up to stick a thorn in his testicles.

Cursing, Jim started moving fast, pushing the bike forward, really leaning into it. The brambles rose up around him like pointy waves of ocean and tore at his clothes and his skin. It was like crawling through barbed wire.

The dog was running now. He could see that, and it was almost on him. Jim pulled the bike around behind him, turned backward so that he could hold the bike in front of him. He used the back of his body to push through the last of the brambles and briars. They tore at him like teeth, but he kept pushing backward. A dark shadow leaped into the air and came at him.

The dog hit the bike like a missile; its jaws clamping around the frame so hard it nearly came loose of Jim's hands. Jim held on and pushed back at the dog, but it was like trying to win a push fight with a rhino. The dog let go and stuck its head through a gap in the bike and grabbed Jim's T-shirt with a snap of fangs and tore the front of it off so quick it was like a magic act. Jim thought, one less layer of cotton, and I would have been disemboweled.

The dog struck again, this time grabbing the frame of the bike near the seat, tugging at it, almost taking it out of Jim's hands yet again. Jim could see into the dog's hot, yellow eyes. He was so close he saw dark flakes moving there, sailing about like schooling piranha. The muzzle was huge and wrinkled. Muscles rolled under the dog's fur like machinery cogs, and the fur was matted with dirt, as if the monstrosity had come from somewhere down deep in the bowels of the earth. And it did not altogether look doglike. There was something odd, unidentifiable about it. Even its stink, which was considerable, was not doglike, but stank of something Jim couldn't identify. Something that was beyond the stench of defecation and decay. The huge teeth gnawed at the frame, and Jim fought to hang on to it.

"Let go, you devil!"

But the beast did not let go.

I'm dead, thought Jim. *I'm going to die out here, eaten by a dog.*

Struggling backward, the briars still tearing at his now shirtless body, Jim managed to put a foot on the trail he had longed to reach.

The dog let go of the bike and lunged. Jim raised the bike and pushed. When the dog hit it, he was jarred backward. The brambles snapped around the dog and entangled him, causing him to lose footing and to fall, the foliage closing over him briefly.

Jim jumped on the bike, pushed off, began to pedal. He looked back, saw the dog twisting out of the brambles, pouncing onto the trail, running after him.

He could see that the trail did lead to the lake, and the lake lay down before him like a big wet, blue eye. He could see a two-story lake house off to the right, up on high water support posts. A woman was out on the landing, sitting in a lawn chair, a cup in her hand. She stood up, put a hand to her eyes and looked in his direction.

Jim gave it everything he had. He had often imagined being a real bike rider, a racer, and now he had something to race for. His life. Blood pumped in his ears, and the wound in his testicles throbbed, and he began to feel all the scrapes and scratches that covered his body. Blood ran down his arms from cuts, flowed onto the bicycle grips.

He slid up to the house, dropped off the bike and charged up a run of stairs, made the landing. The woman, who was middle-aged and under normal circumstances would have been pleasant-looking, dropped the coffee cup, shattering it. She put a hand to her breast, looked at him. Jim knew he had to be a sight. Shirtless, sweaty, covered in blood from the brambles, breathing with a sound like a busted boiler.

He looked back at the trail and pointed. The dog, running at what could only be described as a gallop, was almost to the house.

Taking a deep breath, Jim said, "That dog got after me. For life's sake, let me inside."

The woman looked out at the dog, nodded, jerked open the door, and the two of them charged inside. She threw the lock.

"Jim," he said, tapping his chest, as if an introduction were in order. The woman did not respond. She moved to the window, pulled back the curtain. The dog was topping the stairs, moving onto the landing, then out of sight. There was a loud bump at the door, and another. And another.

"My God," the woman said. "He must be rabid."

"I don't think so," Jim said.

"He's trying to ram the door. What animal does that?"

"This one."

"Holy Heaven," she said. "He stinks like death. I can smell him from here."

The booming grew louder and more frequent as the dog struck the door. Then, there was silence.

"Maybe he gave up," she said, and her body trembled as if an electric current had passed through her.

They eased to the window. She pulled back the curtain. The dog's head rammed through the glass and snapped at her, causing her to stumble back. Jim grabbed her, pulled her to her feet.

"Upstairs," he said.

Pushing her before him, Jim nudged her to the stairs and they both went up. Behind them, the dog was working its way through the window, glass clattering to the floor.

Upstairs, on the landing, the woman pointed at an open door, and they went through it. She slammed the door and locked it.

They were inside a small bedroom with one window over the bed. The room smelled of fresh-washed sheets. Jim grabbed a dresser, worked it across the floor and against the door.

He leaned near the door jam and listened. The dog, walking heavy, was on the landing. He could hear it breathing, growling.

"Is that your dog?" the woman asked.

Jim could barely make his mouth smile. "No, lady. That is not my dog. I assure you."

Then the door was hit.

They jumped back, startled. The door was hit again, so hard it caused the dresser to slide back a few inches.

"What is that thing?" she said.

This was followed by a cracking sound. Jim angled himself so that he could see between the dresser and door. The dog was gnawing at the wood from the bottom. Somehow, it had turned its head and caught its teeth in the wood, and was tearing it out in chunks.

Jim pushed the dresser back, kicked the door. "What did I ever do to you!"

The wood cracked, and now Jim could see the dog's snout. The door began to crack away in chunks. Jim pressed the dresser back into place.

"Get out of my house," the woman said.

At first Jim thought the woman was yelling to the dog, out of fear, but then he realized she was talking to him.

"What?" he said.

"Get out. It doesn't want me. It wants you. It's your dog."

"I assure you, he isn't my dog."

"He wants you. It's you he wants. Get away from me! You're not my problem!"

The woman darted toward the closet, went inside, and closed the door. Jim stood stunned. She was right. He knew it instinctively, the dog wanted him. The beast was like a heat-seeking missile, and he was the target.

Now the door was torn away at the bottom, and the dresser was pushed slightly aside, enough that the dog could stick its head through. Jim got a good look at the dog, and the dog got a good look at him. Its eyes seemed huge and hard, not liquid-like at all. Its mouth snapped at the air, tossing spittle thick as whipped cream onto the carpet.

Jim jumped forward, turned the dresser over on the dog's head, and felt a small sense of satisfaction when it made a whelping noise.

He darted to the bed, jumped on it, ran to the window behind it, kicked the glass out with a few quick kicks, climbed through the frame, a ragged piece of glass tearing at his arm, and stood on the landing. He looked back through the window as the door cracked away in two pieces and the dog shoved all the way through. The dog turned its head toward the closet where the woman hid.

"Come on, you bastard," Jim yelled at him. "It's me you want. Come on."

The dog appeared to understand. It turned its attention back to Jim, leaped onto the bed. Jim raced around the landing until he came to the stairs at the front of the house, bounded down them toward his bike. As he settled himself onto the seat, he looked back to see the dog was at the top of the landing, poking its head through the railing, glaring down at him. It crouched and let out with a growl that would have shamed a lion. The dog raced for the stairway.

Jim kicked off and leaned forward on the bike, pedaled for all he was worth. There was nowhere to go but the lake, and he thought, that's it. The lake. I've got to make the lake. He pedaled furiously. His heart swelled in his chest. He could not only feel it beating, he could hear it. It sounded like a tom-tom.

He ventured a glance back. The dog was almost on him, running so hard; its great body was low to the ground. When it shot out its front legs it looked like a racehorse galloping toward the finish. Then the bike slowed. He couldn't figure it. He was peddling like hell, but . . .

The tire. That was the problem, the front tire. The air was going out of it. He wasn't quite on the rim, but soon would be. He looked back. The dog was right behind him. Its head was higher than the bike, and its mouth was open, teeth barred. Looking down the beast's throat was like looking down a manhole to hell.

Jim jerked his attention back to the trail, peddled even harder, his legs aching, feeling as if they were about to cramp. Pain shot from his ankle to his groin. He thought for a moment the muscles in his leg were going to seize up, but he managed to push through it. Then the bike began to drag.

Glancing back, he saw the dog had hold of the back tire. The bike began to wobble, go off course, but just as all appeared lost, the tire snapped free of the dog's mouth, and he was moving again. But the back tire, punctured by the dog's teeth, was going flat. Jim felt himself dropping lower to the ground as air went out of both tires. He was practically riding on the rims, just inches from the dog's snout and nail-like teeth.

The lake grew larger in front of him, and the trail played out. He looked right and left, hoping for anyone, or anything that might aid him.

Nothing.

He saw the pier before him, jetting out like a sick gray tongue over the water.

He rode directly for it, bumped over some rough ground, went airborne, hit the pier with a thud, the bike wobbling furiously. The boards beneath him rattled like knucklebones in a cup.

Jim didn't look back, couldn't. He fancied he could feel the dog's hot breath on his back, warming the sweat on his shirt. Certainly he could hear it panting, and he could hear the dog's huge feet thudding on the boards, coming ever closer.

The pier was coming to an end. He thought: *This is it. This is the moment of truth.*

He rode off of the end of the pier, and for a moment he felt as if he were pinned to the sky. The air was sweet and cool, and the sky and the water seemed to blend into one big blue moment. He took a deep breath, and then he dropped, the bike falling out from under him, hitting the water first. He came down behind it, banging his knees on the handlebars. He went down into the clear water, and looked up.

A mammoth shadow blocked out the blueness of the lake and the light from the sun. The dog had leaped. It came down with a loud splash, causing the lake around it to vibrate. Jim watched, horrified, and a moment later, his feet touched bottom.

Not too deep here, but deep enough, he thought. If I can just hold my breath a little longer the dog will go away.

Jim kept staring upward, watching. The monster dog-paddled about on the surface. Jim turned his head in the direction of the pier. He couldn't see anything there, just darkness. He thought: *I'll swim that way, maybe find a pier post for support, slide up it to the surface, get a breath, come back down, out of way of the dog. Eventually, the bastard has to give up.*

He looked up.

The dog was swimming straight down toward him.

Jim moved, but . . . his feet were caught. Something had him. He realized it was his bike. He had his foot twisted up between the spokes. He had stepped down right on top of the wheel. He squatted, grabbed his ankle with both hands, and pulled back with all his strength.

He felt something snap in his ankle, and a pain like someone jamming a hot rod through the bottom of his foot all the way up into his intestines shot through him until he thought he would lose his last bit of breath, open his mouth to scream and fill up with water.

But he was loose. He swam along the bottom, his ankle throbbing. Then his head was snapped back violently.

The dog had lunged at him, its teeth tangling in his long hair, then, just as quickly, he was freed as his hair was ripped lose.

The surface. He had to make the surface. He was on his last breath.

He pushed up, and just as he broke the surface of the water, he let out with a scream. The dog had bitten his leg just below the knee, and it was pulling him down. The pain was excruciating. He could feel bones shifting in his leg. He had just enough time for a breath before he went under.

How? Jim thought. *How can the dog breathe and bite me too? How is that? How can that be done?*

The pain subsided slightly, and Jim saw the shape of the dog move in the water, go past him for the surface.

Finally, thought Jim, the demon has to have air too.

Jim dove deep, began to swim toward the dark shadow of the pier. He hurt to move his legs, but the alternative was worse than the pain. He hadn't swum far when there was a tug on his foot, snapping his tennis shoe off. He whirled in the water, looked back.

The dog was on him. He could see its shape, and he could see the shape of his shoe coming free of the animal's mouth, falling toward the bottom.

In that moment, he realized that his heel was shooting with pain; the dog had gotten more than shoe.

The dog made a kind of porpoise-style lunge for Jim's face.

No more, thought, Jim. *No more.*

As the dog came forward, Jim grabbed at its throat, clenching both hands around it. But the dog continued to push forward, turning its head like a shark about to roll, its mighty jaws clamping down on Jim's face like a vice. Jim could feel bones shifting in his skull, teeth tearing into his cranium, the side of his jaw. He pounded at the dog with his fists, hitting as hard as he could.

The dog squeezed harder.

Jim managed one hand above the dog's snout, found an eye, pushed his thumb into it with all his might. The dog shook him like a rag, but Jim hung on. Kept pushing with his thumb. Jim felt as if his head were swelling, as if his chest was about to explode, but he didn't let go.

It was the dog that let go and fought to the surface.

Jim went up behind him, broke the water just after the dog, clamped his arms around the animal's neck and latched his teeth on the dog's ear, filling his mouth with a foulness he couldn't imagine. Then the blood hit the back of Jim's throat, and he began to gnaw, jerk his head, taking off a piece of the ear. The dog let out with a sharp bark, tried to twist, but Jim wrapped his legs around the dog's torso, hooked his ankles together, squeezed his arms with all his might, shifted sideways until he could bring his teeth into the dog's throat.

The dog thrashed and rolled in the water. They went under fighting, the dog snapping and Jim biting.

They floated to the bottom, struggling. Jim released his grip, tried to swim for the surface for some air, but he was jerked down. He thought at first it was the dog, but he could feel it was some kind of weed on the bottom that had wrapped around his ankle, holding him.

The dog swam at him. Jim tried to strike the dog with his fists, but underwater the blow was weak. He dodged the dog's muzzle, clamped his arms around its neck, stuck his cheek against the behemoth's neck. The powerful dog writhed, tried to tear lose, couldn't. It broke for the surface. Jim clung to it. The weed around his ankle snapped free, and the dog brought him up.

They broke into the sunlight.

Jim twisted his head, bit the dog in the throat, jerked his head from side to side. A sound like growling came from his mouth. The dog growled too, rolled over and over in the water, but Jim clung with his teeth, his mouth filing with hot gore.

Then the rolling ceased, and the dog twisted on its back, floating. Jim came loose of its throat, grabbed at its chest, tried to pull himself on board, striking out with his fists as he did.

The dog began to slip beneath the water.

Jim paddled his feet, worked his arms, stuck his face into the water, and looked down.

The giant dog was floating toward the bottom, face up. Jim thought he could see the yellow of its remaining eye, but decided it was an illusion, because in the next moment he could only see the shape of the animal and the odd shape of his bike below, the dog coming down on top of it, rolling, then churning, being gently carried away by the underwater current.

Jim painfully swam toward the pier, but there was no getting out there. The support posts were too tall. He hung onto a post for a moment, than swam toward shore. He crawled onto the sandy bank, discovered he couldn't walk. His ankle was broken. A bone in his foot too. The knee of his right leg wouldn't work either. His face was on fire, and his jaw crunched when he moved. He crawled over the sand until he was on the pier. He kept crawling until he reached the tip of the pier. He lay there on his stomach, looked out at the water.

The dog did not appear.

Jim grinned; his broken jaw aching, his teeth full of dangling, dark, dog flesh.

Jim the Conqueror, he thought.

He let out with a wild, bloodcurdling, primal scream that echoed across the lake and into the trees beyond.

THE ACCOMPANIST

JOHN HARRISON

I never thought I would tell anyone this story. I convinced myself no one would believe it. It would surely be dismissed as fantasy, or worse, hallucination. But perhaps the real reason is that I wanted what happened to remain a secret of mine, precious and inviolate. There hasn't been a day in almost seventy years I haven't thought back to that December evening to marvel at what happened.

Now that Liberty is gone and my days are certainly numbered, I suppose there's no good reason to keep it to myself anymore. Besides, I'm too old to give a damn whether anyone believes me. It's hard enough holding this pencil.

I was only eighteen when I first met him. I'd been hired by The Mutual Life Insurance Co. as an apprentice accountant in their Pittsburgh office. Those were heady times for a young man like me. The country was booming, life was swollen with possibility, fortune was easily within reach. It was a dangerous time, too; more so than we realized at the time. We were lurching into the modern age. Seeds of economic chaos and social upheaval were already rooted in that fertile soil of ambition and self-assurance. Soon, we'd reap the riotous harvest of that discontent.

My first impression of him was curious, to say the least. I'd been forewarned by the office manager, Zack Smith.

"You'll like Matthew Perdu. He's a brilliant man with numbers. Maybe the best we got. He's a little, how shall I say, distracted. But you'll learn a great deal, don't worry 'bout that."

I'd expected a nice old gentleman with thick glasses and thin voice. Instead, I was shown a man no more than thirty, with eyes as sharp as polished crystal and penetrating as the most intimate question; with a shock of unruly hair that seemed, as I noticed later, to rise and fall as he spoke. "He may not be with us much longer," Smith had said with sincere regret. "His, uh, habits don't quite conform to our standards, I'm afraid."

"Habits?" I asked, fearing . . . no, hoping for some scandalous revelation. At my age, I craved the unusual, the taboo.

"His hours are irregular . . ."

Aha, I thought enthusiastically.

"I've put up with it because he *is* good, and, frankly, I like him. But you can't run an office allowing individualism its head. Bad for morale, you know."

Well, by now I was thoroughly intrigued, and my first view of him did nothing to dispel the curiosity. He was sitting at his high desk tapping methodically on a set of company books with his pencil as if working out some intricate musical pattern. He never heard us come in. He simply stared off through the window in front of him, tapping and swaying; humming, too, I believe, although it sounded more like chanting. As we stood there and watched, I thought I saw Smith smile affectionately.

"Ah hem," Smith coughed.

Perdu turned and I swear his hair stood up a bit when he saw us.

"This is Justin Redding, Perdu, the young man I told you about."

He smiled gently and came right over to me. "Yes, of course," he said, almost singing.

"Matthew is aware of your background, Justin, and knows what you should do. Mark him well. You will learn. You will learn."

I got the impression he meant more than bookkeeping.

Matthew was indeed the skilled and patient teacher that Smith had predicted. His sense of humor made the days fly as he punctuated his coaching with remarks on all manner of things, usually barbed with what I considered an appealing and healthy cynicism. No fool this man. He was highly educated and could comment reasonably on most subjects, even though his habit of drifting off mid-sentence to a place only he could go was, at times, a little embarrassing for me.

I soon discovered his real passions were music and the cinema. They called it moving pictures back then, and it was considered a rather low-class form of entertainment. His interest in it only served to feed my fascination with him. So when he invited me to his home for supper one evening, I accepted immediately.

He had a small apartment in the same neighborhood as my boarding house, and it appeared extremely well kept and comfortable, not the quarters of a bachelor with the absentminded qualities of Matthew Perdu.

"I want you to meet my wife, Liberty," he said as he led me to the kitchen.

She was standing over a counter in the center of the room preparing supper. I think my heart must have stopped for a split second because I almost fainted. My mouth went instantly dry, and I heard a marvelous tone rush by my ears.

"I've brought a friend home for dinner," Matthew said. "Justin Redding, the new young man at the firm."

How do you do's were difficult but I managed. She had a smile that could melt iron and that wonderfully thick hair folded on the back of her head framed a magnetic expression of utter calm. Her voice was almost a whisper, but it wasn't timid. I had never seen such a beautiful woman.

Matthew must have sensed my innocent infatuation with his wife, but he carried on in his inimitable way talking about this and that. Liberty was quiet most of the time, only occasionally commenting on what he was talking about. They seemed to know each other profoundly. I just sat there and marveled . . . at both of them.

"Are you the spirited sort?" he asked me over coffee.

"I'd like to think so," I said eagerly.

"Good. In a moment we'll go downtown."

"Downtown?" But he was already up and out of the room. He returned a few minutes later carrying a stack of music manuscripts and signaled me to come along. I made my way to the kitchen and stammered with thank-you's and see-you-again's.

Liberty smiled broadly at me. I'll never forget that smile. It never faded until the day she died.

Matthew and I took a trolley downtown and got off at Smithfield Street. He explained on the way that he had another job at night, one which he loved more than all else except it paid too little money. He'd met a man indirectly through our firm, a Mr. J. P. Harris, who had a number of ventures in the entertainment field, one of which was a storefront shop (he called it a Nickelodeon) where he exhibited motion pictures to paying customers. When Mr. Harris found out that Matthew was a pianist of some skill, the older man asked my friend to consider accompanying the shows at his establishment. It was an offer Matthew accepted on the spot.

I'd heard about this "movie" experience but was never allowed to go. My parents were a bit puritanical. Oh, I'd sneaked into the burlesque hall around the corner on Forbes Ave. once with several other boys, and at the time that was something to see, let me tell you. But I had no idea what to expect from this adventure.

Mr. Harris's Nickelodeon was not the spare, odorous theater I'd expected. Not at all like the burlesque hall. In fact, this place had a certain class and charm, which, I found out later, was the owner's expressed intention. He fully expected the movie industry to flourish, and he wanted to encourage the proper sort of people to attend.

As soon as we arrived, Matthew got me a seat and quickly disappeared. I caught sight of him moments later sitting at a piano near the front of the room. There were several other men in the room waiting patiently for the program to begin. All appeared to be veterans of this type of amusement.

After a few minutes the room darkened. I could hear movement and behind me somewhere, the cranking of machinery starting up. Suddenly a flickering light shot out over my head in a beam, exploding on the wall in front of me with the most magical set of moving photographs. The play was entitled *Tess of the Storm Country*. A dynamic young woman named Pickford had the lead. I can't remember too much about the movie itself (it was a flop, it turns out), but the dizzying experience in that theater irrevocably changed my perception of the whole world. I instantly became a devoted enthusiast of the motion picture.

My only recollection of Matthew during the movie was as a figure off to the side of the room swaying back and forth to the rhythms of music and story. In fact, his music and the images on the wall became inseparable to me. His movements seemed to correspond exactly to the emotions on the screen. When the action was passionate, so was he; when it was calm, he seemed at ease. I was embarrassed to tell him this afterward because I felt I'd betrayed his invitation by not concentrating solely on his playing. On the contrary, he was delighted with my "review."

I left him there for a second performance and returned home alone. Made the trip in an exalted state and didn't sleep much that night. But I wanted to talk with Matthew more. I wanted to see more movies with him.

I wanted to see Liberty again.

Matthew was late for work the next morning.

It was a mild summer that year, and Matthew and Liberty often took me with them on their weekend rides into the country for picnics. We went to concerts together, and exhibits at Carnegie's new museum. I loved their company and still treasure those memories as some of the happiest of my life. I continued to be astonished at Matthew's store of knowledge, and Liberty seemed to grow more beautiful every day. I also learned that there was a certain impishness to her. She was a practical joker at heart, but never cruel or condescending.

I also went to the movies a lot that summer. In the beginning I'd accompany Matthew, but later on I began to go by myself, arriving just before the performance to sneak into a seat before he noticed. I'd become accustomed to this infant art form and soon developed a crude sophistication about it. I could distinguish the difference in the qualities of movies. I became familiar with the names of the New Jersey companies that made them. I was a fan of certain performers, especially the Pickford girl.

But I soon realized how great a part Matthew played in my enjoyment. One night when he was ill and couldn't play, I watched a movie I'd seen twice before (I was a repeat offender, you see). I enjoyed the story without Matthew's music, but surprisingly not as much as before. Somehow I felt the movie was not exactly the same one I'd seen earlier. Now, I always went to the Nickelodeon sober. I watched carefully. I studied, you might say, and this was the third viewing of this particular story. But there were minor differences. Sometimes these discrepancies were simply my emotional response to a scene. For example, in the previous viewings I'd been outraged by the behavior of a particular male character toward his wife. On this occasion, however, I felt somewhat sympathetic to his situation. Other differences were more manifest. I remembered an entire section of the plot happening differently from what I witnessed that night. On my way home I was angry with myself for the confusion. I'd come to think of myself as a bit of an movie aficionado. But what kind of an aficionado can't remember a movie from one night to the next? I puzzled over this for some time.

When I told Matthew about this later, he only smiled enigmatically.

I'd often sit in his apartment and watch him practice at the piano while Liberty prepared our supper. His repertoire was extraordinary, all of it memorized. Composers I'd never heard of: Satie, Webern, and some truly challenging stuff by a man named Schoenberg who apparently liked mathematics a whole lot more than melody.

"I practice scales and intervals constantly. Liberty has to leave the house and take a walk sometimes," he smiled gently. "Says it makes her feel odd. But this constant repetition reacquaints my fingers with the keyboard so that I never have to look . . . or think. I'm more interested in sound and texture than melody or chord progression."

I had no idea what he was talking about. But once during a routine practice of scales, he played something that made me twitch.

"What was that?" I cringed.

"It's a tritone," he laughed. "An augmented fourth. Meant to be annoying. *Diabolus in musica.*"

"Diabolic . . . .what?"

"The devil in music." He lowered his voice melodramatically. "An illegal interval in the middle ages . . . when music was the dominion of ecclesiastics and monks."

He played it again, and I winced again. Couldn't help it.

"Not very pretty, is it? But it has its uses, as you've noticed," he chuckled. "I like it."

Matthew would also work for hours on a style of improvising he called "spontaneous composition." It was astonishing to hear. He said he wanted to use his music to cause a transmutation in the soul of the audience, a metamorphosis during which people would be transported to another place, another time. His theories were couched in a kind of spiritualism with which I wasn't very comfortable, but I listened patiently as he attempted to convey his vision of a perfect marriage of music and cinema. He was convinced that the eventual alloy of the two would have a mystical effect on people.

I told him I thought his aspirations seemed to have theological origins.

"The artistic urge is essentially a spiritual urge," he quickly replied.

I'd become so much a part of Matthew and Liberty's household that

I felt like a member of the family. Had I known what was about to happen I would have stayed away.

Or . . . maybe not.

Alone one night with Liberty while Matthew was at the theater, I quizzed her about Matthew's theories, and she told me he'd been struggling with them for as long as she'd known him. To illustrate, she told me of their honeymoon. He took her to France, and, of course, she was thrilled. But his alternative reason for going there, she soon discovered, was to meet the inventor, George Melies, who had a movie studio in Paris. Matthew had seen a Melies movie based on Verne's *Trip to the Moon,* and it had galvanized his thoughts. Although Liberty didn't really mind the excursions away from their romantic pursuits, it was then she realized she'd forever share her husband's love with another force.

Something else occurred during the honeymoon, which I found fascinating. Matthew had somehow gotten tickets to the premiere of a ballet by the composer Stravinsky. Liberty said it was called *The Coronation of Spring.* Apparently, this was quite a coup on Matthew's part, and the couple prepared for the evening with the greatest enthusiasm. For her part, Liberty's knowledge of music was parochial, but Matthew explained that Stravinsky was sure to be a giant in music, and their chance to see this premiere was a once in a lifetime thing.

Her eyes glowed as she told me the story, how they dressed to the teeth, how Matthew hired a private cab for the trip from the hotel to the concert hall, how he'd showered her with flowers from street vendors all evening and generally acted the love-sick fool. She was invigorated by it all. Then, the concert . . .

There had been some controversy surrounding the ballet arising from critics' reaction to dress rehearsals, so the hall was filled with tension and anticipation. There were whistles and shouts before the curtain even rose. The first minutes of the performance were uneventful, but at one point a few members of the audience began to protest. It was extremely modern music, and from the way Liberty described it the choreography was quite suggestive. The hall lights came up, and the crowd quieted down, but within minutes a veritable riot broke out.

Supporters and antagonists yelled at each other across the aisles. Matthew leapt to his feet in defense of the music and was punched by a man in front of him. Nevertheless, they stayed until the end, at which point Matthew screamed, "Bravo" for a good five minutes. (She told me his hair stood straight up on end.) He positively shuddered with excitement over the next few hours. He'd never experienced any music with such extreme visual power, he told her. It was evolutionary. A new way. He couldn't remember much about the dancing.

That event and the trip to Melies's studio convinced Liberty she'd married an artist. She was deeply in love with him then and still was now. But I detected a certain sadness in her voice, and I suddenly appreciated the simultaneous closeness and distance she felt about Matthew Perdu.

"I love him," she murmured, not looking at me. "But it's a changed love . . . not . . . not the love of a wife."

I could barely hear her last words but the meaning was clear enough.

One night I arrived at the theater late, cold and wet. Things had been harried at the office, and Mr. Smith was especially perturbed at Matthew for leaving early. I made a lame excuse for my friend, then angrily completed both my assignment and the one he'd left unfinished. His tenure at Mutual was fast coming to an end, that was sure. By the time I got to the Nickelodeon, the first performance had already begun.

I rushed the purchase of my ticket, dashed through the lobby hoping I'd only missed a little bit when Matthew's playing stopped me dead. My sense of space and location suddenly vanished. Time evaporated. Images flooded my mind. Moving images. As if I were having some kind of waking dream. As if a movie were playing inside my mind.

"Aren't you going in?" The manager interrupted my reverie.

"Oh, yes, of course." How long had I been standing there? What had I been doing?

"I wish he'd stick to the text, you know," the pudgy man said. Matthew had introduced me to him once, although he rarely came out of his tiny office off the lobby. "It's . . . it's disorienting, that . . . that crazy stuff he plays. Sometimes have to close my door or I can't concentrate."

"Have you had complaints?" I asked.

"No," he murmured, "but he's doing it more and more. Sooner or later he's going to drive a customer away. I'm going to have to speak with him."

I went in and watched the rest of the movie. And that's when I realized I hadn't missed a thing. I knew exactly what the story was about.

I startled a gentleman in the lobby afterward by grabbing his arm and asking him to listen to my synopsis of the early part of the movie, the part I thought I'd missed. He listened patiently then told me my recollection was correct.

On the way home I told Matthew of my experience. He smiled at me with that enigmatic grin again.

"Yes. I'm getting there. It's working," he said, adding nothing further.

By November Matthew was spending almost all of his free time at Harris's Nickelodeon; hour upon hour in a dreary cell of a room beneath the theater where he'd wait between performances, studying strips of film provided by the projectionist with whom he'd established an enduring friendship (founded, I believe, on the old man's love of whiskey and Matthew's ability to provide it). It was a dank place, that dungeon. The smell, the graffiti on the walls, the harsh glare from that single bare bulb above him gave me the impression illicit activities went on here in his absence. I never understood why he preferred to lounge there instead of the lobby, or even outdoors.

"It's quiet," was his only explanation, ignoring the hiss of steam pipes, the "clank" and "bang" of monstrous furnaces somewhere . . . which always made me jump. But there he'd sit, quietly as if meditating, pieces of music and film scattered about the floor randomly.

Liberty seemed to be withdrawing. She was always so patient with him, but as he obsessively pushed closer and closer to some elusive goal only he could see, he was leaving her further and further behind.

I spent a lot of time with both of them, but separately, not together as during our leisurely summer months. My presence seemed to lift Liberty's spirits, but *I* was treading on slippery and dangerous emotional ground.

"Wouldn't it be great if we could hear them talking?" I said while watching him tinker with his film in that tiny room below Harris's Nickelodeon.

He suddenly turned to me with an expression I'd never seen before. A cold, unpleasant darkness swept into his eyes. And I swear his hair throbbed.

"It would add so much . . . ." I stammered.

"That's theater," he hissed. "You want to hear people talk, go to the theater. This is a different art, an art of international language . . . like music. It needs no . . . *dialogue*."

He said that last word with an unmistakable tone of contempt.

"Almost like dreaming," I muttered absentmindedly.

"Yes. That's it. Collective dreaming," he said. And his eyes were gleaming once again. He continued to work for a moment, then he paused and bowed his head.

"They'll do it, you know."

"What?" I asked, troubled by the non sequitur.

"They'll make the pictures talk. Sooner or later. To satisfy people like . . ."

"Me?"

He looked up. He tried to dismiss the accusation with a slight smile. It came off as a grimace instead.

"The promise of cinema will have been betrayed," was all he said.

When I watched the movie later that night, I completely forgot that it played without a single title card. You see, he had cut them all out! But I understood it perfectly.

For the next few weeks Matthew was fanatic about his work at the theater. All else seemed a distraction to him. I covered for him at the office. He became gaunt, his eyes lost their penetrating quality. Their vision had turned inward, I believe.

But on Thanksgiving his old spirits seemed to revive briefly. Liberty had prepared a wonderful meal, and Matthew was actually witty and animated, not at all distracted and aloof.

Liberty and I hoped he might take an evening off from the Nickelodeon but our hopes were short-lived. A new film was scheduled, and he couldn't wait to see it. We watched unhappily as he stepped out into the snowy cold.

Liberty and I sat in front of the fire with our brandy saying nothing for the next hour. I was extremely uncomfortable. My heart, my mind, my nerves were a jumble of conflicting impulses. I wanted to say something, then held back. Silence was a sentinel against my stampeding feelings. Finally, though, it was she who overwhelmed my defenses.

"I'm so lonely, Justin."

My heart shattered. I was in love with this woman. I had known it for some time, but I'd learned to live with it. Seeing her unhappy was something I could not.

Words failed me completely. I wanted to reassure her, dispel her fear, make everything right. But each time I tried willing my mouth to work, it refused.

Suddenly, I was in her arms. I don't know how it happened. Not a word was spoken. My hand had reached out to caress her face. An innocent gesture, I meant, but she leaned into it easily, hungrily. And we melted into each other.

There, in the arms of another man's wife, *my best friend's wife,* I was horrified and excited at the same time. I could feel her heart. I was frightened by her passion. How had it come to this? We began to make love.

"My God," I whispered as I buried my face in her luxurious hair, "what are we doing?"

"We're going to hell," she panted.

But as I looked deep within her eyes, it wasn't hell I was seeing.

For a long time afterward we just lay there in each other's arms. Listening to the fire . . . until she finally leaned over me, caressed my face.

"It's all right now." And she smiled.

I hurriedly left the apartment in a daze. How could I have done such a thing? How could she?

Before I realized it, I was standing in front of J. P. Harris's Nickelodeon on Smithfield Street. Had I meant to come there? Had I been propelled by some imp of the perverse, excited to see me confront the friend I'd just betrayed? Had I been lured here by some external force . . . drawn inevitably by my perceptive friend who wanted to stare into my eyes and silently ask . . . "Well?" . . . as if he'd been sure what would happen after he left? Could he have somehow wanted it to happen?

What kind of madness was this? Were they both demons . . . set out to test me . . . each one pricking the soft tissue of my conscience to see if it would yield?

My mind ached more than my heart.

And that's when I saw Williams, the theater manager, trotting impatiently up the street ahead of me.

"What's the matter, Mr. Williams," I asked as I fell into step next to him. "You seem upset."

"You'd be too if you'd been dragged away from a warm holiday meal into a night like this."

"What's wrong?"

"That's what I'm about to find out. Some street urchin arrived at my door with an urgent message from Bellows. Said I had to come to the theater right away."

At the Nickelodeon everything appeared normal. Except Bellows, the old projectionist, was in the vestibule pacing back and forth like an expectant father. He was extremely pale. And when we came in he stuttered incoherently, which made Williams even angrier. The manager brushed past his tipsy employee and went into his office.

Inside the theater, Matthew's music filled the lobby. I could see the manager through the cracked doorway of his office going over books and papers. He looked distracted. Matthew was playing like a man possessed. I'd never heard anything so disorganized, unrecognizable. Shrill and piercing, all in the upper registers one moment, then low and growling the next. It made no traditional sense, but it thrilled me anyway.

I felt like I'd stepped into another dimension. Everything around me took on an intense glow, and everything seemed to slow down. Williams came back out of his office carrying the nightly receipt card, but he and Bellows and the ticket girl all looked out of whack. The music overtook all other sound. I could hear nothing else. The walls began to vibrate, then melt. Color saturated my vision.

Suddenly I was no longer standing in the lobby. I found myself in a battlefield. The dead and dying were everywhere, and a green gas permeated the atmosphere. Men gagged, horses danced madly in the throes of death. Explosions rocked the earth. But for some reason I was calm and unafraid. A brilliant white light appeared on the horizon and began to come toward me. I tried to approach it, but my legs wouldn't move. Then it began to change. For a moment I thought I was facing a beautiful woman. Then it was something else I can't describe, but it too was beautiful, magnificent. Then the light reappeared. All this occurred within the same instant. The charred, lifeless earth had disappeared in the light. Voices spoke in reassuring, serene tones, but the words were unintelligible. I was swept over by an extraordinary, utter peace. There was music . . . no, not music . . . some unidentifiable sound. It came from everywhere, was everywhere, was everything.

And then it all came to an indescribable crescendo . . . and stopped. I gasped as if coming up for air after being held underwater too long. I looked around. The others appeared to have undergone a similar experience. Williams was sweating profusely.

And that's when we heard it. The applause. A great roaring wave of it.

The door to the theater swung open, and the audience burst out. Some were in tears, others were laughing raucously. Several were shaking their heads in wonder. Not one, NOT ONE, seemed unmoved.

"So, why am I here, Bellows," Mr. Williams demanded waving the nightly receipt card. "We have a full house. They obviously . . . enjoyed the movie." He said this last sentence glancing sideways at me with a bit of embarrassment.

"What is so important that I should leave my home and come down here?" he shouted at the quivering old projectionist.

I stared at this audience of excited people as they walked by. I heard comments like "astonishing," "never seen anything like that," "extraordinary." What a wonderful movie it must have been.

"But you see, that's just it," Bellows stammered. "That's just it."

Williams and I exchanged a suspicious glance.

"There was no movie," the old man protested.

Williams's mouth fell open.

"There was no movie," Bellows carried on. He was slobbering now. "It never got here. I didn't know what to do. We sold the tickets, and I sent a boy to the train station to see if it was there. When he came back empty-handed I sent him to you. But then . . . but then," he nodded at the theater, "*he* started playin'. And they didn't leave. You hear me, they wouldn't leave. I saw 'em through my hole back here. He was playin' like a madman. His hair was standin' straight up in the air. Lord Jesus, I never saw nothin' like that. I heard 'em laughin' and cryin'. They'd shout, then be quiet. And his playin', Mr. Williams . . . you heard it. But there was no movie. It never got here. There was no movie!"

On the way home Matthew and I rode in silence. I couldn't think of anything to say, and I couldn't look directly at him. But he seemed serene, peaceful, as if all was right in the world.

When we neared our stop, he took my hands in his and turned to me for the first time since we left the theater. I was shocked. His eyes had gone totally white . . . like albino eyes. They were soft and gentle looking, but the sight of them almost made me cry out.

"Don't be frightened, Justin," he said. The tone of his voice calmed me. "It's wonderful. Believe me. It's wonderful. I can see everything now."

"What's happened to you?" I wept.

"I've succeeded."

And he said nothing more.

We got off the trolley, and I walked him toward his apartment. At the front door he turned to me again.

He smiled and touched my cheek with his hand. His eyes almost appeared to glow. "I love you both." That was all he said.

He walked slowly up the stairs and fumbled with his keys in the lock.

I never saw Matthew Perdu again.

We got a letter from him several years later. It was the first we'd heard since he moved to California that January. Liberty and I were married shortly after he left and two sons and a daughter followed in predictable order.

In his letter, Matthew sounded totally content, although he worried that his career as an accompanist might be coming to an end. The studios were committed to talking movies, just as he feared they would be, and the services of musicians on the set for actor inspiration would soon be dispensed with. As a blind man his job opportunities would be limited, especially in the movie business.

In the meantime he was working continually. In demand, he told us, by many of the top stars, some of whom would not appear in front of a camera unless Matthew Perdu were on the set. Most recently, though, he'd disappointed a number of these talents by signing an exclusive contract with an actor named Lon Chaney.

"When he plays," Chaney told the studio bosses, "I see the whole movie all at once."

We only heard from him intermittently after that. Mostly postcards encouraging us to go see this movie or that. After 1927 we didn't hear from him again. He disappeared.

Liberty and I never went to movies after that either.

That was the year a movie called *The Jazz Singer* came out.

WHERE THERE'S A WILL . . .

ROBERT MASELLO

Michael got the message from one his three housemates, scrawled on a Post-It note. "4 o'clock. Your mom called—your dad died. Come home." It was stuck on the door of his room.

Michael rented what used to be the dining room of the house, and he had crammed every inch of it with movie scripts, books on writing movies, magazines on the art of screenwriting (Michael felt that he had mastered the craft, but that he still needed to work on the art part), a computer on which to compose his own scripts, a photocopying machine on which to make copies of them. The copy machine had been his one extravagance, but after he'd calculated what he was spending to produce enough copies of each of his scripts to blanket the agents, producers, and studio execs all over town, he figured it was a smart investment.

Now he'd have to come up with the money for a plane ticket home. He'd put aside a few hundred dollars for the next Robert McKee screenwriting seminar, and although he hated to use it up, he really didn't have a choice. If he had to ask his mother, or worse his brother, to send him a ticket, they'd know he wasn't quite the Hollywood success story he'd been claiming to be. And that would be about the only thing that could make this whole situation even more depressing than it already was.

The door to his room swung open a crack—it was, after all, a dining room door—and Kevin poked his head in. "You got my note?"

"Yes."

"Yeah, well, I'm really sorry."

"Thanks." Michael waited for him to leave, but the head remained.

"So, are you going back to Chicago?"

"Looks like it."

"'Cause I've got some friends coming in from out of town," Kevin said. "Okay if they crash in your room while you're gone?"

Michael knew that even if he said no, Kevin would go ahead and do it, anyway. "As long as they don't touch my computer or the copy machine."

"Cool," Kevin said, rapping his hand on the door. And then he was gone.

The next morning, Michael caught a flight out of Burbank airport; blissfully, the seat next to him was empty, and he was able to just stare out the window and think about what lay ahead of him. None of it was pretty. His older brother, Richard, would be lording it over one and all, and his mother would be disconsolate and lost. When he'd spoken to her on the phone, she'd sounded like she was a million miles away. Michael wondered what the funeral arrangements would be, and how long he'd really have to stay. Even though he'd grown up there, Chicago had always given him the willies.

As had his father.

The old man was one of those larger-than-life figures, a big man with a loud voice and large hands and a way of greeting everyone, even his worst enemies, with "how goes it, my friend?" He'd clap people on the shoulders, grip their hands between both of his, and smile down at them like he just couldn't look at them long enough or hard enough. But Michael had his number—he was just reeling them in, making a sale, and he couldn't have cared less whether they lived or died. His heart was as hard as the imported stone—marble, granite, limestone, slate—that he sold, and his will was pretty much unstoppable; Randolph J. Mountjoy always got what he wanted.

Their house, in fact, was something he'd designed himself, and to Michael it had always resembled a mausoleum—it was grand and vast and, of course, made of more quarried stone than any building outside of Washington, D.C. When the cab pulled up outside the gateposts—ponderous columns with recumbent lions on top—Michael took a long breath before pressing the buzzer. His brother's voice came over the intercom, and after Michael had identified himself, the front gate unlocked. His brother was waiting in the open door at the top of the stone steps.

"Mom said you wouldn't be here till later," he said.

"I got the first flight."

Neither one of them knew whether to shake hands, embrace, or revert to form and pretty much ignore each other. Richard was two years older, and he'd been everything Michael was not—tall, strong, a star athlete, president of his jock-filled fraternity, and for many years his father's right hand in the business. It was called "Mountjoy & Sons Stone and Building Supplies," but Michael had never worked there for anything more than the occasional summer, and even then unhappily. The stone was heavy and hard, and he was forever hurting himself—barking his shins, fouling up orders, getting on the wrong side of the foreman—and his father had never let him forget it.

"Mom's sleeping," Richard said. "I gave her some Valium."

The entry hall was as cold and unwelcoming as Michael remembered it, except that now there were some flowers and wreaths laid around.

"She was sort of out of it when I called," Michael said. "But she said he had a heart attack?"

"Massive," Richard said. "Dropped like an ox, right on the loading dock."

Not a terrible surprise—he'd had two minor "coronary events" in the past year, and Michael had known another could happen at any time. "Were you there?"

"I was out with a client. By the time I got to the hospital, they'd already done everything they could."

Well, Michael thought, *at least he went just like he'd have wanted to.* And then he thought, *What a cliché. Is everything I think or say this week going to be a cliché?* He told himself to take some notes—if he happened to think of anything original over the next few days, there might be some good screenplay material in it.

"Is Sissy here yet?"

"She's driving down from Milwaukee after work." Sissy—or Cyndie, as she vainly insisted on being called by her brothers—was a year younger than Michael, and worked as a dental hygienist for a married man they all knew she'd been sleeping with for years. Like their father, he was a big, overbearing son of a bitch, and Michael always found it hard to believe she'd gone out of her way to replicate the old man.

"You can use your old room," Richard said, and Michael nodded, then started trudging up the winding stairs with his duffel bag.

"I'll fill you in on the funeral details later," Richard called up at him. "I've got to go back to the office now."

"Okay, see you later. Thanks for handling all this." Richard had always been the handler, even when Michael had wished he wasn't.

"No problem, my friend," Richard replied. "Who else was gonna do it?"

Michael couldn't help but notice now—his first note for the screenplay—his brother's instinctual use of his father's catch-phrase, "my friend." How long had that been going on?

At the top of the stairs, he turned into his old room, which looked out onto a wooded side yard. This had been his sanctum, and his mother had kept it like a shrine, with everything exactly where he'd left it. His old Oberlin banners still adorned the wall, his theater awards still shone in their glass case, his old clothes still hung in the closet. He moved a few hangars aside to make room for his funeral suit, put his other things in the top drawer of the dresser, then sat on the edge of the bed, next to the wide window. Outside it was another of those cold, bleak Chicago days, with bare black tree limbs etched against a slate gray sky. Michael felt like he was thirteen again.

He was napping when he heard a soft rap on his door, and his mother's voice. She came in looking ten years older than when he'd seen her the summer before. Her face was pale and haggard, her blue eyes were going gray, her hair—normally coiffed and expensively tinted—was in disarray. Even the silk robe she was wearing was uncharacteristically rumpled.

"You should have told me you were here," she said, sitting on the edge of the bed and putting one palm—cool and dry—against his cheek. It reminded him of when she'd feel for a fever when he was a kid; sometimes, even when he was faking it in order to miss a test, she'd claim he felt hot and let him stay home anyway. He knew she knew, but they had a bond—two sensitive souls, trapped in a cold, hard place, turning to each other for warmth and understanding.

He sat up and hugged her—her bones felt fragile through the robe—and for a few minutes they talked about his work in Hollywood. Michael assured her his agent had lined up several promising projects, before they circled back to the grim matters more at hand. "Richard is making all the arrangements," she said, "and I don't know what I'd do without him. I do know the services will be at noon, tomorrow, at the Covington Funeral Home."

The fancy place, Michael thought, where all the best families went.

"And the interment will be at Lakeview Park, in the family mausoleum."

But this was news. "The family mausoleum?"

His mother took a shredded tissue from the pocket of the robe, dabbed at her nose, then said, "Yes. Your father had been building it for the past six months. Of course no one knew it would be needed so soon. Didn't Richard tell you about it?"

"Not a word."

"Well, you'll see it tomorrow. It's at the highest point in the cemetery, surrounded by trees, overlooking the lake."

A family tomb? Michael had to suppress a shudder. What was this, some Edgar Allan Poe story? (Another note for his screenplay that he dutifully filed away.) But he shouldn't have been surprised at this, either—his father had supplied the stone for more mausoleums and tombstones than anyone in the Midwest.

At dinner that night, they ate take-out from an old Italian place their father had always liked. No one wanted to cook, and only Richard seemed to want to eat. Sissy, true to form, was "watching her figure." She had her mother's pretty features, but she'd inherited from her dad a large frame and a tendency to put on weight. Over the years, she'd held a lot of jobs, gone adrift at times, and officially declared bankruptcy twice. But this hygienist gig was apparently going to stick, so everyone was more than willing to overlook her little indiscretions with Dr. Schmidt.

"I keep telling my friends at work that my brother writes for the movies, but they always ask me what movies," she said, carefully scraping the breading off a chicken cutlet with the side of her knife. "Is there anything I can tell them to go see?"

"Maybe next winter," Michael said. "You know, movies take a long time to get made."

"But what are you doing for money in the meantime?"

Starbucks was the word that immediately came to mind: Michael worked the morning shift six days a week. "The thing about the movie business is, a lot of times you do rewrites, but you don't get a screen credit."

He didn't have to glance over at Richard, who had assumed his father's seat at the head of the table, to know that he wore a skeptical expression.

"Have you seen *Vacation in Hell*?" Michael asked.

"Not yet, but I've seen the commercials. Did you work on that?" she asked, eagerly.

Michael tilted his head, modestly; as long as he didn't actually say he'd written something he hadn't, he didn't consider it an outright lie. And he did know the guy who'd written the movie—he always ordered an Espresso Macchiato and a molasses scone.

After dinner, Richard retired to his father's office—did he ever go home to his own place, Michael wondered, a sleek bachelor pad on Lake Shore Drive?—and Michael sat up with Sissy and his mom in what was called "the great room." Michael's private joke had always been, What's so great about it? It was big all right, but soulless, and over the stone hearth (with a gas-fed flame), there was a huge family photo portrait. His father, of course, occupied pride of place, in a dark suit and a bright red tie bearing the sign of the Masonic Lodge he belonged to—"Whoever heard of a stone salesman who's not a Mason?" he'd said more than once. "That's a no-brainer, my friend." Everyone else in the picture stood uneasily in his shadow. Michael was off on the lower left, and as he had often noted, his image was the only one that did not actually touch or impinge upon anyone else in the picture. Depending on his moods, he had thought that stance to be proudly self-sufficient, or unbearably sad.

His mom kept looking at him with the most mournful expression, and twice got up and squeezed his hand as if she were wringing the last drops of water out of a sponge. Sissy prattled on about the wonders of Milwaukee and something called "fish fry Friday"—"I don't eat all day Thursday, just so I can go out and have some real fun the next night"—and occasionally dropped some hints about how hard it was to get by on her meager salary. Michael knew that his father had been supplementing her income for years, and it was a source of pride that he had never asked him to do the same for him.

Privately, he had also feared that he'd be turned down.

When he went back upstairs, he took his Zoloft for depression, his Ambien to help him sleep, and then put on his headphones—he liked to drift off to Lucinda Williams or Tracy Chapman—but tonight it wasn't working. There was too much to sort through, from the general anxiety he felt whenever he was back in the ancestral home to his conflicted feelings about the death of his own father. Weren't you supposed to be shattered? Or at least shaken up pretty bad? All Michael felt was a vague sense of numbness, a suspension of sorts in the pit of his stomach, like you'd eaten something that you weren't sure was going to agree with you later on that night.

And apart from his mother, who seemed expectedly devastated, he hadn't gotten the impression that Richard or Sissy was exactly reeling. Richard, he knew, would relish the perks—sitting in his dad's office, having his own secretary, driving, no doubt, his father's prized Bentley—but then he'd also have to run the business, and he was nothing if not incompetent. The only times he'd been nice to Michael when they were kids was when he needed help with his homework; even though Michael was two years younger, he was still able to master the algebra or geometry that stumped his brother much faster than his brother could, and he did the homework just to buy some peace for awhile.

Sissy, on the other hand, would be chiefly concerned about the loss of her monthly subsidy. She got along okay with her mother, but she had always been Daddy's little girl. Michael wondered what his father would have thought if he could have seen her tonight, scarfing down a cannoli—she'd saved the calories, she announced, by not eating any of the breading or pasta—with him not even in his grave.

Or mausoleum, to be precise.

Sometime after midnight, Michael got up to take another half of an Ambien, and thought he heard voices coming up the stairs. He put his ear to the door. His mom was crying, softly, and Richard was saying, "Either it works, or it doesn't. No harm done either way."

"But it's so . . ." She never finished the sentence.

"The greater good," Richard said, in a low voice, "think of the greater good."

What on earth could they be discussing? Signing the whole company over to Richard? The one who couldn't figure out a ten percent tip at a restaurant?

He heard his mother's bedroom door opening, and Richard saying, "Just get a good night's sleep. It's a long day tomorrow."

Her door closed, and Michael held his breath; he could tell that his brother had walked over to his own door now, and was standing right outside it. He could see the shadow of his feet under the door, and he could hear him take a long breath. Was he going to knock? Michael was riveted in place, then saw the door handle jiggle, almost imperceptibly. From force of habit growing up, Michael had always locked his door, and he was very glad he'd done so now. The handle turned slightly, then stopped, and Richard let it return to its normal position. Michael heard him sigh—in sadness? frustration? weariness?—then walk down the hall in the direction of the guest room. Michael exhaled, and padded back to his bed.

The next morning, Michael woke up late—the Ambien had finally caught up with him—and by the time he'd made some quick notes for his screenplay and gone downstairs, things were already underway. In fact, passing through the great room he saw some empty glasses and snack remnants, as if there'd been a late-night conference to which he had not been invited. His mother was in the kitchen, wearing a black jacket over a long black skirt, instructing a couple of Hispanic women on what to straighten up, what to serve when the guests came back from the funeral, what to put where on the buffet table in the dining room. Sissy was holed up in his father's home office with Richard, poring over some papers. What was that all about? Michael wondered. Was she coming into the business, too, now?

"You still on Hollywood time?" Richard said when he saw him in the doorway. The papers were openly, but swiftly slipped into the top desk drawer.

"There's some crullers in the kitchen," Sissy said. "And coffee."

"But eat fast." Richard glanced at the grandfather clock in the corner. "We've got to get going soon."

Michael was already in his own dark suit—a lightweight cotton, suitable for California, but not up to Chicago standards—and he took some breakfast up to his room, just to get out of everyone's way. His mother had a weird, hectic flush on her face, ineffectually disguised by too much makeup, and she didn't seem able to look him in the eye. Another note to make. When Richard bellowed for him from the front entry hall, Michael closed his notebook, put on his old parka that still hung in the closet, and went back downstairs. That vintage black Bentley, his father's most cherished possession, stood gleaming in the front drive. His mom got into the front passenger seat, and Michael climbed into the back with Sissy. Richard plopped into the driver's seat with a satisfied grunt, and Michael studied the back of his head. His dark hair was perfectly cut, straight across, as if with a razor, and the velvet collar of his topcoat lay smoothly across his broad shoulders. But the sight was nonetheless jarring; Michael had never seen anyone but his father in that seat. Even at the country club, no valet was ever allowed to sit there; his father parked the car himself, in his own reserved spot.

The services were predictably solemn and the crowd, for a man of Randolph Mountjoy's outsized character and achievement, smaller than Michael would have expected. His father's own sister, Michael's Aunt Helen, had called to say she wasn't well enough to come all the way from Seattle. And the eulogies were short and sounded, to Michael, more like biographical sketches than loving tributes. More than one of the speakers mentioned his father's signature line, "How goes it, my friend?" though it failed to elicit any tears from anyone but his mother.

The procession then moved on to Lakeview Cemetery, and up the long winding drive that Michael had traveled many a summer, when he was supposed to be overseeing the installment of a tombstone or grave marker. Michael couldn't see the newly erected mausoleum until the car stopped and he got out, and it was just what he thought his father would have erected. It was a grand tomb of white marble, in the classical style, with rounded columns on either side of the double doors and winged angels perched on all four corners. Michael didn't remember there ever being a point this high in the cemetery, and he figured his father must have paid to have the hill made higher, so as to afford a more expansive view of the cold gray waters of Lake Michigan beyond.

The gleaming casket was removed from the hearse, with only a few close friends of the family remaining in attendance, and Richard himself opened the mausoleum doors; they appeared to be made of heavy, opaque glass, overlaid with an elaborate black iron scroll-work—a design, as far as Michael could tell, similar to the one on his father's favorite necktie. There was some uncomfortable maneuvering among the pallbearers to get the casket, which looked to Michael to be somewhat oversized, through the doors. Standing just outside, he could hear Richard giving instructions—"Here, just below the round window—gently now"—and the scraping of shoes on the floor, the sliding of the polished mahogany box onto presumably some marble shelf. The hired men filed out, as Michael waited with his mother and sister on the hard-packed earth of the gently sloping hill. On closer inspection, he noticed now that the four figures atop the mausoleum weren't angels at all; they were owls, with furled wings and curving beaks. Moments later, his brother emerged, and quickly turned to secure the doors with the kind of key—black and large—Michael would have imagined locking the gates of Bedlam. Another note.

Michael was taken aback at that—he had imagined that he would be allowed to go inside, and the fact that his brother hadn't even offered him, or anyone else, the opportunity, was galling. "What's it like inside?" he asked, hoping his brother would realize his omission and relent.

"Nothing in there you need to see," Richard said, "but the workmanship is top notch. Dad wouldn't have allowed for anything less."

Taking his mother by the elbow, Richard led them all back down the hill and drove them home in the Bentley—to the reception due to begin very soon.

Most of the people there Michael barely knew or only dimly remembered—he had seldom come home after college. A few asked him about his career "out there in Tinseltown," and Michael had to make the obligatory remarks, meant at once to suggest success while modestly claiming none. Thank God they didn't know how well warranted the modesty was. After less than an hour, he was able to discreetly leave the room, and retire upstairs, where he quickly made notes about the day's events.

But as he laid back against the headboard of the bed, scratching his thoughts on the pad, his mind kept going back to certain moments—the whispered conversation on the stairs, his brother concealing the papers in the office, or barring his entrance into the tomb. It had been years since he felt so keenly his brother's bullying, or his own general estrangement from the family. Even his mother, once his only ally, was too devastated by the sudden loss of her husband to be much help. It was as if his father's strong will had been the one thing keeping the family intact, the planets in alignment, the stars in their assigned positions, and now that he was gone, everyone was off balance and looking for some new order to be imposed.

Michael made some more notes, went downstairs for a quick snack from the buffet now that the guests had gone, and intended to make it an early night—he hadn't slept well the night before—but found that he just couldn't calm down. He watched some TV in his room, took a long hot shower, but instead of getting into bed, he found himself getting dressed again and creeping downstairs. He was annoyed; no, he was angry, he told himself. Something that had been building for years was now, at last, coming to the fore. He wasn't as resigned to his fate as the family outsider as he had always pretended to be; he was pissed about it. He wasn't above the fray, after all; he'd just been afraid to stand up for himself. And now, he was going to. ("The protagonist of your screenplay must ACT," ran through his mind, from one of his screenwriting tapes, "not be acted UPON.")

And that's what he was going to do—act. Richard, he knew, had at last gone back to his own apartment for the night, and his mother was no doubt zonked out on Valium. Sissy was in her old room—he could hear "Top Chef" on her TV—and when he went into the home office, he found the top desk drawer unlocked. He took out the papers Richard had been looking at, and for a second didn't realize what he was seeing. It was clearly a new letterhead and logo for the business, but it was only on closer inspection that he discovered the company was now called "Mountjoy Stone and Building Supply." No "& Sons." And certainly no "& Brother."

Was that what he'd been whispering about on the stairs last night? Was that why his mother was crying—at this further, and final, betrayal, of her younger son?

He started to stuff the letterhead back into the drawer, then remembered to do it gently, so as not to leave any evidence of his having been there. And it was then that he noticed the black, iron key, the one that Richard had used to lock the mausoleum. He picked it up and weighed it in his hand, and as he did so, he felt his resolve strengthening. Maybe it was time to start asserting himself, after all. He'd just figured out what his brother's plans were for the family business, and now he could find out what, if anything, was so damn important that he couldn't be allowed inside the tomb to see it.

Even now, he was too afraid to drive his father's Bentley. And trying to find the keys to his mother's car, much less opening the electric garage door, would give away his plans. So he quietly put on his parka, stuck a flashlight in his pocket, and took his old bike through the side door of the garage. The back tire was almost flat, but it would make it—the cemetery was only a mile or two away.

What he hadn't counted on was the snow that began to fall when he was only a block or two from the house. It started out as a light flurry, the flakes sticking to his glasses and the backs of his hands. He put up the hood on the parka, and pedaled faster, but the wind was starting to pick up now, too, and it was hard to make much headway on the increasingly slick streets. The back tire didn't help any, either. By the time he reached the cemetery it was really coming down, and he was coated with wet snow. Leaning the bike against a side gate, he punched in the code he remembered from his summer jobs there, and slipped inside.

He didn't want to turn on the flashlight for fear he might be spotted by a night watchman, so he made his way very slowly, and very carefully, among the graves and headstones. The ground was quickly becoming covered with an even layer of snow, and his footprints reminded him of the ones left by Claude Rains as "The Invisible Man." Something to enter in his notebook. His sneakers crunched across the fresh flakes, and then traced a path up the winding drive toward the highest point in Lakeview—where the mausoleum stood.

Surrounded by snow now, the tomb looked barely real, like a white ornament atop a white wedding cake. Even the black ironwork over the door was dusted with snow, and Michael had to brush some away from the lock before inserting the key. He turned it first to the right, to no effect, and then to the left, which resulted in the sound of a heavy bolt being withdrawn. Another turn, back to the right, and he was able to swing the heavy doors apart and open. It wasn't until he had stepped inside and closed them again after him, with a satisfying *whump*—it sounded less like a door than an air-lock—that he dared to turn on the flashlight.

The marble interior was as bare and antiseptic as he might have expected. Against both walls, there were eight or ten empty shelves—each one deep and dark—and although it was too high to afford any view, one small, round window facing the lake. Who'd be looking out of it, anyway? Michael thought, with a sudden shudder.

He slapped his arms against his sides, to loosen the snow, and warm himself. But still, he shuddered again. And laughed. It only now occurred to him that his mission was pretty damn odd, and spooky, and if he hadn't been so pissed and determined, he might have considered these things sooner.

Especially what he'd feel at the sight of his father's casket, resting in pride of place, on a separate shelf just below that window. He turned the flashlight beam toward it—and only then discovered that the casket had been draped in a purple cloth, with gold tassels; some words were embroidered in silver in the center of the cloth. He stepped closer. They were in Latin, which he could not read. "*Velle est posse.*" Huh. Surely, his brother, who must have placed it there, would know what it meant. And wouldn't it be a neat trick to ask him?

He turned the flashlight on the walls, and now he could see there, too, other inscriptions, but in even more foreign tongues. Some looked like Hebrew, or Arabic, others were simply glyphs. Birds in profile, and wooden boats with black sails. What was all this? Some sort of Masonic secret code?

He heard a soft rustle from somewhere in the chamber, and quickly swept the floor with the flashlight. It was impossible that there'd be a mouse, a squirrel, or even a bug, in such a newly sealed and artfully designed structure. His father always built to tight specifications, and, as in all things, he got exactly whet he wanted. Nobody ever questioned his orders—at least not successfully. Michael had seen him demand that an entire foyer be torn up and redone because the plinth was a quarter inch too short and one of the slabs was not perfectly laid.

The rustle came again, and this time Michael zeroed in on the purple cloth. Had a draft disturbed it? That, too, seemed highly unlikely; the place seemed hermetically closed—and, on a night like this, terribly cold. Outside, Michael could hear the muffled sound of the wind ripping off the lake and howling around the stone walls of the mausoleum, like a pack of wolves trying desperately to get in. Heavy, wet snow slapped against the glass of the doors and coated the one round window above the casket.

Michael started to wonder what he was doing there. What exactly was he hoping to find? And having successfully penetrated the tomb, couldn't he simply declare victory and leave now?

A tassel on the edge of the purple cloth moved, almost imperceptibly. Michael assumed he had disturbed the air. He stood stock still, his breath fogging in front of his face, and now several tassels swayed. And Michael could swear he'd heard something, like a voice, under the gusting wind. A chill literally went down his spine—and even though it was true, something so clichéd could never go into his screenplay. He bent his head over the casket, and heard it again. Like a sigh.

His head instinctively jerked back, and the flashlight nearly fell from his grasp. Could it be? Could he have heard . . . something like that? No. He couldn't have. The Poe story, the one about the premature burial, jumped to mind. But that was a story—and that was before embalming was routinely done—as had, most certainly, been done here.

He touched his fingers to the purple cloth—it was silk—and it swiftly slid from the casket, like a curtain being drawn back to begin a play.

On the roof of the tomb, Michael heard, unmistakably, the hooting of an owl. No, two or three owls. A veritable chorus.

The burnished mahogany of the casket gleamed in the reflected beam of the flashlight. Michael was torn between running out the door, and putting his ear closer to the smoothly beveled wood.

His mind raced for explanations, and came up with one—the body was settling. Hadn't he read that all sorts of terrible things went on after burial? That bodies swelled with gas, that hair and nails continued to grow, that liquids—real and artificial—oozed out of pores and orifices? On that show, *Six Feet Under,* they were always throwing in weird shit like that. And what he was hearing—or thought he'd heard—had to be that, and nothing more.

"*Lift.*"

The word was as clear in his mind as a ringing bell.

His breath froze in his throat.

But he couldn't be sure if he'd heard it spoken, or it had simply been . . . transmitted, somehow, into his head.

He waited . . . but there was no other sound.

Even more astonishingly, the word had been uttered in his father's voice—in that gruff, imperious tone he had so often used, in life, with Michael.

And as if nothing had changed in that respect, Michael felt the same unquestioning obligation to do as he was told.

But lift what? The lid of the casket? What else could it mean?

But that would be crazy. Who would do that?

Why would he do that?

"*Lift.*"

More impatient this time. Demanding.

And definitely his father's voice. The same voice he'd used when dressing down Michael for going out for the school play instead of a sports team—"acting, for God's sake? Why don't you just wear a skirt?"—or choosing to attend arty-farty Oberlin College instead of a real school like Notre Dame.

Michael's mind was reeling. That was his father in there—didn't he have to do what he was being asked? My God, how could he refuse? Especially when it was such a simple request. Just lift the lid of the coffin.

What harm could it do?

The owls hooted, over and over and over again, as if urging him on. The wind picked up and beat like fists at the double-doors.

"*Lift!*"

And Michael felt, as he had felt for his entire life, nearly powerless to resist that voice. His hands, so cold now that he could barely move the fingers, reached for the lid of the coffin . . .

At 5:30 A.M. the next morning, Richard drove from his Lake Shore Drive apartment building straight to the family house. No one was up yet, but he quickly made his way to Michael's room, rapped on the door, and then waited—several seconds—before pushing open the door.

Michael wasn't there, and the bed—to Richard's delight—looked unslept in.

In the home office, he found the order papers for the new company logo right where he'd conspicuously left them—and the key to the mausoleum, as he'd hoped, missing.

He couldn't keep from whistling on his way into the kitchen to make some coffee.

Once Sissy and his mother were up, he bundled them all into the Bentley and drove, as fast as the still unplowed streets would allow, to Lakeview Cemetery. The main gates were barely open before he fishtailed through, and then up the long, winding drive that led to the Mountjoy mausoleum. It was a bitterly cold but clear day, and apart from a maintenance truck, he saw no other vehicles, or people, anywhere on the grounds. His mother was sitting beside him, with a look of mounting trepidation on her face; in the rearview mirror, he could see, and hear, Sissy devouring a Quaker Oats Breakfast bar. Reflective, she was not.

At the top of the hill, he stopped, and was careful to put on the emergency brake; the ground was icy and slippery.

"Do you want to wait in the car?" he said.

His mother nodded, holding a handkerchief to her nose, and Sissy said, "Yeah, you look. Tell me what happens."

That was the way Richard would have preferred it, anyway. No other witnesses, no intrusions, no unexpected reactions. He got out of the car, regretting that in his haste he had forgotten to wear boots, and crunched across the snowy ground toward the mausoleum. If Michael had left any tracks, they were obscured now by the snow that had fallen later that night. At the doors, he stopped, took a long breath, and then, before removing the spare key from his overcoat pocket, tried the handle. It turned.

When he cracked the doors open, he did not know what he would find, though it was fair to say he had not expected to see Michael lying on top of the casket, the purple cloth thrown like an afghan across his legs.

"Maybe we should have put in a heating system," Michael said.

Richard was dumbstruck. If he'd found his brother passed out cold, he wouldn't have been surprised. If he'd found him gibbering in fear, that wouldn't have shocked him, either. But this . . . well, he just didn't know what to make of it yet.

Although he did feel his spirits buoyed.

Michael swung his legs off the casket, letting the purple cloth fall to the floor so that the inscription lay face up. When Richard had asked his father what it meant, he'd said, "It's Latin, for 'Where there's a will, there's a way.' It's going to be the new company motto."

That was fine with Richard, although he wasn't quite sure how it pertained to the imported stone business.

"You bring the others?" Michael said, stepping down onto the cloth itself.

"They're in the car."

"Then what are we waiting for?"

Richard's hopes continued to rise, though he still felt he had to simulate some greater shock or even disapproval. Just in case he was wrong.

"But what are you doing in here?" he asked, and the withering look that Michael threw him told him everything he needed to know. Everything had worked, after all.

"Do we really need to go through this?" Michael said, crossing the threshold with a more assured stride than Richard had ever seen him use.

Once outside in the fresh air, and after that long night in the gloom of the mausoleum, Michael had to close his eyes for a few seconds to adjust to the bright sunlight glinting off the snow; he also needed a moment to compose himself. If he was going to carry this off, he was going to have to remember everything he'd ever learned about character and action and tone. And he would have to conceal everything he was feeling, the resentment and rage, compounded by the sense of utter betrayal, that was roiling inside him.

It was worse when he came closer to the car—with Richard trailing a few awestruck yards behind him. Sissy just sat slack-jawed. *Wait'll he told her there'd be no more monthly stipend,* he thought. And his mother looked at him with an intensity he had never before seen—she was studying everything about him, from the expression on his face to the length of his stride.

Well, let her look all she wants, Michael thought.

When Richard started to go around to the driver's side, Michael said, "Where do you think you're going?"

Richard stopped dead in his tracks, confused.

Michael held out his hand, palm up, until Richard realized he was supposed to put the car key into it.

Richard meekly got in back with Sissy, and Michael took the driver's seat, next to his mother. She tentatively reached out her hand to touch his, and even though he recoiled inside—*the greater good? he wanted to snarl, you were willing to sacrifice me for the greater good?*—he let their hands remain where they were.

"Was it . . . hard?" she asked him.

"What do you think?" he said, in that dismissive tone his father had so often employed.

She seemed oddly comforted by his peremptory tone.

Yes, there was a lot he was going to have to get used to . . . but if he could say, "No" to his father's last request, if he could sit on the lid of that coffin until the voice inside it died away altogether, then how hard, really, could the rest of it be?

STACY AND HER IDIOT

PETER ATKINS

1

Y ou know, soon as the fat guy mentioned his contact in the 18th Street gang, I should've just walked away.

Wasn't that I gave a shit who he knew or didn't. It was the naked and stupid *pride* in his voice—you know, pulling that outlaw-by-association crap that only people who've spent their whole lives *without* association with outlaws can be bothered to pull. So he was bullshitting. BFD. Except that bullshitting is just a polite term for short-order lying, which meant that this fat sack of shit—who I'd known for all of three minutes—was already fucking lying to me.

Like I cared where he scored his drugs. Like it's my business. Here's how it should go. Money. Drugs. Thanks. Seeya. Have a nice life and try showing some mercy to the Cheeze-Whiz, you fat fuck. But no, he's got to start in with the anecdotes about his gangsta compadre. Which means I'm bored and annoyed so I do something stupid. I don't take a line. Don't even open the bag. I just want out of there as fast as possible. Real dumb. Felony level dumb. But I got two things in mitigation: I'd been clean and sober for ninety days so I didn't want to risk even a sample buzz; and I'd gotten this lardass's number from Paulie Benson, and Paulie and me had never had a problem. So I cut Shamu off mid-story while he's gearing up to tell me just how many guys his guy has killed in the course of his illustrious career down there on 18th Street, throw him the money, take the packet and fuck off.

Takes me forty minutes to get back to Silverlake because some moron tries to make a left on Cahuenga at Franklin and gets side-swiped by the '92 Camaro that had the light. Jimmy Fitz and Stacy are spitting at each other in come-down by the time I let myself in and throw the packet at them. Stacy's right there with the mirror, the blade, and the straw—because, you know, nothing else really matters—but Jimmy looks at me hopefully.

"Change?" he says, like it's actually a possibility.

What fucking planet did Stacy find this guy on? I do him the kindness of not laughing out loud and head for my bedroom. Neither of them were going to be needing me for the next couple of hours.

Stacy was the sister of my best friend back in Jersey, so I was kind of obliged to like her, or at least to let her crash in my living room on this little California excursion of hers. But this Jimmy Fitz character was just some douche bag she'd let pick her up somewhere along the way, and I didn't owe him jack shit. So you can imagine how happy I was when it was his voice that woke me less than half an hour later.

". . . The *fuck*?!" he was saying. ". . . the *fuck*?!" And he kept saying it, little louder each time, until I finally got the message that it was for my benefit. It was the retard version of a gentle knock on the door and a polite "terribly sorry to wake you, Ms. Donnelly, but there's something we need to talk about."

I got up without bothering to throw any extra clothes on so I didn't realize I was treating J-Fitz to the classic halter top and panties peep show until he gave me that look. You know, *that* look. Seen it all my life from dipshits like him. *Too bad you're a dyke,* it says, *because, man, is that an ass I'd like to tap.* Prick. Stacy noticed it too and didn't seem to be much happier about it than I was, but she was much more concerned with the other little problem, the one that had gotten her boyfriend all worked up in the first place.

I'd already guessed the coke was fake—junkies rarely wake you up for any reason other than the absence of a fix—but it was a little odder than that. The package I'd brought was split open on the coffee table, and the powder was scattered everywhere, which I'd normally have put down to the little tykes' adorable eagerness to get at the goodies. This time, though, it also allowed me an unobstructed view of the packet's surprise Crackerjack gift.

It was a severed finger.

Guy's finger from the look of it—hair above the knuckle and shit—and it appeared to be have been removed by a knife that could have been sharper and cleaner. It was still wearing a gold ring, which meant that whoever put the finger in the package meant for the ring to be part of the message. It was a signet ring, pearl inlay on black onyx, with a simple design—a central upright, like a capital "I," with a curlicue at the top shooting off to the right and another at the bottom, shooting off to the left.

"I've seen that before," I said.

"The *finger?*" said Stacy.

"Don't be stupid," Jimmy Fitz said. "She means the ring."

"Oh," said Stacy, all offended. "Like the ring isn't on the fucking finger?"

"Yeah, but if the finger was on a fucking *hand,* and the hand was on a fucking *person,* then it's not quite the same as . . ."

"Shut up, both of you," I said. "I don't mean the finger or the ring. I mean what's on the ring."

"That sign thing?"

"The symbol, yeah."

"Where'd you see it?"

"It was on a wall."

"Like, painted?"

"Something like that," I said.

I'd figured it was gang graffiti. Not a tag I'd seen before but it's not like LA was, you know, running out of gangs any time soon. It was the same symbol as on the ring, though a little less well rendered. But then blood isn't as easy to paint with as you might think.

It was scrawled on the bare wall just above the head of the corpse, which was lying on the stripped bed in the second bedroom of some rented house in the Valley that one of Dominic Kinsella's crews was using for a porno shoot. Proponents of the good old American work ethic will be glad to know that the shoot was continuing uninterrupted on the other side of the wall while the body turned blue. And the icing on the are-you-fuckin-kiddin'-me cake was that the door to the room with the body wasn't even locked. I'd been delivering some high-end candy for cast and crew and had wandered in there by accident because I'd thought it was the door to the bathroom.

I had about five seconds to stare at the corpse—practically bisected by a close-range shotgun blast—before the Second Assistant Director followed me in there and closed the door carefully. He gave me an apologetic grimace, the semi-embarrassed kind, the kind that's more suited to a Maître D' telling you there's going to be a ten-minute wait for your table, and raised his finger to his lips.

"The fuck is this?" I said, quietly enough.

"It was here when we came to set up," he said. "We're keeping the door closed so as not to upset the girls. Mister Kinsella's been informed."

Oh, well that was alright then. Long as Mister Kinsella had been informed. "What's *wrong* with you?" I asked, somewhat rhetorically.

"Look," he said. "It's nothing to do with us. It's going to be taken care of. Would you just *leave,* please? People are trying to work here."

So I left.

The hell else was I going to do? No rats in the Donnelly house.

But no fucking idiots either. I'd had a fine old time in the underworld, but I was done. Done using. Done dealing. I mean, it wasn't like I was going to get, you know, a *job* or anything—it's not like there weren't plenty of other interesting ways for a girl to make an undeclared living, but from that point on I was staying in the shallow end. And I'd been there safe and happy, three months clean, until Stacy and her idiot showed up needing a favor and having no numbers of their own to call. And now this. Nice.

"What does it mean?" Stacy said.

"It's a rune," said James Fitzgerald, PhD.

"Whoa. Gold star, Frodo," I said. "Been getting down with your dad's copy of *Led Zeppelin IV* or something?"

"Fuck you," he said. Guess he was over his little crush on me.

"But what does it *mean*?" Stacy asked again. Jimmy shrugged, shook his head. They both looked at me.

I had no idea what the stupid *symbol* meant, but I could unfortunately make an educated guess as to what was going on. That fat motherfucker had been so busy jerking himself off with his second-hand thug life stories that he'd given me a packet intended for someone else, someone for whom the fake drugs and the signet ring would be a very clear message.

"Reprisal killing," I said. "Gang war."

2

Now, how stupid would Jimmy Fitz and Stacy have to be to turn around the next morning and go back for their money?

Yeah. That stupid. Which is exactly how fucking stupid they were.

Crack of dawn they were gunning their car, full of caffeine and attitude, pumped and primed to head over to Hollywood and teach my new friend Orca that they're the sort of people around with whom one does not fuck.

I was still sleeping and knew nothing about it, of course, or I would've strapped them in the kiddie chairs and distracted them with cartoons and Vicodin. Figured they'd probably gone sight-seeing when I got up. The beach, maybe, or Grauman's Chinese. They wouldn't be the only strung-out white trash trying their Skechers out for size in John Wayne's footprints. The packet, the powder, and the unlucky bastard's finger were still on the coffee table. It wasn't until later that I remembered what *wasn't* still on the table—the Post-it note with Roscoe Arbuckle's address on it—and that was long after I'd driven over to see Paulie Benson to try to get a handle on just what kind of trouble we might be in the middle of.

Paulie'd moved into a movie star's house for the summer. Least that's how he described it to people. I mean, nice house and all, but "movie star" was probably stretching it. Longtime customer of Paulie's who was up in Toronto shooting a couple of straight-to-video action flicks back-to-back. It'd keep him busy eight or nine weeks, and so Paulie got to play Lord of the Manor for a couple months in return for leaving a few Red Cross packages in strategic locations around the house for when not-even-Vin-Diesel got back.

It was still mid-morning, but Paulie's party never stops. Pretty boys and girls in and around the pool. Customers and colleagues drinking and snorting. I managed to get Paulie alone, though, and run things by him and the good news was he saw it my way. Figured me and the morons were just crossfire pedestrians who wouldn't be anybody's problem provided we played nice, gave the man his ball back, and kept our mouths shut. He calmed me down enough that I hung out a while, had a shot or two, and thought about flirting with any of the girls who looked they might be interested in playing for my team. Some Spanish chick was telling me about her last incarnation when I suddenly remembered the missing Post-it note and sobered up real fast.

I made it back from the Hills in a pretty impressive eighteen minutes and grabbed my phone. Jumbo picked up on the first ring.

"Harold," he said.

"That your *first* name?" I said. Because, you know, really.

"It is," he said. "Who wants to know?"

"Harold," I said, "we met yesterday. Helped each other out on that retail question?"

"Uh-huh," he said. Real noncommittal real quick.

"There was an item, unsolicited and surplus to requirements, in the recent order. I'm an honest person, Harold, so I want you, and anybody else it may concern, to know that I'm going to return it. And that I'm very cognizant of what is, and what isn't, my business. Do we understand each other?"

"Uh-huh," he said again. Little friendlier this time.

"Would now be convenient, Harold?"

"Uh-huh," he said, and hung up.

He hadn't mentioned any other visitors he might have had that morning, and I'd figured that was best, too. For all I knew, they'd got lost or distracted, and I could get it all dealt with before they fucked it up for everybody. Or they might be dead. Dominic Kinsella, or whoever it was that was pulling Harold's strings, might have already had people over at the fat bastard's place once he'd been apprised of yesterday's little mix-up.

I thought for a brief moment about getting hold of a gun. But here's what I know about guns. First; an exit wound is bigger than an entrance wound. Second; if you're checking out put it in your mouth not at your temple. Third; don't point it at someone unless you're damn sure you've got the balls to pull the trigger because, if you don't and they do, they'll take it off you and send you straight to that corner of hell reserved for dumb fucks who shouldn't play with guns.

That's it. Double it and add tax and it's still sweet fuck-all. None of it *bad* information, but none of it front-end practical like, you know, loading, cocking, aiming, firing. So I was going to go on good faith, on the principle that if everybody kept their heads, we'd be fine. I blew the excess talc off the finger, put it in a baggie, shoved the baggie in my pocket, and headed over.

Harold disappointed me. I'd been polite and upfront with him and was walking into his place alone and unarmed to do the right thing. But Harold wasn't alone. There was another guy in there with him. Young, muscular, tousled hair all Brad Pitt blonde with dark roots. I could give a shit. His muscles looked like they'd been sculpted in a high-end gym rather than earned on the street, and he'd dressed himself in a camo jacket and steel-toed boots to look tough. Yeah. Real tough. Abercrombie & Fitch go Baghdad.

"Thought we were going to have a private chat," I said to Harold.

"Shut up, you dyke bitch," the kid said, which spoke well for his gaydar if not for his manners. I jabbed two stiff fingers into his Adam's apple without taking my eyes off Harold. Call me touchy. Girl's got feelings.

Harold was kind of cool. Didn't even look down as his Seacrest-on-steroids hit the floor gagging. Maybe this wasn't going to go as badly as I thought.

"Stay down, Matthew," Harold said, and treated me to the ghost of an admiring smile. "The lady apparently knows her business."

I reached for my pocket. Harold backed off a couple of feet. "I'm just here to return this," I said, my fingers closing around the baggie.

"Why don't you just hang onto it?" said Harold. He moved fast for a fat guy. The Taser was in his hand before I even registered the odd and eager glint in his eye, and the stinger hit my chest before I could move. The voltage slammed through me, driving my body into a spastic dance, and I blacked out.

3

Don't know if you've ever gone any kind of distance bound and gagged in the trunk of an Oldsmobile, but I don't recommend it.

The ride was rough enough to begin with and the last twenty minutes—which, from the feel of it, was over the kind of ground yet to be reached by civilization—was actually painful. Still, I had lots to think about, and it helped to distract me. Harold. Fucking Harold. Had to hand it to the fat prick, he was the motherfucking King of Misdirection. Not just small-scale—the asshole Malibu muscle to keep my attention off his boss getting the drop on me—but big-picture shit, too; all that crap about his 18th Street buddy the night before must've been just snow, a little blizzard of bullshit to encourage my contempt and stop me from reading Harold right while he handed me exactly the package he wanted me to have. Still didn't know *why,* of course, but I knew that Harold wasn't what I'd thought at all. Harold was a player. Problem was I had no idea what the game was.

The car stopped, and I heard the driver and passenger doors slam, and footsteps come around to the back. The desert light was blinding after the darkness of the trunk, and it took me a few seconds to bring Harold and Matthew into focus. They were both standing there and looking down at me. I've had better moments. Harold had a proprietary excitement in his eyes that I didn't like at all. Matthew was excited too, but in a more immediately understandable manner. He'd unzipped his pants and his cock was right out there in full view. He was stroking it. Not enough to get it leaking but enough to keep it interested while he pled his case.

"Just let me put it in," he was saying, trying hard to make it sound like a reasonable request. He was, by the way, talking to Harold not to me. "Just straight in and up. Just enough to let her know. Remind her who's in charge here."

Harold didn't answer him, though he did throw an apparently casual glance at his muscle's love-muscle that was enough to tell me more about Harold than I really needed to know.

Matthew grinned down at me. "Middle of the Mojave," he said. "Miles from anywhere. Go ahead and scream." He reached down and pulled the duct tape off my mouth. I neither screamed nor said a word, just kept my eyes fixed coldly on his.

"Think you're tough, don't you?" he said. "How about I shove this in your mouth?" He gave a demonstrative tug on his dick. I opened my mouth, wide, and then slammed my teeth together hard and fast in a little preview of what he could expect if he tried it. He flinched instinctively and raised his fist, ready to smash it into my face.

"No," said Harold. "We don't mark the meat." He turned and headed away from the car, speaking to Matthew over his shoulder. "Zip it up. Behave yourself. And bring her."

4

The only structure anywhere in sight was a shack, which I guess is where Harold had changed into his black robe, but the event was scheduled to take place behind it, out in the open, in a small and shallow basin-like depression in the sandy soil. That's where Matthew had brought me and where, after first pressing the Taser hard against my throat to discourage any funny business, he'd surprisingly slashed the duct tape off my wrists and ankles with a serious-looking knife and then, keeping the Taser in plain sight, backed off to the perimeter of the basin, leaving me standing in the center.

Harold was on the perimeter, too, but he and Matthew were a good twenty feet apart, triangulating me.

"As you can see," Harold said, already sweating like the fat pig he was in his heavy black robe under the low desert sun, "the ground has been prepared."

Yeah, well that was one way of describing the various bloody pieces of Jimmy Fitz that decorated the four corners of the area as if marking the bases on a ballpark diamond in hell. Poor Jimmy's idiot head stared at me from home plate, dead eyes still holding an echo of astonishment, jaw held open by a swizzle stick and the cave of its open mouth filled with small rose petals of a delicate and almost translucent yellow. The petals would have struck me as, you know, an unusual grace note but forgive me if I was a little low on appreciation of aesthetic fucking incongruity right at that moment.

"Where's Stacy?" I asked.

Harold glanced at his watch. "Oh, I'm sure she's back with Paulie by now," he said, and smiled.

I didn't say anything, and I hope to Christ I didn't let him see anything, but he knew I was feeling it all right, and he took a moment or two to let it take a good firm hold.

"If it's any consolation," he said eventually, "you don't have long to worry about being played for such a fool. The sun is soon to dip below the earth and the betrayal of friends will be far from your mind."

I might have laughed at the strange formality that had crept into Harold's speech if I wasn't busy realizing that I might be quite seriously fucked here. I still didn't know exactly what Harold had in mind, but I was pretty fucking sure I wasn't going to enjoy it. Still, Stacy and Paulie were on my list now. They'd served me to this insane bastard like a party favor, and I found a little comfort, or at least distraction, in thinking about how slowly I was going to kill them if I managed to get out of here alive.

The back door of the shack opened, and an old woman came out.

At first glance, she could have been some ancient relative of mine from the old country. Big Black Irish bitch turning brick-house solid in her final years. She walked, poorly, with the aid of a stick, the ornamental handle of which was the dry skull of a dead hawk. One of her eyes was sea-green. The other was dead. And the skin of her face was white. I don't mean pale. I mean *white*. White as the paper you're reading this on. White as the roof of the world.

She reached the perimeter and stopped, keeping the same kind of semiformal distance from Harold and Matthew as they did from each other. Her head swiveled on her neck to face Harold with a leathery creaking so brittle-sounding that you'd swear there was nothing liquid inside her.

"I have come as contracted," she cawed at Harold, "to bear witness to the keeping of your covenant."

Harold inclined his elephantine head as elegantly as he could. "The offering has been brought," he said, "unmarked and unbound, and bearing the sigil."

Christ on crack, what was this? A fucking Masonic lodge? The desiccated old crone turned to look at me.

"Welcome, child," she said. "I am The Planet Trilethium."

Believe me, I'd love to have laughed. But her voice had no humor in it, nor any trace of self-consciousness. She was speaking her true name, and, as she did, it seemed that her dead eye glistened for a second as if there were a light far behind its surface, as if it was watching from a very long way away.

And I swear to God the sand beneath my feet shifted in response.

And sighed.

I felt it all almost drain out of me then, felt the way you have to figure the prey feels when the predator's jaw closes on it. You've seen it, right? In those nature films? They just go limp at the last, accepting it, letting it happen. There's probably a comfort there.

But, as my sainted mother used to say, *Fuck That Shit.*

Considering Matthew was the only one with actual weapons in his hand—the Taser and the knife—I must have looked like a moron running at him instead of one of the others. But I figured him as the nearest to an amateur and, besides, what the fuck did I have to lose? I belted toward him, fast, straight, and furious. And sure enough, the dickwad instinctively fired the Taser immediately instead of waiting for me to get close enough. I hardly even had to sidestep. The look on his face when the stinger went wide was so fucking sweet that I almost paused to savor it. But I didn't. Because that would have meant less momentum when I drove my boot into the kneecap of the leg he was putting his weight on. He screamed like a girl and, starting to go down, swung wildly with his knife, which was just what I wanted. I got a clean grip, snapped his wrist in two, grabbed the knife from his useless fingers and took a whole luxurious second to let him have a good look at it and see what was coming.

I didn't get a clean swipe at the fucker's eyes, because Harold's three hundred pounds suddenly slammed into me from behind, but even so the blade ended up hilt-deep through Matthew's upper cheek and it must have been angled upward enough to sever something important in what passed for his brain because he suddenly stopped moving altogether.

Harold grabbed at me before I could either steady myself or get the knife back, and I only managed a half turn before he had me in a bear hug. We did some half-hearted wrestling, my forearms flapping around pretty uselessly, grabbing at his robe and his jacket beneath, and I tried to get my knee up to find wherever his balls hid beneath his mountainous gut, but it was no use. After a few seconds of letting me struggle, he slammed the flat of his arm against the side of my head, and I went limp long enough to let him carry me back to the center of the basin and drop me there, still semi-dazed.

Harold was back at the perimeter before I could get to my feet. I saw him give an apologetic look to The Planet Trilethium, but she seemed, if anything, mildly amused.

Despite my ringing head, my blood was up now, and I'd have been perfectly happy to take another run at the fat sack of shit, maybe try and sink my teeth into the meat of his throat and rip his fucking windpipe out, but the desert had other ideas.

The sand was rippling.

Slowly. Not like an earthquake. Like an ocean. Like an ocean with its depths disturbed, as if something far below was waking and moving and would soon break surface.

The Planet Trilethium sighed in anticipation, the breath rattling in her ancient open mouth like a reptile hiss.

Behind me, the sun was flattening as it reached the horizon.

"You have come to the appointed place," Harold called out. "You have come to the appointed hour."

It was actually hard to keep my footing now, the desert beneath me bucking and dipping, and the speed of its impossible movements increasing. Harold had one last thing to say.

"And you bear the sign of the appointed one."

I planted my feet apart enough to let me keep my balance and stay upright as I found his eyes in the vanishing light and locked on them.

"Check your pocket, bitch," I said.

What, you think I wrestled the fat fuck to cop a feel?

Harold's hand flew beneath his robe to ferret in the pocket of his jacket, and I could tell the precise moment that his hand closed around the baggie with the severed finger by the way his face crumpled past anger and disbelief into something much more satisfying.

I began running out of the center of the basin, hurdling the raging earth, and Harold—screaming like a baby, I'm delighted to say—ran to intercept me, holding the baggie out like he was going to force the ring on me again. But the Sun was gone. And rules is rules, right? Appointed hour, and all that shit.

The Planet Trilethium opened her mouth. Real wide. And a tongue the color of bruises and the length of a garden hose flew at Harold, wrapped around his throat, lifted his massive bulk effortlessly, and slammed him, back first, onto the bucking desert floor in the center of the basin.

I'm a girl who watches her manners, so I'd like to have stopped to thank her but, you know. Busy running. And I really don't think she did it for me anyway. I was utterly irrelevant now, thank fuck, both to her and to whatever was rising from beneath the desert floor. They didn't need me. They had Harold.

I didn't stop running till I reached the Olds on the far side of the shack. I didn't look back even then. You couldn't have paid me to look back. Because, God knows, the sounds were bad enough.

I was ready to hotwire the car if I needed to—because, you know, I've got mad skills—but the key was right there in the ignition. I had no idea which way the freeway was but as long as The Planet Trilethium was behind me then I was going in the right direction.

I drove for a long time. Let midnight come and go. It was after I'd stopped for a burger somewhere off the I-10 that I discovered there was a cell phone in the glove compartment.

I seriously thought about giving Paulie a call.

But, you know, why spoil the surprise?

AMUSEMENT

TANANARIVE DUE

I wonder how eunuchs go to the toilet," Nicola said as though it naturally followed their conversation on the genocide in Darfur.

At first, Paul couldn't help being pleasantly surprised that Nicola knew what a eunuch was and, further, that she could use the word in a sentence. That aside, his ears glowed hot. They were eating curry with Charles and Anne, who had enjoyed more than one occasion to question his judgment. Nicola's comment had come like raw chicken dropped unwanted on their plates. Perspiration dampened the backs of Paul's thighs as Charles ventured a cutting glance that said, *Well, I can see your tastes haven't changed.*

"With difficulty, I would imagine," Paul answered. Nicola must always be addressed as if they were alone, no matter what the level of discomfort. She pouted when she was ignored. "Depending on what's left down there, of course."

In Nicola's unbecoming shrug, Paul could read her displeasure at eating with Charles and Anne, whom she always derided as pseudo-intellectuals who made her feel like a case study, and in her apparent boredom lay the ever-present threat that she would not ask Paul to stay with her tonight. Even after six months, he could never rely upon an invitation, which she doled out like treats. Paul's discomfort turned to annoyance.

He raised his glass to drink and watched Nicola's smooth, long face flatten and deform through the cloudy glass. A shout rose from the back of the curry house as water and lager flew in an argument between drunken students.

"That's our next cue to leave, don't you think?" Anne asked Charles, with special emphasis on the word *next*. She kept her eyes only on Charles, waiting for an answer before reaching for her purse or even unfolding her hands. Watching them, Paul thought of a finely-tuned mechanism; each maintained and deferred to control, and Paul suffocated in envy of them. The fact that they were both novelists—and that Paul had been a Booker finalist—only heightened his thinly buried resentment.

"Yes, I think this conversation is finished," Charles said. "You, Paul?"

"Quite," Paul said, rising. "Let's go."

All of them stood and gathered their coats. Except Nicola.

"I'm not finished with my pint," Nicola said. A half-inch of lager and lime lay diluted at the bottom of her glass.

"Of course, darling. Take your time." Paul sat, bumping against the table in his haste. His curry-stained plate fell before he could catch it, shattering on the floor.

"What was that bit about eunuchs?" Paul asked Nicola when they were alone in his car, but she seemed captivated by her rain-dotted window. Her hair hung in loose, dark strands past her shoulders, the soft tips tickling the soft mounds of cleavage she always exposed, no matter what the temperature. She did not answer right away. Sometimes she gave no answer at all, forcing him to repeat his questions. This time, he wasn't sure he dared.

"Oh, I dunno," she said at last. "You remember palace eunuchs, like in Shakespeare. I've always wondered how they can piss. Do they have a hole and squat like girls?"

At last, he understood: As much as he condescended to her and enslaved himself to her second-rate beauty, she was resorting to insults. He wanted to remind her that she would be damn lucky to find a lover half as good, that what he lacked in her childish concept of masculinity he made up for in stamina and stability. Paul locked his teeth, remembering that she had only allowed him to sit beside her at the Three Horseshoes, the pub where they met, because he mentioned that he was a movie screenwriter. This alone had sustained him for two months, until Nicola began to realize that the movies he wrote had nothing to do with his life.

"How could you write this if you'd never been to Rwanda?" she asked of *Battle Cry,* his first and most well-received film.

"Research," he answered, and saw something like disgust curl the sides of her lips. Then the disillusionment set in. Driving her home, he felt the familiar urgency to stem her boredom; as hopeless a battle as hoarding a ball of sand between his fingers by squeezing more tightly.

"It's early," was all he said.

"I know, but that place gave me a headache. Can you drop me off home?"

"I'll take you to meet a real one, if you're so curious," he said, one last squeeze.

"What's that?"

"A eunuch."

Malcolm was an American half-caste, "half Jamaican and half Californian," as he described himself, a cinematographer's assistant in his mid-twenties, UCLA film school grad, always cheerful. His hair was a crown of red-tinged spirals, and he was tall enough to be a basketball star. In the early days of the shoot, Paul avoided him because friendships and respect came with guileless ease to Malcolm, and he alone seemed immune to the rivalries plaguing them behind the set. Paul disliked almost everything about Malcolm, particularly his soft, high-pitched voice that made him sound like a Michael Jackson impersonator, and his lazy American mumble: "That's some script you put together, dawg." In Paul's eyes, Malcolm's flattery made him dangerous.

All of that changed when Paul found himself waiting beside Malcolm in a queue for the bar at a cast party. "We just can't win in this world, Paul," Malcolm said. "I told the girls I was gay so they'd lay off, and now word's gotten to the guys."

Paul was unsympathetic and told him so. The words *sod off* burned on his tongue.

Malcolm took Paul's arm and Paul felt his warm, alcohol-laden breath tickling his earlobe. "Listen, I'm only telling you this so you won't think I'm a conceited jerk: I can forget about a sex life," Malcolm stage-whispered. "My balls got infected when I was ten, and I didn't know nothin' about a doctor. Went on too long. So the next thing I know, my parents are sitting me down to tell me I have to have 'an operation.' In the process, the asshole with the scalpel cut the nerves . . . so let's just say I lost my virginity at a very young age. Getting laid is not a huge priority in my life."

Paul stared at him in wonderment and skepticism, but Malcolm's whiskey-laden eyes were earnest. "You feel me?" Malcolm finished.

Paul nodded, once he realized the phrase was another Americanism and not an invitation. He swallowed back a distinctive wave of nausea, excusing himself. The confession had been a blast of rank air, the chaotic ringing of someone else's life. But Paul felt terrible about the way he fled. Later, he found Malcolm digging his hand into a bowl of crisps and murmured an apology.

"No worries," Malcolm said, his eyes darting behind Paul as though the apology was akin to a broadcast. "I was out of line, anyway. I've always wanted to tell someone—for some reason, it was you." He grinned boyishly.

Malcolm's honesty struck Paul as noble, and nobility was compelled in return. "You confided in me," Paul said in a sober voice, clasping Malcolm's tawny hand, "and you won't be betrayed."

They began to take tea together during breaks in the shoot. "You know, I never drank this shit at home," Malcolm said, "but now I feel like a freak if I don't have two cups a day." *Of course you're not a freak,* Paul thought—and very nearly said—precisely, of course, because poor Malcolm was one. But pity turned to a friendship, of sorts. They compared the movie industries in the U.K. and the States, and even compared dreams. "You should come back to Hollyweird with me, Paul. You write, I'll direct, and we'll make films worth making."

Paul came to relish these fanciful thoughts of Hollywood in the hours spent in pubs with Malcolm, until the curse of his unmolested loins drew him closer to Nicola and he discovered that it would take all of his free time to keep her.

Xavier woke Paul at exactly three A.M., and Paul was enraged. It had taken him a hot bath and a frustrated bout of masturbation to get to sleep, all destroyed when Xavier jumped on his chest and began bloodcurdling mews. His cat's enlarged pupils glowed red, not unlike the eyes of a demon. A glimpse of the animal's true face.

Paul had never liked Xavier. Charles had given him the full-grown Siamese cat so he wouldn't be lonely in his flat after he finally moved out of his mother's house, but the building didn't allow pets. Paul was always afraid his landlord would find Xavier during a routine inspection, so he closed Xavier in his bedroom whenever he was away. Subsequently, the room bore a slightly pissy smell Paul could never find the source of, a constant source of irritation. Paul also resented being forced to break building rules in exchange for nothing except Xavier's listlessness and neutral blue-eyed stares. Paul had never kept a cat, so he had been surprised that they did not jump up and run to you when you came home; nor did Xavier seem to like him all that much, except at feeding time.

At three in the morning, Paul felt a clarity that had eluded him before.

"All right, then," he said.

Xavier mewed again as Paul grabbed the handful of fur at the scruff of his neck and swung the cat off of his chest. He walked the three steps to his window, pulled it open with a squeal, and tossed the scrabbling Xavier down six stories into the dark. Xavier didn't make a sound on his way down, and the moist faint cracking a second later might only have been his imagination. The whole thing was over before Paul could blink, and for a moment he stood leaning out of his window into the icy night air, wondering if he had only dreamed what he had done. A deep scratch across his forearm was the only evidence of his waking state. His hands trembling slightly, Paul went back to bed, where he slept much more soundly than before.

Xavier had fallen to the car park, so the next morning his neighbors thought he was a stray who had been run over. The sight of his cat's broken, wide-eyed carcass forced Paul back inside his flat. He cried into his pillow like a schoolgirl.

With no one else to confess to, he called Nicola and told her the story.

"Jesus, what time is it?" she said.

It was only eight-thirty, and Nicola rarely rose before ten.

"Did you hear what I said? I threw Xavier out of my window."

"Is he dead?"

"Of course he is."

Nicola yawned. "I'd have never thought you had it in you, Paul," she said, her voice thick with the Yorkshire accent she did not soften when they were alone. But even mired in the thick yoke of an upbringing in Leeds, he could not mistake the sound of admiration.

"Well, it's not something I'm proud of," he said, but he realized that was a lie—suddenly he was quite proud of it. His earlier tears seemed puerile and silly. He imagined Nicola pleasuring herself with the telephone receiver, slowly rubbing the mouthpiece between her thighs. "Come over today," he said.

"When will I meet that mate of yours?" she said. "Malcolm?"

"Soon," he promised.

Nicola sighed. "I'll be there at half-two. You'd better have food this time." Suddenly, her voice lost its razor-edge of irritation. "Did you really do that to your cat?"

He assured her that he had.

"Tell me what else you've done, Paul. Maybe I don't know you as well as I think."

Paul's momentary elation faded as he realized that he had just told her his only secret, and there was nothing more to him. He was quite easy to know in only a glance.

Paul winced under the too-hot stream of water in his shower as he waited for Nicola. The trembling that had begun with his fingers last night had moved to his knees, in uneven tremors. But he didn't think Xavier was troubling him; his thoughts were only of Malcolm. How could he have encouraged Nicola's interest in him? What kind of man would offer a friend, and a good person, as a side-show freak? He was mad if he thought Nicola would ever love him, even after a parade of dead cats and eunuchs.

No, Paul decided as he dried his slightly pudgy and soft body, he would not, could not, introduce Nicola to Malcolm. Settling the matter made his trembling cease.

Then Nicola was in his flat with her pale ampleness, dressed in a snug mini-dress intended to entice him, touching his face as if she was savoring the smooth contours of marble. "Paul? When can I meet Malcolm?" she said, licking his neck with an electrified dart of her tongue.

"Soon," he said, assuring himself it was only a convenient lie.

"How soon, Paul?" Her pelvis cleaved to his, massaging his erection.

Paul swallowed the eager spittle in his mouth. "He might be at the wrap party on Friday. I'll introduce you then."

Paul felt awkward as they made love in the very bed where Xavier had awakened him only a few hours ago. Xavier's white hairs covered his bedspread, clinging to the perspiration on their skin. Nicola was not wet when he plied himself between her legs, so she inhaled in a soft hiss between her front teeth. "I'm sorry," Paul said. His hip bone dug into her fleshy thigh. She shifted slightly and said, "There," sounding relieved. Paul thrust. Their machinations felt like an exercise.

"I have a secret, too, almost like his," Nicola said, as if they were sitting at the breakfast table instead of pressed against each other's nakedness.

"Sorry?"

"That hole you're in, it isn't real," Nicola said, and Paul paused. His spine turned to ice. Here, he thought, was when Nicola would tell him she had been born a man and had an operation. He might never trust a woman again.

"I'm not a tranny," Nicola assured him, running her fingernails across his shoulder blades. "I still didn't have my period when I was fifteen, but I did have God-awful cramps and pains. So my mum took me to a doctor. Know what he found?"

"Not a clue," Paul gasped. He felt his erection fading.

"I didn't have a hole where I should. All the blood was trying to come out, but it was blocked. So the doctor had to cut the hole himself. That's probably why I'm so small." Paul came, which felt like a minor miracle although it was far too soon, dissatisfying. Nicola smiled at him as he hurried to cover himself beneath the sheets. "Paul, is this Malcolm bloke really a eunuch?"

"Exactly like in *Twelfth Night*," he said.

"We're kindred, then, you see? You'll really let me meet him at the party. All right, Paul?"

He heard himself saying *Yes, yes, Nicola. Of course, Nicola. Anything you wish.*

At first, Paul thought that by some divine mercy Malcolm might not turn up after all. After a contentious shoot, the party was only moderately attended, its guests segregated by cliques within several rooms of the posh Persian restaurant rented for the occasion. Nicola fidgeted at Paul's side. She had long since lost her fascination with watching actors eat and drink, especially since she had seen most of them without their makeup and in ill humor by now. The high-pitched whir of Persian pop music goaded Paul's nerves.

"You said he'd be here," Nicola said, her voice accusing.

"I said he *might*."

Nicola sighed. "If he's not here in fifteen minutes, we should leave. I wish you had told me this was casual." Nicola was conspicuously overdressed in black lace stockings and a strapless satin cocktail dress. *Served her right*, Paul thought.

He was about to suggest they should go when Nicola took his hand and pressed hard, her palms warm and wet. "Look, Paul. That's him, isn't it? He's like you said, absolutely beautiful. And a giant, no less."

Malcolm was approaching, drink in hand, with the same grin that had endeared Paul to him. "Well, shit on me," Malcolm said. "Look who's here, after you said you wouldn't be caught dead at another party."

"This wrap was worth celebrating," Paul said, trying to sound bright instead of miserable. "Malcolm, meet Nicola." Paul's legs threatened to collapse as Nicola and Malcolm stood opposite each other. "Shall we sit?" Paul asked weakly, indicating the rose-colored wingchairs behind them.

Paul watched Nicola's eyes, which were directed at Malcolm's lap as he bent his long legs to take his seat, as though she could see through his loose-fitting linen trousers. Paul nearly nudged her, but stopped himself. He put his arm around her instead.

"I'm afraid Nicola has finally seen the truth about the world of cinema," Paul said loudly, hoping to jolt her from her mesmerized state.

Malcolm grinned. "And she's never even been to California."

Nicola raised her eyes to Malcolm's, much to Paul's relief. "An American girl from New York works in my office," she said. "But she doesn't care much for California." Her Yorkshire accent slipped in; *much* sounded like *mooch*.

"No one likes California except Californians," Malcolm said.

"Is there an east-west divide in the States?" Nicola said, and Paul felt himself breathe. He took Nicola's hand and squeezed like a proud father.

"East-west, north-south, black-white, you name it," Malcolm said. "America is one big divide."

"Is it true the Ku Klux Klan is still active?" she said.

Malcolm said. "In some places in the South, sure."

Nicola shook her head. "That's hard to believe, isn't it?"

"Why?" Paul said, and neither answered. His question, meant to be philosophical, had the mortifying affect of stopping the conversation cold.

In the silence, Nicola cast her eyes again toward Malcolm's lap, so indelicately that she did not notice whether or not Malcolm was watching her. He was. In a quick glance, Malcolm saw Paul's anxious start. Realization soured Malcolm's expression. The men's eyes locked. Paul's lips parted slightly, but he could not make a sound.

Malcolm gazed back at Nicola. "Excuse me a moment, will you?" He left abruptly, his walk rigid.

Paul's heart thundered, making him feel both dizzy and sick to his stomach. He could not remember feeling so badly about anything. "Congratulations. Now you've done it," he told Nicola.

"Done what?"

"He knows you know."

"Don't be daft," she said. "He'll come back."

Nicola was right. Malcolm soon returned with a plate of chicken kebabs. He pulled the meat free and popped the cubes into his mouth in quick succession, his jaw chomping constantly, like a tic. He didn't meet Paul's eyes as he sat beside Nicola.

"You have a very hot girlfriend, Paul," Malcolm said, and slipped his arm around her waist. Paul felt awkward with his arm so close to Malcolm's, so he moved his away. Malcolm scooted closer to Nicola, his thigh touching hers.

Paul thanked him for the compliment, finding his voice. Nicola smiled at Malcolm with the admiration Paul lived for. She leaned toward Malcolm to give him a closer glimpse at her bosom. She was flirting with a goddamn eunuch.

Malcolm chewed thoughtfully, his face impossible to read. Had Paul been mistaken to believe he was angry earlier? Perhaps Malcolm had no idea his confidence had been broken. God, if only that were true!

"I think your girlfriend is bored, Paul," Malcolm said.

"Not at all," Nicola said with a coquettish giggle.

"What do you propose we do about that?" Paul said.

"Let's go to my apartment and smoke a couple of bowls."

"Very Sixties," Paul said, foolishly. He had not smoked since he was a teenager.

"Ooh, I'd like that," Nicola said.

And so it was decided.

Malcolm's was an attic flat, its ceiling carved from the angles of the building's roof. Posters from *Apocalypse Now, Pulp Fiction, Kill Bill, Taxi Driver* and *The Cotton Club* formed a checkerboard across the slanted ceiling behind his sofa. Malcolm's lust for Tarantino, Scorsese, and Coppola had dominated many of his pub conversations with Malcolm, and the posters filled Paul with nostalgia. The rest of the room was alive with potted trees and baby palms. "To remind me of home," Malcolm explained.

"Had a good look yet?" Malcolm said, not moving from the doorway behind them. Paul didn't know how to respond—was he referring to Nicola's shameless gazes at his trousers? Suddenly, Malcolm flipped the lights off. "At home I have black lights, but we can sit in the dark. The streetlamp outside makes the room orange."

"It's brilliant," Nicola said, as if Malcolm had invented Light itself. "Do you like it, Paul?"

Paul reached for her hand, but he misjudged the distance between them, so his fingertips only brushed her dress. "It's all right, actually," Paul said.

"Well, have a seat. I'll get the Bud. Paul, you want me to grab you a beer out of my fridge? I think I've got bitter, if that'll make you happy." His voice was as soft as the patter of spring rain.

"An American with a real drink?" Paul called as Malcolm vanished into darkness.

"Couple of footballers brought it by last weekend," Malcolm called back.

Nicola remained standing, but Paul sat on the futon beneath the posters. They did not speak, as if they were actors waiting for cameras to roll. Paul was relieved when Malcolm returned with a can of bitter in one hand and a bong in the other.

"This shit's strong," Malcolm told Paul. "Don't cough."

"Piss off," Paul said.

Nicola giggled before she took her turn, then she coughed. All three of them laughed. The sound of joviality made Paul realize that everything might work out fine. He was spending a rare evening with Malcolm, like the old days, and simultaneously making Nicola happy. What was the harm in it? It was so like him to be living a perfect evening and fail to realize it until it had passed, he thought. Maybe he was learning how to enjoy life, just like Mum said he should.

"I love to watch *The Sopranos*," Nicola said. She puffed, inhaling and exhaling in quick bursts. "But that accent! You know, when I watch that, I have to put on the subtitles. I'm not joking."

"Hold it in, Nicola, or you won't feel anything," Malcolm said gently from where he sat beside her.

Paul chuckled. Nicola's comment struck him as genuinely funny. "Do you really?"

"I never told you?" In the darkness, he felt her squeeze his knee affectionately. "But I do fancy it. You should watch it, Paul."

"Paul thinks American television is 'rubbish,'" Malcolm said.

"He likes to watch those documentaries about the African bush," Nicola said. "He's going to write another movie about Africa and pretend he was there."

"I will go sometime," Paul said defensively. He felt the marijuana suddenly, an anchor lifting in his skull, allowing him to float free, and he wasn't angry at Nicola for her teasing. He really should have spent some time in Rwanda, after all. He started to say this, but forgot the relevance before he could speak.

After two more hits and the can of bitter, Paul had lost track of himself entirely. He stared glassy-eyed at the palm shadows on the wall; oddly waving fingers moving in the breeze from the fan on the floor. Nicola and Malcolm chattered like old friends about subjects Paul could not follow. He was proud that he didn't mind seeing Nicola's head resting on Malcolm's shoulder.

"Why don't any of Paul's other friends have any personality?" he heard Nicola ask Malcolm. She could be speaking from the other end of a long tunnel.

"Because Paul has enough for all of them. Right, Paul?"

"I have no friends," Paul said. Watching the plants' shadows, he thought about Africa, feeling excitement and resolve. What was to stop him from looking into it? The shoot was finished, rewrites were behind him, so why not book a flight to Kenya for the two of them? He was about to ask Nicola what she thought when he heard her say: "Did he tell you he threw his cat out his window?"

It was such a non-sequitur, Paul heard himself laugh.

The futon shook with Malcolm's startled motion. "No way," he said.

"That's a secret, Nicola," he said, pretending to scold her.

"See? It's the truth," Nicola said. "Six stories down. The poor thing's dead."

Malcolm leaned over Nicola to try to see Paul's face in the dim light. His mouth hung open like a large fish, and Paul looked away from him so he wouldn't laugh again. "Is she serious? That's crazy, man," Malcolm said. Paul didn't answer, lifting the can of bitter to his mouth even though he had emptied it long before. Malcolm leaned back, shaking his head. "Damn. Don't ever have kids."

Paul tried to smother his chuckle with the can, but it only sounded amplified.

"I'm serious," Malcolm said.

"Isn't it awful when you get to know people," Nicola said, "and you learn all their secrets?" Her voice faded, dripping into a whirlpool. Paul closed his eyes, and the wooden floor beneath him shifted like the deck of a ship at sea. He secured himself in place by curling his toes tightly. He could sleep for a month, he thought.

"I know your secret," Nicola said to Malcolm.

Malcolm laughed. "Then I guess it ain't no secret, huh?"

Paul must have slept briefly. He snapped awake when he felt a tugging at his arm. Malcolm was gone, and Paul's subconscious reminded him that he had heard Malcolm excuse himself to use the toilet.

"Could you make me a vodka and orange, Paul? Please?" Nicola said.

Paul doubted he could make a glass of ice water in his current state, but he didn't have the energy to refuse. He brought himself to his feet and stumbled in the direction he thought the kitchen might lay. It took a lifetime to fix the drink because each phase had its difficulties: finding a glass in unfamiliar cupboards, finding the vodka, opening the can of juice. The streetlamp outside the kitchen window stretched odd shadows around him, making him pause each time they caught his eye. He stood a moment gazing at his own profile caricatured against the striped wallpaper.

The futon was empty when he returned. He wondered how much time had passed. With a sigh, he set the drink on the table in a sloppy motion that spilled liquid in a ring. He felt disoriented, realizing that he was alone in another man's flat. His eyes were drawn to a stream of light from the hall.

The light wasn't coming from the toilet, he discovered when he approached the boxlike room and peeked inside. He needed to piss, and badly, but he followed the sharp pyramid of light slicing across the floor from the crack in the doorway of what he guessed was Malcolm's bedroom. The flat wasn't as big as his, and the bedroom was the only room unaccounted for. That was where they were, the two of them.

Paul's heart sped. Careful to be quiet, he pushed the door open.

The brightness blinded him for a moment, and then forms began taking shape. Nicola and Malcolm didn't see him, or they weren't bothered about it. As he had expected, they were both reclined on Malcolm's bed. Paul was not even surprised, not really, to see Nicola stripped to her lacy black pants. Her modest breasts were upturned, nipples crimson.

What did surprise and transfix Paul, however, was the sight of Malcolm without his trousers. He lay cherubic and still, nude from the waist down. His long, spindly legs looked unfinished and pale.

Paul thought he shouldn't watch, but he followed Nicola's hand as she brushed her fingertips to Malcolm's pelvis. Malcolm's tiny penis was barely visible; it was thin and flaccid, exactly like a boy's. Nicola ran her hand gently along the ridges between Malcolm's legs, touching the healed and hairless flesh where his scrotum should be.

"Don't you feel anything?" Nicola said.

"No," Malcolm said. He didn't move. His voice was slightly muffled behind a pillow he held up to his face, as if to hide from her.

"You don't miss not doing it?" she said.

"You can't miss what you've never wanted," Malcolm said.

Nicola smiled, leaning over him. When she moved, her eyes shifted; suddenly, she saw Paul in the doorway. Her breasts bobbed above Malcolm's face. "Feel me, then," she said to Malcolm. All the while, she looked at Paul. She winked.

Paul turned abruptly and walked away without realizing he had made the decision to do so. He walked with the assured purpose of a blind man in his own home until he found the futon and sank there. He reached for Nicola's drink, careful not to spill any, and began to sip as he remembered the drinking adage he had learned from an American friend at Sussex: *Liquor on beer, never fear. Beer on liquor, never sicker.* The phrase ran around in his head. He finished the drink before he knew it. He wished he had another. He wanted to wash out his eyes.

The shadowy palm fronds on the wall waved and winked at him, mocking. He stared at his watch until his eyes adjusted enough to see that it was after three. He hadn't realized it was so late. He hoped Nicola and Malcolm wouldn't be much longer, because they really should be off soon. Paul already had his morning planned out: He would call the travel agent's and find out the cost of a return flight to Nairobi. He would buy two tickets, no matter what the cost. They would see elephants and Kikuyu warriors living in the birthplace of mankind, unchanged by the passage of centuries. He would tell Nicola his plan as soon as she came out of Malcolm's room.

Nicola would be shocked, he knew. And delighted.

GREAT WALL:
A STORY FROM
THE ZOMBIE WAR

MAX BROOKS

The following interview was conducted by the author as part of his official duties with the United Nations Commission for postwar data collection. Although excerpts have appeared in official UN reports, the interview in its entirety was omitted from Brook's personal publication, now entitled "World War Z" due to bureaucratic mismanagement by UN archivists. The following is a first-hand account of a survivor of the great crisis many now refer to simply as "The Zombie War."

THE GREAT WALL: SECTION 3947-B, SHAANXI, CHINA

Liu Huafeng began her career as a sales girl at the Takashimaya department store in Taiyuan and now owns a small general store near the sight of its former location. This weekend, as with the first weekend of every month, is her reserve duty. Armed with a radio, a flare gun, binoculars and a *DaDao,* a modernized version of the ancient Chinese broadsword, she patrols her five-kilometer stretch of the Great Wall with nothing but the "the wind and my memories" for company.

This section of the Wall, the section I worked on, stretches from Yulin to Shemnu. It had originally been built by the Xia Dynasty, constructed of compacted sand and reed-lined earth encased on both sides by a thick outer shell of fired mud brick. It never appeared on any tourist postcards. It could never have hoped to rival sections of the Ming-Era, iconic stone "dragon spine." It was dull and functional, and by the time we began the reconstruction, it had almost completely vanished.

Thousands years of erosion; storms and desertification, had taken a drastic toll. The effects of human "progress" had been equally destructive. Over the centuries, locals had used—looted—its bricks for building materials. Modern road construction had done its part, too, removing entire sections that interfered with "vital" overland traffic. And, of course, what nature and peacetime development had begun, the crisis, the infestation and the subsequent civil war finished within the course of several months. In some places, all that was left were crumbling hummocks of compact filler. In many places, there was nothing at all.

I didn't know about the new government's plan to restore the Great Wall for our national defense. At first, I didn't even know I was part of the effort. In those early days, there were so many different people, languages, local dialects that they could have been birdsong for all the sense it made to me. The night I arrived, all you could see were torches and headlights of a few broken-down cars. I had been walking for nine days by this point. I was tired, frightened. I didn't know what I had found at first, only that the scurrying shapes in front of me were human. I don't know how long I stood there, but someone on a work gang spotted me. He ran over and started to chatter excitedly. I tried to show him that I didn't understand. He became frustrated, pointing at what looked like a construction sight behind him, a mass of activity that stretched left and right out into the darkness. Again, I shook my head, gesturing to my ears and shrugging like a fool. He sighed angrily, then raised his hand toward me. I saw he was holding a brick. I thought he was going to hit me with it so I started to back away. He then shoved the brick in my hands, motioned to the construction sight, and shoved me toward it.

I got within arm's length of the nearest worker before he snatched the brick away. This man was from Taiyuan. I understood him clearly. "Well, what the fuck are you waiting for?" He snarled at me, "We need more! Go! GO!" And that is how I was 'recruited' to work on the new Great Wall of China.

(She gestures to the uniform concrete edifice.)

It didn't look at all like this that first frantic spring. What you are seeing are the subsequent renovations and reinforcements that adhere to late and postwar standards. We didn't have anything close to these materials back then. Most of our surviving infrastructure was trapped on the wrong side of the wall.

On the south side?

Yes, on the side that used to be safe, on the side that the Wall . . . that every Wall, from the Xia to the Ming was originally built to protect. The walls used to be a border between the haves and have-nots, between southern prosperity and northern barbarism. Even in modern times, certainly in this part of the country, most of our arable land, as well as our factories, our roads, rail lines and airstrips, almost everything we needed to undertake such a monumental task, was on the wrong side.

I've heard that some industrial machinery was transported north during the evacuation.

Only what could be carried on foot, and only what was in immediate proximity to the construction sight. Nothing farther than, say, twenty kilometers, nothing beyond the immediate battle lines or the isolated zones deep in infested territory.

The most valuable resource we could take from the nearby towns were the materials used to construct the towns themselves: wood, metal, cinderblocks, bricks—some of the very same bricks that had originally been pilfered from the wall. All of it went into the mad patchwork, mixed in with what could be manufactured quickly on sight. We used timber from the Great Green Wall* reforestation project, pieces of furniture and abandoned vehicles. Even the desert sand beneath our feet was mixed with rubble to form part of the core or else refined and heated for blocks of glass.

Glass?

Large, like so . . . [she draws an imaginary shape in the air, roughly twenty centimeters in length, width and depth]. An engineer from Shijiazhuang had the idea. Before the war, he had owned a glass factory, and he realized that since this province's most abundant resources are coal and sand, why not use them both? A massive industry sprung up almost overnight, to manufacture thousands of these large, cloudy bricks. They were thick and heavy, impervious to a zombie's soft, naked fist. "Stronger than flesh" we used say, and, unfortunately for us, much sharper—sometimes the glazier's

---

*The Great Green Wall: a prewar environmental restoration project intended to halt desertification.

assistants would forget to sand down the edges before laying them out for transport.

(She pries her hand from the hilt of her sword. The fingers remain curled like a claw. A deep, white scar runs down the width of one palm.)

I didn't know to wrap my hands. It cut right through to the bone, severed the nerves. I don't know how I didn't die of infection; so many others did.

It was a brutal, frenzied existence. We knew that every day brought the southern hordes closer, and that any second we delayed might doom the entire effort. We slept, if we did sleep, where we worked. We ate where we worked, pissed and shit right where we worked. Children—the Night Soil Cubs—would hurry by with a bucket, wait while we did our business or else collect our previously discarded filth. We worked like animals, lived like animals. In my dreams I see a thousand faces, the people I worked with but never knew. There wasn't time for social interaction. We spoke mainly in hand gestures and grunts. In my dreams I try to find the time to speak to those alongside me, ask their names, their stories. I have heard that dreams are only in black and white. Perhaps that is true, perhaps I only remember the colors later, the light fringes of a girl whose hair had once been died green, or the soiled pink woman's bathrobe wrapped around a frail old man in tattered silken pajamas. I see their faces almost every night, only the faces of the fallen.

So many died. Someone working at your side would sit down for a moment, just a second to catch their breath, and never rise again. We had what could be described as a medical detail, orderlies with stretchers. There was nothing they could really do except try to get them to the aid station. Most of the time they didn't make it. I carry their suffering, and my shame with me each and every day.

Your shame?

As they sat, or lay at your feet . . . you knew you couldn't stop what you were doing, not even for a little compassion, a few kind words, at least make them comfortable enough to wait for the medics. You knew the one thing they wanted, what we all wanted, was water. Water was precious in this part of the province, and almost all we had was used for mixing ingredients into mortar. We were given less than half a cup a day. I carried mine around my neck in a recycled plastic soda bottle. We were under strict orders not to share our ration with the sick and injured. We needed it to keep ourselves working. I understand the logic, but to see someone's broken body curled up amongst the tools and rubble, knowing that the only mercy under heaven was just a little sip of water . . .

I feel guilty every time I think about it, every time I quench my thirst, especially because when it came my time to die, I happened, by sheer chance, to be near the aid station. I was on glass detail, part of the long, human conveyor to and from the kilns. I had been on the project for just under two months; I was starving, feverish, I weighed less than the bricks hanging from either side of my pole. As I turned to pass the bricks, I stumbled, landing on my face, I felt my two front teeth crack and tasted the blood. I closed my eyes and thought, *This is my time*. I was ready. I wanted it to end. If the orderlies hadn't been passing by, my wish would have been granted.

For three days, I lived in shame; resting, washing, drinking as much water as I wanted while others were suffering every second on the wall. The doctors told me that I should stay a few extra days, the bare minimum to allow my body to recuperate. I would have listened if I didn't hear the shouts from an orderly at the mouth of the cave.

"Red Flare!" he was calling. "RED FLARE!"

Green flares meant an active assault, red meant overwhelming numbers. Reds had been uncommon, up until that point. I had only seen one, and that was far in the distance near the northern edge of Shemnu. Now they were coming at least once a week. I raced out of the cave, ran all the way back to my section, just in time to see rotting hands and heads begin to poke their way above the unfinished ramparts.

[We halt. She looks down at the stones beneath out feet.]

Here, right here. They were forming a ramp, using their trodden comrades for elevation. The workers were fending them off with whatever they could, tools and bricks, even bare fists and feet. I grabbed a rammer, an implement used for compacting earth. The rammer is an immense, unruly device, a meter-long metal shaft with horizontal handlebars on one end and a large, cylindrical, supremely heavy stone on the other. The rammer was reserved only for largest and strongest men in our work gang. I don't know how I managed to lift, aim, and bring it crashing down, over and over, on the heads and faces of the zombies below me . . .

The military was supposed to be protecting us from overrun attacks like these, but there just weren't enough soldiers left by that time.

[She takes me to the edge of the battlements and points to something roughly a kilometer south of us.]

There.

[In the distance, I can just make out a stone obelisk rising from an earthen mound.]

Underneath that mound is one of our garrison's last main battle tanks. The crew had run out of fuel and was using it as a pillbox. When they ran out of ammunition, they sealed the hatches and prepared to trap themselves as bait. They held on long after their food ran out and their canteens ran dry. "Fight on!" they would cry over their hand-cranked radio, "Finish the wall! Protect our people! Finish the wall!" The last of them, the seventeen-year-old driver held out for thirty-one days. You couldn't even see the tank by then, buried under a small mountain of zombies that suddenly moved away as they sensed that boy's last breath.

By that time, we had almost finished our section of the Great Wall, but the isolated attacks were ending, and the massive, ceaseless, million-strong assault swarms began. If we had had to contend with those numbers in the beginning, if the heroes of the southern cities hadn't shed their blood to buy us time . . .

The new government knew it had to distance itself from the one it had just overthrown. It had to establish some kind of legitimacy with our people, and the only way to do that was to speak the truth. The isolated zones weren't "tricked" into becoming decoys like in so many other countries. They were asked, openly and honestly, to remain behind while others fled. It would be a personal choice, one that every citizen would have to make for themselves. My mother, she made it for me.

We had been hiding on the second floor of what used to be our five-bedroom house in what used to be one of Taiyuan's most exclusive suburban enclaves. My little brother was dying, bitten when my father had sent him out to look for food. He was lying in my parent's bed, shaking, unconscious. My father was sitting by his side, rocking slowly back and forth. Every few minutes he would call out to us. "He's getting better! See, feel his forehead. He's getting better!" The refugee train was passing right by our house. Civil Defense Deputies were checking each door to find out who was going and who was staying. My mother already had a small bag of my things packed; clothes, food, a good pair of walking shoes, my father's pistol with the last three bullets. She was combing my hair in the mirror, the way she used to do when I was a little girl. She told me to stop crying and that some day soon they would rejoin me up north. She had that smile, that frozen, lifeless smile she only showed for father and his friends. She had it for me now, as I lowered myself down our broken staircase.

[Liu pauses, takes a breath, and lets her claw rest on the hard stone.]

Three months, that is how long it took us to complete the entire Great Wall. From Jingtai in the western mountains to the Great Dragon head on the Shanhaiguan Sea. It was never breached, never overrun. It gave us the breathing space we needed to finally consolidate our population and construct a wartime economy. We were the last country to adopt the Redeker Plan, so long after the rest of the world, and just in time for the Honolulu Conference. So much time, so many lives, all wasted. If the Three Gorges Dam hadn't collapsed, if that other wall hadn't fallen, would we have resurrected this one? Who knows. Both are monuments to our shortsightedness, our arrogance, our disgrace.

They say that so many workers died building the original walls that a human life was lost for every mile. I don't know if that it was true of that time . . .

(Her claw pats the stone.)

But it is now.

WORDS, WORDS, WORDS!

GARY BRANDNER

Hamilton Baxter sat behind the table piled with fresh copies of *Mischief Afoot*. It was his latest book and featured a nice garish dust cover and his name spelled correctly. The dozen or so youngsters across from him in the bookstore were not a Stephen-King-size autograph line, but they were, he supposed, better than nothing.

Baxter pulled his long, lean face into what he hoped was a convincing smile. When one of the young wannabes presented a book he scribbled his practiced autograph, adding some meaningless dedication if requested. Most of these kids, he knew, were English majors hoping to someday see their own name on a book cover. They had sat patiently through his reading aloud of chunks of his prose. It was a drill he hated, but which seemed to be expected. At the end of the day maybe some of these dipshits would actually come up with the $24 to buy his overpriced hardcover.

Amid the babble of fawning praise and trite questions from the fans, Baxter waited patiently for the inevitable "Where do you get your ideas?" While other writers, *real* writers, groaned at this chestnut, Baxter enjoyed it. It gave him a chance to bloviate and pontificate all the meaningless slogans and shibboleths spouted by writers since, well, probably since Plutarch. All the crap about using your life experience, writing from the soul, distilling the one true word from random thought. Empty words, but they ate it up, these writer groupies. So on this occasion when he opened his mouth to lay some platitude on the eager young faces, he was as surprised as any of them to hear what came out.

"Where do I get my ideas? I steal them."

There followed a moment of stunned silence in which it seemed you could hear the non-ringing of the cash register. Then the laughter began as the group of youngsters concluded that the semifamous writer was making a joke. A beat later Baxter joined the general merriment, hoping his own laughter did not ring as false as it was. For what he had just told the assembled fans was the truth. He was a thief.

It was in his freshman year at one of the California state colleges that Hamilton Baxter discovered his knack for taking the work of other writers, changing some words, restructuring a few sentences, and rearranging paragraphs. He could then present the piece as his own and be assured of an acceptable grade. As his skill at word thievery grew, Baxter sailed through college and graduated with a degree in English without producing a single piece of original writing.

On graduation Baxter discovered the career opportunities for English majors were severely limited. He had but one real skill, and he concentrated on some way to use that in making a living. It did not take long for him to settle on fiction writing. There were untold millions of stories in long-forgotten books just waiting to be lifted. Baxter was careful never to use the work of an author whose name people might know, or a story too familiar to the public. He haunted the back shelves of used-book stores and the dusty stacks of unread works in the library. He avoided the Internet as a source because there were too many ways an inquisitive geek could nail him there.

For fifteen years now he had made a comfortable, if not sumptuous living, using the words of others. He was content to be a midlist writer, never breaking into any bestseller list, winning no prizes, selling his work moderately and occasionally playing Author for small groups like the one at the bookstore today.

Shaken now by the inadvertent blabbing of the damning truth to his young fans, Baxter excused himself, pleading a meeting with his publisher. No such meeting was scheduled, but he felt the need to escape before he revealed any more embarrassing facts.

An hour later, in his library refuge, Baxter inhaled the bookish air as a diver might suck in oxygen on emerging from the depths. The smell of the pages, the bindings, and the words themselves invigorated him. The building was new and bright, but the warm musty smell was as old as literature. The friendly middle-aged woman at the desk greeted him with a smile.

"You're later than usual today, Mr. Baxter. No problem, I hope?"

"No problem, Claire. I had to stop off and sell a few books. The artist's curse."

The woman laughed dutifully as Baxter headed for one of the little cubicles at the rear. He was relieved to see that his favorite space was not occupied. He laid his worn briefcase on the desk between the shoulder-high partitions and headed back among the shelves. He was to begin a new book today, and he planned to search among some old material for inspiration. He picked out a volume of stories from long-out-of-print pulp magazines. The writing was rudimentary, but those old penny-a-worders came up with some solid plot ideas. A volume of twentieth-century biographies would provide background for a cast of characters. Play scripts from the 1920s and '30s would juice up his dialogue. An anthology of pretentious fiction from obscure literary magazines would impart a touch of class.

With an armful of stealable literature Baxter returned to the cubicle and settled in. He opened the first book and snatched his hand back with a yelp of pain. A fresh paper cut sliced his forefinger. Damn, on his writing hand. too. He sucked at the wound, blew on it, swore at the drop of blood that oozed out and plopped onto his shirtfront.

Baxter looked around quickly to see if he had disturbed any of the other patrons. Not that he cared, but in his position it did not pay to attract attention. He was relieved to see that no one had looked in his direction. He picked up the book for a closer look at the page that had cut him. Puzzled, he frowned. The paper was old, soft, and pulpy, not the kind of slick linen that inflicted a cut. Whatever the cause, he had a deep nick in his finger that throbbed in time with his heartbeat.

With his left hand he opened another of the volumes. Emitting a strange grunting sound, the heavy cover slammed shut on his hand with bone-cracking force.

"Ow, goddammit!" He tried to pull back, but the book kept his hand clamped where it was. Only when he jammed the book under his right arm and pulled did his hand come free and let the book snap shut. He examined his bruised knuckles and looked around. Again, no one took notice of his outburst. These idiots had to be deaf, or too immersed in their own stupid reading, or maybe they were deliberately ignoring him. Baxter found himself unreasonably angry with these people for not acknowledging his irritation.

All right, to hell with them. Get some work done.

Baxter opened the book, cautiously this time. He was relieved that no page sliced his finger, no jaw-like covers snapped shut on him. It was just an ordinary old book. Relaxing a little, he turned to the title page. The letters there blurred as though he were trying to read through Vaseline. Automatically he touched his temple to be sure he was wearing his glasses. He was. He took them off, huffed on the lenses, and wiped them vigorously with a clean handkerchief. He replaced the glasses and looked down again at the page. No longer blurred, the letters stood out in bold black type:

jzsopkn jsrekk poknjjnsd
mw
ljkhodss pnn sijemdoj

"What the holy hell?"

Baxter realized he had spoken aloud, but he didn't care. Nor, it seemed, did anyone else in the library. Had he somehow picked up a book in some foreign language? No, those random letters looked like no earthly language. He flipped through page after page. Nothing on them but the apparently random scattering of letters, sometimes in wordlike clumps, sometimes in solid blocks down a whole page. Not a bit of it made sense. Crazy.

He pushed the book away like some venomous creature and opened another. It held the same meaningless jumble of letters. The remaining books were just as indecipherable. Baxter sat back in the plastic chair, sweat seeping through his shirt at the armpits. He had carefully chosen each of these volumes from the shelves, checked their pub dates and flipped through the pages before selecting them. Everything was as it should be. There were real words on the paper that had formed themselves into meaningful sentences and para-graphs. Now nothing had meaning.

Baxter closed his eyes and forced himself to draw in four deep breaths and hold them as he had learned to do while plagiarizing a book on relaxation. When he looked again at the pages they were the same incoherent mess.

He lurched up from the little cubicle and stumbled back into the stacks. At random he pulled first one volume then another from the shelves, riffled through the pages, and dropped them one after another to the carpeted floor. Not *a one of them was remotely readable. Am I going mad?* He thought. *Or am I the victim of some dreadful cosmic joke?*

Something nudged him from the rear. Baxter spun around, his shoulder slamming against the opposite steel shelf, which had been a comfortable distance away when he entered the aisle. With a grinding, growling sound the tall, heavy shelf edged closer to him. A horrifying vision swam into his head of his body caught there, crushed until his bloody entrails spilled over the books.

He squeezed out from between the shelves, barely escaping before they clanked together. The bright and airy library had darkened as shadows crept in from all sides. The pastel walls now looked like gray stone; the ceiling was lost in murky darkness. The people at the tables and in the cubicles were hunched over their books; silent and unmoving as stone images. Baxter stumbled toward the front desk.

The graying head of Claire the librarian brought him a flood of relief for the sheer familiarity. Something was definitely wrong here, but Claire was an anchor to reality. He coughed, trying to clear his throat.

Claire looked up. It was her face, but it was not the face she wore minutes ago. Something in the eyes was wrong. Very wrong. The heavy brows slanted down in a deep V. Her mouth stretched in a smile. And stretched. And stretched. Until the terrible orifice spread literally ear to ear. Brown and broken teeth protruded from suppurating gums. Baxter staggered back, his own mouth hanging open.

A rasping croak rattled from the ghastly mouth of the librarian. Nothing resembling words came out, though there was a rising inflection suggesting that this hag was asking a question. She extended a clawlike hand toward his face.

Abandoning all attempts at composure, Baxter leaped back and bolted for the door. Through the glass he could see the outside world where the sun shone on soft green grass, cars rolled past on the street, ordinary-looking people strolled on the sidewalks, pigeons pecked at the remains of a popcorn bag. A boy ran happily by playing with a black and white dog. Baxter fought for composure. Once he was back out there in the familiar world of reality everything would be all right.

He hit the bar with both hands to open the door, and bounced back. The bar was fixed in place; the door did not budge. He tried again with the same result. Whimpering, he pounded on the heavy glass with his fists until the pain shot up his arms. He kicked at the door with all his strength. His trendy jogging shoes made no impact.

Crying openly now, Baxter threw himself against the glass. He rebounded, blood dripping from his nose. As he gathered himself for another lunge a heavy blue-clad arm barred his way. The arm was attached to the powerful shoulder and uniformed chest of a security guard. The man was well over six feet tall with a broad, clean face. Baxter had never seen him here before, but on this nightmarish day he seized on the man as a savior.

As panic seized his throat, Baxter tried wildly to pantomime his distress and the need to get outside the heavy glass doors and away from the nightmare world his library had become.

For a moment he thought he had at last found an ally. The guard looked down at him with an almost sympathetic expression. Then the smile began. As with Claire the librarian, the terrible grin stretched and spread across his cheeks, up and back, until the corners of his mouth met his ears. The revealed teeth were long and sharp, not human at all. The ghastly maw gaped wide and a series of short growling sounds spilled out.

Baxter jerked his arm away from the guard and ran back past Claire, still wearing the hideous grin, past the silent lumpish patrons, past the tall murderous shelves filled with gibberish, to the tiny cubicle where he had left his briefcase and the four dreadful books that had kicked off this terror. He fumbled through the briefcase, found his cell phone, popped it open, and thumbed the button to activate it. The familiar tinkly tone came through, but Baxter scarcely noticed. He was staring at the logo on the tiny screen. It read:

womzilj

That was certainly not the name of the company that manufactured his phone. Nor was it any word in any language Baxter knew. He was not even surprised when the short list of names for his frequently called numbers made no sense. It fit with the bizarre world of non-words he had somehow fallen into. Gripping the little phone with one hand he stabbed at the numbered keys with his split forefinger. After a couple of fumbled tries he hit 911. An almost comforting electronic buzzing ring sound came through immediately. A click sounded as a female voice answered on the other end and said . . .

What the hell *did* she say? There were only crackling, meaningless syllables in his ear. Baxter flung the instrument away from him and turned to the dark interior of the library. There the lumpish people at last began to move. As in slow motion they rose from their seats and turned toward him. He opened his mouth to scream at them, get their attention and plead for help if there was a sympathetic soul among them. Then as they came at him he saw their faces. Oh my God, their faces!

The sounds he made were the burbling prattle of an idiot child. Try as he might, Hamilton Baxter, who liked to say, "Words are my business," could not form a single intelligible utterance. He fell back in the plastic chair and let his head bump forward on the surface of the desk. He heard the shuffling sounds of the others advancing on him. He cried like a baby as his world exploded.

The two men in white uniforms eased the gurney with its motionless burden down the steps of the library. The shorter of the men, who steadied the front end, said to his partner, "Did the doc say what killed him?"

"Who knows. Sometimes they just go, poof, like that."

"They say he was some kind of a writer. Sitting there surrounded by books. I guess he died happy."

BETWEEN EIGHT AND NINE O'CLOCK

RAY GARTON

Eric Volker walked into the Fox and Hound on the night his wife was to be killed, and smiled into the crowded English pub. It was located at the northern end of the small California mountain town of Newbury, fully decorated for Christmas, and noisy even on this, a Tuesday night. It was the kind of place that had a lot of regulars, people who came in weekly, or nightly, and they did not come only for the ale. They came in after work for the music and dancing, to play darts or pool or air hockey with friends or even strangers, or to sing on Thursday nights when the pub engaged in that most drunken of all bar activities, karaoke. They came to see friends, to get out of the house and away from the television, to laugh, to have one of Maggie's "exploding onions" with their drinks. They came because the owners, Denny and Maggie Jollie, always made them feel welcome. It was an open, roomy, well-lighted place that was usually fairly crowded and full of comfortable laughter. A good place to get your mind off the fact that your wife was about to be murdered.

Make sure you're seen by plenty of people Tuesday night, the hit man had said. *I'll be doing the deed between eight and nine o'clock. Make sure you're someplace where people can see you between six and ten. You'll need as many witnesses as you can possibly get. More than that, if we can swing it.*

Eric took in a deep breath and moved forward into the pub. He saw familiar faces and smiled, waved to some, spoke to others briefly on his way to the bar.

In the rear of the pub, on a small wooden platform, a local quartet called Jazz Socket played jazzy Christmas songs. The tree was huge in a corner of the pub, decorated only in sparkling red and black. There were garland, tinsel, and small twinkling white lights everywhere.

"Eric, honey!" Maggie called. "Where's Alma tonight?"

"I left her home tonight, came out by myself." He perched on a stool and slipped off his long black cashmere-blend coat Alma had bought him so many Christmases ago, and let it drape over the stool's back. He leaned forward, folded his arms on the bar.

"Everything okay?" Maggie said, leaning close so she wouldn't have to shout to be heard.

Eric took in another deep breath, then shrugged as he exhaled. "Same as ever. You know. Same old stuff."

Maggie was in her early sixties, with short, curly, lightening red hair. While unlined, her entire pale face, with its brownish half-moons under the eyes, sagged as one down her skull. In the wrong light, it appeared to be melting. Age was part of it. Maggie and Denny were both heavy drinkers, and that was part of it, too.

"I still think it's communication," she said, putting a hand on Eric's hand. Her breath smelled of wine. Denny was a whisky drinker, but Maggie loved her wine. She claimed that was because she was born in the Napa Valley. "You two just need to *talk*. That's all."

He shook his head slowly as it sagged heavily forward. "We've done so much of that, from every conceivable angle, and what it comes down to is this—she doesn't love me anymore. She won't admit it, but that's the problem."

"How about you?" Maggie said. "You love her?"

After several long seconds, without meeting her gaze, Eric simply shrugged. "The usual, please."

She stepped away and came back seconds later with a pint of Guinness. The mug thunked to the bar in front of him when she set it down.

"I want you both to come to the Christmas party, okay?" she said. "Please? Will you do that?"

He pulled a few bills from his right pants pocket, plucked out a five, and put it on the bar for the ale. He stuffed the rest of them back into his pocket with the change that kept jingling annoyingly in the bottom. "When is it?" he said.

"Same as always, Eric, Christmas Eve."

He frowned as he took a few healthy swallows of the ale. He put the mug down and took a napkin from the dispenser on the bar, wiped his foamy mouth. "I'm pretty sure we have plans for Christmas—"

"Honey, everybody has plans for Christmas Eve. All I ask is that you stop by for a couple drinks. We got this *way* cool band coming in from out of town, from Redding, and Luigi's Deli is catering the whole thing, so there's gonna be lotsa good stuff to eat. Just come by for a little while, okay? Both of you?"

He smiled. "Wouldn't miss it."

"Aw," she said as she leaned over the bar and planted a sloppy kiss on his cheek. "That's sweet. Look, I'll see you around, honey." Then she was gone, off talking to someone else, and then someone else, each little conversation quickly leaving her wine-soaked mind to make room for the next. She would come to him again later and tell him the same things and ask the same questions, and give him the same advice, all over again, with no memory of having said almost exactly the same thing a couple hours before.

Eric took a few more swallows of his ale and noticed it was almost gone already.

Slow down, he thought. *You're going to be here awhile.*

He looked at his wristwatch. It was only fourteen minutes after six. It was still early. The evening was very young.

And I, Eric thought, *feel old.*

Eric's first meeting with the killer was on a Sunday morning at the Newbury Artisan's Market. It was an open-air flea market with rows of covered stalls from which the merchants sold their wares. Some weekends, Eric had a stall there at the market, where he displayed under glass his mint-condition first-edition Cornell Woolriches and David Goodises and Jim Thompsons and Dan Marlowes and Dorothy B. Hugheses and many others, some signed. But of course, it was just an excuse to get out of the house. Other than selling some of his regular used paperbacks, all in very good condition, for half the cover price—the James Pattersons and Stephen Kings and Elmore Leonards and John Sandfords and both the Kellermans and the Tony Hillermans and Carl Hiaasens and many others—he barely made back the rental of the stall. He'd had a small store in the Newbury Mall once, but not for long. Books always pulled people in, but as soon as they saw the prices of the rare collectibles, they were gone. No curiosity whatsoever as to *why* they were so expensive, no interest at all in any of the writers they'd never read before. Nothing. It disgusted him, and he was so sick of it by the time he had to close, only seven weeks after opening, that he was glad to be rid of the place. Alma had been glad, too. Oh, she'd been so happy, she threw a party for all their friends. It wasn't the first hateful thing she'd done lately, but it was one of the meanest. She'd been ashamed of the store, because she was ashamed of the books he loved so much. "You can tell by the covers they're *trash*!" she'd declared more than once. Now Eric did all his business online, where he made plenty of money, and where he was connected to other people with the same interests, people interested in trading books.

People like HardBoiledGirl. These days, Eric's thoughts returned to HardBoiledGirl often. After all, she was the reason he was doing all this . . .

Eric had no idea what Judas looked like, but he discovered that Judas knew him. Eric walked slowly through the market that Sunday morning, stopping at each table to look at the items for sale, whether he was interested in them or not, and to look around him, too—mostly to look around him. The next time he stopped and looked around, a man was standing beside him, looking at him. He was a little shorter than Eric, who was six-one and lanky, with a pot belly that was impossible to hide. Judas stood about five feet, nine inches. He had on a broad-brimmed hat and a long grey coat, black pants, and shiny black shoes. He wore silver-framed glasses with lenses tinted just enough to make it impossible to determine his eye color. His face was oval-shaped, and his nose was straight, but ended in a bulbous, bisected knob. He wore leather gloves on his hands and smoked a long, narrow, black cigar that smelled like some kind of roadwork to Eric.

"Hello, Eric," he said.

Eric recognized the voice immediately. It was deep, and just beneath that deep voice was the sound of sandpaper against stone. Something, at some point, had happened to Judas's throat. That's what Eric had decided after talking to him on the telephone. He wondered exactly what had happened to cause the damage to his voice—his imagination hopped from one ludicrous, melodramatic possibility to the next.

"Heh-hello," Eric said.

"I'm Judas. Come on, let's just walk along slowly and browse the tables, okay?"

So that was what they did. They said nothing for a while because Eric was waiting for Judas to talk, and Judas was waiting for Eric to talk.

"How did you know me?" Eric said finally.

Judas cleared his throat. "I knew who you were, where you lived, what you looked like, what you did for a living, where you went to school, and whether or not you were banging anybody at the moment before I even returned your first phone call, Eric. It's my business to know you. I don't go into business with just anybody. Some do. They don't care. Not me. I care. I don't go into business with psychos and nutburgers. So I had to make sure you weren't one of those, or some other kink of human nature. If I didn't want to do business with you, you never would've heard from me, and you'd never be able to contact me again. But, of course, that's not how it worked out, is it?" Judas smiled.

Eric said, "Is that your real name? Judas?"

Judas stopped and had a close look at a painting, a colorful abstract. He sniffed once, then said, so quietly that Eric had to strain to hear him, "You aren't by any chance writing a book about me, are you?"

Eric chuckled. "No, sir. I'm simply curious. I didn't mean to pry. Feel free to tell me to shut up."

"Shut up."

"Okay."

Judas asked about Alma, her habits, her schedule. Eric answered all his questions without hesitation.

"Okay, listen. Can you do that? Listen?"

"Yes."

"Here's what's going to happen. I'll show up between eight and nine o'clock Tuesday night. That's this coming Tuesday, the day after tomorrow. I don't set exact times for myself because in this profession, it doesn't work out that way. Never. Sometime during that hour, I'll show up and do the deed. Now, you gotta tell me—is there any chance, any chance at *all*, that there might be someone else there with her?"

"Well, frankly, um, yes," Eric said, nodding.

They spoke in tones so low, they were almost buried by their own footsteps on the gravelly ground.

"And who might that be?" Judas said.

"My wife's sister, Marianne."

Judas sighed. His sigh was louder than his words. "*Now* you tell me."

"Hey, look, really, that's not a problem. If she's there? Please, for the love of God, go ahead and ki—"

Judas broke into a fit of loud coughs, cutting Eric off. When he finally calmed down, he leaned close and whispered into Eric's ear, "Don't ever use that word out loud. I know what you're talking about. No need to use the word."

Eric realized he was trembling a little from the surprising jolt of Judas's coughing fit. "All right," he said. "I won't."

Eric had not thought about his sister-in-law Marianne. They did not get along, but that was beside the point. The best part of getting rid of Marianne, too, would be that she would not be able to contest Alma's inheritance.

"Now, you were saying there could be *two* problems on the premises?" Judas said.

"That's right. Although I really hadn't thought about it until now. I'm glad you brought it up."

Judas shook his head with frustration, then said, "Yeah, me too. Now, you say you'd like me to solve *both* of these problems. That's never been discussed before."

"I'm sorry I didn't bring it up sooner, really, but it just didn't occur to me until now. My wife's sister—she seems to spend half her time at our place."

"You've only paid me to solve one problem, Eric."

"I'd be perfectly willing to pay you for the second one, too. If it's there. We can't be sure. There's no way of knowing when Marianne is going to show up, she's like a Jehovah's Witness, or a plague, but when she does, the two of them sit there at the bar and all they do is talk about me, denigrate me, demean me. You know, there was a time—a brief time, yes, but a time, still—when I was considering asking *Marianne* to marry me. Now I wish I'd run the hell away from the whole family. I'm telling you, Judas, they're all crazier than shithouse rats."

"You can't possibly think I care about any of this," Judas said.

"Oh." Eric coughed. "I'm sorry."

"Where will you be?"

"Excuse me?"

"Make sure you're seen by plenty of people Tuesday night," the hit man said. "I'll be doing the deed between eight and nine o'clock. Make sure you're someplace where people can see you between six and ten. You'll need as many witnesses as you can possibly get. More than that, if we can swing it. Is that perfectly understood?"

"Yes. I'll need witnesses, people who will remember me."

"That's right. Where will you find them?"

"There's a pub I go to pretty regularly. Sometimes she goes with me, but not always. I know a lot of people there. It wouldn't be unusual for me to go there and just sit around for a few hours, play some games—they have pool, and darts, and—"

"You want to be remembered so you go to a room full of drunks?" Judas said.

"It's not that kind of place, and they're not that kind of people. Most of the people, they're parents, they have kids at home. I can't remember the last time I saw anybody there get *that* drunk. It's the perfect place, really. I'll be up to my neck in witnesses."

Judas nodded. "Okay. That sounds good."

They talked awhile longer, going over every little detail, every possibility.

"Contingency plans," Judas said. "You've gotta have contingency plans. You don't? You're fucked."

So they made up some contingency plans.

They walked through the entire market twice, slowly, talking so quietly they could barely hear each other.

Then they were walking slowly through the parking lot, their conversation winding down. It was a cold, grey day. The ground was spotted with the white of snow left over from the season's first snowstorm. Now, big dark clouds threatened rain. Eric's and Judas's breath misted before their faces when they exhaled.

"Well, Eric, it's about time for us to part."

Judas stopped and turned to Eric. He tipped his hat back a little and made his face more visible. The lower half of his oval face was unshaven and stubbly. He slid his glasses up on his forehead and squinted at Eric with red-rimmed grey eyes that were puffy underneath, as if he hadn't slept in awhile.

"I started calling myself Judas at the age of fourteen, when I figured out what a big favor Judas did for Jesus," Judas said. "I hated my real name, and I really liked the sound of Judas when I first heard it in Sunday school, but my mother was horrified by that, saying he was the man responsible for getting Jesus killed. So I read the story for myself. Didn't seem that way to me at all. Jesus *had* to die. If He hadn't, I don't see Christianity getting beyond the surrounding neighborhoods, you know what I mean? If Jesus had just gone on living, and grown old and fat, and maybe got married? No, there's nothing compelling about a religion built around *that* guy. Jesus *had* to die. Judas made that happen. Judas made Christianity possible. To me, that's a pretty amazing guy, a guy who changes history like that. So I started calling myself Judas." His face split into a dazzling smile and for a moment, his tired eyes lit up. "I also liked it because it pissed off my mother."

The glasses dropped back into place and he brought the hat forward again. "You won't be seeing me again, Eric. If there is a second problem, then you'll hear from me to arrange the extra payment. If not, we're through. It's been a pleasure. Oh, one more thing. You might not want to be the one who discovers her. It's going to be bloody, Eric. Nice and bloody."

Then he turned and walked into the rows of cars to the right.

Eric hurried to his car to get out of the cold. He got into his Honda Civic, started the engine, and turned on the heater. It was a great heater. It warmed up fast and would have the cab toasty in no time at all.

He could feel the heat coming from the vents at his legs. He could feel the cab becoming warm. But it did no good. He still felt chilled to the bone. He began to tremble. The trembling quickly grew worse. His teeth chattered together like machinegun fire in his head.

The heater was working . . . but not for Eric.

He sat behind the wheel, and his entire body spasmed with shivers, and he suddenly felt short of breath, and he realized what was wrong—he was having a panic attack.

He'd just arranged to have his wife murdered, and he was having a panic attack.

Clumsily, he reached over to the glove compartment and opened it up. There was a bottle of Xanax in there. He grabbed it, shook out two of the tiny oval-shaped white pills and popped them into his mouth. There was some Diet Dr. Pepper left in the can in the drink well between the seats, and he drank it down, flat and warm, to swallow the pills.

Then he sat there and waited for it to pass.

Jill, Eric thought as he sat at the bar in the Fox and Hound. *Why isn't she here yet?*

He looked at his wristwatch. It was four minutes after eight. He gasped at the time, and his eyes bulged, and his jaw went slack for a moment. But only for a moment. He caught it all and pulled it back in and hoped to God that no one had seen it.

. . . *between eight and nine o'clock,* Judas had said.

In the last couple hours, he'd played some pool—a couple games with regulars he knew, and a couple with friendly strangers. Then he'd gone back to his seat at the bar, marked for him by his long black coat, and ordered a second Guinness.

After taking a couple swigs of the ale, he sat there awhile and stared at it on the bar in front of him. He decided he would call Jill.

Eric did not carry a cell phone. He hated the damned things. He was convinced that at some point down the line, people were going to start getting some kind of really aggressive brain cancer—brought on, of course, by the frequent use of cell phones. He would get up and go to the pay phone in the basement, where the restrooms were located. In a little bit. He wanted to think first. Think about what to say. It was enough to have Alma angry with him. Alma was always angry with him. But he did not want to say the wrong thing to Jill and make *her* angry, as well. He didn't want to demand that she come down to the Fox and Hound, not like some possessive, grumpy husband. At the same time, he wanted to see her, he craved her company.

He tipped his mug back again and took a few more swallows of ale, still thinking about Jill . . .

Eric played a game of air hockey with a friendly guy named Chuck Wagner who obviously needed someone to talk to about his wife, and talk he did. It seemed Mrs. Wagner, a beautiful blonde named Clarice, did not understand Chuck. He tried his best to understand her. He knew how important her candle making was to her and he did his best to encourage it, to support it, and appreciate it for the talent that it was. Her candles had won awards. They were works of art. He was proud of them. She'd turned a little hobby she'd indulged in while the kids were napping, back before they were in school, and turned it into a profitable online business. People looked forward to getting Clarice's candles as Christmas and birthday presents. Clarice's Candles—that was the name of the Web site, the name of the business. She was quite a little whirlwind, his wife.

Chuck, on the other hand, was quite passionate about his particular hobby—metal detecting. He got together with like-minded friends on the weekends and scoured parks and playgrounds all around the area. They weren't interested in finding change, they were after old coins, jewelry, interesting little pieces of history. From his metal detecting, Chuck had become quite the numismatist, with an impressive collection. But when it came to *Chuck's* hobby, the thing *he* liked to do, Clarice was not only uninterested, she mocked it.

Eric remembered what Maggie had said to him earlier, and he suggested to Chuck that what he and Clarice needed was communication. It was the only thing that would save them. Chuck needed to tell Clarice how he felt, or she would never know.

Of course, the truth was, Eric had no idea whatsoever how Chuck could solve his problems with Clarice. He was just talking because Chuck had stopped, and because he thought Chuck expected something. Problems like that—who knew what the solution was? Anyone who said they had all the answers was full of shit, including and *especially* Dr. Phil.

And yet Eric found himself pontificating about marital communication, as if he were some kind of expert, as if he'd even given it some thought. Then as he spoke, he glanced at the door, and Jill did not stand there, looking for him, and his words faltered, and he stopped talking and frowned.

"You waiting for someone?" Chuck said.

Eric nodded vaguely. Then he smiled at Chuck and said, "I'm going to go outside for a smoke, Chuck. I'll be back in a little while."

"Sure, man. See you later. And thanks for the advice. You're good at that, you know?"

"Glad to help."

Eric went to his barstool and was about to take his coat from it and put it on, but stopped and thought about that a moment. It was going to be cold outside, but he had to leave his coat there because he wanted to give the illusion of not being gone long, even though he was probably going to be gone a little while.

Is that wise? he thought. *Being in this pub is your alibi.*

He could hurry, he wouldn't be gone long. People would see his coat on the stool and know he was still around, right? Was that enough?

He had to see Jill, he craved her, hungered for her. No one at the pub knew about his relationship with Jill, so they could not be *too* familiar there in the Fox and Hound. But just to see her, be near her, smell her perfume, to maybe sneak outside for some furtive kisses and embraces.

He *needed* it.

He held his hands out and looked down at them. They trembled.

His nerves were frayed. Seeing Jill—just being around her—would calm him down.

He left the bar, got into his car, and left the parking lot . . .

HardBoiledGirl lived, it turned out, in Hope Valley, a town just to the north of Newbury. She shared Eric's love for pulp fiction and comic books. They spent a lot of time in a private chat room, getting to know each other. That process was expedited online. People said things to each other online that they would never say to someone in person. They revealed themselves more easily and sometimes were more honest about themselves online than in person. Eric and Jill, her real name, got to know each other quickly, and they both liked what they learned. She was twenty-seven years old and had never been married and had no children. She worked in the Barnes & Noble in the Newbury Mall. She had a cat named Twain and some tropical fish. She had an impressive collection of film *noir* on DVD and VHS—she'd sent him her entire catalog and he'd read some of the harder-to-find titles with envy—and she watched the dark, moody films over and over again. Just as Eric would if he had such a collection. Of course, Alma would never approve.

"I can't believe how much money you've spent over the years on books that were considered trash back when they came out in the thirties!" she'd said once.

He said quietly, "The fifties, most of them. The fifties."

"What*ever*."

Eric once had tried to read her one of his favorite pulp novels, *The Grifters* by Jim Thompson, but she wouldn't have it.

"I don't want to hear that trashy crap," she said. "It's hateful and sexist. I've seen those awful covers. You should be *ashamed* of yourself!"

He tried to explain to her how boring his life was at work. He was an accountant for Macy's at the mall. It was a deadly dull job. As he worked, he looked forward to going home and losing himself in an exciting novel about ruthless crooks, sleazy private eyes, seductive *femme fatales,* crooked cops, nervy psychos. The books were vividly-written pieces of escape fiction, that was all.

But of course, she only used it to insult him, saying that of *course* his favorite "escape" would be to a sexist world of the past when women were nothing but sex objects.

They had been married for fourteen years. Eric was thirty-six years old, Alma thirty-four. It had been such a wonderful marriage at first.

She had been such a loving woman, so affectionate. She'd wanted so much to be a mother, and he knew she would be a great one. They'd tried those first two years. They'd tried hard. The doctor said it was his fault. He was sadly lacking in those little swimmers so necessary to the baby-making process. He was treated for it, and they kept trying, but with no result. So they gave that up and went straight to adoption. The wait for a baby was endless. But if they were willing to take an older child, it might be possible to match them up with one very quickly.

They brought Andrew home when he was four years old. He was an adorable child, angelic—wisps of golden hair all around his head, enormous bright blue eyes that absorbed everything, and that amazingly complex smirk that came shortly before a big smile. Eric found him mesmerizing.

Back then, Alma used to tease Eric about not being able to do anything without her. He would wash the dishes for her, then put the dishes away—in all the wrong places. She would come in and have to do it all over again, putting them where they belonged. She'd poke him in the ribs and say, "What would you do without me, huh?" And he would laugh, then embrace her and kiss her. It didn't bother him because it was so clearly done with love and affection. There was no meanness, no bitterness. No contempt.

When Andrew was six, Alma left him with Eric for one hot summer weekend while she went to see Pam, her best friend from school days. Pam lived in Eureka—sometimes Alma went to see her, sometimes she came to see Alma. They took turns. It was Alma's turn to visit Pam. And of course, she joked before she left about him being helpless without her. And he laughed before giving her a big, long kiss.

That Saturday afternoon, Eric fired up the barbecue in the front yard and started grilling hamburgers and hot dogs. It wasn't long before neighbors began to wander over, as he'd known they would. Somebody brought beer, somebody else brought chips. Before long, they had a party. Kids were playing on the lawn. Somebody brought over a boom box and turned on the oldies station.

The squeal of brakes seemed so out of place there, with all the laughter and chatter, and the good music, the sounds of playing children—the shrieking brakes did not belong there at all.

The sound cut through the gathering like a scalpel through flesh, and everyone fell silent, leaving the music the only sound in the yard.

Then the scream, some woman near the street.

Eric saw his adopted son under the front wheel of a silver Chrysler. Eric went insane then, just lost his mind and went completely crazy, screaming at the driver to back up, please back up, and when the driver did, Eric bent down over the boy who lay clearly broken and torn open on the bloody pavement. He screamed for help, pleaded with someone to call an ambulance. Someone assured him that an ambulance had been called, and kept assuring him, but it did no good, he did not hear the assurances. He heard nothing. His ears were ringing, and his head throbbed, as if there had been some kind of deafening explosion, even though there had not. The explosions had been inside Eric. They had begun when he first saw Andrew lying beneath that tire. They had not stopped yet. They kept going off inside him, in his chest, in his gut, deep inside his head.

Andrew was clearly dead. His eyes were open, and his face had been splashed with blood when it had exploded from his mouth. Eric picked Andrew up in his arms, and the boy's head flopped lifelessly to one side.

Eric heard an awful sound, a high, wailing sound that quavered as it dragged on and on, and after awhile, he realized the sound was coming from him, because it only stopped when he had to breathe.

When Alma came home, she would not speak to him at first. He had no idea why, and it made him furious. He shouted at her, but that did not work. She remained silent, clearly suffering by the look of pain on her face. He wanted to suffer with her, together. But she would not let him.

Then she blew. As dusk was passing and the windows looking outdoors became completely dark. He was following her down the hall to the bedroom, trying to talk to her, and suddenly, she spun around with a look of such wide-open hatred on her face that Eric stumbled backward as if he'd been struck.

"Are you really so helpless?" she cried. As she spoke, her voice grew louder and louder, until she was screaming. "I couldn't leave you with him for a weekend? One lousy weekend? You're so helpless that you couldn't even keep our son *alive* for a weekend? You're *useless*!" Then she'd gone into the bedroom, slammed the door, and locked it against him.

Things had never been the same since then. Alma had never been the same. She hated him, and she made no attempt to hide her feelings. He suggested divorce, but she said she'd never divorce him, that they were going to be together forever, just like they had vowed at the altar. Alma was a devout Catholic and had been all her life. There had never been a divorce in her family—and Eric had never seen a more miserable, unhappy group of people because of it. Of course, he did not need her permission to get a divorce, but he put it off. He kept putting it off, and time passed.

Alma's father had opened a donut shop when she was a little girl, and by the time she was in high school, he'd turned it into a chain from Eureka to Sacramento, a very popular chain because Alma's father poured on the icing, double what other donut-makers used. By the time she graduated from college, he'd sold the chain to a big conglomerate for an enormous sum of money, which was to be split between Alma and her sister Marianne once their parents were gone. By the time Alma's family got rich, she and Eric were engaged. They'd fallen in love long before all the big money came in, so they all knew he was not after her money.

Not then.

But things changed.

He met Jill.

They'd agreed to meet at a Denny's in Hope Valley. It was a safe, public place. Eric felt like he already knew Jill—they had exchanged pictures of each other online. He already knew she was an ivory-skinned, raven-haired beauty. Her hair was shiny-black and fell straight down her back, so thick that as soon as he saw it in the picture, he wanted to touch it.

They met in front of Denny's, out by all the newspaper vending machines, and he touched her hair. She reached up and touched his face. Next thing he knew, they were kissing, and their hands were moving all over their bodies, their tongues going wild inside each other's mouths.

There was a Best Western Inn right next to Denny's, and that was where they went before even entering the restaurant.

It had been a long time since Eric and Alma had had sex. And the last few times, so long ago, had been very uncomfortable. She'd been so stiff, lying there like a corpse with her arms down at her sides, her face all screwed up, as if she were determined not to enjoy it, or even participate in it.

Alma's parents had died in the first decade of their marriage, first her father of a brain embolism, then her mother of breast cancer. All that money was Alma's and Marianne's after that. They did not change the way they lived. Alma refused to spend it. She did not want to lay a finger on any of it. So they didn't.

For a while, it was all Eric thought about, that money. He dreamed about it at night when he slept, and he daydreamed about it during his work at Macy's. All that money, more than any one person could spend in a lifetime, no doubt. An obscene amount of money. All locked up because she didn't want to touch it. But it was hers to do with as she saw fit. And the only thing that would change that, of course, would be Alma's death.

After that first time in the Best Western, Eric and Jill lay with arms and legs intertwined, their naked bodies shimmering with sweat as they panted like worn-out dogs, the sheet and blanket and spread all humped up at the foot of the bed. They kissed as they panted and ran their hands through each other's hair, and he bent forward and buried his face between her voluptuous, upturned breasts and laughed like a little boy getting away with something. Her skin was like satin, her lips tasted vaguely of strawberries. She made things unravel inside him that hadn't unraveled for a long, long time. She made him feel like himself again, the way he *used* to feel back when he had friends and he and Alma would go to the pub two or three times a week. Jill brought him back to life, and she did it in one coupling, one exchange of energy. She had reinvigorated Eric.

Finally, they both fell still, propped up on elbows facing one another, and stared into each other's eyes, faces just an inch or so apart.

"You've changed me," he said, breathing the words. "From just this one time, you've changed me already. I haven't felt this good in years, Jill." She bowed her head a moment, sniffled, then lifted her head again. The light caught one of the moist trails down her cheek. When Eric saw her tears, his eyes widened and he said, "What's wrong? I'm sorry, what did I—"

"You didn't do anything," she whispered, shaking her head. "I mean, you didn't do anything *wrong*. You definitely did *some*thing. I'm not sure what yet, but . . . something."

"How . . . how are we going to handle this?"

"I'm not sure yet. I guess it's really up to you. You're the married one."

"Yeah, I guess I am, huh?" He lightly dragged his fingertips down the edge of her body, from the side of her breast, down over her ribs, to the luscious curve of her hip, then down her thigh to her knee. "I'll have to start lying to my wife, for one thing."

"Is that going to bother you?"

"You have no idea how my wife treats me. It's not going to bother me at all."

"But we can't keep that up very long."

Eric's eyebrows rose high over his eyes. "We can't?"

"No, of course not. You'll have to tell her the truth. And soon. So we can be together all the time."

Eric ran his fingertips back up the edge of her body, but said nothing.

"Look, Eric, I don't want to be involved in some long-term deception, okay?" Jill said. "Do you understand? Either the plan is to tell your wife at the right time, or there's no plan at all. Because if you don't tell her, Eric, I will."

Now there *would be an interesting scene,* Eric thought.

Jill's declaration worried him a little. He was not sure how he could tell Alma. And *why* would he tell Alma? It would most likely get between him and her money. But he had to tell Jill something for now, something to satisfy her, to get her off the subject.

He leaned over and brushed her hair back with his fingers and put his lips to her ear. "Don't worry, sweetheart," he breathed into her ear. "Don't worry."

Eric had managed to keep the relationship going without any big revelations to Alma for seven months, but Jill was getting impatient and even a little angry.

That was when Eric began to think about other solutions to his problem. No more waiting around.

The heater in the car made the cab *too* hot, and Eric turned it down. It started to rain, and he turned on the windshield wipers.

The whole thing passed through his mind now, how he got where he was at that moment. After Jill came along, he came to see Alma as a problem that needed to be solved. He'd thought long and hard about it.

Eric had a lawyer friend in Newbury, Max Randible, a shady kind of guy, a criminal defense attorney with questionable connections, who would bend over backward for Eric—they'd known each other since high school. They had lunch once a month. On his next lunch date with Max, at an Italian restaurant called Angelo's, he'd said, "I've decided to try my hand at writing a novel."

"You're shitting me," Max said as he ate spaghetti. He had floppy, shaggy dark hair and always seemed to have a five o'clock shadow.

His face was jowly, with a nose that hung low over his thin-lipped mouth, like the face of a friendly dog. "A novel? You?"

"Yeah. You know how I love pulp fiction. Well, I'm going to write one of my own."

Max laughed a hearty, encouraging laugh. "Hell, good for you, man, that's fantastic! What's Alma have to say about it?"

"She doesn't know. She'd laugh. Look, I've got a question for my novel. I've got this guy needs to get hold of a hit man. See, his wife has been murdered, and he thinks he knows who did it, and he wants revenge, but he knows he can't do it himself, so he needs to hire someone to kill this guy. How does a regular guy go about doing something like that? My character, he's a construction guy, you know, a contractor. How would a construction contractor find a hit man?"

As Eric spoke, the smile on Max's face slowly disappeared. He stared at Eric for a long time, unsmiling, his head tilted slightly forward and to one side, locks of his shaggy hair falling on his creased, frowning forehead. "A hit man," he finally said, flatly, with no expression.

Eric nodded. He was pulling all of this out of nowhere. He fought to keep up with it, tried not to trip himself up with anything too complex. "Yeah. You know, to kill this guy who killed his wife."

Max slowly nodded his head. Then he reached into a pocket, produced a cell phone, and flipped it open. From his shirt pocket, he produced one of his business cards and a pen. He punched in a number, hunched forward, head low, and spoke in a very low tone. He wrote something on the card, then flipped his cell phone closed and put it back in his pocket. He wrote something else on the card, then put the pen back in his pocket. He picked up the card and handed it across the table to Eric.

On the back of the card was the name Judas, and below that, a telephone number.

"You did not get that from me," Max said, leaning forward over the table. He scooped in a mouthful of spaghetti, sucked up the strings of pasta dangling from his mouth, and chewed for awhile, then with the food making his cheek bulge, he said, "If you ever said you did, I'd deny it up and down. And I'd never speak to you again. You say you need a . . . " He lowered his voice to a whisper for the one word: " . . . hit man? Well, there he is. The rest is up to you, you're on your own from now on. I don't want to know *anything*."

He continued to chew, then swallowed. He mopped up some spaghetti sauce with a slice of garlic bread, then took a bite.

"Look, Max," Eric said, but Max did not let him continue.

"I'm not asking," Max said, "because I don't want to know, okay? I'm going to forget we had this little exchange, and we'll just go on from there. Understood?"

"But Max—"

"You don't have to explain, you don't have to say a word."

Eric wanted to continue the lie and insist that he really *was* writing a crime novel, that was all, but Max would not let him.

"I'm happy to be able to help, Eric," he said. "You say you need that, well, I'm glad I could provide it, for whatever reason it is you need it. But like I said, we'll forget all about it from this moment on. Okay?"

"Well . . . okay. If you insist."

"I insist."

Eric had called the number that very day, and for the first time, he'd heard the raspy, damaged voice of the hit man who called himself Judas, because he thought the Lord's betrayer was a pretty cool guy.

Eric got on the freeway and pressed the speed limit of seventy until he got to the first Hope Valley exit and he took the cutoff. He got to Sycamore Arms, her apartment complex, at 8:13.

He parked on the street and got out, hurried across the courtyard and up the stairs to the second level. He hurried along the outdoor walkway that passed all the apartment doors. He stopped at 209 and knocked hard, his knuckles *crack-crack-crack*ing on the door. He heard no movement inside, no sound at all.

Eric took his keys from his pocket as his breath plumed before him, chose the right key, and slipped it into the doorknob of door number 209. He turned the key and pushed through into the apartment.

"Jill?" he called. He closed the door behind him and locked it again. "Jill, it's me!"

Nothing. No response, no movement. The apartment was dead silent. The shower wasn't running. The television and radio were off.

The apartment was empty.

He went down the short hallway, then turned left into the living room. A note was taped to the television screen. Frowning, he crossed the room, snatched the note off the screen, and read it.

Dearest Eric,

By the time you read this, I will probably
be sitting down with Alma, telling her the
truth about our relationship. It needs to
be done, Eric, you know that as well as I
do, and you're not doing it. So I'm going
stop waiting and do it myself. This will
finally bring everything to a head. Finally,
you and I will be able to live in the open.
I'm doing this for both of us, Eric.

I love you,
J.

Eric cried out, a sound of agonizing pain. He dropped the note to
the floor and ran back through the apartment, looking for the phone,
which was not on its base in the living room. He found it in the
kitchen on the counter by the microwave. He picked it up and
punched in his own phone number. He missed a number, severed the
connection, then tried again, and missed the same number. He swore
out loud as he tried a third time, and finally got it right.

"Hello?"

"Alma!" he shouted.

"Eric?"

"Alma, listen to me, please."

She said nothing.

"Are you there?" he said.

"How could you," she said, just above a whisper. "How . . . *could*
you?"

Then she hung up.

"Oh, *fuck*!" Eric shouted as he slammed the phone down onto the
counter. The plastic panel that held in the batteries came off and clattered to the floor. He paced in the kitchen a moment, then went back
to the phone and picked up the receiver again. He looked around for
the rectangular plastic panel, found it, and put it back in place on the
back of the phone. He punched in his number again. He got the
repetitive sound that indicated a busy line. He waited awhile longer,
then tried again. The line was still busy.

She took the phone off the hook, he thought.

He turned and left the kitchen, went back down the hall, and out the front door. He stormed down the walkway without locking the apartment behind him, then down the stairs to the courtyard.

He felt panic move through him like some possessing demon. It settled in his knees and made them weak, in his chest, which suddenly felt tight and breathless. Back on the street, he opened the car door and practically fell into the driver's seat. He fumbled with the keys, started the car. He put his hand on the gearshift, but then he stopped and thought. He had to figure out where he was first, which direction he'd have to go. Once he had his bearings, he drove away from the sidewalk.

Going back the way he came, he got back on the freeway, then floored it.

He thought, *A perfect alibi for tonight's killing—I get pulled over for speeding with strong ale on my breath.*

He looked at the speedometer, and when he realized he was going over eighty miles an hour, he quickly slowed down.

He passed a sign that read ROAD WORK AHEAD, then another that read PREPARE TO STOP.

"Oh, shit," he muttered.

Another sign: RIGHT LANE CLOSED AHEAD.

He wondered where the construction had come from. It had not been there earlier—apparently they only did their road work during the night these days.

The traffic was fairly light, until the right lane closed, then the cars and pickups and SUVs bottlenecked

Three quarters of a mile along the single lane, the cars slowed to a stop. And there Eric sat, waiting. He turned the radio on—the oldies station was playing something bouncy and upbeat from the eighties.

Coherent, sensible thoughts came hard, he had to work for them, weed them out from all the loud, yammering fear in his head. That was all he could feel—fear.

The minutes clicked by slowly on the digital dash clock: 8:26, 8:27, 8:28, 8:29, 8:30, 8:31 . . .

Judas would arrive at the house, if he hadn't already, and find Alma there with another woman. He would assume it was Marianne, Alma's sister, and he would go ahead and kill her, too, just as Eric had told him to, just as Eric had insisted.

The dash clock read 8:32.

You might not want to be the one who discovers her, Judas had said. *It's going to be bloody, Eric. Nice and bloody.*

"Oh, dear God," Eric groaned as he felt trapped there in that frozen car, unable to move forward or back, just frozen, crippled. His entire body felt like quivery Jell-O.

Suddenly, the cars began to move. Slowly at first, but then gradually picking up speed, until suddenly the traffic on both lanes was back to normal. Eric drove the speed limit along the freeway until he got to the second Newbury exit. He took the cutoff, which put him on DeNancie Street. He turned right and forced himself to resist the urge to slam the accelerator to the floor. "Not yet, Judas," Eric said as he drove, "please not yet."

He went two miles down DeNancie, then turned left on Emberson Park Street, past the park and into the residential district in which he and Alma lived in ranch-style house with a circular driveway in front. He shot into the driveway, then hit the brakes and the car skidded forward over the gravel for a bit, then stopped—right behind Jill's Toyota. Alma's car was in the garage, to the left of the house, just off the circular driveway.

Eric threw the car door open and tried to jump out of the car, but he could not. A second later, he realized his seatbelt was still on. He unfastened it, tossed it aside, then promptly fell out of the car, gravel biting into the palms of his hands. He scrambled to his feet and ran around the car, leaving the car door to slowly swing back into place—it stopped a few inches short of closing.

Eric kicked up gravel as he ran, wobbly at first, then straightening up and heading straight for the front door. It was unlocked, and he burst into the house.

"Jill?" he called. "Alma?"

The living room was to the right of the front door, and it was empty. Two lamps were on, and the television played with the volume turned down to a vague murmur. The Christmas tree stood in the front window, its tiny colored lights twinkling like stars. Down the hall ahead of him, Eric saw light spilling from the kitchen doorway at the other end.

Eric's shoes thunked on the hardwood floor of the hallway as he ran down to the kitchen. He turned right, went through the doorless doorway, took three jogging steps in, and suddenly his feet were up in the air and his tailbone hit the kitchen's tile floor, sending an explosion of pain up his spine.

His hands smacked to the wet, sticky floor and slid over the slick surface a few times as he tried to sit up. He managed to roll over onto his hands and knees, and there he stayed for a long moment, not moving, not breathing as he stared down at the red floor.

But the floor was not red, it was not *supposed* to be, anyway. The tiles were an earthy brown-and-tan. At that moment, though, the floor was red, and it was a wet red. And the red had a smell—a cloying, pungent, coppery smell. There was another smell in the room—the smell of feces from bowels that had gone slack at the moment of death.

Eric's hands slipped out from under him, and he fell flat, then struggled further until he was up on his knees, then on his feet. He looked at his hands, his arms, the sleeves of his coat, his pants—he had blood all over him. A moment after he stood up straight, he bent rigidly at the waist and vomited onto the floor.

There was a tiled bar that separated the kitchen from the living room, cluttered with newspapers and magazines, a couple paperback novels, a half-drunk beverage in a glass, a coffee mug. On the floor just under the bar lay Alma, next to an overturned bar stool.

The phone rang. Eric was surprised to find it operating again after getting the busy signal a couple times. On the third ring, the answering machine picked up.

"Hello? Eric? Alma? It's Betty Macomber next door. Anybody there?"

That busybody, Eric thought, clenching his teeth. Betty Macomber was their most annoying neighbor, a woman who lived to gossip. Alma was too nice to ignore or avoid her, but Eric avoided her like a bad road.

"Well . . . " She sounded worried. "I heard the screams, and I called the police, so they should be coming soon. I . . . I hope everything's okay."

A cold explosion went off in Eric's gut. *The police.*

The answering machine ended the message with an abrupt beep.

"This just happened," Eric whispered. Gooseflesh erupted all over his back when it occurred to him that Judas might still be in the house. He stood and listened for a moment. He heard nothing—the house was empty. Eric was familiar with the house's emptiness, knew when someone was moving around in it somewhere.

He was alone with Alma. He looked down at her corpse.

Her eyes were open, her head tilted back to reveal an enormous open gash where her throat used to be. The corners of her bloody mouth were pulled back so that it echoed the deep smiling slash of her throat—two unnatural smiles, both in death. She wore a pale-blue sweat suit—she usually worked out on the stationary bike in the early evening. The sweat suit was punctured in several places in front where she had been stabbed repeatedly. Very little of the suit's pale blue color remained—it had been obliterated by all the blood.

"Oh my God, Alma," he said, mere breath forming the words. The next words were too jagged and sharp to speak aloud—they would cut his lips to ribbons—so he simply thought them: *What have I done?*

A sound.

Wet and gurgling.

Eric looked around, trying to determine the sound's source.

It happened again—a soggy, gurgling cough.

He hurried through the doorless doorway beside the bar and into the living room, turning sharply right. He looked down and found Jill sitting on the floor between two bar stools with her back slumped against the front of the bar, head tipped back just enough to reveal the bloody gash across her throat. Her arms were limp at her sides, her legs sprawled in her roses-on-black-print skirt below a red sweater. There was a lot of different kinds of red and Eric squeezed his eyes shut for a moment, rubbed them with thumb and finger, then opened them again. The red roses, the red sweater, and all that other red, that glistening, dribbling, smeared, and splashed red.

It's going to be bloody, Eric. Nice and bloody.

He had planned it this way—Judas had known ahead of time that it was going to be this cruel bloodbath. Was that necessary? Eric did not think so. The only possible explanation he could think of was that Judas enjoyed that, had fun doing it that way, nice and bloody. The way it looked to Eric—Judas was a sick fuck, a genuine psychopath, but a very *clever* psychopath who had figured out a way to get people to pay him big bucks to do the very thing that got him off.

"*Glorp!*"

The wet coughing sound came from Jill and was accompanied by a gout of blood from her mouth as her head dropped forward.

Then that awful sound again—"*Glorp!*"—as more blood came from her mouth and dribbled from the gash in her throat. She seemed to be bleeding everywhere, having been stabbed repeatedly.

"Oh, thank you Jesus, you're alive!" he said, with relief in his voice so intense, it made the words sound painful to utter, turning them into what almost sounded like a groan. "Oh, God, Jill. Jill?" He hunkered down beside her and pulled her away from the front of the bar. She was able to lean forward a little under her own power, but she seemed very weak. She'd lost a lot of blood. Fortunately, Judas's knife had managed to cut her throat without severing anything too important—a little farther along on either end of the slice and she would have been dead within seconds of being cut.

"It's me, honey, it's me, Jill, it's Eric, you're gonna be okay, you hear me, you're gonna be fine as soon as we get you to a hospital," he said as he eased her out from under the bar, whispering as he rambled on, as if he were afraid of being heard. He realized he was whispering and did not understand why, but he could not stop—it simply did not feel right to speak out loud.

"Come on," Eric whispered as he put his right arm around her shoulders. His elbow hit something that did not belong there. He pulled his arm back, lowered it, reached with his hand and—

—his fingers closed on the handle of a knife sticking out of Jill's back, and he was so horrified by it, so deeply offended by its presence there that—

—without thinking, without wondering if it was a good idea and before examining the possibilities—

—he pulled the knife from her back.

Jill cried out and more blood came from her mouth, dribbled over her dark-red chin and down over her throat and onto her red sweater.

Eric clutched the knife in his right hand as he scooped Jill up in his arms.

"C'mon," he said as he carried her across the living room, "I'm gonna get you to a hospital." He took a moment to get his balance, first swaying right, then left, wobbling like a crippled penguin.

He went down a mental list—his keys were in his coat pocket, the car was unlocked, St. Elizabeth's Hospital (aka Queen of the Mountain) in Hope Valley would be the closest and the best. He was only halfway across the living room and he was already thinking of the best route to take, wondering if he should hit the freeway, or take the surface streets he knew fairly well. He decided the surface streets would require too much thinking, and he didn't need that tonight, no more aggravation, thank you very much, and he decided to take the freeway.

"Please don't die, Jill, I need you, do you hear me? I *need* you, Jill. You can't die on me, you hear me?" He continued to plead with her as he crossed the living room, a trek that seemed to take forever, as the front door retreated farther and farther away in the distance.

His cheeks were wet, but not with blood for a change. The tears fractured his vision for a moment as he reached out with his left hand and turned the doorknob on the front door

A beautiful kaleidoscope of colored light danced through his tears when he opened the front door—blue and red lights swirled and spiked and became sunbursts of color. Eric sniffed and blinked his eyes a few times, blinked away the tears that clung instead to his eyelashes now.

The lights were on police cars in the driveway.

Eric refocused his eyes on the black hole at the end of a gun held by a police officer.

"Put the woman down!" the officer shouted.

"But officer, she's hurt, I-I-I just fuh-found her this way, and she needs medical attention immediately, she's lost a lot of bluh—"

"I said put the fucking woman down *now,* asshole!"

Jill made a terrible sound then. A deep gurgle in her throat that came to an abrupt end. Then she stopped breathing.

"Jill?" Eric said, looking down at her face. "*Jill?*"

"Do you hear me?" the cop shouted, his voice breaking at one point. "I said *put*! The *woman*! *Down*!"

It was such a final sound, that gurgle.

She'd chosen that particular moment to die. As if she'd looked around, then said, "Oh, fuck, *cops*? You're on your own, honey." And then expired with that death rattle in her throat.

Another police officer had joined the first one on the porch. He, too, aimed his gun at Eric and shouted at the top of his lungs, "Put the woman down or I blow your fuckin' head off!"

Eric wanted so much to say that she needed help. But she didn't, of course. She was beyond ever needing help again. He could not hide behind her wounds.

He was holding a corpse.

"Put down the fuckin' woman and—"

"Goddammit, are you *deaf*? Do you wanna *die*? Are you—"

"—get down on the floor!"

"—a fuckin' retard, huh? Let go of the woman and—"

"I got a bead on your fuckin' face!"

Eric turned to his left, gently bent forward, and placed Jill on the floor, out of the way of the open door.

The shouting stopped for a moment. Then one of the officers went wild with shouting again: "Weapon! He's got a fuckin' weapon!"

"Drop the weapon, asshole!"

"Drop it! Throw it down!"

"I will put a fuckin' hole in your Goddamned head if you don't—"

"Drop that fuckin' knife, asshole!"

At first, he had no idea why they were still shouting at him. He was unaware of holding the knife in his right hand, the handle clutched in his fist, the blade serrated—something from the kitchen, Eric guessed—and dark with Jill's blood.

His fingers were stiff, but he opened them up, let the knife drop to the floor.

The two cops were on him then, tackling him to the floor, shouting, "Hands behind your back!"

"Stop *resisting*!" one of the cops shouted, then punched him in the kidney before Eric could say, "I'm not resisting!" Pain exploded from the point of the fist's impact and radiated all through his abdomen. It made him retch.

They cuffed his hands behind his back, then jerked him to his feet. One cop put a hand to the center of Eric's back and pushed him while the other dragged him along by the elbow.

The cage-grating that separated the front seat from the back in the patrol car cast webworks of shadows across Eric's face as light shifted and passed through the moving car. He leaned forward—he'd been talking to the two police officers.

"Why'd you do it?" the cop in the passenger seat asked.

"I *told* you, I didn't *do* it!" Eric insisted, speaking loudly now. I *found* them that way."

"Then how the hell did you get all that blood all over you, huh?" the cop asked. "What'd you do, roll in it?"

"Well . . . kind of, yes. I, uh, I fell."

"You fell." The cop reached across and slapped the shoulder of the cop at the wheel. "He fell."

"Yeah, right," the driver said.

"Alma was already dead, and Jill was just hanging on." Eric's throat was soar, and his eyes were damp and puffy. He'd waited for what seemed a long time in the back seat of the patrol car before the two cops got in and started driving. During that time, he'd done a lot of crying.

"And you just happened to be holding the murder weapon," the driver said.

"I-I pulled it out of her back!" Eric said, a note of pleading in his voice.

"You *idiot*," the passenger said. "Don't you know you *never* pull a knife out of somebody's—"

"No, I *didn't* know."

"Boy, you better get yourself a really clever lawyer," the passenger said. "'Cause you're gonna need one. Even then, I bet you get the needle."

Slowly, Eric leaned back in the seat, even slumped a little, but all very slowly. He chuckled. The chuckle got a little louder, and quickly turned into a laugh. He pressed his lips together and tried hard to hold the laughter back, but he could not. It burst from his closed lips, and he tilted his head back as he laughed and laughed. He tried to stop again, but it only got worse, and pretty soon, tears of laughter rolled down his cheeks.

"I'm glad you think it's funny," the passenger said. "Because if you ask me, you're fucked three ways from Sunday."

Eric continued to laugh. He bent forward and held his cramping stomach as he laughed on and on.

"What's so fuckin' funny?" the driver shouted.

Between laughs, trying not to stutter, Eric said, "I-I—I might as well have—" He laughed some more. "—I might as well have done it myself!"

He continued to laugh the rest of the way to the police station.

FIRST BORN

JOHN FARRIS

Hello? Miriam?"

"No, this isn't Miriam, Gregory. No doubt you're surprised to hear my voice again. Eye expected you to forget. But today is the very day Eye told you that Eye'd be giving you a call. Doesn't time fly when you're conquering the world? Exactly twenty years have flown by. Two great decades. Has any of this rung a bell with you, Greg?"

"Fella, I have no idea who you are or what—"

"What Eye'm talking about? Ah well. Eye'll pause now to let the hurt sink in."

"This is a private number! How—? Only my wife and my—oh, no. Oh Jesusss! Has something hap—"

"You sound a little out of breath. You must've just finished your morning fifty in the pool."

"—happened to Miriam? Is that why you're calling me on this—"

"Breathe easy, Greg. No cause for alarm. Miriam's fine. It's Friday. She's having, as usual, the works at her spa. Big doin's tomorrow night at the Dorothy Chandler. Congratulations on your Humanitarian Award. Wish Eye could be there, but it's a tough ticket for nobodies like me."

"Is this about one of my kids? Who are you, goddamn it! Better give me a name or—"

"If you hyperventilate you'll pass out and crack your head on the pool apron. You might even scar that immensely valuable face. Now calm down and listen. No harm has come to the wife and kids. Your adorable Livy is at a call-back for the new Bruckheimer show, which Eye believe is to be a mid-season replacement on Fox after the pro football season. Now this is confidential. Livy is going to get the part! Isn't that exciting news? But we both know how talented she is."

"J—Josh—"

"Joshua, by my reckoning, has just finished up his physics lab at the Harvard School. Bright boy. Like his father. Eye'm curious, Greg. How could you not have recognized my voice? No one can say it's a voice that is easily forgotten. Once you've placed the voice, of course, the face is easy. And, of course, the circumstances of our one and only meeting."

"All right, fella. So where are you going with this? You seem to know so much about—so what have you been doing, stalking my—"

"Good grief. Eye'm not a crazy person. Nor am Eye a shakedown artist. So what if Livy has done a little sniffy from time to time. It doesn't concern me. Matter of peer pressure. She'll soon outgrow the desire to experiment. Thankfully, she is not an addictive personality. Now, last but by no means least, to put your mind completely at rest: Eye don't do kidnappings."

"That's it. I'm hanging—"

"'Hanging up?' Quaint. Those *were* the good old days. Incredible, isn't it, what technology has wrought in a mere twenty years? Cell phones. But it would not be wise to end our conversation prematurely, Greg. There are no 'call-backs' in my profession."

"Your?"

"Profession."

"Which is?"

"Eye befriend people in desperate need. Does that joggle your memory? Bet it does. Take a couple of deep breaths, Greg. Should you need to put the phone down and finish toweling off, Eye'll gladly wait. But we are enjoying a lovely warm day, so even though you do take your solitary swim in the nude there's little chance you'll catch cold. A perfect day like this—that does make LA-LA Land bearable the rest of the time. Do you remember the unseasonable monsoon weather the night Eye saved your life?—Ah, there it is! That little catch of the breath. It's almost as if Eye'm right there with you. *Marvelous* technology. So it *has* all come back to you. The thunderstorm.

Lights flickering in that seedy little bar of Moe Bacon's, down at the slovenly end of Robertson. Other than the couple in the corner booth who were mostly in the bag, there were only you and me and the comely barmaid."

"Kimmy?"

"Good for *you*, Greg. But of course you remember Kimmy. Her situation so much like yours, except Kimmy did have a part-time job. Both of you past thirty and frayed at the edges from having been knocked about and chewed on by the Action—the treacherous, remorseless, soul-devouring Hollywood Action."

"*Kimmy*. Dear God."

"That sounded more than a little wistful. She did attempt to get in touch once it started happening for you. But you couldn't make time for her. She never meant all that much to you anyway, did she, Greg? Just someone to sleep with, who commiserated because she also knew what failed dreams did to the luckless and needy. Maybe you could have helped her on your way up. But that's not what Eye've called about."

"This is bullshit, and I—"

"Greg, Greg. Eye've given you twenty of the most wonderful and productive years you could ever have hoped for! Now it's time for gratitude—and, of course, the agreed-upon recompense. Then we can discuss renewing your contract."

"What contract? I never signed anything with you. I've been with CAA for—"

"There is no denying that you owe part of your success to that storm-trooper agency. But Eye knew what they could do for you once Eye put you in Mike's hands."

"Now you're telling me you knew *Mike Ovitz*?"

"And so many like him, not a few of whom have been kicked to the wayside in this dog-eat-dog town. As for actors, how does the saying go? 'It's not enough to want it, you gotta need it.' Portrait of Gregory Wales, age 33. Profession: unemployed actor. The Place: Moe's bar on Robertson. Greg's situation: beyond desperate. Oh, there Eye go again, channeling Rod Serling. Let us dolly-in for that long-ago close-up. Greg Wales, slumped at the bar. Down to his last dime to call a hack agent who can't do anything for him. Down to his last shot of cheap scotch, on the cuff courtesy of the *simpatico* Kimmy. And let us not forget that stolen bottle of prescription Seconals in the pocket of Greg's tattered trench coat. Enough Seconals to provide the final exit in the dingy melodrama of his life. But wait! Here comes the turning point! The defining moment that began Act Two in the life of Greg Wales. In the person of . . . Yours Truly!"

"You're a fucking wack job. Channeling Rod Serling? Seconals? Okay, okay. Now I get it. I've been punk'd. So who put you up to this, Miriam? But enough is enough already, so—"

"Remember my warning about cutting me off, Greg! Deep breath. Another. Good. Is it necessary to review Act Two, now that you've reached the Super Bowl of Stardom?"

"No. I would like to get dressed now, if you'll—"

"But don't you still get that nagging feeling? All of you, no matter how powerful you become—or as a consequence of that power—get it sooner or later. Dick Cavett once asked Bob Mitchum about the ruling passion of LA-LA Land. Was it sex, money, drugs? The lust for immortality? No, Mitchum said. *Fear.* Fear of losing it all. The whole big-star package. Star-bright, limelight, the red carpets, the G-5 jet, the little sweetmeats on the side."

"Nobody's taking what I've earned away from me."

"Just bear in mind before we square the account that it was Eye who rescued you after you had downed twenty Seconals in that noisome little toilet of Moe's, thereafter sent you streaking into Hollywood orbit."

"Yeah, *right.* Let's get this straight. I never took any damn Seconals. And whatever conversation we may have had couldn't have amounted to much because I don't even know your name. And you won't tell me who are you, will you? Because you know I have people who deal with people like you, pal. And this conversation is—"

"Going on too long? Yes, yes, you're right. Shall we say tonight at eleven sharp? Moe's, Eye think. For old times' sake? Eye still do a considerable amount of business there. Where the heart-worn and desperate meet in a community of denial. Who knows? Gorgeous as the weather is now, by eleven tonight it could be raining. That little touch of *film noir* ambience. Speaking of, Eye don't suppose you still have that shabby Burberry you were practically living in? Of course not; just messin' with you."

"You've had your fun! Fun's over. I'm not meeting with you tonight or any time! If you try getting in touch with me again, I swear—"

"Eye would like Livy to wear white. Casual, not too trendy. With some frivolous gold bling and her hair brushed down past her shoulders. Most becoming. White happens to be a passion of mine, and because your daughter technically is still a virgin—"

"*Livy?*"

"Olivia Raquel Wales. Age sixteen. First born of Greg and Miriam Wales. Promised to me on this very day twenty years ago, in exchange for the deluxe Gregory Wales Star Package, which you must admit has been a tremendous value."

"You sick, miserable piece of—"

"Don't, Greg. We should also talk about—"

"Fuck you, little man!"

And Greg Wales snapped his cell phone closed.

After a few simmering moments he reached back, then threw the compact phone high and far into a grove of Italian cypress on a steep hillside. Far below a twelve-foot stone wall that surrounded his fiefdom lay the city of Beverly Hills. Greg's four acres occupied some of the most expensive real estate on the planet. At certain times of the year he and his family dwelled, literally, above the clouds.

The Olympus-style home of Greg Wales, two-time Oscar winner.

Naked now at poolside, trembling from anger.

The extension of the house phone played a perky tune. Also a very private number. Greg's shoulders drew together as a defense to the chill snaking up his backbone.

They had caller ID. But instead of the caller's number appearing in the little window of the handset there was a text message, which he unwillingly read as it scrolled.

Eye think you should know that the world has just changed, Greg. Instead of Act Three beginning, you're just not there any longer. Why don't we let that sink in for a few moments, hey Greg? Then when you're ready to have things back as you've become accustomed, just press the pound sign on your headset. See you and Livy tonight at Moe's.

Still furious, but with that crawly feeling changing to fear, Greg was about to hurl the wireless handset after his cell phone. But he stopped when he heard children laughing and splashing at the shallow lagoon of the huge pool, near a stair-step waterfall. They sounded much younger than his two.

He'd been alone, just seconds ago. Hearing nothing but a small plane over the valley, some players on Denzel Washington's tennis court. Stunned, he looked around at the shady lagoon.

Three kids. The oldest, a red-haired girl, probably not more than twelve, pre-pubertal shapely. He'd never seen her or the two boys before.

One of the boys, wearing yellow flotation cuffs on his upper arms, was paddling idly in Greg's direction, squinting up at him. The sun was behind Greg, backlighting him to good advantage. He was really buff for a fifty-three-year-old man, kept the tan glowing year around. And he had one of the world's most recognizable faces. But the kid didn't react to him. Not a flicker of expression as he changed direction in the pool.

Greg became aware of other, low voices. He whipped his head around, meeting resistance and getting a jolt from his arthritic neck. Probably time to stop making so many action movies. But they were enormously profitable.

He didn't only have children for company: half a dozen adults were gathered around a long-legged beauty on a chaise. They weren't just having brunch, lazing around. A photo shoot was in progress. Tamed, focused, shadowless light. The kind of concentrated, suspenseful activity that might accompany the opening of an important tomb. Greg knew the photographer: small, gnarly, a desert-rat look. He had recently shot Greg in Morocco for a six-page layout in *Vanity Fair*'s April—

Greg felt a whiplash shock. It blurred his vision momentarily, left him light-headed. He refocused on the woman on the chaise, object of everyone's expertise. From the degree of deference being paid, she had to be top-tier showbiz. Greg had no clue as to who she was or what she might be doing here in his—another shock, of indignation, registered belatedly. What the *hell* had they done to his garden? Instead of tropical blooms and plantings, he saw formal little hedges, topiary—as if the garden had been ruthlessly redressed by a team of—

Topiary? He hated—

Then he couldn't think of the word, or any words. His mind suddenly a void, as if he were experiencing the worst attack of stage fright in the history of his profession, a lockjawed, cold-cocked numbness.

He felt the sun on his angular nakedness like a spotlight. He blinked helplessly. What scene was this? Rolling. Speed. And . . . *action*. They were all waiting for him. He felt the pressure of their expectations.

As if he'd heard and must respond to an insistent prompt, Greg drifted around the pool and approached the garden, where statuary framed an entrance. They were all doing a damned good job of ignoring him. The children played and chattered in the lagoon. His frozen perceptions began to thaw. He was over his unreasonable fright. He smiled a mean, knowing smile. Okay. So this had to be an elaborate punk too, probably with Miriam's wholehearted cooperation.

Mir—?

Who was that? Who did he say? The void was back. No words words words. He trembled and felt frail in summer light, ephemeral, disappearing. He had no more pain his arthritic neck. That was something . . . but it was a blessing followed by sheer horror, because when he looked at himself there was nothing to see. Fingers, hands, feet . . . and his fabled sword! He wasn't conscious of having a body at all. And yet, and yet—his blood was high, full-flooded with colliding emotions: fear, grief, anger.

The red-headed woman being prepped for the shoot (there could be no doubt that she was the mother of the girl in the pool) smiled as the makeup artists eliminated an unwanted highlight on one cheekbone. They were great cheekbones. The woman was at work too, small changes of expression, settling into the Right Face, communing with her artistic spirits. Her appeal was lusty, shading to an eldritch romanticism. He must know her, but what was her name? There had been hundreds of beautiful women in his personal life, complementing his art; either he had acted with her or fucked her or both, but . . . but . . .

The woman's Romany eyes shifted slightly as requested by the photog. She looked past a crouching assistant with a light meter to where Greg was, or felt he was, about twenty feet away between two brutally disjointed marble statues. Her gaze as remote as the chiseled blank of goddess eyes.

Whether or not he still had a body, which he couldn't confirm, he still had eyes, and they were weeping.

Tears the woman was unaware of. If she were seeing him, he would have noticed some nuance of reaction. So he just wasn't there for her—not only wasn't there, he realized with a dismal failure of heart and nerve, but hadn't been, not in twenty years. When it would have been so easy to give her hope. A simple act of remembrance, gratitude perhaps, a returned phone call.

He'll know who I am. We used to

Kimmy.

He might have whispered her name, but he didn't hear himself. Couldn't hear a thing any more. Not the voices, the wind surfing through tall cypresses. The kids sporting in the pool.

But if she was Kimmy, here, in *his* place of sumptuous celebrity, if indeed it was Kim who had taken the treacherous little man's Star Package deal, then what had become of Greg Wales?

Those damned Seconals.

The photographer was ready. Kim lifted her chin, smiled as the shoot team drifted respectfully back from her idol space.

Greg smiled too. Truly heartbroken for her.

In that moment of decision the scene changed again. The photo shoot in the garden became a faded tableau, like a frame taken from a bad print of an early-thirties film. There was a sensation of blood and flesh returning to him after that terrible interval of nowhere, nothing, *gone,* white-faced and stone-cold on the dirty floor of Moe Bacon's toilet. His other Eternity.

"Kimmy. You look so beautiful. And I'm so sorry."

Greg lifted the telephone handset. It seemed welded in his grip. Powerful. Magical.

An eye appeared on the small screen. The eye winked at him. There was amusement in that wink, but basically it was insulting.

Ready for another ten years of close-ups, Mr. Wales? Pay my price.

"Sure. You'll get what you have coming to you. My end of the bargain."

As he had been instructed, Greg pushed the pound sign, instantly banishing Kimmy and retrieving the life he could not bear to part with.

Lester had accompanied Livy to the call-back for the new Bruck-heimer TV series, and he drove her home afterward. Lester had worked almost ten years for the Wales family. Before that he'd been a boxer, staying with it too long, sometimes one fight away from a heavyweight title shot, but never able to win that crucial bout. At age fifty he had begun to shuffle a little when he walked.

"I'm going out tonight," Greg told him. "I don't want any paparazzi picking up my trail. Can you borrow your brother's Hummer for me to drive?"

"No problem, Mr. Wales."

"I want you to meet me at a place called Moe's down on South Robertson. Drive your own car. Park a block away but don't come in. Be there a little before eleven."

Lester nodded. He was often complicit in the Byzantine maneuvers of the superstar when Greg needed a few hours of total privacy or secrecy. He also understood intuitively that this time trouble was involved, but he asked no questions.

Livy was at her desktop computer catching up on schoolwork when Greg walked into her suite. She wore headphones, orally conjugating French verbs. She gave Greg a preoccupied smile and held up the spread fingers of one hand: *five minutes*.

Greg went outside on her balcony and looked at the moon rising over the Valley, although it wasn't yet full dark. A clear night, the moon full or almost full, a vivid yellow. *Good*, he thought, then shuddered, although the air at this altitude had no bite. The Valley lights seethed like a blanket of live coals.

"What's up, dad?" Livy said, slipping an arm around his waist and giving him a quick kiss. "The Scorsese deal didn't fall apart, did it?"

"No, and I'm not about to let it happen. Acting in Marty's movie, it's like breaking bread with Jesus."

"You look kinda worried, that's all."

"Probably hunger pangs."

"I haven't eaten anything either. Stomach's still a little nervous from the audition."

"Mom's out for the evening, Josh said he's spending the night at Colin's, so—looks like just the two of us. Date?"

"Sure! Where do you want to go, the Ivy?"

"I was thinking about the little Chinese place in Studio City. Been a year, at least."

"Chinese. Mmmm, *yes*!"

"How did the call-back go?"

"There must have been thirty people in the room this time."

"Producers and Network, mostly. You pick out one face to—"

"I know, and ignore the rest. I did okay. Actually I think I did *great*."

"I could give Jerry a call, see how it's going."

Livy grabbed his elbow. "No, you won't! That's why I use mom's maiden name. Livy *Jefford*. If I'm gonna have a career it'll be because I earned it, like Bryce Howard did . . . Dad?"

"What?"

"You've got that look again. Something's wrong, I *know* you."

Greg shook his head and responded to his cue for a reassuring smile. In the auto courtyard where Lester had parked the borrowed

Hummer, which needed a wash job, Greg offered the keys to Livy. She shied away as if he had dangled a shrunken head in her face.

"Dad—we're not taking *that thing*?"

"Why not? Have you ever driven one?"

"And I never will!" she said indignantly. "Global *warming*, dad! And that—that is an ecological Frankenstein!"

Greg laughed, and looked up at the moon. It wasn't an image of Universal Studio's venerable monster that came to his mind just then. Nothing make-believe. Infinitely worse.

He wondered how he was going to get through the next few hours without going mad.

The little man, with a ruddy face as round as the moon outside, was holding forth at the bar when Greg walked, alone, into Moe's at two minutes past eleven. He was chattily entertaining a couple of barfly regulars in his childishly treble voice while keeping one blue eye on the door. He gave no sign of recognition when Greg appeared, but his small mouth tightened ominously.

Greg chose a booth, signaled for a beer. He didn't have long to wait for the little man to join him.

"*Where is she? Where is Olivia?*"

"We had dinner together at a little place on Ventura Boulevard. Then . . . I put her in a limo and sent her home."

The little man squeezed into the booth opposite Greg, letting out his breath in a catlike hiss, riffling his fleecy beard. His eyes glittered. Greg watched him calmly, unblinking, focusing on a small wen between the fulminating blue eyes. An actor's trick. Greg knew fine clothing and great tailoring. The little man, for all his hard-to-fit butterball size, was sartorially splendid. Double-breasted red blazer with handcrafted gold buttons featuring bas-relief dragons, a shirt that gave off highlights when he breathed, curled and uncurled his chubby hands on the chipped formica tabletop.

"You never said who you were. I'd like to know."

"*Eye* have *nothing* further to say to you. *Eye* am not accustomed to being treated this way! Even for an actor you are notably bereft of scruples or honor. Your reward will be oblivion. The floor of Moe's toilet is much too good for you."

The little man raised his left hand. An ancient ring with a fiery stone overwhelmed the pinky. Within the stone a dark eye opened malevolently. Greg braced himself.

"Now hold on just a minute, Shorty—"

He was showered with radiance from the ring's eye, forced to shield his own eyes. After a few seconds the light abruptly failed, and the eye closed, perhaps disappointedly.

The little man shook his hand, yelping as if he were snakebit.

"Yeah, I'll bet that stung," Greg said amiably.

The little man stared at his baroque ring. Then at Greg.

"But—but you can't still be here!"

"Why shouldn't I be? I've done everything you asked of me. I *have* brought you my firstborn. She'll be walking in the door any time now."

"What?"

The little man looked around at the entrance to Moe's, outlined in twinkling Christmas lights that were never taken down. The door remained closed. The little man faced Greg again with his cupid's bow mouth pursed angrily. He trembled as if in the first stage of a tantrum.

"The ring knows, doesn't it?" Greg said. He took an envelope from his coat pocket and tossed it down in front of the little man.

"What is this?"

"The birth certificate of my firstborn. Jennifer Ellen Garmon, age twenty-five. Born in Ruttlen, Utah. She doesn't go by my name, but I am on the birth certificate as her father."

"Ridiculous! A lie! A clumsy ruse—" The little man rose half out of his seat, then shook the hand with the ring again. "Ouch! All right." He settled down, confounded, beginning to perspire.

"You have had only *two* children! Eye should know. Eye never make mistakes. Eye know everything about each of my—"

"Clients? Victims?" Greg took out another dun-colored envelope. "DNA tests. Mine. Jenny's. A match."

The little man wheezed and fumed. "Anything can be faked."

"Maybe. If there's enough time. The DNA tests for proof of paternity go back four years. Jennifer *is* my daughter. Not that you will have any doubt of it once you've seen her. My true firstborn, Shorty."

"Stop calling me that! I am . . . *Shalamanázar!*"

"I'd never have guessed. Okay, Shal. I know you've had your heart set on Livy. But a deal's a deal, right."

Shalamanázar dabbed sullenly at his sweaty face with a large handkerchief.

"Jenny is not exactly someone you, ah, 'settle for.' I think you'll agree as soon as—oh, here she comes."

Jennifer Garmon had made her entrance. Immediately she claimed the attention of everyone in Moe's who wasn't blind drunk or under a table.

As Greg had said, her paternity was obvious in her face. But the long lissome body, her dark raffishly chopped hair, her large, luminous, dreamy eyes were all woman.

Jennifer looked around the semi-dark bar, acknowledged her father with a slight, almost timid wave, then looked with a delighted smile at a pair of pinball machines.

"Just finishing up some business here, honey," Greg called to his firstborn. "Go ahead and play if you want to."

She waved again, *Thanks, daddy,* then went quickly to the candy-bright, glowingly futuristic machines, studied each carefully while deciding which one to play.

Shalamanázar drew a long wheezy breath. His face was an incandescent pink. His expression tipped Greg that he'd instantly been smitten.

"Jennifer? Does she understand—"

"That she's going with you tonight? Yes."

"Well, then," the little man said, sparing Greg a glance but unable for long to take his eyes from his unexpected prize. His flush was deepening. He twitched in anticipation.

Greg looked at his watch. "But try not to rush her. Pinball is her favorite game. Let her enjoy a game or two."

The suggestion made Shalamanázar uneasy. He passed his other hand over the bulge of the ancient ring as if to quiet a deep-lying rumble. "Eye suppose a few more minutes won't matter."

"Do you have far to go?" Greg asked casually.

"Only a short cab ride to—" Shal looked up with a hint of suspicion as Greg stood. He laid a set of car keys on the table.

"A little something extra for you. It's the black Hummer in front of the launderette across the street."

"Really? That is . . . awfully decent of you, Greg. Eye must admit eye was too hasty in denigrating your character."

"So I'm renewed for another ten years, top-tier at the box office? And after that—"

"After that, enjoy a long-lived retirement in the company of your lovely wife, numerous grandchildren, and your third Academy Award. Or, if you choose, you may run for public office. Success is assured."

"Wow."

"As I speak, so is it written. Good night."

"Good night to you, Shal. By the way, a small favor? Jenny looks mature, but she has always been, ah, exceptionally shy."

"I understand. Say no more." Shalamanázar's gaze was momentarily softer as he watched Jennifer rock a pinball machine, jockeying her point total to stratospheric numbers, showing surprising strength in spite of her gamin slenderness.

On his way out Greg paused to kiss the back of Jennifer's neck. She smiled absently, absorbed in her game.

Lester was in his Chevy Colorado parked two blocks south of Moe's. Greg got in beside him.

"Miss Jenny be all right?"

"Yes."

"What now?"

"I don't think we'll have long to wait."

Five minutes passed.

"Ain't that big ole moon somethin' to see," Lester said forebodingly, his misshapen fingers tapping on the steering wheel.

Shalamanázar emerged from Moe's behind Jennifer Garmon, who stood about a foot taller than Shal. He spotted the Hummer and hustled her across Robertson. Traffic was sparse, the hour closing on midnight.

"That the dude?" Lester said. "Look like Santy Claws."

"Jennifer's always wanted to meet Santa."

Lester grumbled in his throat, then said, "Why not just let me take care a him for you?"

"There's a protocol to be observed. Besides, he's got this ring. I don't want to fuck with his ring."

Lester looked dubiously at Greg as Shalamanázar helped Jennifer into the massive vehicle, which looked as if it had been imagined by a team of designers in a permanent state of road-rage. He hustled around to the driver's side and climbed aboard.

"I think he's under some kind of time restraint," Greg said. "Just a hunch. Okay, there he goes. Follow them, but don't give us away."

"Like I needs to be told that."

Shalamanázar lived in Rancho Park, south of Pico and not far from the Fox film studio. It was a street of small, well-kept one- and two-story houses. Shal's was tan stucco, with a flat tile roof and a three-foot concrete wall around it, topped with ornamental iron grill-work. An automated gate guarded the narrow driveway. There was a lighted porte cochere into which the Hummer would have fitted like a bullet in the cylinder of a revolver. Shal left the Hummer in the street in the only available space, at the foot of his own drive. He escorted Jenny into his house. From Greg's vantage point, where the pickup idled in the mouth of an alley near Pico, his daughter seemed willing to be with Shalamanázar, although she kept her head down. Greg's heart was cold from anxiety, his hands clenched.

"Boss?"

"According to the Almanac, the moon won't be at its fullest for another seven and a half minutes."

"Oh Lawd. This be makin' me mighty nervous."

"Tell me about it."

Lester grumbled in his throat, but otherwise was fretfully silent.

Ten minutes passed.

"All right! Pull up in front of the Hummer. We're going in for Jenny."

"Hope we ain't too late."

The gate at Shalamanázar's driveway was closed, but it was no trouble for either of them to get over the wall. There was a dog walker up the street, but his back was to them. Greg had no further concern about prying eyes in nearby homes. He was focused on his firstborn.

They went through the porte cochere to a kitchen door at the back of the house. Curtains covered the glass; Greg couldn't see inside. He stepped back and nodded to Lester.

Lester broke in.

There was a light on over the sink. No evidence of an alarm system. Greg doubted that the wizard, or bane thaumaturge, or whatever he was, had need of one.

The kitchen was small, with glass-front cabinets, not a cup or spoon out of place. And it was suffocatingly hot. A low rumble below caused the house to tremble. Next to the pantry a door to the basement was slightly ajar. Reddish light flickered down there.

"What he need a furnace on in summertime?" Lester said, taking out a handkerchief to wipe his brow. His other hand was on the butt of the pistol he wore on his belt.

"I don't think it's a furnace, Lester. But we're not going down there to find out."

"Oh Lawd," Lester moaned. "Miss Jenny is gone already, ain't she?"

"Don't say that. Come on." Greg left the kitchen, calling: "JENNY!"

No reply. They searched the house, which took only a couple of minutes. They discovered several stuffed black cats in attitudes of agitation and, in the larger of the two bedrooms, a standing oval mirror that gave off turbid light that distorted reflections. The mirror frankly scared the hell out of Greg.

They retreated to the hall outside, breathing heavily in the heat, staring hopelessly at each other.

In the kitchen glass broke.

Greg got there first. The refrigerator door stood open, vapor gusting into the kitchen.

Jenny frowned at a shattered bottle of orange juice on the tiles at her feet. She looked at Greg. Then down at her bloody hands.

"It's so hot down there," she said. "I was thirsty. But the bottle slipped. I should've washed my hands first." She began methodically to wipe them on her blouse, which already was soaked with blood. Tears fell from her eyes.

"Don't worry, Sweetheart," Greg said.

"I'm s-sorry, daddy."

"It's all right. Let me get you cleaned up."

"I was bad again, daddy." She looked at the door to the basement. Lester walked around her to the sink and wetted a couple of dish towels. "Daddy?"

"Yes, Sweetheart?"

"He w-wasn't really Santa Claus."

"I guess he had me fooled, Jen."

Greg took the towels from Lester and began to clean his daughter's hands, forearms, and spattered face. Not for the first time in her twenty-five years.

"I brought you a change of clothes. After you're dressed, what do you say we get a chocolate shake and something to eat at the Burger King?"

"Yes!" she said, with a quick smile. Then she winced, pink teeth pressing into her lower lip. She looked hesitantly at her father.

"Then I have to go back to The Place, don't I?"

"But you like it there, Jen. You feel safe at The Place."

She shrugged. "I guess so. Only—"

"What, Sweetheart?"

"The pinball machine's broken, and nobody's come to fix it."

"Know what I'm going to do? First thing in the morning?"

"W-what?"

"I'll have *six* new pinball machines sent over, so you can play as much and often as you want to." He cleaned a spritz of Shalamanázar's blood from above her brow line. Some of the hairy growth on her forehead rubbed away with it, leaving fresh pink skin. Another twenty minutes or so, she would be her old self. Flawlessly young, dewily beautiful.

Lester slowly closed the door to the basement and stood with his back to it, arms folded. The house continued to tremble as if from a mild earthquake. Jennifer didn't look at Lester or the door. Most likely, Greg thought, except for a headache and torn nails she had no physical reminders of the horror she'd been through. And only a vague, nagging memory of it.

That was the blessing that accompanied her curse.

Jennifer put her cleaned arms and now hairless hands around Greg's neck and kissed him joyously.

"You're the best daddy in the world!"

"I have my moments," Greg said. "Now why don't we go change your clothes, brush your teeth, get that bad taste out of your mouth?"

As he was leaving the kitchen with Jen he glanced at Lester. Lester sighed and opened the pantry door, looking for a pail and a mop.

A HOST OF SHADOWS

HARRY SHANNON

*The individual has a host of shadows, all of whom resemble him and for
the moment have an equal claim to authenticity.*
—SOREN KIERKEGAARD

T HIS MAY HURT a bit." If Dr. Neumann is aware of the cliché, he
hides it well.

The surgeon is a squat, balding gnome with yellowing, uneven
teeth like chipped piano keys. The patient on the table is confused
and frightened and does not remember anything except his name.
Neumann turns from the table with busy, white-gloved hands. Mean-
while, the helpless man's senses telescope as a wickedly long needle
approaches and freshly starched medical greens whisper obscenities.

"Wait." Quinn despises himself for sounding frail. "Not yet. What
are you going to do to me?"

Neumann purses that ruined mouth, cocks his head. "Mr. Quinn,
we have been over this a number of times."

"I don't remember."

"This we know."

"Are you comfortable?" There is a tall, coltish nurse, who would
normally be considered attractive in a surfer-girl kind of way, but at
the moment, standing in the corner, half covered in shadow, she most
resembles a preying mantis. She is tactful, sotto voce; asking if Quinn
needs more medication. He likes the hushed drug glow just fine, hell
it's better than a pitcher of martinis at Happy Hour, he's nicely fucked
up, but any more and he's likely to fade out completely . . . and then
what happens?

Quinn realizes he has waited far too long to answer. "No, I'm comfortable. I want to stay awake."

"Remember, we can do this either way," Dr. Neumann says, crisply. "But we must deal with your delusions once and for all." He dons a thick pair of glasses, positions the needle sideways on a glittering silver tray. "It would certainly be helpful to have you cognitively present to contribute to this examination, but that is not absolutely essential to the success of the procedure."

"Are you certain?" *Convince them you're fine.*

"Excuse me?"

"Certain this is necessary, and that I am . . . hallucinating."

Nurse Elizabeth glides spider-sideways out of the gloom, pats his arm just above the taped IV. "Be calm, sir."

And Dr. Neumann says: "Oh, but you are already far more rational on the Haldol, yes? Mr. Quinn, one of the drugs you have received is a powerful antipsychotic. You have been suffering from some quite spectacular delusions. You must allow us to help before it is too late."

"What if I'm not crazy?" *You're not. Don't let them do this to you.*

"Excuse me?"

"Have you got the right guy? This could be a mistake. You did read my file, right? Jesus, you're not about to operate on the wrong man are you? I've read about stuff like that, amputating a perfectly good leg."

"Let me offer an example." The good doctor leans down and Quinn can see himself reflected in large, oval lenses. "You told us that you believe you have seen some kind of an unknown parasite. You are convinced that it causes violent behavior in humans. Yes?"

"Yes. No. I'm not sure."

"Well, my dear Mr. Quinn, I can assure you of one thing. That was not a delusion. In point of fact, such creatures *do* exist."

Large rush of adrenaline, time slows like a drool of cold syrup. The man who knows himself as Quinn squints up at the surgeon, one eyebrow raised. Images appear. His tongue abruptly feels carpeted. "Parasites that cause violence?"

"Astrocytoma is a rare but efficient tumor in the frontal lobes, Mr. Quinn. As I've said, it can cause severe emotional disturbance, dizziness, mental confusion, and both auditory and visual hallucinations. I believe you have such a tumor, and cancer may certainly be viewed as a parasite. All we need to do now is explore how to best attempt to remove the astrocytoma with a minimum of collateral damage."

"Without turning me into a potted plant?"

No answer. The air thickens. Quinn swallows dryly, sleepily. "I just can't believe it's come to this. Someone I don't know from beans is going to saw a hole in my skull and dig around in there with some shit that looks like an electric toothbrush and a tuning fork, and he says it's going to hurt. God, why this is happening?"

"Now, now." The nurse wipes Quinn's feverish brow with a cool cloth. With economy of movement, Dr. Neumann busies himself with a tower of lit electronics that glitters like a blackened Christmas tree. He taps a monitor with two gloved fingers then slaps it with his palm. The screen flickers on, a blurry smear of color, and confirms that at least one of the probing devices will contain a miniature camera. Neumann keeps his back turned as he covertly tests something.

RRRRrrrrrrRRRRRrrr. Quinn vaguely hears the nasty, tenor snarl of a small bone saw. He writhes, whimpers.

"I think . . . I'm going to be sick."

"Now, now." It's Nurse Elizabeth, again wiping his moist brow, *that's her name, Elizabeth.* Quinn thinks: *This bitch is like one of those goddamned Disney robots.* His fear is rapidly becoming palpable, stronger than the medication, and again all he wants to do is delay. Talk. *Stall.* "Did you read the report on me, Doc? All the way through, I mean?"

The surgeon still turned away, hunched over, the bone saw growling again—*RRRrrrrRRRR*—even more aggressively, this time. "We all did."

Quinn goes blank. "Did what?"

The surgeon and the nurse exchange knowing glances. He says: "Read the report."

"Wait! I remember now." Quinn begins to babble. And in a way, he does remember. "I started getting these headaches, you know? Right smack in the middle of my forehead, where they used to say there was a third eye. Ha. Nobody could find anything wrong with me, though, not at first. They wired me up and stuck me with needles and did every test they could think of before saying it was all in my head. That's one sick joke in itself, right? All in my head."

"Now, now." Female fingers on his temple.

"Stop saying that!" Quinn knows his voice has gone up an octave or two, kind of a soul scream, and he's rambling now but can't seem to stop talking. "It came out of nowhere. I was talking to one of the physicians, some specialist named Edison, a big guy with white hair.

And he looked out the window, and I saw something coming out of his right ear. It was kind of like a small earthworm, but with antennae, and all black and shiny. It wiggled for a second and then went right back in."

"Just so." Apparently satisfied, Dr. Neumann brings the small bone saw over to the silver tray. He sets it down on the table, next to the hideously long needle. "And obviously, something like that is illogical and absurd. Yes?"

"Perhaps, but . . ."

"You must not agitate yourself," the surgeon offers, gently. "Staying calm is best. Your mind will produce less dissonance that way."

"Doc, you don't need to do this. I can get better on my own." Again, Quinn hears the desperation, that frail voice. And again, it shames him. Because Quinn does not know anything for certain, has begun to lose faith in his own sanity. *But if I believe I'm crazy, I'm not crazy anymore, right? I read that somewhere.*

"Now, now."

Quinn moans. "Nurse, please, let me have some water."

"We can't do that," she whispers, efficient as ever. "You might aspirate and strangle on your vomit. It won't be long now."

"Wait. Wait." Now Quinn *needs* to finish the story. "I really do remember. I didn't say anything at the time, I mean everyone would have thought I was crazy, but that weekend I was watching the basketball game and I changed back to the local news at halftime, and . . ."

Dr. Neumann raises the needle, caresses the plunger, a jet of clear liquid ejaculates into the frigid air. His huge glasses now reflect something or someone squatting behind Quinn's head, in a clenched fist of darkness well behind the nurse, but a second later it is gone. *Wait, who was that?*

" . . . Anyway, the news said this doc named Edison had gone completely bonkers over the Fourth of July weekend."

The nurse feigns interest. "Really?"

Quinn pauses to breathe, his eyes crossing to focus on that freaking needle, willing it to freeze in space and time. "He poisoned his whole family. He put something medicinal in the party punch, related to curare, that 'rendered them immobile,' the news said. Something commonly used in surgeries, I think. And then he cut them up with scalpels while they were paralyzed but could still feel everything."

"How ghastly, did they ever catch him?" Dr. Neumann asks. It is clear he either does not care or already knows the answer. The long needle moves closer to the trembling flesh of Quinn's exposed vein.

"No, he got away somehow." *No, don't!*

"Tragic." Was that voice male or female? Actually, Quinn is not sure anyone spoke the word. Perhaps he imagined it.

"Amazing." *Who said that? Are there others in the operating room?*

"So, so." Neumann masks his lower face, reaches forward with the syringe. "And now we begin."

"Wait!" Something else has occurred to Quinn, something deeply disturbing. "Didn't you just hit that dirty monitor with your fingers?"

The doctor shrugs. He examines the needle again, checking a second time for air bubbles. Satisfied, edging closer, he bends over and cloaks Quinn in velvet shadow. While groping for a vein, he finally responds. "The monitor can be uncooperative at times."

"But that means your gloves aren't sanitary anymore, doesn't it?"

"No worries," the doctor whispers, feigning a mediocre Aussie accent. The nurse clamps down on Quinn's bare shoulder. Someone else is nearby. A male moans in a low voice, the sadist in sexual ecstasy.

"Wait, I mean, you're about to fuck around with my *brain* for God's sake! Wait. And what's in that thing? What drug are you giving me?"

The needle penetrates and his entire body slides into a deep puddle of warm, loose mud. Now Quinn can recall having been worried about something recently, but has no idea what; even when the saw roars to life, he remains calm and indifferent. A few more pinpricks render his face and forehead numb.

RRRrrrrRRRRRrrr. He is neatly scalped and feels some tugging. The top of his skull is gently removed with a sticky *pop.* Quinn grunts; his eyes float lazily to the monitor and register pulsing red and blue patches and the tip of a long aluminum probe.

"Now, I need to know exactly what happens," the good doctor whispers, "when I touch this . . ."

. . . He is thirsty beyond description. The heat slams down hard, splintering the rocks ahead into fragments that glow like gleaming shards of broken mirror. There is a miniscule pocket of shade lurking beneath the stunted row of browning tamarind trees, over to his left. Quinn stumbles that way, licking dry lips, hoping to find water. The sun has been up for nearly two hours. He will have to rest. It is already too hot to make good time. Quinn makes for the shade and aims his deerskin boots at flat rocks to hide his tracks. He crawls

under the half-naked trees, pulls dried sage over his body and covers his eyes. He wants to rest but he can still hear the tormented, feeble screams of that mule skinner the Apache roped to a wagon wheel, the one they are slowly roasting to death. Quinn cannot understand that need. Killing a man is one thing, necessary from time to time, but taking pleasure in his extended suffering . . .

Pebbles rattle in a nearby arroyo. His heart kicks hard. Quinn clings to the big-bore Hawken rifle and its nearly exhausted pouch of ammunition. On the other side of the slope, the Mexican boy shrieks on and on without respite or release. Quinn's hands are shaking as he brings the barrel to his own mouth. He swallows dry spit and resolves to shoot himself rather than be captured by the savages. He waits. Listens . . .

"Mr. Quinn?" Dr. Neumann seems irritated. "You must remain focused for this approach to be effective. What happened when I touched you there?"

"Bright light," Quinn manages. Gags. "I was somewhere else." He is very thirsty. "It was very hot, like a desert. I heard my feet moving in the dirt and a noise like someone screaming from far, far away."

"Ah." The doctor seems satisfied. "We have both light and sound, then. And we certainly all know who was screaming, now don't we? Very good, thank you."

The instrument teases new tissue. Its image on the monitor quivers, as if the probe were somehow aroused. "And what happens now?"

. . . The old man is looking down at withered arms and spotted hands that cling to a dented walker. His brown slippers whistle-thud along worn shag carpet streaked with sunshine and shadow. With every forced step, he grunts darkly. Some dim and still furious part of him remembers being young. He hates what his body has become. He wants to make it to the front window; wants to be looking out that window not trapped in his own shit and piss in the bed in the room with the others who have become as helpless as infants. He wants to drink fresh water. There is light outside, birds and colors and fresh, clean wind . . .

"Wind," Quinn says in a voice startlingly loud. He thinks: *Where was I just a moment ago? What was I dreaming?*

Dr. Neumann's eyes crinkle slightly above the white mask, which bellows and sucks with increasingly rapid, very shallow breathing. He seems agitated, but also genuinely puzzled. "That one made you hear it as the wind? Odd."

Quinn sees the monitor, struggles to make sense of it, starts to object but then comes another touch of the probe—again no immediate pain, in fact this time just a whirling dervish of color and sound . . .

. . . *A sunny day but not a dry one—he sees a stretch of damp, sparkling backyard grass and the twirling hiss of a lawn sprinkler. Quinn drops the shovel and blinks away sweat. Pleased, he watches a bronze young woman with long, brown hair and almond eyes dancing through the cool spray. She wears a man's white tee shirt, and the wet fabric flatters her body and reveals tantalizingly pert nipples and a wet triangle of her sex. She smiles broadly, winks and waves. He looks down, examines his hands and finds them calloused; his arms are strong and roped with a younger man's muscle. She approaches, her hips swaying, and he moves to touch her but the world turns black and his hungry fingers touch empty space, and a bitter emptiness . . .*

"Not that, not the emptiness," Quinn cries. Her abrupt absence renders him inconsolable. *I was really there that time, not imagining it.* "Please no." *Take me back.* He means to beg them for more but emits a sobbing cough instead. "I'm so thirsty."

The nurse clucks her tongue and dabs his brow. She offers something likely intended to reassure Quinn. What emerges is a garbled drone. Time warps. The universe crackles like tinfoil. Dr. Neumann adjusts the white mask. He scratches his face, shakes his head. "What emotion did you feel just then, Mr. Quinn?"

"Please don't do that again," Quinn gasps. *Please, don't bring me back here. Not to this room. Leave me with her.*

"The . . . emptiness?"

"Not that." Quinn cannot make them understand. He begins to cry. "The emptiness."

Neumann chuckles. "I see. Well, obviously that place you call the emptiness has served to make you feel very, very sad." He looks up and away as if playing to an invisible audience. "We are getting closer, yes?" He writes something down on a notepad.

Closer to what? Who else is here? "Who are you people?" Quinn shouts. "What are you doing to me?" He is suddenly full of terror because the answer is abruptly coming to him, knowledge that has Quinn fearing his own swollen heart might burst. He begins to fight for his sanity, his life. He struggles, kicks.

The medical team chirps and soothes as the patient bucks mightily against frayed canvas restraints. The fresh flow of cold adrenaline helps bring clarity. Now the man called Quinn knows that he has not been ill at all, that he does not belong here and that this operation is a fraud. He's being drugged, tortured. He bites down on his own cheek; hard and again, harder. The pain snaps him into focus.

There are secrets he must keep.

Then a jarring paradigm shift allows Quinn to take it all in; first a miasma of odors ranging from pungent disinfectant to urine and excrement, then the truth of his surroundings. The operating room is not pristine at all; it is a dusty basement or garage of some kind, filled with odd equipment gone orange with rust. The floor is concrete and stained with what appears to be dried blood. He has soiled himself repeatedly.

"Enough foreplay." Someone offstage, addressing Neumann. "Let's make the little traitor talk."

Quinn stiffens himself. Now he has another, vital piece of the puzzle. He knows that voice, although he cannot place it right away. He tries mightily to concentrate and finally pictures an athlete gone to seed, a tall man wearing a uniform with the garish epaulets of the Secret Police, a colonel.

Christ, my cover is blown, I've been captured. The patch must have held, so they're trying to break me this way.

Dr. Neumann hurries closer. *Is this real?* The surgeon seems visibly afraid of officers seated in the darkness as if picturing his own fate should he fail. Perhaps his assignment is to devise a way around implanted suggestions, programs that place a subject's secrets beyond the reach of physical pain. If that's true, the frantic surgeon must open the human lockbox prone on the gurney and retrieve the secrets buried there, or take Quinn's place in a torture chamber.

Quinn gathers what saliva he can assemble and when Neumann bends closer, he spits in his face. "Fuck you!"

Dr. Neumann turns away, a little unnerved. "This one is strong." He searches for more anesthetic. "We must calm him."

"No. No more drugs." The colonel's voice again. "We want him to suffer."

Someone tightens the clamp on the vice holding Quinn's head in place. It does not hurt, but he feels something in his skull crack and slide down and sideways a bit. He no longer fears death—just the long, nightmarish journey ahead.

Quinn hears the raspy scratch of a match and a few seconds later catches the scent of an expensive cigar. Everything is vivid, clear. Something in Neumann's approach has worked, just not as they'd intended. Panicked, Quinn swims up as if from the bottom of a deep, cold well and remembers that his real name is Neil Cassidy, and the identities and locations of the others in his group, including his lover, Martine. *No!*

He is fully present in the torture chamber now, and that stark reality horrifies him. Within moments he will have no defense. Without the patch he is certain to break and give them everything they want.

He attempts to swallow his tongue. The nurse jams a stick in his mouth.

"Again." The eager voice of the Colonel, followed by the wicked touch of that electric probe . . . *Frozen water everywhere and Cassidy stands at the top of a crystal white mound, surrounded by pine trees bowed down, heavily weighted with fresh, sparkling snow. The boy whoops for sheer joy and watches as a long plume of dragon breath pops from his mouth to dissipate in the crisp morning air. He looks down the slope, and his small hands, now gloved in blue wool, grip the sides of the sled. He kneels right to the edge of the slope, takes a deep breath and pushes himself over, roars down the chute like a cannonball. Then he becomes afraid of crashing into a tree, being seriously hurt, being crippled or killed. He hollers from fear, not excitement, now. His ears are so cold they hurt and the air screams defiance, a high-pitched wailing sound, or maybe it is not the air, maybe it is someone's voice, maybe his own voice . . . ?*

"Give the gentleman some time," the Colonel says, almost pleasantly. "I see no point in being rude."

But this time Cassidy/Quinn cannot stop screaming. On and on, the ghastly sound continues unabated, as if wrung from the soul of a tormented Mexican roasting on a wagon wheel under the blistering Texas sun; or perhaps it's the wail of a proud man rotting in the body of a stranger, or a good man torn from the embrace of his wife forever. No, it is the freezing wind in the ears of a small boy headed for a rendezvous with death. The awful shriek bounces off concrete walls and echoes across two hundred and fifty years before finally coming to rest beneath Cassidy/Quinn's ragged, labored breathing.

"No more." *Who said that?*

He will betray his friends, of this there is no doubt; babble and wail incoherently until he has spilled everything and anything to avoid what Neumann has been doing with that probe, those needles and the drugs. It must stop.

I was really there, the prisoner thinks, frantically. *I was not here I was really there, back in that mound of snow.* He swallows, forces words: "I'll talk."

A chair squeaks as the colonel shifts around in the gloom. "But of course you will, Cassidy. Why not? Most of your friends already have."

"Bullshit."

"Give me their names."

"Please. I can't."

"No?" The chair again, complaining. "Apparently you need more motivation. Neumann? We may as well give him that last one again."

The prisoner suddenly comes to a decision. "Okay, okay," he cringes, "but please not the emptiness again. Not that. I can't bear it."

Dr. Neumann slows for a second, absorbing the content of the sentence. He quickly consults his notes, locates the area now specified as "emptiness," and looks for permission to return to that particular section of exposed brain. Apparently the Colonel nods, for Neumann adjusts position and resumes probing.

The surgeon actually whispers, "I'm sorry" as he presses down . . . *a bronze young woman with long, brown hair and almond eyes is dancing through the cool spray of the backyard sprinkler, it is Martine and she wears a man's white tee shirt, the wet fabric flatters her body and reveals tantalizingly pert nipples and a wet triangle of her sex . . .*

"What's going on?"

"I don't know, sir."

. . . *Martine smiles broadly and she winks and waves. Cassidy looks down to examine his hands and finds them calloused; his arms are strong and roped with a young man's muscle . . .*

"Answer me damn it, what's wrong?"

. . . *She approaches, her hips swaying, and he walks to meet her, and both space and time are standing still . . .*

"Did you lose him?"

"I don't know what happened."

"Look at him. He's a drooling vegetable, that's what happened."

"Some form of catatonia, perhaps?"

. . . *The sun beats down on bare skin lathered with sweat and sunscreen and a body loosened by enjoyable physical labor . . .*

"Idiot! He is of no use to me like this."

"Doctor," the nurse calls, urgently, "the patient is no longer breathing."

"*What?*"

"Flatline."

"Bring him back!"

"We are trying. Clear. Clear."

"Doctor . . .?"

. . . It is sunny day but not a dry one—Cassidy sees a stretch of damp, sparkling backyard grass and hears the twirling hiss of a lawn sprinkler. And then she is there again, smiling.

Martine.

Free. I am free . . .

Wait.

The patient opens his bloodshot eyes. The surgeon is a squat, balding gnome with teeth like chipped piano keys. Quinn is confused and frightened and does not remember anything, anything at all, except for his name.

The surgeon pats his hand in a macabre parody of bedside manner.

"This may hurt a bit."

WHAT THE DEVIL WON'T TAKE . . .

L. A. BANKS

H OWLING WINDS WHIPPED at the hem of their black robes. Voices escalated in a cacophony of assent. "Let it be so!" Stern faces, etched hard with determination, were washed pale in the moonlight. Twelve men of means stood shoulder-to-shoulder united in a clearing. One had come upon an ancient book given to him by a bereft victim's family.

The woman had made a scene before them. She had shrieked out her complaint as she was carried away. "If you don't believe, call it! Tell the truth and shame the Devil! You know what happened to my child!"

Curiosity drove them to hear the woman's impassioned plea. Anger and indignation made them honor it. She needed twelve men to perform the ritual after innocent blood had spilled. Her daughter's blood had soaked the ground of a crime scene. That was a fact. But they were learned men, men of reason. This was not reasonable. And there was plenty of doubt.

What they called was something that the Devil wouldn't take and the angels had left behind. The entity was a netherling, something left over from the early days of the Titans, a justice harbinger that could do great harm or great good, both in one, based upon the whims of the caller. Alone, the entity was neutral. But once summoned, it could be lethal. That's what the book claimed.

They had all talked about it over cigars and brandy, each with their own theories. Another had it appraised at Sotheby's and found that it was the real McCoy . . . something worth millions simply based on its historic value. It had been given to them with witnesses. They could sell it and share in the profits; ownership had transferred. But before they reaped the lucrative benefits from the ill-begotten text, one scholarly member of their very small fraternity decided to have a read. Then another wanted to test the authenticity of the eerie verbiage contained therein, placing a wager on the content.

Initially it was all folly, all interesting conversation amid so much boredom and the mundane.

Twelve frustrated judges stood in a wooded clearing, clearing their consciences, clearing their dockets, clearing the way for absolute justice, having learned over time that what was legal wasn't necessarily ethical, and what was ethical wasn't necessarily legal.

But every single one of them was tired of watching the guilty walk on a technicality. Every single one of them was ready for a netherling to attend their court proceedings. Every single one of them wished they could have convicted the serial killer that snuffed out young women's lives in the most gruesome way . . . wished they could have comforted that anguished mother's wails, wished they could have put a barbarian in the chair.

Unfortunately, polite society had rules, and the shadow of a reasonable doubt hadn't been established. Wailing families, disturbed juries notwithstanding, they all had cases that haunted them, and would, till their graves. Child molesters, serial killers, domestic abuse that ended in death. Drug kingpin hits, drive-bys that took women and children along with rival gang members. Faulty evidence collection, frightened witnesses, shrewd attorneys, the lack of DNA. These old men were so tired. Were so disillusioned. It was just a parlor trick to amuse their bored lives. It couldn't really work; the true value was in the antiquity of the tomb, not any real magical powers it held. Or so they thought.

The call went unanswered and they closed the book discouraged— each never telling the others their secret hope was that what was written was true. Then they went back to their lives and their day jobs on the bench. Went back to business as usual. No justice, no peace. They cashed out and quietly sold the book to a museum, disappointed. It had all been folly.

San Francisco . . .

He had gone clear across the country to get away from the hostile community, now that the trial and allegations were over. It made sense to lie low and let things cool off for a bit. FBI would be watching; local cops were also a pain in the ass. Who cared about some drugged-out hookers anyway? They needed salvation, needed his brand of death. Each one of them was shameless in their sensuality.

Glimpsing his reflection in the mirror behind the bar shelves, he rolled his athletic shoulders and finger-combed his dark brown hair into place. He had Hollywood good looks, if he did say so himself. His idol was Ted Bundy, serial killer extraordinaire. He'd break Bundy's record before it was all over. He was only thirty-one and had a lot of living yet to do. The whores always came to him; it was easy pickings.

Every single last one of them made him wrap his hands around their pretty necks to choke the life out of them. But not before making them beg, not before torturing confessions out of them. He loved to hear them tell him all the nasty, carnal things they'd done for money while whimpering on the floor. That their families sat in court and cried made him nauseous. He brought another shot of Jack Daniels up to his lips and took a very patient sip, watching.

Why hadn't these grievers mourned the loss of their daughter's innocence? Why hadn't those drunken moms and molesting dads and concerned siblings and cousins and aunts and uncles done anything to make their prostitute daughters' lives better? Why did they think they had a right to sit up in court and seek justice through his imprisonment or lethal injection, when they had been the ones to set the wheels in motion? He just finished the job—dead woman walking. Why weren't they being held accountable for the lives they'd ruined by what they did or didn't do?

He watched another one come into the bar. Blonde, just like all the others. Dressed like a real whore. Breasts pushed up so the creamy swell of her tits spilled over the black lace edge of her bra, and he could see through her filmy red shirt. Short, tight, black leather skirt, doing fishnets in red stilettos. Mouth a perfect scarlet O when she cooed in a potential customer's ear. He'd love to see it make that shape when he was choking the shit out of her.

She had red fingernail polish, too. He liked to save the nails, especially the acrylic ones. Her eyebrows were arched delicately and also blonde. She might be a genuine one; her nipples might be pink. It was so disappointing when he found out later they weren't, were really brunettes.

As she bent over to reach for her dropped purse, his cock stirred. With the trial and the move, and having to lay low from the cops, it had been so long since he'd done it, had any cold, tight, ass. The wheels of justice ground so slowly, over a year it took. A year held without bail, no porn to tide him over. Too much crazy shit going on in the joint, but nobody insane enough to try him. Him not wanting any trouble. A year of jacking off thinking about their pale, lifeless bodies. Then, she caught his eye.

He nodded. As always the gentleman. That's how you had to be if you wanted to lull them into a false sense of security. She came over and sat beside him. For a whore, she smelled good.

"Buy you a drink?" he asked, glimpsing her from the side.

"Yeah, that can work," she said, sounding entitled. "But I sure could go for a cigarette. This smoking ban is bullshit."

He hailed the bartender, wondering if it was just idle chitchat she made with all her prospective Johns, or if she really wasn't from the area.

"I thought all Californians were health nuts?" He smiled at her while she smiled at him but adding a scowl.

"I wouldn't know. I am *so* not from here."

"Ah . . . didn't think so. What'll you have?"

"Johnny Walker, Black." She gave him a challenging look.

He nodded to the bartender calmly, and the man withdrew. This bitch was just asking for it. "So, where are you from?"

"Vegas," she said, beginning to fidget in her purse for a compact.

He looked her over, noticing how her taut little nipples pressed against her sheer blouse. "How long are you in town for?"

"Depends," she said in a matter-of-fact tone, accepting the drink and bringing it to her lips.

He watched it make her lips moisten, watched how the red lipstick stained the glass.

"You from here?" She batted her long, mascara-laden lashes at him and let her gaze take him in.

"Depends," he said with a half smile. This one liked to play. He might enjoy her for a while. Pulling out a huge wad of cash, he peeled off a C-Note to make sure she understood that being in his company could be lucrative.

"You know where I can get some cigarettes?" Her eyes went to his cash wad and then to his eyes. "Or anything else?"

"Depends." He put away his cash and went back to his drink.

She leaned in. "I can't openly solicit in here, or I'll get put out, got it? I'm new and don't have a place yet. Can't work the streets without a man, or I'll get my ass kicked over turf."

"You wanna go get those cigarettes after you finish your drink?"

"Sure." She tossed back her drink and stood.

"How much?"

She smiled. "Depends."

Normally he was cooler than this, more patient. But it had been a long time. Plus she was so eager and kept touching him in the elevator. This wasn't his normal way of doing things. He liked roadside motels, the ones where you could pull a car up to your room door. The pay by the hour places were too closed in. He was feeling claustrophobic, hadn't brought all of his tools. But maybe that was a good thing, if he changed his MO a little in a new location.

Besides, he was so hard he couldn't stand it. Her slender hand burned where she squeezed. She'd unbuttoned her blouse a little so he could see a half moon glimpse of her pink nipples. Let him kiss those creamy breasts in the elevator; let his hands glide over the high-set mounds. Let his fingers trace up her black fishnets to find her wet snatch barely concealed behind a thong. Exploring her folds as the elevator lumbered to a halt, he wondered if it was him or the promise of cash that had dampened her, or if it was just lubricant that all prostitutes probably used to make a client think he was turning them on?

The stench of urine in the hall made his eyes water. Soon she'd be cold, and he could have his way with her, as soon as the last of her life was choked away.

He opened the door with a smile and closed it behind her.

"I need to shoot up, too, Daddy," she said, unbuttoning her blouse and exposing her half-covered breasts that were almost out of the cups. She quickly unhooked the back clasps and let them bounce free.

She did have an impressive body. Really was a beautiful woman.

"I'll give you enough for that, like I promised . . . You take care of me; I'll take care of you."

She walked over to him quickly, rubbed herself along his body and began working at his buckle. The moment she freed him, she dropped to her knees.

This was the worst part, subduing his carnal nature as the victim began sucking. It felt so good, but he had to make her cold to make it right.

"Get up," he ordered through his teeth. "Get on the bed."

They liked that, whores did—liked it when you bossed them around. This one *really* liked it. She'd smiled brightly as she stood up. She was much prettier than the others, hard to think of her as a junkie. No tracks, no dark circles under her eyes. Beautiful, that's why desecrating her body in this profession, with the drugs too, was such a punishable crime. That's why he'd torture this one worse than all the others. As soon as he got the pillow case into her mouth. He had to do it quickly, though. He had to cum soon, had to get off.

"Lie down and open your legs."

She smiled wider and did what he'd asked, watching him stroke himself. This bitch seemed to be enjoying his pain. He had to stop jerking off so he could kill her.

"You are so dead," she said calmly.

"What did you say!" he shouted, unable to stop moving his hand up and down his shaft as he stared at her breasts and exposed thatch of blonde hair between her legs.

"I said, you are so dead," she whispered and rolled over on her side with her elbow bent and head resting on her palm.

Now he was pissed off. He tried to take his hand away, but couldn't. It hurt so badly he had to move it faster, up and down, trying to chase the throb.

"Why did you kill all those women?" she asked with a sad smile. "They might have been prostitutes and junkies, but at one point, they were somebody's child. It wasn't your place to do that, Bob. Really, it wasn't."

His heart was beating triple-time in his chest. He looked down and opened his mouth to scream but no sound came out. He'd rubbed the skin off his dick; blood was dripping on the floor, exposed veins and flesh and muscle was in his grip. Then came the pain so severe he dropped to his knees.

"Remember the cigarette burns?" she cooed.

An invisible force stronger than him pulled his face toward her. She was covered with burns and then just as suddenly as he'd seen the image, he felt them being inflicted on him. Still he couldn't make a sound, could only whimper in pain. From out of nowhere, she produced a cigarette case and withdrew one. She simply looked at the end of the cigarette she held, and it began to glow.

Calmly she brought a lit cigarette to her lips, holding it between her slender fingers as her crimson nails began to lengthen. She pulled a long drag off it, and her mouth made a perfect O as she exhaled a smoke ring. Every sensitive place on his body sizzled and smoldered as the stench of burning flesh filled his nostrils—but no scream was allowed to escape.

Panting from the agony, still clutching his bloody stump, he couldn't speak as she slowly sat up. Pure terror kept him staring at her. Yes, he remembered what he'd done to each girl. But who was this bitch, what was she? How did she have such power!

"Remember the cuts, all the long slices that took off fingernails and nipples and ruined gorgeous faces?"

He closed his eyes and shook his head no, tears rolling down his cheeks. A plea stabbed into his brain as he felt a cold blade against his left nipple, slicing. But when his eyes popped open, she was standing across the room next to the bed bleeding with a missing left nipple.

"Bob," she murmured, with a yellow-fanged smile, sauntering over to him and turning into the most hideous, green-skinned gargoyle-like creature he'd ever seen. Her once-perfect body was now misshapen by wings and claws and a spaded tail, her ghoulish skin marred by every wound he'd ever inflicted on a victim. His whimpers seemed to delight her.

"You made them suffer for hours, made them cry, and made them beg you. Made their families cry. I wonder how many women you went to trial for and how long each one of them took to die? Remember what I told you when you asked me how long I was in town for . . . and I said it depends?"

Sunday morning golf was a tradition among the twelve friends. Sometimes only a few of them made it, but most assuredly, there was always a game at the club to be had. Six of the twelve had made it to the green this morning. Cell phones were off. Concentration in full swing. It was their sanctuary . . . it was near the place where they'd tried their boyish prank in the clearing and failed.

But a swiftly approaching golf cart carrying a good friend at the Bureau made them all turn to stare. There was something in John's ashen complexion, something very troubled in his hazel eyes. He hardly waited for the cart to come to a stop before he jumped out and approached them, looking five ways. His dark suit was rumpled like he'd been up all night. A departure from his normal, crisp, professional look, his wheat-hued thicket of hair was unkempt, matching his five o'clock shadow at ten A.M. All the judges shared a worried glance.

"You all right, John?" Walter asked. As most senior member of the group of judges, anything that had gone awry he should have known about first. He stared at John McDevitt hard. John knew he had political aspirations, so he should have called him at home if there was a problem.

"Gentlemen," John said, glancing around the suddenly solemn expressions. "We've got a real nutcase on our hands. It seems as though there's someone going through all of your past cases . . . any ones that were . . . questionable." He raked his mass of disheveled hair with his fingers. "I don't know how to tell you gentlemen this, but anybody that was most likely guilty, and didn't get convicted, or got out early on a bullshit walk—we've got 'em in our morgues."

"What?" Jim murmured, and looked at Bill.

Brad began walking in a tight circle. "Jesus H. Christ . . . You have got to be kidding."

"I wish I were," John said, glancing around the group. "This is gonna be a problem for all of you."

"Hold it, I know you're not implicating us," Tom said, glaring at the FBI Director. "I want my attorney present."

"*Of course* we're not *blaming* you," John McDevitt said, looking confused. "What do you think we're stupid, Tom? Like twelve judges paid to put hits on their cases that didn't end in convictions? Be serious. We're pulling our hair out trying to figure out how to protect twelve U.S. Judges from some nut that has gone berserk. We came here to personally warn you, because if they've gone after your dismissed cases, or those overturned on appeals, they might just be crazy enough to come after you . . . blaming you in some way." He motioned with his chin toward agents in the distance. "We've got all sorts of psychological profilers looking at this from every angle."

Ed sent a troubled gaze around the group. "You said in your morgues, so they went after how many?"

"Fifty top profile cases in a single night. That's the thing," John said, rubbing both palms down his face. "There had to be a network of them, because these are federal cases that happened all over the country—just like the murders were just done everywhere . . . and they tortured the perpetrators just like the notes and evidence from the trials read."

"That's our entire backlog of cases that walked," Brad said, swallowing hard, his pale blue eyes alight with terror. "That many would have to be all of ours, plus Scott's, Joe's, Keith's, Arnold's, Pat's, and Michael's. Divide it among the twelve of us, and we each had *at least* three to four cases during our careers where we *knew* for a fact the defendant was guilty as sin, guilty of heinous crimes, but the law couldn't bring them to justice because of technicalities."

"That's why we're on it, your honor. We can't have vigilante militias roaming around, following high-profile cases and dispensing barbaric, medieval, torture-style justice when they don't like the outcome of a case. Next thing you know, the lawyers that defended them and maybe knew these perps were dirty, might be next on the hit list and tortured, too."

The six judges present shared a knowing, horrified glance.

"Tortured?" Bill whispered, aghast.

"That sodomy case where the nut was molesting little boys—yeah, well, he died of hemorrhaging and a prolapsed rectum. You don't wanna know what we found shoved up there. Same deal with the Robert Doogan serial killer case. They found that sonofabitch in San Francisco with his dick filleted and every wound he'd ever inflicted on the alleged victims was inflicted on him—down to exact number of cigarette burns. Now, we're trying to figure out how they all died in different cities and states at the same time on the same night without a single witness, no screams—some were even shot, but nobody heard a thing."

"Do the other justices know?" Walter Kingsdale asked in a shaky voice.

"We've been informing them one by one this morning, your honor. We'll keep you posted, and we're ordering increased security for you all until we get a break in the leads."

They watched their inside man and friend climb back into his golf cart, and they impatiently waited until he was out of earshot.

"We have to get the book back," Walter Kingsdale said flatly.

"I've heard enough. I'm a believer. The coincidences are just too . . . I don't know." Tom swallowed hard and dropped his voice to a terrified whisper. "In there it said if the netherling acquired its own book back, it would be unstoppable."

The six assembled judges nodded.

* * *

"What do you mean you sold the book to a private collector and cannot divulge who that is!" Walter Kingsdale bellowed. He stood behind his desk, his tall, imposing frame puffed up with righteous indignation as he raked his fingers through his thicket of silver-gray hair.

Eleven distraught faces stared at him in his walnut-appointed study. Decanters of brandy, bourbon, and scotch were carefully set down on polished tables. Crystal rocks glasses and brandy snifters were held midair. The room crackled with high-voltage tension as Kingsdale returned the telephone receiver to its cradle with a bang.

"Walter," Ed said quietly, his gaunt face pinched with worry. "We have to figure out how to send the entity back."

Nervous gazes ricocheted around the room.

"You don't think I know that?" Walter Kingsdale stood and paced to the window. "If what we read in the book is true, after it eats its way up the food chain and addresses injustice that anyone complicit committed, it comes for its owner, if its owner dispatched it—and they have to pass the test of purity or it will seek reparations from the owner."

"That's why it's the only demon the Devil won't take," Tom said in a trembling voice. "Lucifer will never call it, even though he benefits from the swath it cuts through humanity . . . and even though it's doing justice, its methods are so horrible, the angels don't want it. That's why it's called the netherling. A thing neither heaven nor hell wants." He wiped beads of sweat from his brow and popped an antacid before taking another sip of his drink.

"This is fucking insane!" Jim shouted, leaping to his feet. His thinning auburn and gray hair was all over his head like a mad professor's, and he lumbered back and forth, his potbellied frame huffing from the effort. "That means, if we believe this superstitious mumbo jumbo, that every lawyer involved in those dismissed capital cases who knew their client was guilty, will be murdered? Is that what you're saying? Then it comes for us?"

"I want out," Bill said quietly as he blinked nervously behind thick, Ben Franklin-style glasses. His birdlike features drew to a severe point at his chin and nose, and he ran his fingers though his trimmed, sandy-gray hair while rocking where he sat. "I just want out, no matter what it costs."

"I read the book," Tom said, his hands and thick jowls shaking as he poured another Bourbon. "I read it cover to cover when none of the rest of you believed. It draws you in, and that's exactly what it said. Anyone complicit would be their attorneys, accomplices the

DAs' offices couldn't catch—others. The netherling can only be sent back by the primary caller once it's spilled blood, and it demands that person's soul to be given over to Lucifer, if they want to spare themselves the agony of suffering the same fate they'd visited on others. That's the only way. Somebody in this group has to make a pact with the Devil to make this creature go back into hiatus." Tom looked at Walter Kingsdale. "Or else it will keep rampaging until everyone that helped the people we called it up to serve justice against is dead. Then, it comes for the callers. If we don't pass muster—"

"This is complete superstition and bullshit, Thomas. I'll get the book back," Walter snapped, his nerves wire taut. "We'll read what it fucking says, and we'll close whatever dark portal we possibly opened while we were drunk. I for one refuse to be held accountable for the deaths of mobsters and serial killers and drug dealers or goddamned child molesters. They deserved what they got. Let them burn in hell. Didn't we all say that that night? Didn't we all wish we weren't tied to laws and evidence, and could go back to the old days of justice when a man swung at the end of a rope if he did heinous crimes? Didn't we talk about the fact that the Wild West was probably more civilized than putting axe murderers and killers in a facility supported by our tax dollars, with three hots and a cot? We're clean!"

"But what was that stuff you said in the beginning, Walter . . . those words in another language you read?" Tom asked quietly, panic emblazoned in his eyes. "What if that was some sort of pact with Sat—"

"Don't even say it!" Walter shouted. "We were all drunk. None of this is even real. All of this is hypothetical. We don't even know if . . . if—what are we doing here?"

Eleven justices looked at him and then looked away, sending their gazes to the floor. Some had been mute the entire evening. No one knew what to do, no one wanted to take a stand. This had gone too far.

"Well, be that as it may, we knew the bastards we called this thing up to consume were guilty, then," Brad finally said, sloshing his drink. He lifted his aristocratic chin and smoothed his salt and pepper hair back with an athletic palm. His pale blue eyes held no emotion. "Why would it come for us, assuming there's a so-called *it*? You worry too much. This is all hypothetical, like Walter said. Who cares if this entity goes after the dirty counselors, too? As long as our noses are clean, who gives a shit?"

"You don't understand! The text was clear!" Tom shouted, hoisting his hefty frame to his feet. "I've been on the bench for over thirty years. How many men might I have put away . . . maybe knowing they were innocent but the preponderance of evidence—"

Horrified glances went around the room.

"Think about it," Tom said, breathing hard. Tears glittered in his aging, blue eyes. "This thing rights *any* wrong in your life, if you were a caller. *Any wrong.* So sending an innocent man to prison for years is wrong, if looked at in purely black and white terms. That's just one thing . . . what if you caused a suicide, a shooting by your actions, I don't even know all what I might have done wrong. But I know I'm not perfect. I just hope God can forgive me."

"We can't be blamed for the errors made in youth, in climbing career ladders," Ed said quickly, cutting off Tom's outburst. Beads of nervous perspiration had formed on the gleaming horseshoe of his bald head and wisps of brown hair stuck matted to his scalp. "We'd all die." He looked around. "I was in the South during Civil Rights." Ed stood and went to the window. "There was a kid, young fellow no more than eighteen or twenty . . . but the pressures of that day, things were so volatile—I knew in my soul the evidence against him had been trumped up by the local police . . . but . . ." He closed his eyes and took a sip of his drink. "He hung himself in his cell after his first week in the penitentiary. They'd gang-raped him. His mother was a church woman and told me God knows all."

"All right, gentlemen. Let's gather our wits and pull ourselves together," Walter commanded. "We got drunk and were playing with this bullshit like an Ouija board, and I for one refuse to believe that anything supernatural has come to life. I'd rather think it's a vigilante group, a terrorist cell, and I know McDevitt is on it."

"Tom, what was the spell to send it back?" Jim said, trembling so badly now that he held his glass with both hands.

Tom swallowed hard. "I don't remember all of it . . . I just know that you have to call Satan and make a deal with the Devil. Then the thing goes back into its book . . . kinda like an insane genie going back into its bottle."

NATIONAL NEWS REPORT . . .

The string of bizarre murders seems to be taking on a new dimension. A rash of attorneys' deaths is sweeping the nation. The connection is all the same; the first wave of victims were their clients.

Walter Kingsdale clicked off the television, glad that his wife had gone to stay with her brother while the house was being guarded by federal agents. He tried the museum again, speaking to the acquiring curator, his tone more malleable. He had to get the book. He'd sent too many urban thugs to jail, allowing shaky, illegally obtained evidence to wipe the streets clean of the scourge he detested most. They'd called him the hanging judge, and he had a different brand of justice for those who came into his court from certain sectors of society. Like breeding rats, that's how he'd thought of them.

Until now, he hadn't cared what became of their lives, what horrors they'd faced in prison—they'd been illegitimate bastards born of welfare mothers and drug-dependent fathers, and as far as he was concerned, getting rid of them before they'd done anything serious was preventive medicine the urban environs required, like a preemptive strike. Now the netherling would hunt him down, and he didn't even know whatever became of those young men.

"Please," he murmured, once he and the curator had dispensed with formalities. "We think this book could be a part of a very sensitive case, and we need the new owner to at least meet with me—as lead justice, to discuss how it's being used in capital offenses. The identity of the new owner, as well as his investment, will be thoroughly protected, as we know he is not directly involved."

"This is so highly irregular, Judge Kingsdale, and the new owner is a heavy contributor to our antiquities department . . . but given the issues at hand, I will ask him to contact you. That's the best I can do."

Walter Kingsdale closed his eyes and nodded. "Thank you."

WASHINGTON, DC NIGHTLY NEWS . . .

Justice Edgar G. Hunt was found dead in his Alabama summer family home in what appears to be a bizarre, sexually-inspired suicide. The apparent victim of a vicious, repeat sodomy attack, the kidnapped, seventy-three-year-old justice took his own life by hanging himself by a bedroom sheet from a Waterford crystal chandelier. FBI—

Walter Kingsdale hit the remote to click the power off, turned away from the large, flat screen HDTV that graced his office, leaned over the side of his polished mahogany desk, and vomited on the Turkish rug. Dabbing beads of perspiration from his forehead, he clung to the edge of his desk and then pushed himself up with trembling arms.

"Justice is brutal, at times," a deep, baritone voice said from across the room. "Unsettling."

The judge's head jerked up to stare into the shadows where a pair of high, winged-back leather chairs faced the fireplace.

"Who are you, and how did you get in here?" Walter gasped, wiping his mouth with the crisp sleeve of his starched, button-down Oxford shirt.

The figure moved calmly, standing from the chair to walk toward Walter's desk. Under the muted chandelier light, his coal-hued eyes glittered with predatory intensity and amusement, and his elegant style of dress would peg him as one of the wealthiest young attorneys on the circuit. But his cool demeanor was also that of an assassin.

"I haven't seen you in my courtroom before. How did you get past all the security out there to pitch me?" Embarrassed by his bodily fluids left on the rug, the justice stepped around the mess and went to his bar. "I don't need another attorney, and there are ten FBI agents crawling all over the premises."

"I know. I saw them," the unidentified man said. "I may be new to your court, but I'm not new to systems of justice . . . and you are indeed correct. I'd love the chance to pitch you."

Walter Kingsdale poured himself a Scotch. "I'm in no mood. If you want something, you'll have to see me—"

"I want to negotiate with you, kind sir."

Walter took a liberal sip of liquor. "I just lost one of my best friends. If you need a political fav—"

"I'm the new owner of the book." The dark stranger smiled and cocked his head to the side. "Might we share a drink together?"

Slowly the stranger's eyes changed, the pupils becoming slits within amber irises. Walter clutched his chest, horror trapped in his throat, trapped in the silent scream. It felt like his heart was twisting, ripping from the anchors of tissue holding it beneath his breastbone, lungs scorched by his last breath. His ears were ringing with instantly elevated blood pressure; the room became blurry as he weaved a bit, but then caught himself against the edge of the bar. The thing before him smiled.

"I want a chance to negotiate," Walter rasped, sweating.

The entity smoothed its lapels on its designer suit and nodded. "So be it."

Eerie calm befell Walter's demeanor. The netherling tilted its head. This was intriguing.

The justice set his drink down very carefully, his voice catching in his throat as he dabbed away perspiration. "Name your poison."

The stranger inhabiting his study laughed. "I like your style. Bourbon, neat."

The justice complied and handed off the drink, but strangely tasted bourbon scorch his throat as he watched the unidentified man that he knew was the netherling take a sip of it. For a second, everything went black. Like a slow blink. Then everything was so clear.

"What do you want?" Walter whispered.

The stranger looked at him. "The same thing you want—justice."

Walter simply stared at the man.

"I cannot fully use the book without a dedicated caller," the stranger said with a casual sip of his drink. "For years I have been looking for one that could call forth the power and whom could feed the needs therein."

"I do not understand," Walter rasped. "Why not give it to Satan, then?"

The stranger chuckled and leaned forward, his lethal gaze holding the justice's. "He doesn't have a soul," he whispered. "The feeding would be so hollow. That is reason enough. But perish the thought that Lucifer brings out the netherling. If it turned on him, the netherling would be trapped for an eternity feeding off the trail the Devil had left, and none of the sins created by mankind alone would be addressed . . ." He shook his head. "Too much baggage, bad karma. No, no, no, no, no. That is why it's the book that, as they say, the Devil won't take and angels don't want."

With a droll smile, he shrugged. "Angels fear it, because even though they are of pure intent and have no past misdeeds, they believe justice falls only under the purview of One I never name . . . they don't want the responsibility—alas, when this is such an awesome tool." His smile deepened as he looked at Walter without blinking. "And you, my friend, have used the tool very, very well. I couldn't be more pleased. I just wish you were . . ."

Suddenly the stranger cocked his head to the side and narrowed his gaze. "Clean? Totally clean, without a shred of significant sin?"

The two stared at each other for a moment. Again, Walter felt a strange out-of- body sensation, as though watching himself from a very remote place in his mind.

"Who are you?" Walter croaked, his knuckles turning white as he gripped the edge of his desk to keep from falling when his knees buckled.

"I told you, I'm the book's owner. I acquired it for quite a hefty sum from the museum," the stranger said, unfazed. "You were burdened, asked to speak with me. How could I ignore such a . . . vulnerable plea?" From beneath his suit jacket, the stranger extracted a large book that could not have been hidden there. "Call the power often."

"We have to send the netherling back," Walter said, his voice dissolving into a plea. He watched the book slide across the table toward him, its power arching out to make his fingertips tingle.

"I see no reason to do that. It is serving justice in a most blind way, cutting a swath through the country, cleansing the impurities of society without mercy." The stranger leaned in. "Here's another reason why the angels loath this book. It and the entity it contains were created well before the concept of salvation came about. It is very Old Testament in its pursuit. That's one of the things I find so enchanting about it, but let me not bore you with my philosophical rhetoric. I could go on and on *forever.*"

"Sir, if you just tell me your name, we'll provide you with a check for the trouble . . . if we might borrow it for one evening and then we'd even return it to you."

"Oh, I would insist on your returning it to me," the stranger said. "I merely hold it until the right person comes along that *really* needs it and will use it to the fullest. It is always their choice whether or not to court the consequences. That's what I so love about the book."

Walter Kingsdale thrust his hand in a drawer, his eyes never leaving the stranger's dark gaze and withdrew a checkbook quickly, snatching a Mont Blanc pen from his desk blotter. "Your name, sir?" he said quickly, and then waited, poised, ready to write.

The stranger smiled. "Nether Ling . . . but I can cash it under Satan's account, using many other nom de plums." He laughed as the wide-eyed justice began to back up. "Oh, did I mention that I need your soul jotted down in the memo section of the instrument, too?"

Walter quickly wrote out the instrument and shoved it across the desk, and then clutched the book. He stood very still watching the smile slowly fade from the stranger's handsome face as he stared at the check. Human skin pulled back from bared fangs and normal flesh tone gave way to hideous green. The netherling's serpent-like eyes glowed with rage as wings and a spaded tail ripped through the designer suit.

"You tricked me!" it screeched, flinging the check back onto the desk. It stabbed a claw into the signature line of the check, goring the desk. "*Lucifer.* You have to give me back what is mine, because this was not a clean and just trade!"

"As always." The body of the justice opened the book calmly, flipping to the right page. "Walter died right before your eyes of a heart attack. There was no sin in his empty shell while I manipulated it. Oh, the instrument is good, too—I can cover the amount on the check, and you and I both know I'm not about to allow you to rid the planet of all erring humans. *That* would not serve my purposes at all. The trade stands in supernatural law." He leaned in toward the netherling with a smirk. "But you've been such a bad little demon. So hard to find, so hard to contain." Satan chuckled making a tsking sound while he crooked his finger, causing the netherling to twist and squeal as it began to turn into a sulfuric plume of smoke.

He watched the funnel cloud enter the book and finally slam itself shut. Disgusted, he wiped his hands down the front of Walter's borrowed body and then stepped out of it, allowing it to crumple to the floor in a heap. He looked back once and collected the book in his massive talons. "Some crap even I won't take."

THE Y INCISION
A CAL MCDONALD CRIME STORY

STEVE NILES

HENDRICKS WAS BLEEDING to death by the time I reached him near the intersection of sewer tunnels. He'd had his side ripped out like a bite out of a melon. His upper and lower intestines were splashed on the cement like vomited Udon noodles.

He didn't have long.

The *thing* had gotten to him.

I was on my own, in the sewers, against one of the freakiest things I'd ever encountered, and all I had was a Glock with a single full cartridge and a shotgun with two shells.

But as usual, I'm getting ahead of myself. I suppose I should start from the beginning . . .

I knew Henry Thicke was trouble, but I could never pin anything on him, and in all honesty, he'd never done anything to me. I could just sense he was scum. I could smell dead bodies on him. Granted he owned and ran a funeral home, but this was different. This guy reeked of freak.

Henry was from a tenth-generation funeral home business family. He was human, but I liked to imagine his genes were saturated with formaldehyde because he lived and loved his job. So much so he creeped out the ghouls and believe me people, it takes a lot to freak out the undead.

He was tall, at least six-six or taller and thin as a fucking bone. He had this short greasy, slicked hair, gaunt, white face and lips as thin as they were colorless. And when he spread those lips for a rare smile he had these thick gums and two perfect rows of Chicklet teeth.

The last year for me had been one of the worst on record. Two close friends died. One was a cop. Her name was Brueger. She helped me out from time to time, and I helped her out. I let her get too close, and she wound up being the target of one of my enemies, Dr. Polynice. He tortured her and shredded her body with a remote control device attached to his heart.

It was triggered when I blew his rotten brains out.

The other was my girl, Sabrina. She meant a lot to me. Fuck, I'll say it: I loved her, but she had enough sense to walk away after what happened to Brueger. But Sabrina couldn't stay away. She came back and fell victim to a Euro-trash vampire who claimed to be the original Nosferatu. I offed him, but not before he infected Sabrina.

Last time I saw her she was flying away with fangs as long as a walrus.

Did I mention Brueger was a cop? Sure I did, but did I mention she was married to a hotshot city councilman? You can imagine he wasn't too thrilled with me, and he let me know it.

Not only did he beat me within an inch of my suck-ass life, but he also used his contacts to have me cut off from the LAPD, and made me a wanted man while he was at it. He drummed up some fake drug charges and had my place ransacked. They found a small pharmacy of illegal painkillers and other assorted items I like to use to take the edge off.

If you're keeping score, that's two dead friends, one major enemy, and a warrant out for my arrest. And let's not forget homeless. I'd been on the run for a month. Luckily (or unluckily) the Ghouls of Los Angeles found me places to stay.

Oh yeah, my name is Cal McDonald. I'm a private detective currently working out of the subbasement of an abandoned airport in Burbank.

When I got the call from Henry Thicke I was wallowing in self-pity. I'd polished off a bottle of Jim Beam, two bottles of Listerine, some Robitussin, and a package of Excedrin PM. I shoplifted all of it. I had no cash so I couldn't afford any of the real stuff.

I was feeling pretty shitty; loopy and shitty. I had a mattress in the corner surrounded by boxes of files I lifted from my office before the cops took it apart.

It was my little, shitty, self-pity fort.

I stayed in there for a week, drinking, smoking, and ingesting anything I could get my hands on or steal. I asked Mo'Lock to score me some hard stuff. He refused. Cheap bastard. I knew he had cash. If my limbs didn't feel like melted rubber, I would have mugged him.

Who am I kidding? That fucking ghoul was the closest thing I'd ever had to a best friend and a partner. He'd stuck with me through thick and thin and saved my ass on more than one occasion.

It was Mo'Lock who handed me the cell phone.

I pressed it to my face and made a sound that somewhat resembled a greeting.

It was Henry Thicke, the creepy mortician.

"Is this Cal McDonald?"

"Yesh." My tongue felt like a blowfish in my mouth.

"This is Henry Thicke."

He sounded nervous. Even in my state I could hear the quiver in his voice.

"Wuz the ploblem?"

I could barely string a sentence together.

I looked at Mo'Lock. The ghoul shook his head and turned away. I knew him well enough to know he was up to something. With his back to me he took something out of his pockets. I heard a rattle sound and to an old junkie like me that was music. That was the sound of pills in a bottle.

I told the mortician to hold for a second, except it came out more like "Hol on fr a specont."

Mo'Lock begrudgingly opened his hand. There were five black pills, speed. Just the thing I needed to get my shit together. During the best of times taking drugs was like one big chemistry set with my body being the test tube. You had to find just the right blend or the test tube would blow up in your face.

I downed the pills dry and then chased them with some water. Maybe it was my imagination, but I swear I could feel the amphetamine coursing through my blood.

I waited another minute and then went back to the phone.

Henry Thicke wanted me to come down and check out his mortuary. He'd tried calling the police, but they weren't any help which was no big fucking shock. If anything even slightly out of the ordinary was going down, cops were useless. That's why people call me.

I asked Thicke for some details, but he insisted that I come see for myself. Luckily his place was in Burbank, on Victory Boulevard about three-four miles from where I was squatting with the undead.

By the time I hung up the phone the speed had taken over all of the over-the-counter crap. I was all tingly, my head itched, and my pits were sweating like a drippy faucet.

I was ready for action.

I told Thicke I'd be over within the hour. I had a errand I wanted to run first.

"Please hurry, Mr. McDonald."

"I'll be there as soon as I can."

When I hung up the phone Mo'Lock was staring at me. Ever since all the shit went down, the big dead freak had been treating me like his kid more than a partner, and it was starting to get fucking annoying.

"Was that a job?" he asked.

I nodded. "Yeah, Henry Thicke says something's up over at his mortuary."

The ghoul flinched. I told you they were freaked out by Thicke.

The ghoul composed himself. "What was the errand you spoke of?"

That tore it. I don't mind somebody caring for me. Hell, it was nice after three decades plus to have someone(even if he was dead) give a shit about my well-being, but the ghoul was pushing his fucking luck.

I climbed out of my mattress fort and stood in front of the ghoul. He had about a foot on me but I wasn't scared of him.

Besides I was pretty sure he'd never hurt me, and trust me, you don't ever want to be on the receiving end of an angry ghoul. They can dismantle a human like a Marine does a rifle and in about half the time.

I was feeling pretty good. The speed finally made its way around to my eyes and teeth. My eyes were wide, and my teeth throbbed.

I stuck my finger in the ghoul's gray-toned face. "I'm starting to get pretty sick of you playing nursemaid with me, Mo. What's say we get back to being partners, and I'll take care of myself."

The ghoul stared down at my finger, then slowly up to my eyes. "I thought you said we weren't partners."

He was fucking with me. "I'm just saying I'd rather have a partner than a babysitter. I can take care of myself. I've been abusing myself for a long time. I know what I'm doing."

"So the errand is for drugs?"

"Yeah . . . and I need to borrow some cash."

The ghoul turned his head. He didn't have a whole hell of a lot of expressions so it was difficult to gauge what he was thinking.

Then he turned back to me and held out a stack of twenties. "No hard stuff." He said.

I took the bills and shook my head. I knew what he meant. No needles. Nothing that made me into a zombie. Nothing that made me dead. I was cool with that. I'd avoided shooting for years with only one relapse. I pretty much stuck to pills and smoke.

"Thanks, Mo'Lock."

The ghoul just nodded.

I went to stick the bills in my pants and missed. I wasn't wearing pants. I was naked from the waist down.

"Goddammit."

I shot a look at the ghoul, and luckily for him he wasn't laughing or smiling. Not that I could tell if he was, but I would have busted a slug in his belly if he was. Unfortunately, my Glock was holstered to the belt on my pants.

I grabbed my pants, pulled them on, and made sure the weapon was loaded. Thicke didn't say what was up, but that quiver in his voice told me loads. As an extra precaution I grabbed my sawed-off shotgun which tucked into a strap inside my jacket.

When I was ready to go, I noticed Mo'Lock wasn't following.

"You coming?"

"Am I needed?"

I smiled. "It's Henry Thicke, isn't it?"

The ghoul lowered his head. "It is hard to be around someone who smells of the recent dead."

"Why the hell would that bother you?" I asked. "You're already dead."

Hidden in the shadows of the gray cement basement, the ghoul glanced up, his eyes hidden in pits of darkness. "I am undead," the ghoul paused and sighed. "I do not like being around that which I almost was, let alone around someone like Henry Thicke, who revels in the dead."

I didn't really know what the ghoul was talking about. As a team we'd been around dead bodies plenty of times. I assumed it had more to do with the mortician than anything. Like I said, he creeped the ghouls out so I let it lie.

By the time I was dressed and armed, despite not having showered in over a week, I was feeling pretty good. Every inch of my body tingled.

Upstairs I kept the car, my '73 Nova, parked inside one of the old hangars. I hadn't started her up for as long as I hadn't showered, but two turns of the key in the ignition and the powerful V8 roared to life and spit out a single plume of smoke, like a smoker clearing his devastated lungs.

First I'd swing by a dealer I knew in Burbank and grab some happy pills and smoke, then to Thicke's Mortuary to see what the trouble was.

As I'd promised, I arrived at the mortician's place in under an hour. I had a pocket full of pills, uppers and painkillers, and some weed. Later I'd do a little chemistry experiment and find the right balance. At the moment, the speed was doing a fine job.

I parked the Nova around back where Thicke had his hearse backed against a double steel door. I guessed he'd been loading new arrivals, and even from outside with a strong late December wind blowing, I could smell the stench of formaldehyde.

I walked around the front entrance, which was set up like the front of a friendly old house. I assumed this was to put customers at ease.

I rang the bell and waited. Rang it again and waited some more. Then I saw the sign that said to enter and wait in the front waiting area. I looked around, hoping nobody had seen me. It was one of those moments. I felt like an ass, not unlike standing in front of the ghoul with my beans and frank hanging in the wind.

The air was sharp inside, an eye-stinging combo of formaldehyde and Lysol, and the same homey masquerade showed in the décor. The front was set up like my grandma's living room, except anyone with an eye could glance up and see the next room over was a showroom for caskets and other funeral minutia.

On the wall of the inside foyer was another bell, and mounted above in the corner was a small security camera. I pressed the bell around a dozen times to make sure this time. Within seconds I heard movement beneath my feet, in the basement of the mortuary where I assume all of the embalming and other unpleasantness was done. First I heard doors open and close, and then the sound of heavy footsteps coming upstairs toward me.

To my surprise, a panel of the wall clicked and opened; a hidden door, and then Henry Thicke appeared. He was even lankier and creepier than I remembered. He made Mo'Lock look like a fucking Teddy Bear.

"Mr. McDonald," he said with surprising enthusiasm. "I'm so glad you responded to my call."

On second evaluation I discarded the enthusiasm for desperation. He was happy to see me all right, but it was because something had him scared. He was trying to hide it, but if there was one emotion I knew and could spot, it was fear.

"What can I do for you, Thicke?" I muttered. "On the phone you said it was important."

Thicke came toward me and extended his hand. I glanced down to make sure he didn't have blood or some other bodily funk on it, then shook it.

"It's very important . . ." he hesitated choosing his words carefully, "and extremely disturbing. You were the first person I thought to call."

"Gee, thanks."

My whole body was tingly, and my head itched. I wanted to get on with it and told Thicke just that.

"Of course. Please come downstairs with me."

I was afraid of that.

Thicke pushed the wall panel; it clicked and opened again. I wanted to make a crack about the door, but Thicke wasn't a guy I wanted to make small talk with let alone take jabs at. I wouldn't want him to think we were buddies. Mo'Lock was right. The guy reeked of creepy.

I followed him downstairs. At the bottom was a large cement walled room, not unlike the basement I was currently hiding out in, except this room was filled with two embalming tables, a bunch of cabinets with jars of god-knows-what, and along one wall about six of those corpse filing cabinets. You don't usually see those in commercial mortuaries, usually just city morgues.

"What's with the body cabinets, Thicke?" I said, "You saving bodies for a rainy day?"

He laughed, and I got a glimpse at those nasty little teeth. "No, no. I perform services for homeless persons—John Does—and I have to wait 30 days until the bodies are free to be buried or cremated. I had those installed for extra storage."

"Amazing what you can get at Ikea," I said.

I regretted it immediately. Thicke laughed so hard I thought those teeth would shoot across the room and attack me.

I scanned the room. One table was empty but still needed cleaning. There was diluted blood in the drain grooves. On the floor between the two tables was a drainpipe the size of a manhole, where everything was washed down.

There was a lot of blood clotted around the drain and what might have been small bits of flesh.

I took Thicke for a lot of things; one of them wasn't being a slob.

On the other table was a corpse being prepped up for embalming. It was an old woman, in her late eighties if I had to guess. She was completely naked and next to her body was a wash pan filled with water and a large sponge. Thicke must have been washing her down when I rang.

Then I noticed the blood around the drain wasn't entirely coming from either of the two embalming tables. There wasn't much, just a pinkish wash, but some of it appeared to have flowed from those body cabinets in the wall.

By then the whole place was making me nauseous. The smell of the bodies and the chemicals and the fact that I was running on amphetamines made for a nasty combination. If we didn't get on with it, I'd puke for sure.

"So why'd you call me down here?"

Thicke gathered himself and nodded like a nervous pigeon. "Yes . . . well . . ." he started then wiggled his skeletal fingers at the cabinets in the wall. "Perhaps it's best if I just show you."

He walked slowly toward the wall and turned to me. He was nervous, like a guy who had done something wrong once and felt guilty about everything ever since. I knew the type. It meant they were capable of doing more bad shit if they were given the chance.

I followed about halfway to the wall and stopped as Thicke reached for the handle of the first drawer.

"I'd had a couple bodies go missing," he said. "I reported those to the police, but when I found this I thought I'd better call you."

The handle popped and clicked, and then Thicke opened the square steel door. Inside all I could see was darkness and the bottoms of two pale, yellowish feet.

Then Thicke pulled the slide tray out, and I got a good look at the body.

"This is what I found this morning." He finished and stepped back to let me take it in.

The body was a black male. He looked to have been around seventy years old, with thinning gray hair and a matching white beard. He was thin as a rail but with a huge bloated belly.

Problem was, most of the left side his bloated belly was gone now. From below his left nipple to just above the pelvis the flesh had been torn away violently and sloppily, like someone or something had dug it out with a dull fork. A good twelve-inch section of skin was completely gone, and whatever organs had been inside were also missing.

I could see veins and arteries and even a section of his upper intestines lying there like discarded tubing. Not severed or even chewed through, they looked like they had been yanked and pulled until they snapped and tore.

I looked at Thicke. He had backed away and was standing in a section of gray wall between two glass cabinets. He was waiting for a reaction from me.

"How many bodies went missing before this started happening?" I asked. I gave him no reaction besides the query.

He stammered a little bit. "Two or three."

I raised an eyebrow. "Are you saying you're not sure how many corpses disappeared?"

Thicke's mouth was dry. His lips stuck and smacked when he spoke. "No, sorry. It was three," he said. "I'm sorry. All of this is a little . . . disturbing to me."

"Yeah, I bet." I gave Thicke a good long stare. "All three John Does?"

"Yes. Yes, they were."

I leaned in close and gave the wounds a better inspection. The tears were definitely not done with any kind of knife or surgical instrument, and I'd dealt with flesh-eaters before so I could see that the jagged grooves weren't made by human teeth, or even animal for that matter.

The fork image stuck in my head. The skin was ripped away by something repeatedly scraping until it gave way. They might have been made by some sort of claws or even human nails, but my gut and brain told me it was too sloppy even for that.

Thicke remained in his cubby hole between the cabinets. He was watching me very carefully. I could feel his eyes on the back of my head.

"Is this the only one?"

Thicke shook his head slowly.

He was getting his story mixed up, and I was starting to get pissed.

"Where are the others then?" I asked.

I glanced at the mortician, and he motioned his head toward the other body files.

I walked around the one already laid out and grabbed the handle of the neighboring storage unit. It clicked and popped and opened as the other had. Again I was greeted with feet until I pulled the tray out and saw another body, a white male, with his entire midsection shredded away and emptied.

"You found both of these this morning?" I asked.

Thicke nodded and added, "And two more in the two shelves above."

"Christ."

I opened the other two and sure enough, except for being different bodies, they had the same problem: no flesh around the midsection and no internal organs.

I slammed the drawers shut. I'd seen enough.

"What did the cops do when you called about the missing bodies?"

Henry Thicke stayed where he was, between the two glass front cabinets against the wall. "A detective came by," he stammered. "He took a report and that was that."

"The detective leave a card?"

Thicke fumbled for his wallet, flipped it open, and retrieved a card. He didn't give it to me. He just read the name. "He was a Detective Nathan Hendricks."

I laughed. I knew Hendricks. He was a casebook bad cop, always on the take, big drinker; rumor had it he had some bouts with drugs as well. If he wasn't such a scumbag, he might have been my best friend.

But the thing was, with me on the outs with the LAPD, Hendricks was probably the one cop who wouldn't rat me out. I wasn't sure this was my kind of case, and I might want to pawn it off. A bunch of mutilated dead bodies are pretty weird, but not my kind of weird.

I dialed Hendricks's precinct and asked the desk sergeant to get him on the line. When he asked who was calling, I said Al Capone, and the dink didn't even seem to notice I was pulling his leg. He just asked me to hold while he transferred me.

Thicke remained in the same spot. Behind him was one of those huge floor-to-ceiling diagrams of the human body with all of the organs showing.

He noticed me watching and made an attempt at eye contact, but then something above and behind me distracted him. I turned to see myself and saw the monitor that went with the security camera up front.

On the screen I saw three people, a black woman along with a younger male and female, also black.

I shot a look back at Hendricks. He looked nervous, more than before. Now he had little beads of sweat sliding from his hairline.

It didn't take a detective to figure that was the family of the first shredded corpse. Hendricks's reaction confirmed it.

"Oh dear." He said and finally moved from his spot. "I'd better go up."

I gestured to the phone at my ear. "I'll wait here."

Thickc hesitated. He didn't want me down in his playroom alone, but I wasn't budging, and he had customers waiting, so he relented and went up the stairs, leaving me leaning against the table with the old lady.

Finally somebody picked up on the other end.

"Detective Hendricks."

"Hendricks," I said, "It's Cal McDonald."

There was a long pause. A second longer, and I might have hung up. Then he came back, whispering this time.

"You're pretty popular these days. You don't need me to tell you every cop on the street is looking for you."

"It's bullshit," I coughed. "The Councilman trumped up those charges. I'll deal with it later. Right now I'm on a case and your name came up."

That got his attention. "Yeah? What case is that?"

"I'm down at Henry Thicke's Mortuary."

Hendricks sounded disappointed. "This about that missing body? I told that creepy old coot to cool his heels while I filed the report."

"How many bodies he tell you about?"

"How many? Just the one," Hendricks said, speaking louder. "There more?"

I glanced up at the monitor and saw Thicke in the receiving area doing his best to comfort the family. They probably wanted to see their loved one's body. I was half-tempted to show them.

"Get this," I said. "When I asked him how many he said two OR three."

Hendricks laughed on the other end. "What's he up to? You think he's banging the merchandise?"

I paused and looked at the phone. "Okay, first of all, *gross*. Second, how would that make them go missing?"

"I dunno."

Sick fuck. I wished I hadn't called him, but I had him on the line, and the more I thought about it, the more this seemed like a normal, albeit strange case.

That's when I glanced down at the drain between the two

embalming tables. There was all sorts of debris aside from the blood on and around it, but just around the edge it was clean. I gave the grate a shove with the tip of my boot, and it moved.

The drain grate wasn't sealed, and it looked like it had been moved recently.

"You need anything else, McDonald?"

I forgot I was on the phone. "Yeah, sorry, Hendricks," I said. "Listen, how about coming down here? You should see what else Thicke has down in his embalming room. This is probably more up your alley than mine anyway."

"What? No ghosts or witches haunting the place?"

I flipped off the phone.

"You wanna help or what?"

He didn't hesitate. "What's in it for me?" he said in true scumbag form.

I had a couple hundred left from what the ghoul gave me for drugs. I figured it'd be worth it if I could pawn this off on the cops. Besides, the ghoul had plenty more cash where that came from.

"I got a hundred."

There was a half-beat pause, then, "Sure. I'll be down there in fifteen."

As soon as Henry Thicke finished with the family and came back downstairs, I was pointing at the drain in the floor.

"Where's this drain go?"

I either caught him off guard, or he was stalling. He hemmed and hawed for a few then muttered, "To the sewer," he stuttered. "But that's just for hosing the floor. Blood drained for embalming goes to a septic tank that is drained and disposed of legally and properly."

I held up my hand. "Okay. Christ. I just wondered about the drain." I said. "It looks like it's been opened recently."

This is where Thicke blew it. He tried to be too casual, too cavalier, and all it told me was that he was hiding something from me.

"Hmmm," he said. "No I don't believe I've opened it lately."

I stuck out my foot and jammed the heel of my boot down on the side of the drain grill, and it kicked up and clanked back into place ever so slightly. It was heavy, but definitely not secured.

"Looks loose to me," I said, glaring at him.

The mortician moved passed me and again placed himself in front of the anatomy poster between the cabinets. The first time I thought he was just scared. Now I was thinking there was more significance to the location, especially after seeing his fondness for hidden doors.

I pulled out my gun and lowered it on Henry Thicke.

"What are you hiding?" I asked.

Thicke began to sweat like a pig. He raised his hands, not over his head, but just enough to keep them in plain sight. "N . . . nothing." he said. "Please Mr. McDonald, I can explain."

I wasn't interested in explanations. I wanted answers, and obviously the only way I'd get any was to get them myself.

"Step away from the wall."

I guided him with my gun. He did what he was told. The lanky mortician vacated the space between the two glass cabinets.

Keeping an eye on Thicke, I edged to the wall, and with my free hand I gave the anatomy poster a push. It gave, followed by a click and a pop, and the hidden door opened.

I glared at Thicke.

He gave me a weasel smile.

It's happened before, and it happened to be the one thing that pisses me off more than just about anything else: people trying to use me to clean up their own messes. I wasn't exactly sure what Thicke's mess was yet, but with the missing and gutted corpses I guessed it wouldn't be pretty.

I gave him one more chance to come clean. "What's in here?" I asked, gesturing to the partially opened hidden door.

"J . . . just my private workroom."

I shook my head, then walked right over to him and cracked him across the face with my gun. He yelped and went down like a bag of bones and began whimpering on the floor. I was about to give him a boot in the head when I heard another gun click behind me.

It was Hendricks. All three hundred pounds of him. His hair was greasy and combed over a lopsided bald patch on the side of his head. His face was pockmarked, and his eyebrows were one stretch of thick black hair across his clammy forehead. His suit was a rumpled mess of mustard polyester.

"Put down the gun, Hendricks." I said. "I think my client here is shaping up to be more of a suspect."

Hendricks kept the gun on me as he moved into the room. "You still got my cash?"

"Yes."

Hendricks put away the weapon. He had all the morals of a scorpion.

I told him to handcuff the mortician to one of the embalming tables, the empty one, not the one with the old broad on it. Once he was done with that I told him to check out the bodies in the storage units.

Whether it was because he was a seasoned cop or he just didn't give a shit, Hendricks didn't so much as flinch when he saw the corpses with their guts ripped out. He didn't react at all.

But he did have a response. After he looked at the last body he closed the drawer, turned and kicked Thicke in the kidneys.

By that point I'd opened the hidden door and was peering down a short cement hall, no more than a yard or two. I headed inside. Hendricks was on my heels.

The hall led to a small box of a room, but it was too dark to see anything. I fumbled for a light switch and came up empty. Then a string brushed my face. I grabbed it and gave it a tug.

"Christ." Hendricks said as the bulb flickered to life.

The hidden room was a private workroom all right, but the work being done in here was anything but normal mortuary services.

There was an operating table so stained with blood you could hardly tell what the original color was. And not just blood. There was debris, chunks and slices of tissue dried, hardened, and stuck to the table. I glanced down and saw there was no drain like in the main room.

Next to the table was another smaller table with piles of surgical tools ranging from the smallest scalpel to a bone saw. They were about as blood-soaked and clotted with tissue as the table.

But the kicker was what lined the shelves that filled the rest of the room.

There was a Hand of Glory, a candle made from the hand of dead man. It was a legendary article of magic and mysticism, which purportedly allowed its possessors to access any place they wished.

Next to the hand was a statue of Anubis, the Egyptian God of the Dead, and next to that a small black figure of Baphomet, a common Satanic symbol referenced by occultists from the Middle Ages to Aleister Crowley.

The rest of the shelves were loaded with stacks of ancient-looking books and cheap paperbacks, all on the subject of the occult.

Where there weren't books there were jars. The jars ranged in size and contained all manner of sick and twisted shit people generally associated with witchcraft, black magic, and the occult. There was a jar of severed human fingers. I saw eyeballs, probably human, in one, and a human scalp in a larger jar next to it. Stacked on top of the scalp was a smaller jar filled to the rim with what looked like fingernails.

On the left shelves were all chemicals and powders. They were arranged like a macabre spice rack. There were the usual items an occultist worth his salt would own like Tanis Root and Blessed Thistle, alongside Mandrake and Wormwood. There were also some rarer items such as Tetrodotoxin, a powder thought to be used to create zombies from the living, and a vial of the herb Datura, also used to drug people into trancelike states.

I'd seen all this shit before. It looked like Henry Thicke was doing more than dressing the dead up for funerals.

Behind me Hendricks wasn't as relaxed as I was. "What the Christ has that sick fuck been up to?"

I glanced over Hendricks's shoulder. Thicke was on the floor chained to the embalming table, but listening to every word we said.

"I think Thicke was playing with his bodies," I said loudly, "and when his games backfired on him he called you guys to cover his ass for the missing John Does and then me to clean up the mess."

Hendricks just looked confused and disgusted.

I leaned so I could see Thicke. "That sound about right, Henry?"

The mortician just dropped his head and whimpered.

I left the room. I didn't need to see anymore. Hendricks followed, quickly this time. The seasoned old cop was spooked but good.

"What's this mess you're supposed to clean up, McDonald?" Hendricks barked and then added, "And where's my cash?"

I gave him half what I owed him. I told him he'd get the other half when we were finished with the job.

"Finished?" he whined. "I'll drag Doc Sickfuck in and we're done. What's to finish?"

I shoved Thicke aside and reached down for the large drain grate in the floor. It weighed twenty, maybe thirty pounds. I lifted it, threw it aside and stood facing the cop.

"We gotta go down there and find whatever he made and . . . deal with it." I said.

Hendricks looked down into the sewer like a kid who just dropped his ice-cream cone.

I knew how he felt. It seemed like every other case I took on wound up with me slopping around in the fucking sewers. I thought about calling in the ghouls and letting them handle the search, but in the end I'd be the one to have to get my hands dirty, so fuck it, I figured.

I climbed down first. The hole was just big enough for me to slide through. That fat bastard Hendricks had a slightly harder time. I had to stand on the bottom rung of the ladder and pull on his leg to pop his belly through the slot.

I had a penlight on my keychain. I scanned around the tunnel as Hendricks bitched and complained about his ugly-ass suit getting blood on it.

There was blood on the walls, not much but enough to tell me we were on the right track. We were at a dead end so there was only one way to go. I led. Hendricks followed, bitching every chance he got.

About a hundred yards in we came to an intersection. We could go forward, left or right. There wasn't any blood so it was a toss-up. I decided we should split up. Hendricks wasn't keen on the idea, so I gave him the other half of the cash I promised him. He took it, agreeing to go right while I went forward.

As soon as we were separated, I popped a couple more pills and lit a smoke. If I was going to be sloshing through shit, I might as well have a decent buzz.

It was dark, and the smell was a cross between urine and vomit, with rotten meat thrown in for that extra something special.

I used the light from the penlight and my smoke to guide the way, and another hundred yards in I began to wonder if there was anything to find.

Just because Thicke played with the dead didn't mean he got results. For all I knew he'd mutilated the bodies in the embalming room and made it look sloppy to throw me off.

Just as the thought cycled through my speeding brain, I saw something ahead. In the darkness it looked like a pile of garbage or some debris gathered up and clogging the system. But as I got closer I could see it was something else.

I pulled out my gun and spat the cigarette into the water so I'd have a hand for the light and one for the weapon. Then I edged closer.

The pile was two naked male bodies, one black, one white. They were thrown on top of each other face up, and it was clear these were two of the missing John Does, the homeless that Henry Thicke claimed to provide cheap funeral services for.

Their skulls had been crushed in on the left side like they'd been hit by a baseball.

Or a fist.

Both bodies had the post-autopsy Y incision across the chest and down the bellies. Usually these incisions were held together by thick cordlike thread, but somebody had pulled them apart, and inside there was nothing. All of the organs were gone.

All around the bodies was some sort of packing material, excelsior or straw. Some remained inside the empty cavities, but most of it had been pulled out and strewn around.

If I had to guess, it looked like somebody was looking for some organs and came up empty.

Things started to add up: three missing bodies. Two turn up like this, one still missing. And then you take into account that Thicke was messing with some evil hoodie voodie crap, and that meant that there was a third body out there who was probably some sort of undead freak now and looking for more organs, for what reason was anybody's guess.

That was when I heard Hendricks's yell, followed by a gunshot that rang through the sewer tunnels like a sonic boom.

I was deaf for a second and couldn't tell what direction the sounds came from, so I started running back to the intersection where we'd split up. Not long after I could hear Hendricks yowling.

I ran down the tunnel he'd disappeared in and, as I ran, I pulled out the sawed-off in my jacket. Forget the fucking light. I needed firepower.

I didn't have to run long. I found Hendricks bleeding to death by the time I reached him near the intersection of sewer tunnels, his side ripped out like a bite out of a melon slice. His upper and lower intestines were splashed on the cement like vomited Udon noodles.

He didn't have long.

Hendricks looked up at me, blood pouring over his double chin. "I found him."

I didn't feel it, but I flashed him a smile. He wanted to go out brave, and I owed him that much.

Hendricks coughed, and his body shook, pushing out another length of intestines from his gaping wound.

"You want me to call somebody?" I asked.

"W . . . what's the f . . . fucking point?" He coughed. "Besides . . . I'm moonlighting. I'd only get fired."

I looked around and then back at Hendricks as his eyes started to close. "Which way did he go?"

"Ugly fucker . . . and f . . . ast." He stammered and then, "He headed back toward Thicke's place."

I wanted to bolt as soon as he said that, but I didn't want to leave him to die alone. I lit a smoke and stuck it in his lips. He took one drag and then the cigarette dropped into the water, and Hendricks's eyes closed for good.

I left him lying there and ran as fast as I could back toward the hole we'd climbed in through. The tunnels were narrow, and I was hitting cement every other step, scraping my arms and raking my head, until finally I came up on the hole.

I climbed fast and found what I'd dreaded right away. Henry Thicke was still chained to the table. His skull was crushed worse than the two bodies in the tunnels. I could see skull fragments cutting through his scalp and brain matter bubbling through the blood. He hadn't been gutted though. His clothes were torn away, but his belly was untouched—I assumed because I'd shown up and interrupted.

With both weapons out, I turned in the embalming room fast. Except for me, the old lady on the table and Henry Thicke on the floor, the room was empty.

But the hidden door behind the anatomy print was closed. It was open when Hendricks and I went down into the sewers.

I raised the shotgun and the pistol and walked toward the door. I began to extend my leg to release the locking mechanism, a really stupid move on my part, because when the door burst open from the inside, I was thrown completely off balance, backward. I lost both the shotgun and the Glock, and the back of my head smacked against the second embalming table.

I was lying on my back, and standing in the doorway was the third John Doe. He had the same Y incision on his chest and the thick cord holding him together. But his cavity wasn't empty. It was stuffed to the gills with the organs he'd stolen from the other bodies. His whole torso was bloated and distorted.

The black cord and skin was stretched and tight. It looked like either his skin or the cord would give at any second.

In the dead man's hand was a tool with three blood-caked prongs that looked like a hand gardening hoe or rake. It might have been some type of surgical tool, but with the freak coming at me with it I didn't really give a shit.

The dead man lunged, and I rolled, causing him to smack his own head against the old lady's table.

I scrambled to my feet and put the two tables between me and the dead man. Unfortunately my guns were on his side. With nothing left to shoot, I grabbed the largest scalpel I could grab off Thicke's tool tray.

I looked into the dead mans eyes and saw no life. They were covered with gray film, and his lips foamed. Whatever Henry Thicke had done may have brought the dead back to life but that was about it. The thing was a wild rabid killer. Beyond collecting organs, I doubt it had any real thoughts.

I moved first.

I jumped into the open between the two tables with the corpse drawers at my back. The dead man came at me, raising his giant fork tool over his head.

I slashed straight at his chest where the two downward incisions met the one going the length of his belly. The sharp blade sliced through the taut cord like a hot knife through wax, giving off a popping sound as the blade passed through.

The dead man froze as his chest cavity opened and organs began to pour out onto the floor like a dump truck dropping its load. There were multiple hearts, kidneys, lungs, livers, spleens, pancreases, and intestines—all mixed and mashed up in a jumble stew of gore on the floor.

The dead man made the first sound since I'd seen him. It was a kind of pathetic whimper from the back of his throat, as he dove to the ground in an futile attempt to scoop up the organs and cram them back inside his body.

I just backed away and watched the whimpering corpse grab and shove the organs inside his empty body, only to have them fall right back out again.

There was something really sad about it, to tell the truth. I felt bad for the fucked-up freak. If there was anybody to be pissed at, it was Henry Thicke, and he was dead. At least the thing killed him. I suppose there was some justice there.

As the dead man gathered, shoved and dropped organs, I glanced into the secret room and wondered what Thicke had been attempting. Was he tired of dealing with death and struck by a sudden Frankenstein syndrome? Or had his constant exposure to death finally driven him to want to defeat it?

Hell, maybe he was just lonely and wanted to make some friends.

I walked around the other side of the tables and found my Glock under the old lady's table. I holstered it and searched for the shotgun.

I found it lying just behind where the dead man knelt wallowing in his collection or organs and blood.

The thing didn't react when I cocked the shotgun or even when I stepped behind him and placed the double-barrels to the back of his head.

All he did was scoop and shove the organs inside him, only to have them fall back out.

The blast ended the repetitive ritual with a booming explosion and a spray of blood, bone, and brains across the floor.

The dead man flopped forward into his gory collection and went still after a death rattle or two.

Then everything was quiet, and I was alone in the embalming room with a bunch of dead people, and I didn't have a clue who any of them really were or, for that matter, what had happened to them.

I found a cloth and wiped down everything I thought I had touched and backed out of the embalming room and back upstairs where I'd stood when I arrived.

I hadn't noticed it coming in, but there was a sign on the wall that read, "We take care of your loved ones so you can have peace of mind."

I'm not sure why, but I started laughing out loud as I left the building and headed back to my car. Maybe it was the absurdity of the whole thing. Maybe it was the fact that I'd just completed another of many cases I wouldn't see a dime for. Hell, I was out two bills. I'd actually lost money.

And maybe, with the cops on my ass, I couldn't help but imagine what it would be like when they found the scene in the basement of the mortuary and in the sewers.

If I didn't know what the hell had happened, that mess would make their heads spin.

Either way, something was funny about the whole disgusting mess.

THE UNLIKELY REDEMPTION OF JARED PEARCE

JOEY O'BRYAN

J ARED DIDN'T KNOW what the hell he expected to see, but he sure as hell didn't expect to see what he saw. The thing in the back seat had skin with the burnt, fissured texture of blowtorched Naugahide. It also held a big-bore revolver in its gloved hand. Jared guessed that if he didn't follow orders, Extra Crispy would not hesitate to use it. Shrouded in shadow, it was hard to make out much else. Jared's gaze shifted to his own reflection in the rearview mirror, and he drew a sharp breath. A crescent-moon steel blade was encircled around his neck, half an inch between his Adam's apple and the circular edge. It was built into the headrest and appeared a sturdy construction. If he so much as sneezed, the damn thing would no doubt take his head off.

Happy fuckin' New Year's Eve.

Jared had spent the better part of his evening at an AA meeting. It was the smartest place to be on a night where temptation was ever present. He'd left with plenty of time to make it home for the countdown. He never made it out of the parking lot. Last thing he remembered was a bee sting, the prick of a needle as he slid behind the wheel of his Pinto. He'd gone dizzy, the world went black, and next thing he knew his pumpkin had become a carriage. The hood ornament cresting the cherry-red hood confirmed the make of his new ride. It was a boat of a Buick, not his peanut of a Pinto. Parked in an abandoned barn, not a parking lot. His head was pounding. Jared tried to get his bearings. What had it done to him?

"Sodium pennnnnnothal," the thing in the backseat hissed, a wheeze forged in gravel and chimney smoke. "A small dose, enough to relax one's inhibitionssss . . ." Corrugated scar tissue undulated as it spoke, "Starrrt the carrrrrr."

Jared instinctively reached for the breathalyzer under the dash, a force of habit. In the time since the accident, he hadn't been able to start the Pinto without blowing into the device. At first it was a humiliation. Later it became a comfort, a reminder of what he'd overcome. Now a simple turn of the key was all it took to get the engine purring. So easy. Jared's guts churned. He didn't trust easy.

Suddenly, Nat King Cole exploded in his ears as the stereo blared to life. "Hark! The herald angels sing . . ."

Jared flinched, startled, and felt something bite into him as his neck kissed cold steel. His hand flew to the cut but stopped short when he sensed heat blossom from the wound. He sucked in a gasp and froze.

"Carrrrrrreful."

The thing in the backseat motioned to an oversized cassette jutting from the eight-Track player. "My father played this evvvvery Christmas, evvvery New Year's. He played it the night he wrapped our carrrrrr around an apple tree. Branches were fullll, apples rained all arrrround. Thirty-five years ago. I was nnnnnine. The car caught firrrre. My father was killed insssssstantly. I was not . . ."

Too bad, Jared thought.

The thing in the backseat leaned forward and set something between them. Jared glanced down, taking care not to move.

A bottle of tequila. Jared swallowed. Hard.

"You'lll celebrate as he did. We will drive. We will drink and we will drive untillll we crash. Everyyyything must be as it wasssss. If the gas runs out first, you live. Ifff we crash . . ."

Jared couldn't take his eyes off the bottle. "If we crash, maybe you don't make it either . . ." The thing in the backseat was unfazed. "All-llllll the crashes I've been innnn, I've walked away from evvvvvery one . . ." Jared was stunned. "You've done this before?"

"The prrresssssssss calls me Mr. Lucky . . ."

CLICK. Mr. Lucky cocked the revolver.

"Drink."

Jared hesitated, then reached for the bottle. "Annnother driver-rrrrr once turned the bottle towarrrds the floor," Mr. Lucky said, "I shhhhot him before he could empty it . . ."

Jared steeled himself as he tilted the bottle to his lips, years of sobriety about to be undone. The last time Jared had a drink, four people died. A worm floating in the bottle, another reminder of the grave. The Tequila stung as it hit his lips. Something inside him screamed. That's when the worm *twitched*. Jared coughed, surprised, spewing tequila on his shirt. "The worm, it—"

"I make it myself. A little lllleesssssss mescal allows the larva to live." He placed scornful emphasis on the word "larva," correcting the bewildered Jared. "Inside a larva, there is a beautiful butterfly. Inside a worm, nothing but muck. Daddddy was a Tequila Man. He loved to eaaaat them." Mr. Lucky pressed the gun to Jared's temple, forcing him toward the circular blade. Jared tensed, straining against him. "There is but one ruleeeee, and one ruleeeee only: do not stopppp. Stop dddriving, stop drinking, I shoot."

Jared reluctantly pulled the Buick out onto the dirt road, almost clipping the side of the barn in the process. You had to put a lot less thought into cornering a Pinto than a Buick. He was reminded of his old Lincoln, the one he'd totaled. Jared had been into big cars his whole life, but had decided to go with something less threatening after the accident.

"Where we going?" Jared asked.

"You're drivvvving." Mr. Lucky lay across the backseat, revolver never wavering. Jared's mind raced as he pulled onto a deserted rural road, trying to dream up a way out of the nightmare. He took it slow, countryside tracking by at a crawl. The leisurely pace would buy him time to get his thoughts together. He was worried Mr. Lucky might object, but he said nothing. As long as he wasn't breaking the one rule, Jared had only the collar to worry about.

It was enough.

"Ffffirst one, I replaaaaced the sssseatbelt with a curved blade. Number two, steel spikes prrrotruding from the driver's side door. The third, a concussion grennnade where the airrrbag ought to be." Mr. Lucky grinned. Something had tickled him. "Did you know, some believe that when the head is sevvvered from the body, the brain can continuue to function for up to fffffifteen seconds? It's never beeeen proven, though maaany have tried. I hooooope there's some truth to it, for your sake . . ."

A cackle from the backseat.

"Every second is a gift, wouldn't you agreeee?" The cackle became laughter, and soon Mr. Lucky was having a fit. Jared imagined him choking to death, but the pleasure it brought was fleeting. It was Jared's head on the chopping block.

Ol' King Cole was crooning about *The Happiest Christmas Tree.* "Ho ho ho, hee hee hee, look how happy I can be, oh lucky, lucky me!" Jared wanted to punch the tape deck.

He took another swig instead. Tasted like Hell. A Hell in which four kids judged him with angry faces. He could hear them in his head. He should have taken a bullet before a drink. Jared ignored their voices as best he could. What he was, was *alive.* How to stay that way posed a significant conundrum. If stopping earned him a lead lobotomy, getting out of the Marie Antoinette headgear was going to be damn difficult. Eyes shifted from side-to-side, taking in the whole of the interior. Tequila bottle the only available weapon. Too bad he couldn't use it without turning round and cutting his throat. Brute force wasn't going to help him out of this predicament, he'd have to think his way out. Best he could hope for was to attract attention and pray Mr. Lucky folded.

HONK!

A VW bug roared up behind the slowpoke Buick. Horn howling, headlights flashing. It whipped alongside, and Jared's heart leapt. He began to shout, turning as much as he could without injuring himself. "Help! I've been kidnapped!"

"Windows are tinted," Mr. Lucky gloated. "They'll never see you . . ." He was right. The driver shot them the bird, bellowing something incomprehensible. "No, no . . ." Jared reached for the window crank. It came off in his hand. A snicker from the backseat, Mr. Lucky pleased with his ingenuity. Jared strobed his brights at the retreating vehicle to little effect. He sped up to try and keep pace, but the bug was soon lost to the night.

Jared eased off the gas and coasted to a less dangerous velocity. "You're not drinking," said the Devil on his shoulder. Jared slammed the bottle back. No hesitation. Shoveling coal into the furnace of his hate. Hate would keep him going. Jared made up his mind; then and there: no way on God's Green Earth was Mr. Lucky going to get away with this shit. He had to pay. Jared's mind raced through a series of unlikely scenarios, each more absurd than the last, until a more plausible option occurred to him.

Officer Harris.

Harris kept his police cruiser parked behind a rotting Kay's Pancakes billboard beside an onramp to the two-lane 115 Interstate, lying in wait for unsuspecting road racers. It had to be the most predictable speed trap in the state. Jared often passed him en route into Takoma Valley. Locals suspected he just liked his peace and quiet. It was the only explanation that made sense of his stubborn refusal to relocate to a less obvious hiding place. Harris wasn't much of a cop, but he had a gun and a radio, and it wouldn't be hard to get his attention. He was Jared's best chance, maybe his only chance.

Jared carefully turned the car around.

"Where are wwe going, Daaddy?" Mr. Lucky sounded different, affected. If he was trying to sound like a kid, he came off more like Elmo with a scalpel in his larynx. The caricature in no way convinced, but it was damned unsettling.

"Home." Jared said, playing along. No sense in giving Mr. Lucky an excuse to open up the back of his head. "You need to stop drrrrinking, Daddy." Mr. Lucky cooed. "Mommmmmy said you havvvvve a problem. Mommy says you have soooooo many problems since the warrr." Jared did the math. Somewhere between the Stars-and-Stripes dash cover and the boozy ride into an apple tree, Daddy probably got more than he bargained for serving his beloved country and turned to the bottle for comfort. "I don't have a problem, son." Jared replied. The words came easy to him, though the "son" would've been tough without the hooch. He'd said the others before. Too many times, especially before the accident. He'd made more of himself afterward, but the damage had been done. Four dead, the oldest only seventeen. Kids.

Jared had blacked out on impact. He'd gone out to watch a game, but by the time he'd left the bar he couldn't remember who was playing. He took the scenic route through Takoma Valley. Not because he liked the view. It was the quickest way home. He'd felt fine at first, hadn't even noticed he'd drifted out of his lane. The kids were coming home from a late-night bash in Mom's Chrysler. She was mad as hell her daughter took it without asking. It would soon be the least of her worries.

Jared's Lincoln punched them through a guardrail as they came round a corner, sending them over a cliff and into the canyon below. Jared vomited when he came to and saw the wreckage battered against the rocks. He cried, found a shard of glass on the blacktop, and slashed his throat.

Somehow, he survived.

Judge looked at the suicide attempt as evidence of genuine remorse and sentenced Jared to only two years. It was his first offense, and he got out early on good behavior. Eight months jail time, two for each kid. The families were outraged, but there was nothing they could do. Time passed and everyone moved away, hoping to start over in places far, far removed from the tragedies of Takoma Valley.

Probation bound Jared to the land, but he wouldn't have left even if the option were open to him. Living in the shadow of what he'd done kept him on the straight and narrow. If he ever felt tempted to knock a couple back, one look in the mirror was enough to dissuade him, the ear-to-ear scar under his chin a flesh-and-blood reminder of that terrible night.

Late every Thursday, the night of the accident, he'd drive out to Takoma Valley. Even years later, the shiny new section of guardrail stood out from its more weather-beaten counterparts. Once a week, a new bouquet for his victims. There would never be enough. This place haunted him. He dreamt about it every night. In the dream Jared stood at the edge of the cliff where the Chrysler had gone over. It was always the same.

First, the scar across his throat would begin to itch. Soon the irritation spread, and he was scratching all over, like a dog with ticks. Jared would convulse as something glided beneath his skin. His throat bulged impossibly huge until the scar split open, a face peering through the gash, pushing its way out like a baby leaving the birth canal. The old Jared gurgled as a new Jared emerged from within, naked and bloody as a newborn. This new Jared was immune to the laws of gravity, floating skyward as he slid from the shell of his former body as casually as a snake sheds its skin. The burden of the past was replaced by the exhilaration of weightlessness, of limitless possibility.

He was flying. Soaring over the valley. The vista that had before held only pain became wondrous, magical. Then would come the tug of consciousness. The dream would fade, and there was only the reality of the stuccoed bedroom ceiling, the smile across his throat, the breathalyzer he'd have to suck on if he wanted to get to work, and the kids he'd killed.

The scar now seemed less like a grim reminder of the past and more like an invitation, the dotted line drawn by a surgeon that begs "cut here." It was the sort of perfect coincidence only fate could engineer. Perhaps, Jared wondered, this was meant to be. The universe dishing out a little poetic justice.

Perhaps not. On the horizon, Kay's Pancakes beckoned.

The double yellow line between the Buick and the billboard swayed like the larva adrift in the bottle of tequila. The half-emptied bottle of Tequila. Lost in the trance of recall, Jared hadn't realized how hard he'd hit it. *Like riding a bike.* The thought set Jared's soul on fire. Forty-five, read the speedometer. He'd have to get moving if he hoped to spur Harris into action. He wasn't likely to bother with anything under seventy-five. Jared blinked until the road turned from shifting pixels to black mud. In the old days, a few self-inflicted slaps to the face would get the ball rolling toward clarity, but the logistics of the guillotine rendered that old technique inapplicable.

"Did you really killllll people, Daaaddy?" The asshole had done his homework, Jared thought as he leaned on the gas. How long had he been watching him? Jared felt the back of his skull sink into the headrest as the Buick gained momentum. "Mommy sssaid they were baaaaaad guys," Mr. Lucky continued. In his drunken stupor, it took Jared a second to realize Mr. Lucky had not been referencing him, but Daddy. The Soldier. Or maybe, Jared thought, he was lumping them together. They had some things in common, after all. Hell, maybe he was talking about every last sonofabitch he ever put behind the wheel of one of his custom-rigged Buicks.

The speedometer crept past fifty-five, bumps in the road becoming more pronounced. Jared was hyper-alert to every last one of them, each new tremor conspiring to jostle him into the deadly halo enclosed around his throat. He grimaced and stiffened his spine, an imaginary iron bar running from scalp to ass crack. A tab of melting butter shifted into view as the Pancakes drew closer. Eggs smothered with a square of processed cheese, bacon glistening with grease. Jared sensed his supper rising and pushed it back down.

Sixty-two, sixty-three, sixty four . . .

"Daaaddy, you're going too fffffast!" Mr. Lucky was smiling when he said it, half in the moment and half not, enjoying the rush of heightened jeopardy. Nat King Cole was going on like he knew some-thing they didn't, crooning about a world of sin, the thrill of hope, and weary souls rejoicing. Jared read it as a sign in his favor.

The Buick blew past the billboard.

Jared glanced into the rear-view. Nothing. Down at the speedometer. Eighty-two MPH. The air went out of him as Kay's pancakes receded into the distance. Back in the mirror, only darkness . . .

Then, light.

Whirling red and blue shafts caught in a cloud of dust, the police cruiser materializing out of the void, siren screaming as radials rumbled onto the interstate.

Jared allowed himself a glimmer of self-satisfaction as Mr. Lucky rose from the back seat, waving the gun around. *Gotcha, fuckface.* Through the rear window, the police cruiser nipping at their heels. Mr. Lucky turned to the front, more excited than concerned.

"Only one rrrrrrule," he said, beaming.

It wasn't the reaction Jared had hoped for. "Open your eyes asshole, there's no way out of this!" Silence from the backseat. "We stop, we crash, I live, I die, you walk or crawl out of this car, you're done!"

Still no response. "They can *help* you, man!"

The stench of mildew shot through Jared's nostrils as Mr. Lucky lurched over the seat, hot breath on his cheek. "You're ruining it, Daaaaaadddy!!!" He was twice as revolting out of the shadows as he was in, eyes bulging from seared sockets. Instinct told Jared to pull away. The shining silver halo kept him rooted to the spot. By the time Jared thought to swing the bottle of tequila up into Mr. Lucky's face, he had shrunk back out of range, wailing to himself over and over again, "One rule, one rule, one rule, one rule . . ."

He whipped the gun up. "Hey, hey!!!" Jared protested as he took a pull off the bottle. This one went straight to his head, like a needle in the nape of his neck. Jared bit his tongue, pain bringing the world back into focus. He turned his attention to the cruiser, and saw Harris mouthing off into a handset. Jared scored one for himself. Maybe a few more black-and-whites would make Mr. Lucky rethink the one rule.

"We stop the car right now, you give up the gun." Jared took an uneasy breath before the capper. "I don't want you to get hurt, son."

"I should have died," Mr. Lucky said. "I want to die."

"Not like this you don't," Jared countered. "You wanna die in the crash. With me. You wanna keep doing it over and over again 'til you get it right. Well, it ain't gonna happen. 'Cause I'm gonna pull over. I'm gonna pull over and if you crack that cannon the cops are gonna swiss cheese this boat and everyone in it. You're gonna die like a common criminal."

"No, Daddy dooooooon't sssay that!!!"

"Now put down the gun you little shit and let Daddy help—"

Jared stopped talking and punched the gas as he caught sight of Harris swerving toward their back bumper. The cruiser went out of control as it turned into empty space, weaving to and fro. All that downtime hadn't done a lot for Harris's driving skills. The cruiser righted itself and bore down on them. Jared gritted his teeth. Harris was showing uncharacteristic ambition. He meant to bump them off the road. One solid knock would send the car spinning and throw Jared sideways into the circular blade. It might not be enough to take his head off, but it would definitely put him down. Harris had given the advantage back to Mr. Lucky, and Mr. Lucky knew it. He was mugging confidently in the rearview. Jared met his gaze, desperate but determined. *No way on God's Green Earth . . .*

He sped up, weighing his options. Even if he could lose Harris without wiping out, he'd be back to square one. Harris was armed and therefore the only real hope against Mr. Lucky's big-bore revolver. Stopping was a given, but how to do so without killing himself? Slowing down wouldn't work. If Mr. Lucky didn't blow his face off, Harris would sideswipe him into oblivion. He'd have to catch them both off guard. It would have to be abrupt, unexpected, but such a sudden stop would surely pitch Jared onto the blade, no matter how he steeled himself against it. Maybe he could shove the tequila bottle between the blade and his throat. One glance at the bottle dispelled that notion. The body was too wide, and the neck wasn't thick enough. He'd just wind up with a face full of broken glass on his way through the guillotine.

A more gruesome option occurred to him. His hand would fit into the gap. The blade would pass through flesh like Jell-O but bones were another matter. They might not prove resistant enough to keep Jared's head on his shoulders, but it was a better bet than glass. Better maimed than dead, Jared thought. According to Mr. Lucky, he'd only have fifteen seconds to regret it if he got it wrong.

Screw it.

The rest fell into place. Mr. Lucky would be thrown forward. He'd be disoriented. Jared would have a few precious milliseconds to brain him with the tequila bottle. Or snatch his gun away if possible. Harris would need time to stop, get out, and draw—

"Daaaaaaaddy!!!" Mr. Lucky was pointing and laughing.

A fork in the road lay ahead.

Construction. It hadn't been there last Thursday.

No time to think. Jared jerked the wheel. The Buick drifted into the curve, smoke curling from squealing tires. His neck muscles tightened, veins bulging with effort. One hand braced against the armrest, the other on the wheel. He felt his body sliding, the edge of the blade sinking into him. The Buick banked onto the straightaway and gravity yanked Jared in the opposite direction. His throat nicked the adjoining arc of the circular blade. The cuts weren't serious. Blood trickled down either side of his neck, but a Pez dispenser he was not.

The junkyard crunch of stressed steel, smashed glass drew his attention back to the rearview. There he saw Harris's police cruiser cartwheeling round the bend, flipping end over end. He could only watch, horrified, as the car rolled onto its side and lay still. Jared forgot himself. His foot slipped off the gas, and Mr. Lucky leveled the revolver at him. Jared scowled, put the pedal down, and took the detour, a back road winding up into Takoma Valley.

"He'll be okay, I thinkkkkk." Mr. Lucky glared triumphant. Jared wanted to believe he would be, that the airbag and seat belt had done their job, but there was no way to know for sure. He tried to push Harris out of his mind but he wouldn't budge.

"Is thisssssss where it happened, Daddy? Where you killed thosssse people?" Jared didn't respond. He didn't want to think about it. He didn't want to think, period. He tilted the bottle all the way back, frustration eating at his insides. Mr. Lucky was still babbling, but Jared wasn't listening anymore. He concentrated on the road, the bottle. So much time between then and now, yet here he was, driving drunk through Takoma Valley in the middle of the night, another accident in his wake. Should have let Harris run us off the road, he thought, imagining Mr. Lucky either shot full of holes or rotting in jail.

"I wanna know one thing." Jared asked. "Why guys like me? Guys tryin' to turn it around. Laying in wait outside an AA meeting, why not wait outside a bar till you see some liquored-up piece of shit headed out with keys in hand?"

"Daddy thought heeeee turned it arrrrround!" Mr. Lucky snapped. "Mooooore than once . . ." His voice trailed away, tinged with melancholy. Then, as if to reassure himself, "Everything mussssssst be as it wassss—"

Jared cut him off. "I'm not your daddy." Mr. Lucky glared an objection but said nothing. "Besides," Jared added, "no one gets to turn back the clock." It was as much confession as confirmation. Jared smiled and gulped tequila. His insides grew warm. For the first time, he let himself enjoy the sensation.

He skid the Buick through a series of hairpin turns. Mr. Lucky squeaked out a nervous giggle, delighted by the bravura display of recklessness but still troubled by Jared's outburst.

"Thisss is fun. Don't ssspoil it."

Yeah, Jared thought, *just wait.*

He finally felt like he understood the pitiful thing in the back seat. Mr. Lucky loved *and* hated his father. Wished he'd died with him, but wanted to kill him over and over again for what he'd done. A contradiction that perhaps only made sense to those whose scars ran deeper than most. It made sense to Jared. He'd felt like that about himself from time to time. Jared tipped the bottle higher, and the road went distorted through the caramel glass. The squirming larva slid into his mouth as he chugged the last of the tequila. The bottle fell from his hand as the road spun, oils running down a canted canvas.

Mr. Lucky's enthusiasm became uncertainty.

"What are you dooooing, Daaaddy?"

The Buick slammed into the railing. This particular section a little shinier than its more weather-beaten counterparts.

Jared felt the small of his back leave the upholstery. A lightning bolt pulsed through his body, every nerve ending alive and shrieking for one terrible instant. Something warm gushed against his cheeks, and he was surprised how good it felt. He seemed to float out of his body and over the dash, passing through the empty rectangle where the windshield once was. It was as if he was sitting in a movie theatre and found himself catapulted into the screen.

He soared through a star-field of twinkling glass, the remnants of the shattered windshield. Shards gnawed at his chin and forehead but he felt no pain.

Then the glass was gone, and there was only night.

The valley spread out before him like a mural.

Jared felt weightless.

Free.

He was flying.

Flying.

The sensation was better than any dream. The world began to tilt, turning on its axis. Total circumference of the landscape spinning past to reveal . . .

The Buick.

Oh yeah, The Buick, Jared thought, brain blissed-out in a euphoric haze. The guardrail was twisted round it like a bow. Steam plumed from the cracked grill, wheels spinning uselessly as the vehicle crested the edge of the cliff. Jared's eyes narrowed as he caught sight of himself in the front seat. Well, part of himself anyway. His hands were frozen to the steering wheel, locked in a death grip. There was a fountain where his head ought to be, painting the interior dark red. Through the crimson spray, he saw Mr. Lucky. It was hard to tell if he was screaming or laughing.

Maybe it was a bit of both.

A grim smile spread across Jared's lips, which were fast turning a sick shade of blue. Mr. Lucky spun away, and the cliff face came into view, racing past in a blur. Gravity had taken hold. Jared was no longer in flight, but freefall. He had climbed to the top of the roller coaster and was contemplating the plummet down. That was usually the moment his stomach dropped. Of course, with no stomach to upset, he was able to enjoy the moment in a way he never had. The thought made him laugh, but no sound came out.

The ground below whirled into view for a moment before it was replaced by the sky, then the Buick. Jared was grateful to have had a second look, however brief. It was a comfort to know it had gone over properly. Now that he thought about it, the back wheels could've snagged on the guardrail, and he would have died for nothing. The Buick became the cliff face became the sky became the ground as the valley floor rushed up to greet him. Jared wondered how long it'd been. Fifteen seconds, was that what Mr. Lucky had said?

The world spun faster.

Ten? Twenty?

A smear of color swallowed by darkness.

Thir—

God flipped the switch in Jared's head to the off position, glazed eyes staring as head met earth. His skull cracked on impact, head bouncing from the path of the Buick as if by design, the vehicle touching down in a cacophony of screaming metal.

Mr. Lucky failed to emerge from the wreckage this time.

No way on God's Green Earth . . .

Jared's fractured, lifeless noggin tumbled to a stop, still grinning despite having landed in a bed of cactus. He had plenty to smile about. He had redeemed himself. He had killed the bad guy. He had won.

One last snippet of Nat King Cole's Christmas album warbled distorted from fractured speakers . . .

The little Lord Jesus laid down his sweet head,
the stars in the sky looked down where He lay,
the little Lord Jesus asleep in the hay . . .

From the corner of Jared's mouth, the larva inched down his chin and through a minefield of cactus needles. The lonely survivor made its way to the ground, crawled across the soil and into a bed of weeds.

A beautiful butterfly growing inside.

QUEEN OF THE GROUPIES

GREG KIHN

THE ROAD TO rock and roll heaven is paved by the bleached skulls of guys like him," I read aloud from the *Cleveland Plain Dealer*. It was a review of our gig at the Agora Ballroom the night before.

Skull took a drag on his Marlboro. Bass players always ask the right questions. "Guys like who?"

"I guess he means me."

"Well, that's a snotty thing to say. I thought we rocked."

"We did rock. But, different people see the same things differently. Maybe he's into prog."

"What does he know anyway? The little shit can't even play an instrument."

Skull's logic was irrefutable. He would never presume to tell somebody else how to do their job, unless he could do it himself, only better.

Rock critics never truly connect with musicians for that very reason. The code of rock makes them forever outsiders. The code forbids anything even remotely hostile to the "us against the world" ethos to which we swore allegiance. It was the lifeblood of any band. We lived by that code. Sometimes it was the only thing holding the band together. As long as there was another gig, the code stuck. It was, and would always be, "us against the world."

Back in the day, our band stayed on the road for months at a time. We had to; it was the only way to maintain a cash flow. We were on a small record company with a tiny budget. To save money, we always leased old tour buses from a company in Nashville. These were wornout, older coaches with colorful histories and threadbare seats. They smelled too.

We stood in front of the Swingo's Celebrity Palace hotel and waited for our new wheels to arrive for the next leg of an endless tour. A thick, icy fog swirled around the streetlights, which were already illuminated at 5:30 on this bleak January evening.

Skull lit another cigarette as he ground the last one, still burning, into the dirty snow.

"I sure hope this next bus is better than that last piece of shit. The heater never worked the entire time, and I froze my ass off."

I squinted up the street. I heard it before I saw it. The terrible grinding of gears and rattling of linkage sounded almost alive. It snarled at the traffic around it.

Then, the light changed and around the corner came a battered Silver Eagle coughing smoke and belching fire. It emerged from the freezing mist like a ghost ship. Its headlights pierced the fog like two tired eyes after a twelve-hour drive. The front bumper sagged downward into a frown. The brakes hissed, and it rolled to a stop right in front of us.

"This is the worst tour bus I've ever seen," said Skull. "I ain't riding in this deathtrap."

"Oh, yes you are," road manager Brett Krebs said firmly. "We were lucky to get this one. Everything's booked. The next gig's in Minot, North Dakota. That's over a thousand miles from here. It's a two-day drive. We'll be lucky to make it. I'll look into getting us another bus after next week. This one will have to do for now. Sorry, boys. Don't complain to me, complain to management. I'm just a hired hand."

"These dartboard tours are pretty rough on the band, Brett."

"Hey, I don't book this shit, I just make sure you get there on time."

The door to the bus hissed and swung open with a metallic screech. The sound made us jump. It was dark inside. Brett leaned in and said something. The engine died with a heaving sigh. We could hear someone stirring.

A dwarfish man wearing a big, black cowboy hat stepped out. He was no more than five-two, with the hat. He sported a thin Fu-Manchu goatee and carried a half burned cigar between his stubby fingers. His jeans and shirt were wrinkled and funky.

When he spoke, his voice sounded as rough as sandpaper.

"I'm Jimmy. Y'all are the band, right?"

Brett said, "That's us. I've got the contract right here."

"Okay, well, you boys might as well get your gear stowed while I talk business with this gentleman. We're leavin' right away. We got a mighty long drive ahead."

Skull looked at me with a pained expression. He shook his head in disgust.

Jimmy tossed me the keys to the locked storage compartment below the bus. It was a rectangular cargo bay that ran almost the length of the bus, with two big fold-down doors. The undercarriage of the bus was splattered with mud and ice. I squatted and looked at the lock. As I did so, I momentarily lost my balance and my hand shot out for the cargo door to break my fall.

The door was colder than ice. Unnaturally cold. So cold that my hand drew away stinging. I shook it vigorously.

"What the hell?"

Skull said, "Let's get the damn thing open and get the luggage and the guitars in there."

I looked at the lock and examined the keys in my hand. I selected the logical one and, careful not to make skin contact with the door, fit it into the keyhole. I twisted the key, and the door swung down with a sudden bang. Our lone roadie, Cliff, watched with amusement.

"Careful! Those things can bite."

I peered into the belly of the beast and shivered. It was a dark and ominous space. I got a bad feeling. The gloom seemed to pour out of it, as if the darkness there had weight and substance. Then a sharp, sickeningly sweet odor hit me and almost made me gag.

I staggered back from the bus as if I'd sniffed ammonia.

"What's wrong?"

"Can't you smell that?"

"Smell what? There's nothing there. Why don't you go topside and pick out a bunk? Me and Skull can load this stuff."

I didn't want to be near that cargo bay. I went around to the front of the bus and peered inside. Again, an oppressive melancholy feeling swept over me. As my eyes adjusted I could see faded brown upholstery, a fold-down table, and a tiny microwave oven. The interior smelled like stale cigarettes and spilled beer. I stepped up and into the lounge area.

The bus had seen better days. It was scuffed and battered, with duct tape holding a few of the overhead doors shut. In the corner a small television jutted out of the wall. The kitchenette was clean but worn. A half-size refrigerator clicked and farted.

I walked down the aisle and peered into the bunks. They were identical coffin-sized compartments with a reading light at one end and a tiny window. A curtain could be drawn for privacy. There was just enough room to lie down and prop yourself up on one elbow. I picked a lower bunk and threw my bag in to claim it, hating the idea of actually having to sleep in that claustrophobic little hole.

I kept walking until I reached the back lounge. There were two small couches and another TV. It seemed like the least forbidding place on the bus so I sat down and looked out the window. The baggage compartment doors slammed shut, and the rest of the band filed onboard.

Jimmy climbed behind the wheel. He had special extenders so he could reach the floor pedals. He fired up the massive engine, and the bus rumbled to life. We pulled away from the hotel in a cloud of blue exhaust smoke.

"This bus gives me the creeps," I said as Skull entered the lounge.

"It's a Cleveland Steamer."

I laughed. It was a phrase we had learned last night at the gig. It meant a steaming dog turd on a snow bank.

Skull sat down and busied himself rolling a joint.

"Might as well break it in right," he said.

I went to the closet-sized bathroom to pee. There was barely room to stand. I leaned against the door to steady myself in the moving bus. As I finished, I happen to glance up and look in the mirror. I saw a young girl wearing bright red lipstick standing behind me. I looked around, and she was gone. I looked back in the mirror, and she had vanished. I smelled a faint, familiar scent. It hung in the air, and I tried to identify it.

"Did you see a chick in here just now?" I asked Skull.

"Nope. If there was a chick on this bus I would know it, man."

Skull lit the joint and took a big hit. With his lungs full of smoke, in a constricted voice he said, "Maybe it was a ghost."

The miles rolled monotonously under our wheels. Ten hours passed. The bus was like a submarine. *Das Boot*. The band moved around the bus with restless energy. Skull sat with Joey the drummer and lead guitarist Reed Wayne. They drank beer and watched a video of *Dirty Harry*.

I sat behind Jimmy. The strange little man seemed part of the bus. He shoved the pedals down with his extenders and grunted. CB radio chatter filled the cockpit, and Jimmy nursed a cup of coffee. Out in the darkness, guys with names like Greasy Diesel and Road Dog were holding deep and meaningful conversations. In the dashboard light, Jimmy's face took on a surreal, distorted look. I saw it reflected on the windshield against the inky road ahead. He looked positively manic.

More time passed. The bus rolled on through the bleak night, on the Hank William's Lost Highway. When you're constantly in motion, the world is not the same. Ken Kesey was right. You're either on the bus or you're not.

I yawned and tried to push my misgivings out of my mind. I walked back to my bunk. Reed and Joey had already turned in. I flipped on the reading light and looked inside. It looked okay so I climbed in with my clothes on. I pulled a stiff, gray blanket over me and pulled the curtain shut. The stinky little pillow was cold against my cheek. I closed my eyes and tried not to think.

I must have dosed off, because when I opened my eyes, the reading light was still on, and the curtain was still closed. Except now, the bunk seemed much smaller. The ceiling was now inches from my nose. I started to feel claustrophobic. While I watched, the whole sleeping compartment began to shrink around me. The walls inched closer, the ceiling lowered, I reached up and pushed with my hands. It wouldn't budge. I felt panic rise and kicked against the wall with my foot. I rolled out of the bunk and hit the floor with my head. I looked back into my bunk, and it was normal again.

I immediately noticed that I had a throbbing erection. I lay on the floor, wondering if it was all a dream. When the erection began to subside, I climbed to my feet and headed for the restroom. I looked in the mirror right away, but saw nothing. I peered closer at my face. There was red lipstick on my cheek.

I wiped it with my hand, and it came off on my fingers. I looked at it in disbelief. Was I going crazy?

I exited the restroom and saw a light on in the back lounge. Skull was in there swigging Jack Daniels right out of the bottle. He'd been smoking joints all night. He looked up at me in a daze and smiled.

"Hey, man!"

I sat down next to him. "Weird shit's been happening on this bus, man. Just now, my bunk started closing in on me. Then I woke up with a huge boner, and I found lipstick on my cheek."

Skull snorted. "So? That shit happens to me all the time."

"No, I really mean it. The bunk was closing in on me."

He handed me the bottle of Jack. "You need this, brother. May it serve you well."

"I think this bus is haunted."

Skull looked at me with one eye open. "Cool."

He flopped back in the seat and started to snore. I put the bottle down and wandered back to the front of the bus. It was dark except for Jimmy's diminutive silhouette illuminated by the ghostly light.

He was talking to somebody. Then, I clearly heard a girl laugh. I could smell that scent again. Then it hit me: Clove cigarettes. I only knew a few people who smoked Cloves. Whenever you smelled it, you knew one of them was around.

I moved forward into the main cabin like a cat, careful not give myself away. When I got closer, I saw the same girl I had seen earlier in the mirror. She stood next to Jimmy, rubbing his leg. They murmured to each other. She smoked a Clove cigarette.

I heard him say, "You're my pearl, Roxie, and I'm the only one that loves you."

I studied her face. She wore bright red lipstick, the same color I found on my cheek. It was overapplied and went over her lips. It gave her a slightly bizarre look. Apart from the smeared lipstick, she was beautiful, with pale skin and long blonde hair hanging down her back. She wore a little black party dress and white cowboy boots.

At that moment the bus hit a bump, and one of the doors on the overhead bins popped open with a loud bang. Jimmy and the girl looked back and saw me. I stood there, the proverbial deer in the headlights. As I watched, she disappeared.

I rubbed my eyes. Yes, by God, suddenly and mysteriously, she was gone! In the blink of an eye, I saw it, but I didn't believe it.

I walked up to Jimmy's seat. His eyes were now glued to the road ahead, and he pretended nothing had happened.

"Who is she, Jimmy?"

Jimmy looked at me with world-weary eyes. He waited a beat, then sighed. "Her name is Roxie."

"Is she a ghost?"

He nodded.

"You want to tell me the story?"

Jimmy re-lit his cigar and settled back in his seat. "I guess I owe it to you. Y'all are payin' customers. You have a right to know."

He took a puff of his cigar and exhaled a thick cloud of smoke. Jimmy was not good-looking guy, but his face softened, and I think I saw the hint of a tear in the corner of his eye. He took off his cowboy hat and ran a hand through his greasy thin hair. He put the hat back on and cast me a sideways glance.

"Once, a long time ago, this bus was new. It was owned by Billy Boy Soams. I was his driver."

"The legendary country singer?"

Jimmy nodded. "He was a real hell raiser, let me tell ya. Billy Boy had some major demons eatin' away at him, that's for sure. He liked his whisky and his cocaine. And his women. Oh, Lord, the women! He loved bright red lipstick, and he made all the girls wear it. He dressed 'em up the way he liked and had his way with 'em. Billy had parties every night on this bus. His groupies were unbelievable. Crazy, wild, shameless women who just wanted a good time. Billy gave it to them, as long as they wore the lipstick. He was funny about that."

Jimmy paused and looked back to see if anyone was eavesdropping. Satisfied that we were alone, he continued.

"Roxie started comin' around to the gigs. Billy took a shine to her. Who wouldn't? She was a beautiful girl. He took her on the bus from town to town, his own little pleasure unit. She was a wild child, let me tell you, a real spitfire. Among the groupies, Roxie was the queen of them all. But, you know how it is. Billy was always messin' around, and one night she caught him naked with another girl in the lounge back there." He nodded toward the back of the bus.

"Billy always had guns layin' around, and she grabbed one and tried to kill him. She missed, but she shot up the bus pretty good. Anyway, Billy thought she was a little too crazy for his taste so he kicked her off the bus.

"But that girl wasn't done yet. She hitchhiked across two states and caught up with us at the next gig. She caused a big scene. Billy slapped her face, and she stomped off madder than a hornet. When we pulled out that night, nobody knew it, but Roxie had stowed away down in the baggage compartment."

Jimmy looked at me. "It was January, on a night like this. The temperature was down in single digits when we made the long haul through North Dakota. When we got to the next town, I opened the luggage compartment and found her frozen to death. She was blue."

Jimmy's voice cracked. "Poor little thing. I didn't know she was down there. I . . ." His voice trailed off.

I said, "It wasn't your fault, Jimmy. You had no way of knowing."
Jimmy made no reply.

"And now she haunts this bus," I whispered. "A restless spirit caught between worlds."

Jimmy looked at me and frowned. "Now she's revealed herself to you. She's never done that before."

"What does that mean?"

Jimmy's face sagged. "I don't know."

We rolled through the night. All the other guys were asleep. I couldn't make myself go back to the bunk so I stretched out in the back lounge. Skull had crawled to his bunk and was snoring peacefully down the aisle. I had the room to myself. I read until I couldn't keep my eyes open.

As I drifted into slumber, a sweet odor drifted past my nostrils. I recognized the scent of Clove cigarette smoke. Alarms went off inside my head. My eyes jerked open and there she was, naked in front of me.

There was no mistaking her intentions. "Come here," she whispered through smeared lipstick. "I need you."

"What about Jimmy?"

"What about him?"

"He loves you."

"He was the only one who was nice to me. But now, you can be nice to me." She slid into my lap.

I held up my hands. "I can't do this. I just can't."

I felt the bus decelerate. Roxie pressed against me. I tried to stand, but she pinned me down with supernatural force. The bus rolled to a stop, and I heard the parking brake crank. Roxie would not stop. Within moments my face was smeared with her lipstick.

The door to the back lounge kicked open, and Jimmy waddled in with his two best friends, Smith and Wesson.

"I knew it! I just knew it!"

He aimed his pistol at me. It was a blue steel .38 S&W revolver with powder burns on the barrel. My heart pounded. Instantly, a million pores in my skin each secreted a tiny drop of sweat. It happened so fast that it momentarily stung like a thousand pinpricks. In a heartbeat I was bathed in sweat.

I could taste the fear in my mouth. It was the most scared I'd ever been.

Jimmy's voice seemed to come from another world. He sounded distant and distorted.

"That's my woman you're messin' with. Now you gotta die!"

"Hold on, Jimmy! Just hold on a minute! Let's think this out, okay?"

I was talking fast now, like a used car salesman.

"Jimmy! Who are you gonna kill? You can't kill her because she's *already dead.* You can't kill me because then I'd be dead too, and I'd be with her. You don't want us to be together in the afterlife, do you? Well, that's what will happen if you kill me. I'll be haunting this bus too, along with Roxie. You don't want that to happen, right?"

Jimmy's voice was dry and bitter. "What was she doin' with you?"

I wiped the sweat off my forehead with the back of my hand. "She was all over me, man, but I didn't touch her. I can't. I really and truly prefer live women. Swear to God."

Jimmy kept the pistol raised and pointed at me.

I said, "How do we know she didn't plan this?"

Jimmy's eyes narrowed. "Why would she do that?"

"Well, if she wants to get it on with me, the best thing for her to do is get me dead. Then she'd have me all to herself. Now, I gotta figure she knows you pretty well, and she knew you'd fly into a jealous rage and pull your gun if you caught us together. So, it's entirely possible that she engineered the whole thing."

The gun barrel drooped slightly. Jimmy looked at Roxie.

"Is that true?"

Instead of answering, Roxie disappeared. She winked out and left Jimmy alone with the gun in his hand and decisions to make. I could see tears welling up in his eyes.

He shook his head. "My life ain't worth a damn anymore. All I do is drive this rolling shithouse, day after day, year after year. I don't even have a home address, I live on the road twelve months a year."

I didn't answer him. He had the gun. I waited to see what he would do.

"I wanna be with her," he whimpered. "I love her."

Part of my brain could see what was coming. Another part wanted nothing more than for Jimmy to put the gun down. Whatever happened after that was all right, as long as the gun was out of his hand. Yet another, more optimistic part, prayed for any reasonable resolve, one where nobody got shot. But, as soon as the thought occurred to me, I knew it wouldn't be like that. I knew what Jimmy was going to do. And I understood why.

Jimmy stayed the same. He sobbed a little more, but he stayed the same. Minutes passed. At last, he nodded to me.

I nodded back.

He put the gun to his head and pulled the trigger.

There was nothing I could do.

He had figured it out.

The band never traveled by tour bus again. They never quite recovered from waking up to a gunshot and finding Jimmy's brains splattered against the wall. The official investigation concluded that Jimmy was full of pills and depressed, and probably just couldn't take it anymore.

But, I knew better.

The bus was refurbished and leased to yet another unsuspecting rock band, now with two restless spirits permanently onboard. It's probably still out there on the road somewhere, rolling to the next gig.

SEASON PREMIERE

JAMES SALLIS

I T WAS JUST after they hung Shorty Bergen that the rats showed up. No one had ever seen anything like them. They came swarming up over the bank of a dried-up riverbed, must have been close to a hundred of them, traveling all together. It was like locusts in those films of Africa, where the bugs sweep down and leave behind nothing but bare branches and stalks. Only the rats weren't looking for vegetable matter. Johnny Jones lost his whole crop of chickens. At Gene Brocato's they took down five sheep and a young cow.

"Rats don't hunt in packs," Billy Barnstile said. He and his partner Joe McGee were out in one of the power company's trucks, checking lines. They'd pulled off the road to watch as the rats broke into twin streams around the farmhouse, then rejoined to sweep over Gene Brocato's field. Within moments, it seemed, only bones remained where livestock had been.

"Never saw anything like it," Joe McGee said.

Of course, no one had ever seen anything like Shorty Bergen either. He looked like parts of two people glued together, this long, long trunk with a couple of stubby doll legs stuck on as afterthought. "Boy'd had legs to match his body, he'd be eight feet tall," his mother always said. But he wasn't. He was four-and-a-half feet tall, even in the goat-roper cowboy boots he favored. Hair stuck out in bristles from his ears. His real hair, however often he washed it, always looked greasy, all two dozen or so limp strands of it.

What had happened was, Shorty'd taken himself a liking to Betty Sue Carstairs, and there was two things wrong with that. Dan Carstairs was nearabouts the only person in town with anything like real money, and he loved his daughter, who'd come to him late in life, with a fierce pride—that's one—and Betty Sue, for all her beauty—this is two—was simple as a fence post. When Shorty Bergen started bringing her candy and bundles of wildflowers he'd picked on the way through the woods, she babbled and drooled in delight. Didn't have no idea how ugly he was, or that anything might be wrong in it or what he was up to. Her daddy'd always brought her things. Now Shorty did too.

Pretty soon the rats were all the talk down at Bee's Blue Bell Diner, which, if you didn't eat at home, was where you ate in Hank's Ridge.

"They ain't come near town as yet, at least," Lucas Hodgkins said. Some egg yolk and about a third of his upper dentures had slipped his mouth. He reached up and pushed the dentures back in. The egg yolk stayed.

"I hear you." This was Froggie Levereaux, four tables away. People said he ordered that damned beret he always wore from Sears. He sure as hell hadn't bought it in Hank's Ridge. His nose put you in mind of the blade on a sundial. "You never know, though. Onct they get a taste of human blood . . . I seen it happen with huntin' dogs. Even with a goat, one time. Commenced to gobbling up small children like popcorn."

Bee herself, a dry stick of a woman, was in the thick of it.

"Don't like it, don't like it at all," she said. Bee hadn't liked much of anything in well onto forty-six years.

"Where've they been is what I want to know. None of us ever heard tell of 'em."

"I remember when I was little, back in Florida, it used to rain frogs."

"Frogs is frogs. Rats is rats."

"It's like that story about the paid piper."

"Boils be next," Judd Sealey said—a deacon down to the church. "Boils. Then—well, I can't rightly remember. Seven of them, though. Seven plagues."

"Rodents, is what they are." Bud Gooley shuddered. "Teeth don't never stop growing."

The sound of the screen door out to the kitchen swinging shut brought a hiatus to the conversation.

Jed Stanton shook his head sagely. "You ever know Stu Ellum to leave behind a perfectly good bite of pie before?"

Froggie Levereaux ambled over and finished it up for him.

"Man's got him a worry for sure," Bee said.

Dan Carstairs warned Shorty Bergen to stay away from Betty Sue and went into some detail as to what would eventuate if he failed to do so. Thing was, taken as he was with Betty Sue, Shorty Bergen had gone damn near as simple as the girl herself. He'd just stand there smiling up at Dan Carstairs. Nobody laid claim to having seen it, but everyone knew how one Saturday evening when Shorty Bergen came courting, Dan Carstairs proceeded to have his farmhands stretch Shorty out against an old wagon wheel and went at him with a bullwhip, dousing him with salted water afterward. Shorty Bergen never said a word, never once whimpered or cried out. Next day, there he was as usual, with flowers and candy for Miss Betty Sue.

Stuart Ellum lived two or three miles south of town on what had once been a thriving apple orchard. Years back some unknown disease had attacked the trees, moving from limb to limb, turning apples into lines of tiny shrunken heads. Limbs twisted and deformed, trunks bloated, the trees remained.

Stu Ellum also had a daughter, Sylvie. The two of them lived in a shack overgrown with honeysuckle and patched with old tin signs for soft drinks. There'd been a wife too for a while, but no one knew much about her, or just when it was she left, if leave she did. A hill woman, they said. Some of the old women used to avert their eyes whenever she came around.

Sylvie never showed any interest in going into town the way Stuart did a couple of times a week, or really in leaving the place at all. She cooked, cleaned their clothes in the stream nearby. Other than that she'd sit on a rickety chair outside the cabin watching bees, wasps, and hummingbirds have at the honeysuckle, or head off into the woods and be gone for hours at the time.

Then a while back, in one of the hollows where people hereabouts are wont to dump garbage, she'd come across a TV set and hauled it back to the cabin. Its innards were all gone, but the glass in front was still good. Sylvie put it up on an old crate in one corner of the cabin and commenced to carve little tables and beds and chairs and buildings. She'd set these up inside, then go across the room and sit watching. One day when Stuart Ellum walked in, he saw she had insects, a grasshopper, a katydid, sitting at the little table inside the TV, acting out whatever scene Sylvie had in her mind.

Over the next several weeks, Shorty Bergen had got himself horsewhipped a second time, beat with axe handles till three ribs broke, and thrown in the pen, hobbled, with one of Dan Carstairs's famously mean-tempered goats. Each time he popped right back up. Carstairs would head out to check on the ploughing or to buy feed and come back and there that boy'd be, sitting on the porch holding hands with Betty Sue.

Must have been right about then that Dan Carstairs decided on taking a different tack.

He started putting it out that Shorty Bergen had raped his Betty Sue. She wasn't the first either, by his reckoning, he said, and men folk all round the valley had best look to their wives and daughters.

Probably nothing would've come of it, except a couple families over the other side of the mountain started saying somebody'd been getting to their girls, too. Never mind that just about everybody knew exactly who it was had been getting to them. That kind of thing, once it starts up, it spreads like wildfire. Wasn't more than a month had passed before Shorty Bergen woke to a flashlight in his eyes and a group of stern-faced men above him. They dragged him outside, tied a rope around his neck in a simple granny knot and threw the rope over a limb, and a bunch of them hauled at the other end. When the limb broke, they started over, and got the job done, though it took some time.

Now, it happened that Sylvie had taken a liking to Shorty Bergen. One of the ways he scraped together a living was by scavenging what people threw away, everything from chairs to simple appliances, and fixing them. Then he'd take them around and sell them for a dollar or two. He'd only been by Stuart Ellum's cabin twice, since Stuart always told him they had everything they needed and then some, but Sylvie never took her eyes off him either time, and afterward was always asking Stuart about him. Before that, whenever she told Stuart about her shows, they were full of doctors and nurses, rich men who lived alone in great sadness, and young women suddenly come upon unsuspected legacies or gifts, like all those soap operas she'd seen on a visit to her aunt in the city. Once she saw Shorty

Bergen, though, all her shows centered around him. Shorty was running for sheriff, but the rich man who owned everything hereabouts was bound and determined to see him defeated. The doctors at the hospital had done something to Shorty at birth. A withered Native American shook a child's rattle of feathers over his still body and warned that if Shorty were to die, his spirit would sweep like a storm across the land, cleansing it, purifying it.

"Girl? Girl?" What have you done?" Stuart Ellum asked as he ducked to enter the cabin. All the way back from the diner he'd been thinking about what he'd heard there, about that pack of rats overrunning everything, sheep and cattle going down beneath them, a flood of rats laying waste to everything in its path.

"Shhh, it's the news," Sylvie said.

Behind the glass of the TV two rats sat upright in tiny chairs looking straight out into the room. They took turns talking, glancing down at the table before them from time to time, other times looking at one another with knowing nods.

Soon Sylvie clapped her hands silently and turned toward him.

"What did you want to ask me, Daddy?"

As she turned toward him, so did the two rats sitting at the little table inside the TV. Then they stood and took a bow. Their eyes shone—the rats' eyes, and his daughter's.

I AM COMING TO LIVE IN YOUR MOUTH

GLEN HIRSHBERG

> This must be the very pinnacle of good fortune, he thought. To have every
> moment of his death observed by those beautiful eyes—it was like being
> borne to death on a gentle, fragrant breeze.
>
> —YUKIO MISHIMA

I T HAPPENED THE first time during the 4:00 A.M. feeding, and
Kagome believed she was dreaming. This was not unusual; she
almost never slept anymore, and most of her life felt like dreaming,
now. She'd already flushed out Joe's catheter, sponged gently at the
pus that dripped incessantly from the tumor that had devoured his
upper lip, and replaced the nutrient bag on the IV stand. Now she
was sitting quietly, holding his skeletal, freezing fingers in her own.
Briny, Joe's Burmese, lay curled in the permanent indentation he'd
made for himself across Joe's thighs. Once or twice, the cat half-
raised one nictitating lid, flicked its stub of a tail back and forth as
though sweeping the room with radar, and went back to sleep. Out
on the deck, the shadows of the oaks swayed in the winter wind
spooling silently down the San Gabriels, and the Nuttall's wood-
pecker that never left, even in the snow, knocked once against
whichever pine or telephone pole it had lodged in this night.

I am coming, she heard, half-heard, rolling the bones of Joe's fingers with her thumb.

It was like the interferon year all over again. In a way, despite the
realities of the current situation, watching him then had been worse.
He'd slept even more, for one thing, sometimes as many as thirty
hours in a row, and never less than twenty. But his sleep had been
more disturbed, riddled with tremors that wracked him for minutes

on end, haunted by dream demons Joe clearly remembered afterward but rarely described to her. *Tall things,* he'd murmur. *Whisperers.*

Sometimes, that year, the moments when he wasn't shuddering or dreaming were more frightening still. His face had been less drastically scarred, then, but also tended to go sickeningly slack, drain of everything that identified *that* hawk-nose, *these* flippy ear-lobes, this slightly upturned mouth, as Joe's. Looking into it had been like staring at the drawn shades of a house that had been termite-bombed.

And yet. Back then, there'd also been that one, absurd element of hope. That the interferon regimen might just work. Kill every deadly cell inside Joe but still leave Joe.

Whereas now, hours or days from the end—not weeks, she'd been assured, not even one week—Joe rarely so much as twitched. Sometimes, as she tended to him, his eyelids fluttered, but contentedly. At least, Kagome insisted to herself that was the case. And sometimes, right at this moment, he'd actually awaken and look at her, and she'd see that formidable engine in there fire one more time, all that ferocious fight, all those useless things he somehow knew locking into place behind his retinas. Once, he'd told her he loved her, that she was the only reason he was still battling. Mostly, though, he glanced at the feedbag and said, "Kidney pie. Rock on." Or, if they had a chemo or oncologist appointment later that day, "Shotgun."

I am coming to live . . .

She was moving his hand against the inside of one of her wrists, now. Feeling the paper-thin membrane against her smoothness, right where the sleeve of her robe ended. Dazed, she moved his hand to her cheek. Held it there. Stroked once, so gently, down. Back up. Down again. Then she slid Joe's hand to her neck. Down farther, into the V of her robe to brush one nipple. The other. *How long had it been now? Two years? Three? They'd had such sweet touching in the eighteen months before what they'd always known was coming—or, coming back—arrived for good. Such patient touching, as though they'd had all the time in the world.* Now his skin—what there was of it—just felt scratchy and hard, like a dried-out loofah.

I am coming to live in your mouth.

She jerked upright and dropped Joe's hand to the hospital bed that had taken the place of their couch and swung around.

Screaming, she thought. *I should be screaming.*

She couldn't see his face. He was standing in the corner, just where the shadow of the tallest oak spilled through the glass sliding door.

His stained tan overcoat hung too low, all but brushing the tops of his galoshes, which looked shiny and wet, though there hadn't been so much as a mist out there yet this fall. He had his head bent low, the brim of his trilby completely shading his face.

"Get out of my—" she started, and his voice overrode her though it was barely a whisper, hollow as respirator breath in an oxygen mask.

I am coming to live in your mouth. Because you never have anything to say.

Then she *was* screaming, crying, too, *"Out! Get out! OUT!"*

The figure in the corner didn't even lift its head, but it was still speaking, or else those words had rung a resonant spot inside her, because she could hear them over her shouting. *Coming to live. Never have anything . . .*

"What in *sweet God's* name?" Mrs. Thiel snapped from the stairway, and Kagome whirled, her own voice choking to silence but that *other's* still echoing.

At least the mask was down, Kagome thought, watching Joe's mother's razor-thin eyebrows squeeze together like crayfish pincers. For a long moment, she just held Mrs. Thiel's gaze, then remembered and leapt to her feet, swinging around.

By the sliding glass door, she saw the shadow of the oak shaking slightly, as though ravens had just sprung from its branches. Bare floor. The boxes of sterile needles and spare tubing tucked neatly against the breakfront. Nothing else.

I am coming to live in your mouth.

When she turned once more, she found Joe's mother smiling. The eyebrows hung in their carefully separated spaces like precisely hung photographs. The mask, in place once more.

"Jasmine?" Mrs. Thiel said brightly. "Help us greet the new day grinning?"

Moving to the stove, ignoring Kagome's elegant tetsubin tea things arrayed on the shelf by the sink, she filled the utilitarian silver kettle she'd brought with her when she'd finally dropped the pretense and moved in a few weeks before. The kettle made an ugly, banging sound as Mrs. Thiel settled it over the burner.

"Think the newspaper's here? I'll get you your crossword. Or is it more a sudoku kind of hour?"

Instead of answering, Kagome gazed down again at what was left of her husband. Her screaming hadn't roused him. *Would today be the last day? Would the next time he opened his eyes be the final one?*

Good God, had she already had *the final one? When had it been? She couldn't even remember.*

She watched Joe's chest, which just lay flat.

Lay flat.

Lay flat.

Lay flat.

And finally, fitfully, inflated, as though some small child were shoving at it from inside. Joe's mouth didn't exactly open anymore, but part of his lower lip quivered as air slipped past it. He gurgled once, and pus ran down his teeth onto his tongue. Then his chest clamped down again.

Kagome glanced toward the corner. With a brief, discreet brush of her husband's palm with her fingertips, she turned to face Mrs. Thiel. She had no smile in her, and managed one. At least, it felt like she did. "Sudoku, I think," she said. Without even slipping her fuzzy overcoat over her robe, she crossed to the front door and stepped out into the icy mountain air to wait for the paper she knew wouldn't come for at least another hour.

But the cold didn't help. Nor did the shower when she came inside. Nor Mrs. Thiel's superb slow eggs and salsa. The final proof for just how unsettling her 4:00 A.M. encounter had been came as Mrs. Thiel was clearing the breakfast dishes, leaning over her shoulder while Kagome tapped the last unfilled boxes of the Thursday *Times* crossword with her pencil eraser.

"Mulliner," Mrs. Thiel said suddenly, and Kagome stared at the puzzle. The answer was correct, of course. *65 down: Old hat, at the Angler's.* Jobs misspelled to make Wodehouse characters, the theme of the day. *When, exactly, had Mrs. Thiel started nailing crossword clues like that? Never before, in the time Kagome had known her.*

"Get the crazy glue," Mrs. Thiel said, and Kagome grabbed her hand and almost made her drop the dishes. She could feel Mrs. Thiel's scowl on her shoulders—God forbid either of them should actually show any emotion other than radiant, resolute *hopefulness*—but Mrs. Thiel held on, too. For one second, no longer.

Get the crazy glue. It was what Joe said when he turned away from a ball he'd bowled immediately after bowling it, before the ball was halfway down the lane. When he knew he'd rolled a strike, and that the pins would be flying. In the three, maybe four times Kagome had gone bowling with Joe, she'd never seen him guess wrong. "'*Cause there's no guessing involved,"* he'd say. And touch her cheek gently with one finger as he returned to his seat.

I am coming to live in your mouth . . .

The doorbell rang at eleven while Kagome was still combing out her long, black hair and beginning to weave it into the complicated *sakkou* fashion she'd learned from her mother, and that had always hypnotized Joe. Fascinated him. "Like a wild knot," he'd said once, slipping his long fingers in and out of the whirl of loops and crosses she'd made. Then, when she'd lain still long enough, he told her what that was, as she knew he would. A knot built out of infinite sequences, with a seemingly infinite number of edges. "In the actual universe—the physical one—" Joe told her, "there's no such thing."

Abruptly, she came out of her reverie. *Hospice.* She'd blocked that out. Forgotten they were coming. Then she heard the door opening, a single strum of out-of-tune ukulele, and her first real smile of the day spread over her pale, exhausted face. Pinning the last twist of her hair into place, she stepped into the hall and caught a fleeting glimpse, *galoshes sliding silently around the corner, into the guest room they never used, who would come?*

Sprinting for the room, she threw open the door—*closed? It was closed?* —and found the erg machine Joe had ordered to keep his muscles in shape while his skin rotted off and his lungs shriveled and his organs imploded, one by one. Beyond the bare windows, she saw the tops of trees, all but bare now, swaying.

More ukulele strum from downstairs, and Ryan's ridiculous, keening laugh, and his croak of a voice. "Going down, chum. Going down hard." And then that roaring, ripping cough—the cancer growling as it fed—that told her Joe was awake.

Kagome hurried downstairs, ignoring the urge to swing around, just once, to make sure. *She'd made sure. And already knew, anyway.*

"How long has he been awake?" she asked Mrs. Thiel, who was wiping down the kitchen counters, having already washed every dish and tucked away the supplies from last night's feeding. Only occasionally did the woman allow herself a glance toward the couch, where her son, propped up, was trying to get his fingers around the Playstation controller and his thumbs into place. Finally, Mrs. Thiel looked at Kagome. And grinned.

Kagome smiled back. They stood together and watched.

Ryan, in his usual holey black *Warped Tour* skateshirt and Vans, was alternately flipping at his mop of brown hair and fiddling with the television controllers. Eventually, the screen burst into color, and pumping techno music thudded through the room. Returning to his seat, Ryan spied Kagome, waved the ukulele he was still holding by its neck in his free hand, and settled in the chair closest to Joe. On the screen, twin rocket-propelled race cars approached a starting line as the riff in the music repeated itself, then froze as the START NEW GAME? message appeared.

It was hard to remember, watching them, that Ryan had started out as Kagome's friend. He'd been her intern at *Mountain Living*. In some ways, he fit the copy editor stereotype even more closely than she did: glasses, nervous twitch to his fingers, permanent pale-yellow cast to his skin. Computer tan. Except he also wore Vans and played the ukulele, told invented shaggy dog jokes that made Kagome laugh—no mean feat, in this particular era of her life—and kick-boxed.

Four months ago, out of nowhere, hunched over his computer in the midst of a particularly gnarly edit, he'd mentioned his Boggle prowess. She'd said nothing, but brought Joe's travel set the next day and set it wordlessly before Ryan at lunch. It had taken her two rounds to realize he hadn't been kidding, and seven for him to win the match. Which made him exactly the second person she'd ever met to take one from her. She hadn't so much invited him to dinner as thrown down the gauntlet. He'd shown up singing "Tiny Bubbles," Joe had skunked him at Boggle but lost every Playstation game they'd tried and also computer Jeopardy, and that had pretty much been the last time Kagome had spent with Ryan except at work.

When Ryan was at their house, which was almost every night now, he was with Joe. Once the sickness consigned Joe permanently to the couch, Ryan came more frequently, not less. She didn't think she'd ever been happier about another human being's existence except her husband's.

"You'll be wanting me to say I'm lucky," Ryan told Joe now. She watched his eyes flick to the tumor on Joe's mouth. On Joe's lap, Briny aimed an annoyed glare at Ryan, then hopped down and disappeared upstairs.

"Nnuz nuuuuhne," said Joe. He couldn't really turn his head, but Kagome saw his gaze stray in her direction.

"He says, 'Because you will be,'" Kagome told Ryan. Even Mrs. Thiel could no longer understand her son.

Ryan grinned. "Then you're admitting defeat before we begin. It's what I've always wanted from you."

He triggered the game, and on screen one of the racers launched from the start and hurtled out of sight around a curve, while the other spun immediately into a side wall and blew up.

"Nnuk," Joe said. Ryan grinned wider, and kept going.

Kagome saw the panic first, and moved immediately, silently. Mrs. Thiel was right behind her, and Ryan didn't even notice until they were already beside Joe, gently disentangling his catheter tube from underneath him and beginning the several-minute process of preparing to help him up.

"What . . . oh . . ." Ryan said, wrinkling his nose at the smell and standing. "It's okay, dude." He held out his hands.

"He knows it's okay, could you get a water bucket and the sponges?" Mrs. Thiel snapped.

"Under the sink," Kagome murmured. "Thank you, Ryan."

Somehow, once they got Joe to his feet, he managed to stay there while Kagome and Mrs. Thiel bundled up the mess in the sheets, and Kagome scrubbed at the slimy, brown streaks sinking into the pillows. Those streaks seemed so devoid of mass they barely even qualified as shit. When she'd finished, she leaned back on her haunches and brushed her nose with her forearm and looked up at her husband. So thin as to be almost two-dimensional, pale as paper, like an origami approximation of himself. To her delighted surprise, he was fully alert, staring back. *And smiling?*

"Nnnay nur nuky," he said.

"I'm lucky," she whispered, and kissed the bones of his hand.

"How about Tijuana Taco?" Mrs. Thiel chirped as she returned from whatever she'd done with the sheets. *Framed them, probably,* Kagome thought, then chastised herself for thinking it. "Kagome, green chile for you, right?"

"Just soup," she murmured. A few chattery seconds later, Mrs. Thiel mercifully left the house on her errand.

Standing for so long had completely exhausted Joe, and he was swaying and shivering more violently than the trees outside as Ryan and Kagome lowered him back onto the home-care hospital bed he'd chosen to die on and settled his heap of comforters and blankets and coats around him. They weren't enough, and Joe went on shivering even as sleep swallowed him.

Stripping off her rubber gloves, Kagome stood and gazed down at her husband. Behind her, Ryan muted the TV, though from the clicking of the controllers, she knew he was finishing Joe's race for him. Starting right where Joe's car had exploded. After a while, he took up his ukulele again, stroked that quietly. The chords he played changed so slowly, she wasn't sure they were even connected or part of a song until he started half-humming a vocal line, in his strangely sweet croak that was far too old for him.

"*Because you never . . . because you never . . . have anything . . .*"

She didn't mean to hit him, of course she didn't, but the words he had sung didn't register right away, and when they did, she panicked, spun so fast that the fist still holding the shit-rag smacked across his cheek and her knee drove the ukulele out of his hands and across the room. Stunned, streaked with brown and red across his cheeks, Ryan stared up at her, while her free hand flew to her own mouth.

"What did you just . . ." Her brain was screaming back to this morning, and she was crying again, too, seeing the stick-thin, galoshes-guy in the corner. "*Ryan?*"

Even as she said it, she knew it wasn't so. She hadn't seen the trilby man's face. But he'd been considerably taller. And even though his shape had been disguised by his trench coat, it hadn't been Ryan's shape. *No. It had been . . . what? She couldn't remember.* Furthermore, Ryan had been downstairs, just coming inside, at the moment Kagome had seen the trilby man ducking into the guest room. *Because he* had *been there. She was as sure of that now as she'd been that he was imaginary a few hours ago.*

"I'm sorry," she whispered, blinking to try to stem her tears. She bent to wipe at the streaks on Ryan's cheek, and he let her. "I'm sorry," she said again.

"It's okay," he said, though she'd clearly frightened him. "You've been through so—"

"That song." Dropping the rag, she slumped into the wooden chair Mrs. Thiel always sat in, leaving the armchair for Kagome. Precisely the sort of gesture Kagome despised in her mother-in-law, even though it probably had no other motive behind it than kindness. "What made you sing that?"

Now Ryan was staring. "Sing what?"

"What you just sang."

"I wasn't singing. I was barely even—"

On the couch, Joe unleashed a cough that lifted his spine off the pillows and convulsed him with shudders but didn't waken him. Kagome dug under the blankets, found the IV tube, and followed it down to Joe's hand. Then she held on. After a while, she turned her gaze once more on Ryan. Her eyes had dried, her features settling into their comfortable, familiar impassivity. Mrs. Theil's wasn't the only mask, she realized.

"Kagome," Ryan murmured. "I'm sorry. I was just . . . strumming. *Wasn't I?*"

"Yes," Kagome lied, and her heart banged. "I think probably you were."

After that, they sat and breathed and watched for Joe's breaths. At some point, Kagome's free hand found Ryan's, and for a fleeting few minutes, she felt a peculiar, suspended stasis. Not peace, nowhere near peace. But there were people in this room who loved her.

And someone else, too, who was coming to live, and Kagome gripped Ryan's hand and closed her eyes and held still and held on.

"She driving you crazy?" Ryan said. "Joe's mom, I mean? What's she so happy about, anyway?"

For a long time, Kagome didn't answer. Didn't want to. Despite the waves of panic and loneliness and nausea and fear, she wanted to stay right where she was, propped in place, like a birdhouse with birds hopping around and into it, even though there was virtually nothing left inside.

"She's never been happy," Kagome answered. "She just . . . she thinks it's what Joe wants. You know, he's never liked even acknowledging that he's sick. She also thinks it's why he's still here. If you don't look at it, it can't see you. That kind of thing. I think. Maybe she's right. You know he's been told he had less than a year to live since he was seven years old."

"Does she like you?"

The question startled Kagome out of her half-trance. For the first time in who knew how long, her eyes left Joe's face. She looked not at Ryan but the mountainside folding into nightshadow as the November day drained away.

Then that voice was in her ears again, and her bones, too, and the soft tissue of her arms and chest, whispering, scratching. *I am coming to live in your mouth. Coming to live in your mouth. Coming . . .*

"She thinks I'm a vacuum," Kagome said, and didn't cry, or squeeze Ryan's hand. She squeezed Joe's, though. Hard. "She thinks he married me to have a *calming* presence near. Because he finally got scared."

"Does she know you can beat him at Boggle? Does she actually think that *calms* him?"

"Scrabble. Not Boggle. Not ever."

Her eyes flicked to Ryan's face. Behind his glasses, his surprisingly large green eyes seemed to swivel in their sockets like a bird's. To her immense relief, he was smiling, a little. Somehow, in his *Warped* T-shirt, with his long legs bunched up against the hospital bed and his hair falling over his face, he looked completely adrift on the currents in this room, bobbing like a bottle with a message in it. Whether the message was for or from her, she had no idea.

Hospice arrived a little after five, an hour or so after Mrs. Thiel came back. Rising from the wooden chair where she'd stayed all day—to her mother-in-law's visible annoyance, and not once had Mrs. Thiel taken the empty La-Z-Boy—Kagome watched the two nurses and one social worker fan through the room, silent and efficient as the elves in that story about the shoemaker, who come in on a moonbeam. Truly, they were marvels. Even the doorbell when they rang seemed muffled. Even Mrs. Thiel went quieter when they were here, though her ferocious half-grin never wavered.

The two nurses sponged Joe down, changed his bedding; one combed what was left of his hair while the other washed out the tumor over his mouth with a syringe. The social worker brought Kagome tea in one of her porcelain cherry-blossom cups, and may have spoken to her, too. Kagome might even have spoken back. She couldn't be sure, knew only that the muttering in her ears and her blood had gone quiet. She could hear it, still, but barely. As though it were out on the deck in the falling dark, and just once she glanced that way, through the sliding doors, and saw only shadow.

I know you, she thought, and didn't even try to make sense of that.

"You know what hospice does?" Mrs. Thiel had halfway shrieked, when Kagome had insisted on bringing them in. "Hospice kills you. You understand that, right? You think they're coming to help? They're coming to kill Joe. They're the angels of goddamn death."

And of course, she was right. The smothering doses of morphine and methadone that ate away at the brain, the thousand other little drugs they gave that the body couldn't really take, all meant to keep Joe comfortable, mask the pain. The words they used, to settle them all. Get them ready. Or, not ready, there was no such thing, and they would never have used so crude a term. Tranquil, maybe. Sort of. Angels of death they truly were. But why did Americans always focus on the death part? What else did they imagine angels were for?

So pervasive was the spell the hospice workers cast that Kagome only noticed the positions they'd taken and realized what they were about to do a few seconds before Joe woke up. Way back in her throat, a groan formed, and though it came out choked, barely even audible, the sound grated against everything else in the room and rattled Mrs. Thiel to wakefulness. And so Mrs. Thiel realized what was happening, too.

"Get away from him," Mrs. Thiel said, but even her voice seemed to come from under a layer of gauze, as though she'd been gagged. "Get . . ."

Her words sank to nothing as her son's eyes flew open. For one moment, he lay there, blinking, before rolling with surprising alacrity onto his side. His glare was like a bucket of water flung over the hospice workers. They were human after all, Kagome noted; all three flinched back on the chairs they'd arrayed around the bed so that their medical whites formed a sort of picket fence between Joe and the rest of the room. The life he'd lived. Just like that, they ceased to be angels, and their features resolved into ordinary, comprehensible, *human* ones. One of the nurses had a Band-Aid under the lobe of her left ear. The social worker had pretty auburn hair—*just moments ago, it had seemed gray, Kagome had assumed that was a required color for the job, like a uniform*—clumped in an unflattering working bun at the base of her neck.

It was the social worker who spoke, as a new shiver rippled down Joe's obscenely articulated bones. The woman's voice was trained, alright, lulling as a 2 A.M. smooth-jazz disc jockey's, but warmer. At once more detached and more genuine.

"Joe," the woman said.

Beside Kagome, Mrs. Thiel beat her arms against her sides like an enraged mother eagle. But she held her place. Waited.

"Joe, you've fought so hard, for so long. For thirty years, is that right?"

To Kagome's astonishment, Joe answered. And his voice came out fuller, with more of his joyful, prickly *Joe*-ness than at any time in the past two months. Also with more consonants.

"Thirty-three. Got sick when I was seven."

"Thirty-three years, when virtually anyone else would have been dead in six months. Incredible. Please know, Joe. All we want is to help you make meaningful use of every meaningful second, and also provide comfort. To you, and your loved ones. We've been coming here a month. I've never seen anyone fight like you do."

Was Joe smiling, now? Oh, God, was Joe crying? The tumor

seemed to float across his mouth, obscuring it, like one of those black blotches television stations use to blur victim's features on true crime shows.

"So now. Joe." This time, as she spoke, the social worker slid forward on her chair. As if on cue, the others edged forward, also, and Kagome almost screamed, it was like watching hyenas dance in from the edge of a clearing.

"What is your goal now, Joe? Can you tell me that?" At this, the woman gave a practiced but mournful glance over her shoulder toward Kagome and Mrs. Thiel. Kagome watched her auburn bun shake. "What do you still want to do?"

There was no doubt anymore. Joe was crying. If there'd been a smile, too, it was gone. "Survive," he said, in his dead man's rasp. Then he rolled over and went back to sleep.

"You bitch," Mrs. Thiel murmured, and Kagome started to nod right along with her, wanted to raise both fists in the air and cheer or scream, and then realized her mother-in-law meant *her*. "I can't take this," Mrs. Thiel went on. "I'm going to the movies." Already, her voice was molding back into its chirp, as though it were pottery clay she was rounding, relentlessly rounding. "I'll be back soon. Bring you those chocolate stars you like, if they have any, Kagome. Bye, Ryan, see you tomorrow?"

Moments later, she was gone, and hospice, too, leaving a message pad full of numbers to call, *any*time, for help or advice, or just to talk. They promised to be back tomorrow afternoon. Kagome returned to her wooden chair and Ryan to the La-Z-Boy. Ryan left his ukulele on the floor. They stayed there in silence a long time. Full night fell.

Kagome wasn't sure when she realized Ryan was asleep. He had his arms crossed tight across his thin chest, his head twisted at an ugly angle, as though someone had slipped up behind and wrenched it halfway off. His leg, barely touching hers through her skirt, felt almost hot. So palpably *living*. Gently, she reached over, lifted his head, and leaned it in what she hoped was a more comfortable way against her shoulder. When she looked up, the trilby man was watching through the window.

For the second time in less than a day, a scream jagged up her throat, but this time Kagome managed to catch it between her teeth, and her tongue and everything inside her sizzled as though she'd bit down on electrical wire. *How did she know the trilby man was watching, she couldn't even see his face? The hat and the dark hid his features, made her wonder if there was a face under there at all, his head just looked like a blacker circle pasted on the black out there.*

Because it wasn't *out there.* She was seeing his reflection. He was right behind her.

She whirled, banging Ryan's forehead with her own. His head rocked back, stars shot across her eyes, and she swept her gaze wildly through the room but saw nothing. *Wait—near the counter. By the kitchen.* But that was Briny, Joe's cat, creeping back.

Tears poured through her squeezed lashes all at once, as though she'd tipped a vase that had been stored there. She couldn't stop them, felt the shakes seize her. Then Ryan's arms were around her shoulders, enclosing her. She let herself fold forward. For long minutes, she had no idea how long, she just leaned into Ryan and shook. He held tight.

The only thing she was *absolutely* certain of, later, was that she'd started it. And that she'd been looking at Joe when she did. At the stump where Joe's right ear had been, and the black, ball-shaped scar over the hole in his jaw where the second-to-last of the twenty-three surgeries she'd been through with him had focused. The little tumors swelling all over his face, seeming to wriggle when she looked away, like pregnant spiders scurrying over her husband with their sacs of young.

Partially, it was triggered by the awkward way Ryan held her, with his hands seemingly affixed to her shoulder blades like defibrillator pads he was trying to place. For most of the time Joe had been able to hold her, he'd done so like that. He'd avoided dating, most of his life. Hadn't seen the point, he said. And so he hadn't known what to do with his hands, at first. She'd had to show him.

But partially, too, it was Ryan's heat. His pale arms, with her tears streaking them, and the surprising force of his skater's thighs pushing against hers. It was like holding Joe, but a different Joe. Joe *healthy.* Joe capable of expressing the hunger she knew he felt, that was too strong for his frail frame, that he'd been afraid would shake him to pieces every time they touched. She wasn't exactly thinking any of this, but she was conscious of it all as one of her hands slid down Ryan's chest into his lap, and her mouth lifted and found his.

It lasted longer than she could have hoped, certainly longer than she expected. Long enough for her to wonder if they were actually going through with it, and to understand that Ryan hadn't come here only for Joe, after all. His hands had come off her shoulders at last, and they felt so *good* gliding on her back. His eyes were closed, but hers flicked constantly between this boy's sweet, helpless face and her husband's wrecked and sleeping one. It was like touching them both, touching Ryan, yes, but also Joe through him. Their mouths had come open, and she was caressing, probing, had Ryan's belt unbuckled when she saw the *cat* staring at her and froze, just for a second.

Which was far too long. Ryan gagged, his mouth snapped shut, and he banged her head again with his own as he scrambled to his feet. "Oh, Kagome," he said, fumbling at his snap and his belt and not getting either and finally staring down at himself and then her in disbelief. "I'm so sorry," he said, and burst into tears.

"Ryan," she said, and started to stand, and then she was just too tired. She watched him and offered nothing reassuring, just leaned her head into the side of the La-Z-Boy and let her hair droop almost to the floor. She didn't cry, didn't even want to. Mostly, she realized, she wanted to be alone. *When was the last time she'd been alone, for any length of time? A month ago? Three?*

Ryan kept crying, kept saying, "Sorry." Not until he was at the door did he say he'd be back. She couldn't even rouse herself to nod or wave.

Then she was by herself. She closed her eyes and listened. For a moment, she panicked. Even the wind outside seemed to have stilled, and nothing anywhere near her seemed to be breathing, not even her. Then, very low, she heard the rumble of Briny's purr, and after that a sudden, rattling gasp from Joe, followed by another in no rhythm. Then silence again. She couldn't even hear the air entering or leaving her own body. *Maybe Mrs. Thiel was right, and she was more bonsai tree than wife. Decorative and silent.*

And she never had anything to say.

Kagome. Even the name was meaningless, her mother had taken it from some childhood chant.

Opening her eyes, Kagome sat up. She considered dialing her parents in Sendai. But talking to them from this house was like shouting across a mountain canyon. Her mother's health—and, maybe, her father's unexpressed sense of betrayal or just loss that she'd decided to settle here—had prevented them ever from coming. And Joe's health had prevented his going. And years had piled up, like snow in the Snow Country, so deep and so quickly. Kagome didn't have the strength to traverse them tonight.

I know you, she was thinking, nonsensically. She sat.

At some point, she considered calling Ryan. Telling him he had nothing to be sorry for, that it was her fault. If there was fault. That she loved his coming to the house, and knew his presence was at least as crucial to keeping Joe alive as her own. But then she decided she didn't need to say this. Ryan was so bright, so intuitive despite his awkwardness. Like Joe was. Had been.

To Kagome's astonishment, Mrs. Thiel came home raving drunk. She stood swaying a while over her son, glared at Kagome, and Kagome wrapped her in a blanket and took her up to bed. The woman's hands were rigid with cold, as though she'd shoved them in an ice-bucket for the past few hours. As Kagome flicked out the bedroom light, she heard Mrs. Thiel murmur, "Thank you, Kagome. You are, without question, the easiest person in the world to go through this with."

Kagome almost threw herself back across the room, shrieked in Mrs. Thiel's face. *I tried to fuck his friend,* she almost said. Wished she'd said. *Easiest?*

Instead, she shut the door and stood a few silent seconds on her balcony, in her silent house. That would soon be empty for real. Silent for good. She didn't open her eyes until she was halfway down the staircase.

The hospital bed was empty.

At first, the sight made so little sense that Kagome couldn't process it, couldn't begin to think what to do. Then she was flying downstairs, all but crashing onto her face as she leapt the last five steps into the living room and stared around at the kitchen, the deck—*Shit and God, had he thrown himself from the deck?* —and saw nothing, and no one.

"Joe?" she said. Spun back to the stairs, to the deck again, expecting the trilby man to materialize out there, *he'd said he was coming, warned them he was.*

"Joe?"

Then she heard it. One single sob. From the bathroom. Skidding across the hardwood, she rattled the knob, which was locked, beat with her palm against the door. "Joe? It's me."

"I killed Briny."

In mid-beat, with her arm still raised, Kagome froze. "What?"

Sob. Then a sawing, rattling gasp of a breath.

"Joe, please."

"It wasn't me. I couldn't help it." His voice so clear. As though, right at the end, he'd swallowed the tumor whole, or ripped it off in one last savage spasm of defiance.

"Joe."

Sobbing.

Cautiously, squeamishly—which was hilarious, in a way, given what she'd seen and done and immersed herself in ever since she'd married her husband—Kagome glanced around for the cat. Briny was so much Joe's, she'd never developed a deep-seated attachment to it. But she'd loved the way it loved him.

God, did he have it in there with him?

Sinking to her knees, Kagome leaned her forehead into the door and closed her eyes, willing herself through the wood. "Joe. Please."

"It's like I had no control over my hands. Like they weren't my hands, anymore, I wasn't even part of it." Rasp. Rattle. Long silence. Sob.

"I think I pulled her head completely off."

Kagome stifled a sob of her own, felt her fingers curl into claws, as though she could scratch her way through, opened her eyes and saw the cat. It lay curled sleepily in the impression Joe had left in the hospital bed when he'd somehow dragged itself off it, licking a forepaw, watching her through one half-open eye.

"Joe? Joe, Briny's fine. She's right here."

Silence. So long that Kagome caught herself making loud, bellows-like sounds with her breath, as though she could blow air through the wood, around the tumor and into Joe's desperate, deflating lungs. She knew what was happening, now. It had happened so many times. One of the new drugs—who even kept track anymore—had reacted with one of the old drugs. Or had built up in his system, or triggered some unexpected reaction. And now he was having an episode. And there was nothing to do about it except talk him through.

"Kagome?" Joe said, and his voice sounded different yet again, so small, like a seven-year-old's. "Kagome, I don't want to die dumb. Please, I don't want to be—"

"What? What are you talking—"

"What time is it?"

"Huh? 1:15 or some—"

"Date? What date? How long have I been like this?"

Sick? Sad? Dying? She could hear in his wheeze that he was dying. The rattle had changed, gone heavy in his throat, like a motor shutting down. She started to weep, glanced sideways. The trilby man stood at the top of the stairs.

All she could see of him, really, was his galoshes, the bottom of his coat, his legs up to his knees. *No,* she thought, shrinking back, looking frantically around for anything heavy. Something she could swing.

I am coming to live in your mouth.

"Won't," she heard Joe grunt, his breath bubbling. "Oh, God, not this way. How long? I killed the . . . I won't. *HOW LONG?"*

Thumping, as though Joe was pounding his own chest. Or driving his head into the wall. "Joe," Kagome said, starting to weep.

"I don't want to be dumb."

"Dumb?"

"I want to be me."

"Joe, You've been you since the day I—"

"Date? What date? How long have I just been lying there? I killed the—"

"Never," she hissed. "Never, for one second, my husband, have you *just been lying there."* She blinked, and the trilby man was closer. Three steps down from the balcony, visible to the waist now. Without even moving. *I know you.* Even as Kagome thought that, he was five steps down. Absolutely still, with his long arms at his sides. Like she was watching a spliced film.

Because you never have anything to say.

Trilby. Trilllll . . .

She was panicking, frantic, wanting to flee the house and unable to move, rolling that word on her tongue. Over and over. *Trilby. Useless name, for a hat no one wore. No one she'd ever known. Where had she even learned it?*

"I killed Briny. Kagome, *WHAT TIME IS IT?!"*

"Constantinople," she said abruptly, heard her husband gasp and go still.

On the stairs, the trilby man winked closer. Still not moving, hands at his sides. She could see the top of the hat now, the head bent down on the chest, obscuring the face.

"Come on," Kagome muttered. *Which of them did she mean? She didn't know, wasn't sure it mattered.*

"Calcutta," Joe whispered, voice catching hard, ripping on the teeth of his cough, and Kagome threw her head back, almost smiling. Almost.

"Cheating," she said, as tears erupted down her cheeks. "Hasn't officially changed its name yet."

"Just because . . ." Ripping, ravaging cough. Then the rattle, low and long. " . . . the west hasn't acknowledged, doesn't mean . . ."

"Fine. Chennai." The trilby man's rubber soles reached the hard-wood floor. Kagome watched him come. *I will not move,* she was chanting, deep inside herself. *I will not move.*

Trilby.

"*That's* cheating," Joe said.

Through her tears, Kagome watched the trilby man twitch closer, and gripped the doorframe to keep from collapsing. The grin that broke over her face was different than any she'd ever felt there.

"How so?" she whispered. Knowing the answer. Wanting him to tell her. To have the pleasure. To *play,* once more. *Fight,* a little longer.

"It's . . . the name changed. Not the name . . . it was."

"Madras," she said.

"Madras," said Joe. "I'm sorry, Kagome."

The trilby man was five feet away; next time he moved they'd be touching. There was nothing to swing at him. Nowhere to run, and even if there was.

Mulliner. Coming to live . . .

"Sorry?" Kagome said, staring at the hat tipped down, the hidden face. *I KNOW you.* "Joe, you have nothing—"

"For not staying. I can't stay."

"Joe. Let me in."

"Can't . . . reach the door. Sorry. Sorry. Sorry."

Weeping, glaring her defiance, Kagome turned her back on the trilby man, put her mouth to the crack between the door and the wall, and began to whisper. "I love you, Joe. I love you, Joe. I love you, Joe."

Then she remembered.

Where else would she have heard such a nothing word but from her husband? *Tall* things, he'd called them, in the year of his inter-feron dreams. *Whisperers, in trilby hats.*

Angels of death? Walking tumors, whispering in the blood?

Or . . . What had that doctor said?

From the top of the stairs, there was a new sound, now. A whimper, climbing toward keening.

In her ears, Kagome could still hear the slow song Ryan had sung. Sworn he hadn't sung. On her shoulders, she could feel his hands, the way they'd moved, and hadn't moved. And in her mouth, she could taste his tongue. The sweat on his cheek that had tasted so sweet. So sweetly *familiar.*

Mulliner. Never before, not even once . . .

"Kagome?" Mrs. Thiel sobbed.

"It's a myth, you know. That we can't kill cancer. We can kill any-thing. Just . . . not selectively." That's what that doctor had said. *"Now, if your husband could oblige by stepping aside, figure a way to climb out of there, just for a month or two . . . "*

Had he?

Kagome whirled, heart hurtling up her chest, borne on a boil of grief and nausea and loneliness and terror and *hope?*

Joe?

Mrs. Thiel had reached the bottom of the stairs, was staring at Kagome, at the closed door behind her. The rattling in the bathroom had stopped. Had been stopped for too long now. Kagome glared back, across the empty room, past her mother-in-law toward the pine trees outside. All that empty, useless wind.

"No," Mrs. Thiel said, and Kagome felt her mouth curl once more, into a snarl she'd never known she had in her. *Because it had never been there. She'd seen it before, though. In those rare moments Joe didn't think she was looking, and the pain came for him, and he somehow roused that* fury *in there and fought it back one more time.*

Whatever was coming, she thought. It was here.

With special thanks to Norman Partridge for the loan of the nightmare . . .

THE AMMONITE VIOLIN (MURDER BALLAD NO. 4)

CAITLÍN R. KIERNAN

1

IF HE WERE EVER to try to write this story, he would not know where to begin. It's that sort of a story, so fraught with unlikely things, so perfectly turned and filled with such wicked artifice and contrivances that readers would look away, unable to suspend their disbelief even for a page. But he will never try to write it, because he is not a poet or a novelist or a man who writes short stories for the newsstand pulp magazines. He is a collector. Or, as he thinks of himself, a Collector. He has never dared to think of himself as *The* Collector, as he is not without an ounce or two of modesty, and there must surely be those out there who are far better than he, shadow men, and maybe shadow women, too, haunting a busy, forgetful world that is only aware of its phantoms when one or another of them slips up and is exposed to flashing cameras and prison cells. Then people will stare, and maybe, for a time, there is horror and fear in their dull, wet eyes, but they soon enough forget again. They are busy people, after all, and they have lives to live, and jobs to show up for five days a week, and bills to pay, and secret nightmares all their own, and in their world there is very little *time* for phantoms.

He lives in a small house in a small town near the sea, for the only time the Collector is ever truly at peace is when he is in the presence of the sea. Even collecting has never brought him to that complete and utter peace, the quiet that finally fills him whenever there is only the crash of waves against a granite jetty and the saltwater mists to breathe in and hold in his lungs like opium fumes. He would love the sea, were she a woman. And sometimes he imagines her so, a wild and beautiful woman clothed all in blue and green, trailing sand and mussels in her wake. Her gray eyes would contain hurricanes, and her voice would be the lonely toll of bell buoys and the cries of gulls and a December wind scraping itself raw against the shore. But, he thinks, were the sea but a women, and were she his lover, then he would *have* her, as he is a Collector and *must* have all those things he loves, so that no one else might ever have them. He must draw them to him and keep them safe from a blind and busy world that cannot even comprehend its phantoms. And having her, he would lose her, and he would never again know the peace which only she can bring.

He has two specialties, this Collector. There are some who are perfectly content with only one, and he has never thought any less of them for it. But he has two, because, so long as he can recall, there has been this twin fascination, and he never saw the point in forsaking one for the other. Not if he might have them both and yet be a richer man for sharing his devotion between the two. They are his two mistresses, and neither has ever condemned his polyamorous heart. Like the sea, who is *not* his mistress but only his constant savior, they understand who and what and *why* he is, and that he would be somehow diminished, perhaps even undone, were he forced to devote himself wholly to the one or the other. The first of the two is his vast collection of fossilized ammonites, gathered up from the quarries and ocean-side cliffs and the stony, barren places of half the globe's nations. The second are all the young women he has murdered by suffocation, *always* by suffocation, for that is how the sea would kill, how the sea *does* kill, usually, and in taking life he would ever pay tribute and honor that first mother of the world.

That first Collector.

He has never had to explain his collecting of suffocations, of the deaths of suffocated girls, as it is such a commonplace thing and a secret collection, besides. But he has frequently found it necessary to explain to some acquaintance or another, someone who thinks that she or he *knows* the Collector, about the ammonites. The ammonites are not a secret and, it would seem, neither are they commonplace. It is simple enough to say that they are mollusks, a subdivision of the Cephalopoda, kin to the octopus and cuttlefish and squid, but possessing exquisite shells, not unlike another living cousin, the chambered nautilus. It is less easy to say that they became extinct at the end of the Cretaceous, along with most dinosaurs, or that they first appear in the fossil record in early Devonian times, as this only leads to the need to explain the Cretaceous and Devonian. Often, when asked that question, *What is an ammonite?*, he will change the subject. Or he will sidestep the truth of his collection, talking only of mathematics and the geometry of the ancient Greeks and how one arrives at the Golden Curve. Ammonites, he knows, are one of the sea's many exquisite expressions of the Golden Curve, but he does not bother to explain that part, keeping it back for himself. And sometimes he talks about the horns of Ammon, an Egyptian god of the air, or, if he is feeling especially impatient and annoyed by the question, he limits his response to a description of the Ammonites from the *Book of Mormon* and how they embraced the god of the Nephites and so came to know peace. He is not a Mormon, of course, as he has use of only a singly deity, who is the sea and who kindly grants him peace when he can no longer bear the clamor in his head or the far more terrible clamor of mankind.

On this hazy winter day, he has returned to his small house from a very long walk along a favorite beach, as there was a great need to clear his head. He has made a steaming cup of Red Zinger tea with a few drops of honey and sits now in the room which has become the gallery for the best of his ammonites, oak shelves and glass display cases filled with their graceful planispiral or heteromorph curves, a thousand fragile aragonite bodies transformed by time and geochemistry into mere silica or pyrite or some other permineralization. He sits at his desk, sipping his tea and glancing occasionally at some beloved specimen or another—*this* one from South Dakota or *that* one from the banks of the Volga River in Russia or one of the *many* that have come from Whitby, England. And then he looks back to the desktop and the violin case lying open in front of him, crimson silk to cradle this newest and perhaps most precious of all the items which he has yet collected in his lifetime, the single miraculous piece which belongs strictly in neither one gallery nor the other. The piece which will at last form a bridge, he believes, allowing his two collections to remain distinct, but also affording a tangible transition between them.

The keystone, he thinks. *Yes, you will be my keystone.* But he knows, too, that the violin will be something more than that, that he has devised it to serve as something far grander than a token unification of the two halves of his delight. It will be a *tool,* a mediator or go-between in an act which may, he hopes, transcend collecting in its simplest sense. It has only just arrived today, special delivery, from the Belgian luthier to whom the Collector had hesitantly entrusted its birth.

"It must done be *precisely* as I have said," he told the violin-maker, four months ago, when he flew to Hotton to hand-deliver a substantial portion of the materials from which the instrument would be constructed. "You may not deviate in any significant way from these instructions."

"Yes," the luthier replied, "I understand. I understand completely." A man who appreciates discretion, the Belgian violin maker, so there were no inconvenient questions asked, no prying inquiries as to *why,* and what's more, he'd even known something about ammonites beforehand.

"No substitutions," the Collector said firmly, just in case it needed to be stated one last time.

"No substitutions of any sort," replied the luthier.

"And the back must be carved—"

"I understand," the violin-maker assured him. "I have the sketches, and I will follow them exactly."

"And the pegs—"

"Will be precisely as we have discussed."

And so the collector paid the luthier half the price of the commission, the other half due upon delivery, and he took a six A.M. flight back across the wide Atlantic to New England and his small house in the small town near the sea. And he has waited, hardly daring to *half*-believe that the violin-maker would, in fact, get it all right. Indeed—for men are ever at war with their hearts and minds and innermost demons—some infinitesimal scrap of the Collector has even *hoped* that there *would* be a mistake, the most trifling portion of his plan ignored or the violin finished and perfect but then lost in transit and so the whole plot ruined. For it is no small thing, what the Collector has set in motion, and having always considered himself a very wise and sober man, he suspects that he understands fully the consequences he would suffer should he be discovered by lesser men who have no regard for the ocean and her needs. Men who cannot see the flesh and blood phantoms walking among them in broad daylight, much less be bothered to pay tithes that are long overdue to a goddess who has cradled them all, each and every one, through the innumerable twists and turns of evolution's crucible, for three and a half thousand million years.

But there has been no mistake, and, if anything, the violin maker can be faulted only in the complete sublimation of his craft to the will of his customer. In every way, this is the instrument the Collector asked him to make, and the varnish gleams faintly in the light from the display cases. The top is carved from spruce, and four small ammonites have been set into the wood—*Xipheroceras* from Jurassic rocks exposed along the Dorset Coast at Lyme Regis—two inlaid on the upper bout, two on the lower. He found the fossils himself, many years ago, and they are as perfectly preserved an example of their genus as he has yet seen anywhere, for any price. The violin's neck has been fashioned from maple, as is so often the tradition, and, likewise, the fingerboard is the customary ebony. However, the scroll has been formed from a fifth ammonite, and the Collector knows it is a far more perfect logarithmic spiral than any volute that could have ever been hacked from out a block of wood. In his mind, the five ammonites form the points of a pentacle. The luthier used maple for the back and ribs, and when the Collector turns the violin over, he's greeted by the intricate bas-relief he requested, faithfully reproduced from his own drawings—a great octopus, the ravenous devilfish of a so many sea legends, and the maze of its eight tentacles makes a looping, tangled interweave.

As for the pegs and bridge, the chinrest and tailpiece, all these have been carved from the bits of bone he provided the luthier. They seem no more than antique ivory, the stolen tusks of an elephant or a walrus or the tooth of a sperm whale, perhaps. The Collector also provided the dried gut for the five strings, and when the violin-maker pointed out that they would not be nearly so durable as good stranded steel, that they would be much more likely to break and harder to keep in tune, the Collector told him that the instrument would be played only once and so these matters were of very little concern. For the bow, the luthier was given strands of hair which the Collector told him had come from the tail of a gelding, a fine grey horse from Kentucky thoroughbred stock. He'd even ordered a special rosin, and so the sap of an Aleppo Pine was supplemented with a vial of oil he'd left in the care of the violin-maker.

And now, four long months later, the Collector is rewarded for all his painstaking designs, rewarded or damned, if indeed there is some distinction between the two, and the instrument he holds is more beautiful than he'd ever dared to imagine it could be.

The Collector finishes his tea, pausing for a moment to lick the commingled flavors of hibiscus and rosehips, honey and lemon grass from his thin, chapped lips. Then he closes the violin case and locks it, before writing a second, final check to the Belgian luthier. He slips it into an envelope bearing the violin maker's name and the address of the shop on the rue de Centre in Hotton; the check will go out in the morning's mail, along with other checks for the gas, telephone, and electric bills, and a handwritten letter on lilac-scented stationary, addressed to a Brooklyn violinist. When he is done with these chores, the Collector sits there at the desk in his gallery, one hand resting lightly on the violin case, his face marred by an unaccustomed smile and his eyes filling up with the gluttonous wonder of so many precious things brought together in one room, content in the certain knowledge that they belong to him and will never belong to anyone else.

The violinist would never write this story, either. Words have never come easily for her. Sometimes, it seems she does not even think in words, but only in notes of music. When the lilac-scented letter arrives, she reads it several times, then does what it asks of her, because she can't imagine what else she would do. She buys a ticket and the next day she takes the train through Connecticut and Rhode Island and Massachusetts until, finally, she comes to a small town on a rocky spit of land very near the sea. She has never cared for the sea, as it has seemed always to her some awful, insoluble mystery, not so very different from the awful, insoluble mystery of death. Even before the loss of her sister, the violinist avoided the sea when possible. She loathes the taste of fish and lobster and of clams, and the smell of the ocean, too, which reminds her of raw sewage. She has often dreamt of drowning, and of slimy things with bulging black eyes, eyes as empty as night, that have slithered up from abyssal depths to drag her back down with them to lightless plains of silt and diatomaceous ooze or to the ruins of haunted, sunken cities. But those are *only* dreams, and they do her only the bloodless harm that comes from dreams, and she has lived long enough to understand that she has worse things than the sea to fear.

She takes a taxi from the train depot, and it ferries her through the town and over a murky river winding between empty warehouses and rotting docks, a few fishing boats stranded at low tide, and then to a small house painted the color of sunflowers or canary feathers. The address on the mailbox matches the address on the lilac-scented letter, so she pays the driver and he leaves her there. Then she stands in the driveway, watching the yellow house, which has begun to seem a disquieting shade of yellow, or a shade of yellow made disquieting because there is so much of it all in one place. It's almost twilight, and she shivers, wishing she'd thought to wear a cardigan under her coat, and then a porch light comes on and there's a man waving to her.

He's the man who wrote the letter, she thinks. *The man who wants me to play for him,* and for some reason she had expected him to be a lot younger and not so fat. He looks a bit like Captain Kangaroo, this man, and he waves and calls her name and smiles. And the violinist wishes that the taxi were still waiting there to take her back to the station, that she didn't need the money the fat man in the yellow house had offered her, that she'd had the good sense to stay in the city where she belongs. *You could still turn and walk away,* she reminds herself. *There's nothing at all stopping you from just turning right around and walking away and never once looking back, and you could still forget about this whole ridiculous affair.*

And maybe that's true, and maybe it isn't, but there's more than a month's rent on the line, and the way work's been lately, a few students and catch-as-catch-can, she can't afford to find out. She nods and waves back at the smiling man on the porch, the man who told her not to bring her own instrument because he'd prefer to hear her play a particular one that he'd just brought back from a trip to Europe.

"Come on inside. You must be freezing out there," he calls from the porch, and the violinist tries not to think about the sea all around her or that shade of yellow, like a pool of melted butter, and goes to meet the man who sent her the lilac-scented letter.

The Collector makes a steaming-hot pot of Red Zinger, which the violinist takes without honey, and they each have a poppy-seed muffin, which he bought fresh that morning at a bakery in the town. They sit across from one another at his desk, surrounded by the display cases and the best of his ammonites, and she sips her tea and picks at her muffin and pretends to be interested while he explains the importance of recognizing sexual dimorphism when distinguishing one species of ammonite from another. The shells of females, he says, are often the larger and so are called macroconchs by paleontologists. The males may have much smaller shells, called microconchs, and one must always be careful not to mistake the microconchs and macroconchs for two distinct species. He also talks about extinction rates and the utility of ammonites as index fossils and *Parapuzosia bradyi,* a giant among ammonites and the largest specimen in his collection, with a shell measuring slightly more than four and a half feet in diameter.

"They're all quite beautiful," she says, and the violinist doesn't tell him how much she hates the sea and everything that comes from the sea or that the thought of all the fleshy, tentacled creatures that once lived stuffed inside those pretty spiral shells makes her skin crawl. She sips her tea and smiles and nods her head whenever it seems appropriate to do so, and when he asks if he can call her Ellen, she says yes, of course.

"You won't think me too familiar?"

"Don't be silly," she replies, half-charmed at his manners and wondering if he's gay or just a lonely old man whose grown a bit peculiar because he has nothing but his rocks and the yellow house for company. "That's my name. My name is Ellen."

"I wouldn't want to make you uncomfortable or take liberties that are not mine to take," the Collector says and clears away their china cups and saucers, the crumpled paper napkins and a few uneaten crumbs, and then he asks if she's ready to see the violin.

"If you're ready to show it to me," she tells him.

"It's just that I don't want to rush you," he says. "We could always talk some more, if you'd like."

And so the violinist explains to him that she's never felt comfortable with conversation, or with language in general, and that she's always suspected she was much better suited to speaking through her music. "Sometimes, I think it speaks for me," she tells him and apologizes, because she often apologizes when she's actually done nothing wrong. The Collector grins and laughs softly and taps the side of his nose with his left index finger.

"The way I see it, language is language is language," he says. "Words or music, bird songs or all the fancy, flashing colors made by chemoluminescent squid, what's the difference? I'll take conversation however I can wrangle it." And then he unlocks one of the desk drawers with a tiny brass-colored key and takes out the case containing the Belgian violin.

"If words don't come when you call them, then, by all means, please, talk to me with this," and he flips up the latches on the side of the case and opens it so she can see the instrument cradled inside.

"Oh my," she says, all her awkwardness and unease forgotten at the sight of the ammonite violin. "I've never seen anything like it. Never. It's lovely. No, it's much, *much* more than lovely."

"Then you will play it for me?"

"May I touch it?" she asks, and he laughs again.

"I can't imagine how you'll play it otherwise."

Ellen gently lifts the violin from its case, the way that some people might lift a newborn child or a Minoan vase or a stoppered bottle of nitroglycerine, the way the Collector would lift a particularly fragile ammonite from its bed of excelsior. It's heavier than any violin she's held before, and she guesses that the unexpected weight must be from the five fossil shells set into the instrument. She wonders how it will affect the sound, those five ancient stones, how they might warp and alter this violin's voice.

"It's never been played, except by the man who made it, and that hardly seems to count. You, my dear, will be the very first."

And she almost asks him why *her,* because surely, for what he's paying, he could have lured some other, more talented player out here to his little yellow house. Surely someone a bit more celebrated, more accomplished, someone who doesn't have to take in students to make the rent, but would still be flattered and intrigued enough by the offer to come all the way to this squalid little town by the sea and play the fat man's violin for him. But then she thinks it would be rude, and she almost apologizes for a question she hasn't even asked.

And then, as if he might have read her mind, and so maybe she should have apologized after all, the Collector shrugs his shoulders and dabs at the corners of his mouth with a white linen handkerchief he's pulled from a shirt pocket. "The universe is a marvelously complex bit of craftsmanship," he says. "And sometimes one must look very closely to even begin to understand how one thing connects with another. Your late sister, for instance—"

"My *sister?*" she asks and looks up, surprised and looking away from the ammonite violin and into the friendly, smiling eyes of the Collector. A cold knot deep in her belly and an unpleasant pricking sensation along her forearms and the back of her neck, goose bumps and histrionic ghost-story clichés, and all at once the violin feels unclean and dangerous, and she wants to return it to its case. "What do you know about my sister?"

The Collector blushes and glances down at his hands, folded there in front of him on the desk. He begins to speak and stammers, as if, possibly, he's really no better with words than she.

"What do *you* know about my sister?" Ellen asks again. "*How* do you know about her?"

The Collector frowns and licks nervously at his chapped lips. "I'm sorry," he says. "That was terribly tactless of me. I should not have brought it up."

"How do you know about my sister?"

"It's not exactly a secret, is it?" the Collector asks, letting his eyes drift by slow, calculated degrees from his hands and the desktop to her face. "I do read the newspapers. I don't usually watch television, but I imagine it was there, as well. She was murdered—"

"They don't know that. No one knows that for sure. She is *missing*," the violinist says, hissing the last word between clenched teeth.

"She's been missing for quite some time," the Collector replies, feeling the smallest bit braver now and beginning to suspect he hasn't quite overplayed his hand.

"But they do not know that she's been murdered. They don't *know* that. No one ever found her body," and then Ellen decides that she's said far too much and stares down at the fat man's violin. She can't imagine how she ever thought it a lovely thing, only a moment or two before, this grotesque *parody* of a violin resting in her lap. It's more like a gargoyle, she thinks, or a sideshow freak, a malformed parody or a sick, sick joke, and suddenly she wants very badly to wash her hands.

"Please forgive me," the Collector says, sounding as sincere and contrite as any lonely man in a yellow house by the sea has ever sounded. "I live alone. I forget myself and say things I shouldn't. Please, Ellen. Play it for me. You've come all this way, and I would so love to hear you play. It would be such a pity if I've gone and spoiled it all with a few inconsiderate words. I so admire your work—"

"No one *admires* my work," she replies, wondering how long it would take the taxi to show up and carry her back over the muddy, murky river, past the rows of empty warehouses to the depot, and how long she'd have to wait for the next train to New York. "I still don't even understand how you found me?"

And at this opportunity to redeem himself, the Collector's face brightens, and he leans toward her across the desk. "Then I will tell you, if that will put your mind at ease. I saw you play at an art opening in Manhattan, you and your sister, a year or so back. At a gallery on Mercer Street. It was called . . . damn, it's right on the tip of my tongue—"

"Eyecon," Ellen says, almost whispering. "The name of the gallery is Eyecon."

"Yes, yes, that's it. Thank you. I thought it was such a very silly name for a gallery, but then I've never cared for puns and wordplay. It was at a reception for a French painter, Albert Perrault, and I confess I found him quite completely hideous, and his paintings were dreadful, but I loved listening to the two of you play. I called the gallery, and they were nice enough to tell me how I could contact you."

"I didn't like his paintings either. That was the last time we played together, my sister and I," Ellen says and presses a thumb to the ammonite shell that forms the violin's scroll.

"I didn't know that. I'm sorry, Ellen. I wasn't trying to dredge up bad memories."

"It's not a *bad* memory," she says, wishing it were all that simple and that were exactly the truth, and then she reaches for the violin's bow, which is still lying in the case lined with silk dyed the color of ripe pomegranates.

"I'm sorry," the Collector says again, certain now that he hasn't frightened her away, that everything is going precisely as planned. "Please, I only want to hear you play again."

"I'll need to tune it," Ellen tells him, because she's come this far, and she needs the money, and there's nothing the fat man has said that doesn't add up.

"Naturally," he replies. "I'll go to the kitchen and make us another pot of tea, and you can call me whenever you're ready."

"I'll need a tuning fork," she says, because she hasn't seen any sign of a piano in the yellow house. "Or if you have a metronome that has a tuner, that would work."

The Collector promptly produces a steel tuning fork from another of the drawers and slides it across the desk to the violinist. She thanks him, and when he's left the room and she's alone with the ammonite violin and all the tall cases filled with fossils and the amber wash of incandescent bulbs, she glances at a window and sees that its already dark outside. *I will play for him,* she thinks. *I'll play on his violin, and drink his tea, and smile, and then he'll pay me for my time and trouble. I'll go back to the city, and tomorrow or the next day, I'll be glad that I didn't back out. Tomorrow or the next day, it'll all seem silly, that I was afraid of a sad old man who lives in an ugly yellow house and collects rocks.*

"I will," she says out loud. "That's exactly how it will go," and then Ellen begins to tune the ammonite violin.

And after he brings her a rickety old music stand, something that looks like it has survived half a century of high-school marching bands, he sits behind his desk, sipping a fresh cup of tea, and she sits in the overlapping pools of light from the display cases. He asked for Paganini; specifically, he asked for Paganini's Violin Concerto No. 3 in E. She would have preferred something contemporary—Górecki, maybe, or Philip Glass, a little something she knows from memory—but he had the sheet music for Paganini, and it's his violin, and he's the one who's writing the check.

"Now?" she asks, and he nods his head.

"Yes, please," he replies and raises his tea cup as if to toast her.

So Ellen lifts the violin, supporting it with her left shoulder, bracing it firmly with her chin, and studies the sheet music a moment or two more before she begins. *Introduzione, allegro marziale,* and she wonders if he expects to hear all three movements, start to finish, or if he'll stop her when he's heard enough. She takes a deep breath and begins to play.

From his seat at the desk, the Collector closes his eyes as the lilting voice of the ammonite violin fills the room. He closes his eyes tightly and remembers another winter night, almost an entire year come and gone since then, but it might only have been yesterday, so clear are his memories. His collection of suffocations may indeed be more commonplace, as he has been led to conclude, but it is also the less frequently indulged of his two passions. He could never name the date and place of each and every ammonite acquisition, but in his brain the Collector carries a faultless accounting of all the suffocations. There have been sixteen, sixteen in twenty-one years, and now it has been almost one year to the night since the most recent. Perhaps, he thinks, he should have waited for the anniversary, but when the package arrived from Belgium, his enthusiasm and impatience got the better of him. When he wrote the violinist his lilac-scented note, he wrote "at your earliest possible convenience" and underlined "earliest" twice.

And here she is, and Paganini flows from out the ammonite violin just as it flowed from his car stereo that freezing night, one year ago, and his heart is beating so fast, so hard, racing itself and all his bright and breathless memories.

Don't let it end, he prays to the sea, who he has faith can hear the prayers of all her supplicants and will answer those she deems worthy. *Let it go on and on and on. Let it never end.*

He clenches his fists, digging his short nails deep into the skin of his palms, and bites his lip so hard that he tastes blood. And the taste of those few drops of his own life is not so very different from holding the sea inside his mouth.

At last, I have done a perfect thing, he tells himself, himself and the sea and the ammonites and the lingering souls of all his suffocations. *So many years, so much time, so much work and money, but finally I have done this one perfect thing.* And then he opens his eyes again, and also opens the top middle drawer of his desk and takes out the revolver that once belonged to his father, who was a Gloucester fisherman who somehow managed never to collect anything at all.

Her fingers and the bow dance wild across the strings, and in only a few minutes Ellen has lost herself inside the giddy tangle of harmonics and drones and double stops, and if ever she has felt magic—*true* magic—in her art, then she feels it now. She lets her eyes drift from the music stand and the printed pages, because it is all right there behind her eyes and burning on her fingertips. She might well have written these lines herself and then spent half her life playing at nothing else, they rush through her with such ease and confidence. This is ecstasy and this is abandon and this is the tumble and roar of a thousand other emotions she seems never to have felt before this night. The strange violin no longer seems unusually heavy; in fact, it hardly seems to have any weight at all.

Perhaps there is *no violin,* she thinks. *Perhaps there never was a violin, only my hands and empty air and that's all it takes to make music like this.*

Language is language is language, the fat man said, and so these chords have become her words. No, *not* words, but something so much less indirect than the clumsy interplay of her tongue and teeth, larynx and palate. They have become, simply, her *language,* as they ever have been. Her soul speaking to the world, and all the world need do is *listen.*

She shuts her eyes, no longer needing them to grasp the progression from one note to the next, and at first there is only the comfortable darkness there behind her lids, which seems better matched to the music than all the distractions of her eyes.

Don't let it stop, she thinks, not praying, unless this is a prayer to herself, for the violinist has never seen the need for gods. *Please, let it be like this forever. Let this moment never end, and I will never have to stop playing and there will never again be silence or the noise of human thoughts and conversation.*

"It can't be that way, Ellen," her sister whispers, not whispering in her ear but from somewhere within the Paganini concerto or the ammonite violin or both at once. "I wish I could give you that. I would give you that if it were mine to give."

And then Ellen sees, or hears, or simply *understands* in this language which is *her* language, as language is language is language, the fat man's hands about her sister's throat. Her sister dying somewhere cold near the sea, dying all alone except for the company of her murderer, and there is half an instant when she almost stops playing.

No, her sister whispers, and that one word comes like a blazing gash across the concerto's whirl, and Ellen doesn't stop playing, and she doesn't open her eyes, and she watches as her lost sister slowly dies.

The music is a typhoon gale flaying rocky shores to gravel and sand, and the violinist lets it spin and rage, and she watches as the fat man takes four of her sister's fingers and part of a thighbone, strands of her ash blonde hair, a vial of oil boiled and distilled from the fat of her breasts, a pink-white section of small intestine—all these things and the five fossils from off an English beach to make the instrument he wooed her here to play for him. And now there are tears streaming hot down her cheeks, but still Ellen plays the violin that was her sister, and still she doesn't open her eyes.

The single gunshot is very loud in the room, and the display cases rattle and a few of the ammonites slip off their Lucite stands and clatter against wood or glass or other spiraled shells.

And finally she opens her eyes.

And the music ends as the bow slides from her fingers and falls to the floor at her feet.

"No," she says, "please don't let it stop, please," but the echo of the revolver and the memory of the concerto are so loud in her ears that her own words are almost lost to her.

That's all, her sister whispers, louder than any suicide's gun, soft as a midwinter night coming on, gentle as one unnoticed second bleeding into the next. *I've shown you, and now there isn't anymore.*

Across the room, the Collector still sits at his desk, but now he's slumped a bit in his chair, and his head is thrown back so that he seems to be staring at something on the ceiling. Blood spills from the black cavern of his open mouth and drips to the floor.

There isn't anymore.

And when she's stopped crying and is quite certain that her sister will not speak to her again, that all the secrets she has any business seeing have been revealed, the violinist retrieves the dropped bow and stands, then walks to the desk and returns the ammonite violin to its case. She will not give it to the police when they arrive, after she has gone to the kitchen to call them, and she will not tell them that it was the fat man who gave it to her. She will take it back to Brooklyn, and they will find other things in another room in the yellow house and have no need of the violin and these stolen shreds of her sister. The Collector has kindly written everything down in three books bound in red leather, all the names and dates and places, and there are other souvenirs, besides. And she will never try to put this story into words, for words have never come easily to her, and like the violin, the story has become hers and hers alone.

DARK DELICACIES LAST WORD

A Modest Proposal

JEFF GELB

HOW THE HELL do I follow nineteen great horror stories? And a foreword by Ray Harryhausen? And Del's cogent and clever comments about things that go bump in the night and give you a fright? Talk about challenges!

And you know what's really scary? The fact that numerous other authors are waiting in the wings, stories already written, ready to submit. Will these stories even find an anthology home?

It's gotta happen, folks. There are so few horror anthologies anymore; so few places where writers can stretch their talents in new directions. Where young writers can appear side by side with the masters. Where readers can enjoy a depth of ideas that movies can't hope to provide. Movies have to be focused and focus-grouped for maximum appeal to the widest possible masses. That almost always means dumbing it down and playing it safe. As I'm sure you've noticed.

Ironically, millions of people of all ages love to be scared—as long as it's at the movies. Even now they're at the multiplex seeing *Saw IV* or *Hostel 3*—and those are probably the better ones. Chances are they don't even think about the fun they could have reading horror fiction.

So I'm throwing down the gauntlet, guys and dolls. It's up to us to get the masses into horror fiction. No one's getting rich writing for *Dark Delicacies*. Actually, they wrote their stories for *you*. They love horror, and they want to share that love with you and other fans.

So what can you do? For starters, how about buying at least one extra copy of a horror novel or anthology you love, and putting it in the hands of that friend or co-worker who can't stop talking about how scary the latest serial killer/slasher flick was? Dare them to read it at night, in a room lit by a single bulb.

I know I'm preaching to the converted. But it all comes down to us, gang. We've gotta grow this community of horror fanatics. Ultimately, that's the only way we will be able to continue to read the kind of fiction we can't live without.

Is horror dead on paper? Not yet. Is it dying? I'd say it's somewhere between life support and ambulatory. But if people like you can somehow bring some of your love of this genre to more people, we can have the sort of success with horror novels that the box office has with horror movies.

Okay, I'll stop pontificating now. I gotta go. I'm sitting on a stack of unread horror novels by immensely talented folks, like the people who wrote stories in this collection. I like being scared in the way only a great piece of horror fiction can creep me out. And I want to be scared—tonight, tomorrow, and for years to come!

How about you?

ABOUT THE CONTRIBUTORS

PETER ATKINS—Peter Atkins is the author of the novels *Morningstar* and *Big Thunder* and the collection *Wishmaster and Others*. For the screen, he has written *Hellraiser II: Hellbound, Hell on Earth: Hellraiser III, Hellraiser: Bloodline,* and *Wishmaster*. He has contributed to *Weird Tales, Fantasy & Science Fiction, Cemetery Dance,* and *Postscripts,* as well as several award-winning anthologies.

L. A. BANKS—L. A. Banks (aka, Leslie Esdaile Banks) is a native of Philadelphia and graduate of the University of Pennsylvania Wharton undergraduate program, and holds a Masters in Fine Arts from Temple University's School of Film and Media Arts. After a ten-year career as a corporate marketing executive for several Fortune 100 high-tech firms, Banks changed careers in 1991 to pursue a private consulting career—which ultimately led to fiction and film writing. Now, with over twenty-seven novels plus ten anthology contributions in an extraordinary breadth of genres, and many award to her credit, Banks writes full-time and resides in Philadelphia. Look for a full listing of her published works under an array of pseudonyms at: www.vampire-huntress.com or www.LeslieEsdaileBanks.com

GARY BRANDNER—Gary Brandner, born in the Midwest and much-traveled during his formative years, has thirty-odd published novels, more than 100 short stories, and a handful of screenplays on his resume. After surviving the University of Washington, he followed such diverse career paths as amateur boxer, bartender, surveyor, loan company investigator, advertising copywriter, and technical writer before turning to fiction. Since his breakthrough novel *The Howling*, he has settled into a relatively respectable life with wife and cats in California's San Fernando Valley. He is currently involved in a movie project as writer/co-producer.

MAX BROOKS—Max Brooks was a writer for *Saturday Night Live* from 2001–2003 during which time the show won an Emmy Award. His first book *The Zombie Survival Guide* was in its 16th printing last time we checked. His latest novel *World War Z* has been optioned by Brad Pitt's company for a film, and he is currently working on a graphic novel adaptation of it. Both of his books were *New York Times* bestsellers, and in his spare time he works on and is the co-creator of the internet comedy series *The Watch List* which is currently running on Comedy Central Motherload.

TANANARIVE DUE—Tananarive Due is the American Book Award–winning author of seven novels, including *Joplin's Ghost, The Good House, The Living Blood, My Soul to Keep*, and *The Between*. She has been nominated for the Bram Stoker Award and the International Horror Guild Award. *Publishers Weekly* wrote that *The Living Blood* "should set the standard for supernatural thrillers in the new millennium." Two of Due's novels are currently in development at Fox Searchlight studios. Her short story "Patient Zero" appeared in two Best-of-the-Year science fiction anthologies. Due has also published short fiction in the horror and speculative fiction anthologies *Dark Dreams, Dark Matter* and *Mojo: Conjure Stories*. Due and her husband, author Steven Barnes, also collaborate on screenplays and novels. In July of 2007, they published their first mystery novel, *Casanegra,* which they wrote in collaboration with actor Blair Underwood. Due was raised in Miami by two civil rights activists. She collaborated with her mother, Patricia Stephens Due, to write the nonfiction book *Freedom in the Family: A Mother-Daughter Memoir of the Fight for Civil Rights*. Due lives in Southern California with Barnes, her son Jason, and her stepdaughter, Nicki.

JOHN FARRIS—John Farris has been called "the best writer of horror at work today." His thirty-eight titles have sold 22 million copies worldwide in twenty-five languages. His most recent novels are *You Don't Scare Me* and *Avenging Fury,* the fourth and final volume of the Fury Quartet. He wrote and directed the cult classic film *Dear, Dead Delilah,* and has written many other screenplays. He had a short-lived career as a playwright in his twenties. His only produced play, *The Death of the Well-Loved Boy,* Farris fondly recalls as having received "the worst reviews since Attila the Hun."

RAY GARTON—Garton is the author of over fifty books, and the winner of the 2006 Grand Master Award. He is currently at work on his next novel, *Ravenous,* a werewolf story with a twist on the old myth, to be published by Leisure Books. He lives in northern California with his wife Dawn and their brood of cats.

JEFF GELB—*Dark Delicacies Volume 2* is Gelb's 21st anthology as editor or co-editor. He co-created the ongoing, internationally-published *Hot Blood* series (now in its 13th volume) with Michael Garrett, and co-edited the *Flesh & Blood* anthologies with Max Allan Collins. He has also edited several *Shock Rock* editions, and *Fear Itself.* Gelb's one novel is *Specters,* and also has one comic book writing credit: *Bettie Page* Comics, done with Dave Stevens. Gelb lives in Southern California with his wife Terry Gladstone. Their son Levi has just completed his rabbinical studies.

BARBARA HAMBLY—Since her first published fantasy in 1982, *The Time of the Dark,* Hambly has touched pretty much all the bases in genre fiction, including historical murder mysteries, fantasy, science fiction, comic books, a "contemporary occult romance novella" for Harlequin, and scripts for Saturday morning cartoon shows. She continues to write both fantasy and historical fiction: her most recent horror novel is *Renfield, Slave of Dracula,* and her newest historical novel is *Patriot Hearts,* a novel of the Founding Mothers. She grew up on science fiction and fantasy in Southern California, and attended the University of California where she received a Master's degree in Medieval History, and a black belt in karate. She attended the University of Bordeaux and traveled in Europe in 1971–1972. She married science fiction writer George Alec Effinger in 1998 and lived part-time in New Orleans for a number of years. Hambly's interests include historical research, dance, hiking, costuming, and carpentry. Now a widow, she shares a house in Los Angeles with several small carnivores.

JOHN HARRISON—John Harrison began his career directing rock videos and working as first assistant director for famed horror director George Romero (*Night of the Living Dead*). Harrison wrote and directed multiple episodes of Romero's classic TV series, *Tales from the Darkside* before helming *Tales from the Darkside The Movie,* which won Harrison the Grand Prix du Festival at Avoriaz, France. Harrison has written and directed episodes of *Tales from the Crypt, Earth 2,* and *Profiler.* He has written and directed world premier movies for the USA Network and Starz/Encore. Harrison's six-hour miniseries adaptation of Frank Herbert's monumental bestseller *Dune,* which he directed, was an Emmy-winning success in the U.S. Harrison's screenplay for *Children of Dune,* another mini-series encompassing the next two novels of Frank Herbert's mythic adventure series, was another Emmy winner for the SciFi Channel. Harrison co-wrote the animated feature *Dinosaur* for Disney. And he has just completed the adaptation of Clive Barker's fantasy novel *Abarat,* also for Disney. He has also adapted Barker's short story *Book of Blood,* which he will direct. Harrison has written screenplays for Robert Zemeckis and Richard Donner among others, and his writing and directing have been honored with awards from the Writers Guild of America, Houston International Film Festival as well as the Grand Prix at Avoriaz.

RAY HARRYHAUSEN—Ray Harryhausen's body of work is legendary. Universally regarded as the king of stop-motion animation, Harryhausen's magical images have jump-started the careers of more movie directors and special effects technicians than can be counted. Starting with *Mighty Joe Young* in 1949, Harryhausen's work includes too many classic movie moments to list here. Harryhausen has recently added author to his list of accomplishments, with *Ray Harryhausen: An Animated Life,* and *The Art of Ray Harryhausen.* Next up: he has personally supervised the colorization of many of his early films for future DVD releases, and he has developed several new comic book series based on his creations.

GLEN HIRSHBERG—Glen Hirshberg's most recent collection, *American Morons,* was published by Earthling Press in 2006. *The Two Sams,* his first collection, won the International Horror Guild Award, and was selected by *Publishers Weekly* and *Locus* as one of the best books of 2003. Hirshberg is also the author of the novels *The Snowman's Children* and *Sisters of Baikal.* With Dennis Etchison and Peter Atkins, he co-founded the Rolling Darkness Revue, a traveling ghost story performance troupe that tours the west coast of the United States each October. His fiction has appeared in numerous magazines and anthologies, including multiple appearances in *The Mammoth Book of Best New Horror* and *The Year's Best Fantasy and Horror, Dark Terrors 6, The Dark, Inferno, Tampoline,* and *Cemetery Dance.* He lives in the Los Angeles area with his wife and children.

DEL HOWISON—Along with his wife Sue, Del Howison created America's only all-horror book and gift store, Dark Delicacies, as fans and for fans, and they remain among horror's biggest aficionados. They, and the store, have been featured on many television documentaries concerning horror and the nature of evil. As a former photojournalist, Del has written articles for a variety of publications, including *Rue Morgue* and *Gauntlet* magazines, along with a foreword for the Wildside Press edition of *Varney the Vampyre.* His short stories have appeared in a variety of anthologies. He is currently working on two co-editing projects: *The Horror Book of Lists* with Amy Wallace and Scott Bradley and *Dark Screen: Horror Writers on Horror Cinema* with Lisa Morton.

CAITLÍN R. KIERNAN—Caitlín R. Kiernan is the author of seven novels, including *Silk, Threshold, Low Red Moon, Murder of Angels,* and, most recently, *Daughter of Hounds.* A four-time recipient of the International Horror Guild Award, her short fiction has been collected in four volumes: *Tales of Pain and Wonder; From Weird and Distant Shores; Alabaster;* and *To Charles Fort, With Love* (a World Fantasy Award finalist). Her stories have regularly appeared in such anthologies as *The Year's Best Fantasy and Horror, The Mammoth Book of Best New Horror,* and *The Year's Best Science Fiction.* Born near Dublin, Ireland, and trained as a vertebrate paleontologist, she now lives in Atlanta with her partner, photographer and doll-maker Kathryn Pollnac.

GREG KIHN—Greg Kihn was a rock star in the '80s and had several worldwide hit records (including "Jeopardy" and "The Breakup Song"). In the mid '90s he quit his wild man ways and began successful parallel careers in writing and radio. He has published four novels and numerous short stories. His radio show Big Rock Beat is now in syndication. Greg lives in Northern California and does the morning show on KFOX in San Jose. He still performs with his band.

JOE R. LANSDALE—Joe R. Lansdale is the author of over twenty novels and two hundred short pieces. *Bubba Hotep* was filmed from his work, as well as *Incident On and Off a Mountain Road*. Many others have been optioned.

ROBERT MASELLO—Robert Masello is an award-winning journalist, television writer, and the author of many novels and nonfiction books. His articles, essays, and reviews have appeared often in a wide variety of publications, such as the *Los Angeles Times, New York Magazine, New York Newsday,* the *Washington Post, Redbook, Travel and Leisure, Harper's Bazaar, Glamour, Elle, TV Guide, Cosmopolitan, Parade, Town and Country,* and the *Wilson Quarterly.* He has also served as a writer on such popular TV shows as *Early Edition, Charmed, Sliders,* and *Poltergeist: The Legacy.* Among his books are two studies of the occult—*Fallen Angels and Spirits of the Dark,* which was quickly followed by *Raising Hell: A Concise History of the Black Arts and Those Who Dared to Practice Them*—and a number of novels, including *The Spirit Wood, Black Horizon, Private Demons, Vigil,* and, most recently, *Bestiary.* His books have appeared on the bestseller lists of the *Los Angeles Times* and *USA Today* and been translated into eight languages, ranging from Swedish to Korean. For the past six years, Masello has been the Visiting Lecturer in Literature at Claremont McKenna College in Claremont, CA.

STEVE NILES—Steve Niles is one of the writers responsible for bringing horror comics back to prominence, and was recently named by *Fangoria* magazine as one of its "13 rising talents who promise to keep us terrified for the next 25 years." Niles is currently working for the four top American comic publishers: Marvel, DC, Image and Dark Horse. His *30 Days of Night* comic book mini-series is filming as a major motion picture, with Sam Raimi as producer. In June of 2005, Niles and actor Thomas Jane ("The Punisher") formed the production company Raw Entertainment; their first production is *The Lurkers*. Niles and his *Bigfoot* co-creator, rocker Rob Zombie, have sold the film rights to Rogue Pictures. Niles and Zombie will be handling script duties. Also in development are adaptations of *Wake the Dead, Hyde, Aleister Arcane,* and *Criminal Macabre.* Niles resides in Los Angeles.

JOEY O'BRYAN—Joey O'Bryan is a former film critic—for the *Austin Chronicle* and *Film Threat,* among others—turned screenwriter. He worked for iconic figures like Roger Corman and Sammo Hung before co-writing the Hong Kong action hit *Fulltime Killer* for acclaimed director Johnnie To. Honored at the Hong Kong Film Critics Association's Golden Bauhinia Awards as one of the top ten Chinese-language films of the year, it was distributed all over the world following its selection as Hong Kong's official entry into the Academy Awards Best Foreign Film category. He has since optioned three specs and tackled a wide variety of screen assignments, for producers big and small, foreign and domestic. "The Unlikely Redemption of Jared Pierce" is his first published piece of short fiction.

JAMES SALLIS—James Sallis's books include the Lew Griffin cycle, a biography of Chester Himes, and a translation of Raymond Queneau's novel *Saint Glingin,* as well as six other novels and multiple collections of stories, poems, and essays. His most recent books are *Drive* (called by the *New York Times* "a perfect noir novel") and *Salt River* (the third and final installment of his Turner series), and the story collection *Potato Tree.* He was a longtime columnist for the *Boston Globe,* regularly reviews for the *Washington Post* and *L.A. Times,* and contributes a quarterly books column to F&SF. His Web site is www.jamessallis.com.

HARRY SHANNON—Harry Shannon has been an actor, a singer, an Emmy-nominated songwriter, a recording artist in Europe, a music publisher, a film studio executive, and a free-lance Music Supervisor on films such as *Basic Instinct* and *Universal Soldier.* He is author of *The Night Trilogy,* the Mick Callahan suspense novels *Memorial Day* and *Eye of the Burning Man,* and the acclaimed horror/thriller *The Pressure of Darkness.* Harry's horror script *Dead and Gone* was recently filmed by director Yossi Sasson. His Web site is *www.harryshannon.com.*